C0-ALN-643

Scholastic

A Publishing Adventure

Scholastic
A Publishing Adventure

JACK K. LIPPERT

SCHOLASTIC BOOK SERVICES
NEW YORK • TORONTO • LONDON • AUCKLAND • SYDNEY • TOKYO

NO PART OF THIS PUBLICATION MAY BE REPRODUCED IN WHOLE OR IN PART, OR STORED IN A RETRIEVAL SYSTEM, OR TRANSMITTED IN ANY FORM OR BY ANY MEANS, ELECTRONIC, MECHANICAL, PHOTOCOPYING, RECORDING, OR OTHERWISE, WITHOUT WRITTEN PERMISSION OF THE PUBLISHER. FOR INFORMATION REGARDING PERMISSION, WRITE TO SCHOLASTIC BOOK SERVICES, 50 WEST 44TH STREET, NEW YORK, NY 10036.

CASEBOUND: ISBN 0-590-07660-4   SOFTCOVER: ISBN 0-590-30884-X

COPYRIGHT © 1979 BY SCHOLASTIC MAGAZINES, INC. ALL RIGHTS RESERVED. PUBLISHED BY SCHOLASTIC BOOK SERVICES, A DIVISION OF SCHOLASTIC MAGAZINES, INC. FIRST PRINTED IN THE UNITED STATES OF AMERICA IN 1979.

To all

who gave a portion of their lives

to building the foundation

and the structure of Scholastic,

and in particular

to the one who gave the most, Robbie

Contents

Preface

THIS book is an extension and amplification of Thora Larsen's *The First Forty Years of Scholastic Magazines* and of William Boutwell's and Donald Layman's manuscripts updating that record through the 1960's. What I have done is to add detail to their accounts and to acknowledge their own contributions to the progress of the company, something they avoided doing as though they had been — in all their productive years with Scholastic — mere observers of the success they helped to achieve. Yet it is understandable that, in the history of a company written by an insider, the writer will err on the side of omission when it comes to his or her own role in it. The present writer has applied very little of this kind of restraint to the pages that follow. They do not constitute a history in the usual sense of the term, as — in many instances — they lack the interpretation and analysis to be expected of a history.

Events and developments that were painful to the management of Scholastic and nearly fatal to its continued existence are of course included, such as the half-ownership of Scholastic by American Education Press in 1931–32 and the management survey conducted by Booz, Fry, Allen & Hamilton in 1941. Had the latter's recommendations been carried out by the owners — Augustus K. Oliver and George H. Clapp — that deed would have nipped then and there any prospect of the company's becoming what it is today.

Also included here are other episodes that gave the founder and president, M. R. Robinson, many restless days and nights as the company teetered on the brink of bankruptcy or acquisition. While writing about some of these, I would show him a draft of the copy, not for the purpose of censorship but for adherence to the truth as far as it could be documented or recalled. The first time I did this, back came the copy with this message written in the margin: "Jack, excoriate me as much as you like — or even more than you like! — Robbie." I was pleased but not surprised to get this, although his use of *excoriate* seemed to me extreme. There was no reason "to flay, chafe, or gall" him as the dictionary suggested, or to censure him "scathjngly." His comment did reflect his well-known disposition to welcome from his colleagues criticism that is directed toward the improvement of the product or his management of it.

Besides inviting me to excoriate him, Robbie admonished me to keep the spotlight off him, to keep him in the wings and all that. Well, the leading player in the wings is ever on his toes to return on stage, and on those few occasions when Robbie was in the wings, it didn't take a falling piece of scenery to get him into the act.

The longest chapter in this book is the chronicle of attacks that have been made on Scholastic over the years. It may seem strange to Scholastic admirers that more space should be given to the attempts of individuals and organizations to "do us in" than to any other topic. Yet only the most serious attacks are included, and I consider their aggregate effect helpful to an appreciation of Robbie's ability to overcome adversity. Surely the experience in overcoming the tribulations and cliff-hangings of the past has contributed to Scholastic's enduring strength, through which the resourceful and enterprising founder and his staff attained the success they enjoy today.

Overall this is not a chronological record, but a topical one. Each chapter is a topic or feature of the company's first 55-plus years. (There is more chronology to the sequence of the first eight chapters than to those that follow.) Chapter III—"Stockholders Ahoy!" — starts the story of corporate development, to which Thora Larsen gave the title "One Little, Two Little, Three Little Companies . . ." in her Scholastic story. This is picked up again in Chapter VI.

My sources for this book have been the company's archives in Englewood Cliffs, NJ; the files of past and present executives, editors, and managers in all Scholastic offices; and in the Scholastic library in New York, where back issues of the magazines are preserved. I also had occasion to refer to sources in the library of the Magazine Publishers Association in New York and the Library of Congress in Washington. The Carnegie Library of Pittsburgh provided on loan the only known existing copies of *The Western Pennsylvania Scholastic*. The Carnegie Library's Volume 1 (1920–21) contains only the first eight of 24 issues, but Volume 2 (1921–22) has all 28. I am probably the one responsible for the loss of the company's own bound volumes of those two years, as they were sent to me on loan in 1923 by Robbie so that I might absorb some of the Scholastic spirit as I took on a moonlighting assignment for the company while working on *The Pittsburgh Press*. I assume that, in the shuffle upon my departure from the office to New York in 1926, the Scholastic volumes were either lost or stolen. Whoever has them, or their like, may obtain a generous finder's fee by sending them to me.

I have used verbatim the first two paragraphs of Thora Larsen's chapter on the origins of Scholastic because I was frustrated in my attempt to improve them. Readers of both *The First Forty Years* and this book will recognize other snatches from the former.

I gratefully acknowledge the help of many others in and out of the office who checked their records and supplied the missing links of information. I regret that there are still some links that could not be found. I also regret that all Scholastic staff members who have contributed to the company's success are not named in this record.

Besides those mentioned above on whom I have leaned heavily, I wish especially to thank Mary Jane Dunton for designing the book; Lavinia Dobler, Lucy Evankow, and their library associates for locating elusive data; Jane Fliegel, Barbara Kellogg, and Nancy Ragolia for copy editing and proofreading; Eric Berger for his contribution to those parts of the text related to the aspects of the company's growth in which he held a leadership role for more than 40 years; Sturges Cary for a semi-final reading of the whole thing; Nancy Grossman and her staff for typing services; Nancy Smith for putting on the *coup de grâce* as indexer; and Anne Devanie for keeping track of it all so that only the final approved copy went into the production process. Any errors and oversights are my responsibility.

JACK K. LIPPERT
June 1, 1978

CHAPTER I

Origins of Scholastic

FOR a clue in just a few words to what has kept Scholastic running in the right direction since 1920, you need go no further than a remark made by M. R. Robinson himself, without any intent to refer to his accomplishment as founder and chief executive of this company. During a talk some years ago he said, "I cannot recall a day when I did not look forward to tackling the work that was waiting for me in my office." That office has always been Scholastic, although there could have been others if he had been of a different heart and mind about seeing through the job that he had started.

A deep faith in the usefulness of his work, a zest for going hard at it, and a buoyancy of spirit that kept him afloat in the stormiest of publishing seas are qualities that partially explain why Robinson held to his Scholastic course. But why hardheaded businessmen consented to keep the struggling enterprise alive for so many years either casts doubt on their hardheadedness or convicts them of blind faith in it or in its instigator.

Perhaps it was a case of hardheads meeting a harder head. From his college days Robinson had wanted to be an editor or a publisher. Two years' service in World War I

Maurice Robinson (center, first row), editor of the Wilkinsburg High School *Review*, with his staff in 1915, his senior year. He was class president.

had already delayed his graduation from Dartmouth College. In the fall of 1919 he and two classmates, Richard M. Pearson and Raymond F. McPartlin — editor and managing editor, respectively, of *The Daily Dartmouth* — were neglecting senior-year studies to write editorial, advertising, and circulation sales copy, make up dummies, and go through all the motions of creating a magazine. The magazine was to be called *College*, and they proposed to publish it after graduation.

Suddenly the glittering bubble was burst when, on a morning early in 1920, there arrived at the office of *The Daily Dartmouth* a notice of a new magazine called *The Collegiate World*, published monthly by a Chicago group. As it had already been launched, *The Collegiate World* had the advantage of being first of its kind. "Its kind" turned out to be the type of editorial program Robinson, Pearson, and McPartlin had dummied into their proposed *College* — stories and articles by students, anecdotes, college news (athletic and otherwise), jokes, and cartoons — much of it reprinted from the 500 undergraduate

2

periodicals then being published, many of them college humor magazines. Up against this earlier bird, the Dartmouth triumvirate folded their dummy and turned their thoughts to how to earn a living after graduation in June.

The Collegiate World turned out to be a successful national magazine, not under that title, but under the title of College Humor. It happened this way: During its first years (1920–22) The Collegiate World assembled the best of its humorous articles, jokes, and cartoons — plus some it did not have room to include in the magazine — and put it in book form under the title The Best of College Humor. The next year the book title was reduced to College Humor. This proved so popular that the publishers substituted College Humor for The Collegiate World as the mag-

Left: Robinson at Rock Island Arsenal, 1917. He became a second lieutenant in 1918. Right: at Dartmouth, June 1920.

azine title and discontinued the annual book. The *College Humor* magazine was a success for about 15 years. It survived the Depression in a weakened condition and was folded in 1944.

Had there been no *Collegiate World*, would *College* have gone to press? And would its publisher have branched out into the high school field from his *College* base?

After graduation in June 1920, Robinson returned to his hometown, Wilkinsburg, near Pittsburgh, PA. He got a job, starting July 1, at the Pittsburgh Chamber of Commerce, writing publicity and helping the editor of the Chamber's periodical *Pittsburgh First* at $150 per month.

Soon came a day when Robinson was assigned to do a routine story about the September opening of schools. Waiting for an interview in the office of Pittsburgh Superintendent of Schools William M. Davidson, Robinson studied some wall charts showing projected increases in high school enrollments on a local and national scale. His "gotta-be-a-publisher" temperature suddenly leaped from normal to feverish as his mind interpreted the writing on the wall to mean opportunity — now, immediately — for a high school newspaper.

Robinson later revealed his thoughts to Superintendent Davidson and received encouragement and the advice that he discuss the idea with high school principals, whose cooperation would be needed. It was only natural that Robinson turned first to the principal of his old high school, William C. Graham of Wilkinsburg. From him came further encouragement and the signal that this was something that should be brought to the attention of the

Ray McPartlin, first left, and next to him Dick Pearson, Robinson's collaborators in proposing a national magazine to be called *College*.

principals of all 50 high schools of the Western Pennsylvania Interscholastic Athletic League (WPIAL), who, along with the athletic directors, served as league directors. The next move, suggested Graham, would be to talk with Edward Rynearson, principal of Pittsburgh's Fifth Avenue High School and president of the WPIAL. The spirit of helpfulness was catching on, and Rynearson invited Robinson to attend the next meeting of the WPIAL directors to present the idea and a dummy issue.

The idea was clear, the dummy rough but good enough to win the directors' support and their endorsement of the yet-unborn *Western Pennsylvania Scholastic* as the "official weekly newspaper of the Western Pennsylvania Interscholastic Athletic League." The personality of this entrepreneur must have made as strong an impact on these high school principals and their athletic directors as the idea he was proposing. He had won their confidence. No signed documents were necessary, just a handshake.

5

McPartlin and Robinson, 1920.

Now the fat was in the fire. The first issue had to be gotten out fast and thereafter "every Friday of the school year," as the masthead would promise. Robinson wrote urgently to his old friends, Pearson and McPartlin, to ask them to join in this publishing venture. McPartlin welcomed the opportunity to escape from his job as copywriter for the Dennison Manufacturing Company in Framingham, MA, and hastened to Wilkinsburg. Pearson had enrolled in a graduate program at Columbia and chose not to leave.*

It was the Robinson-McPartlin plan to have every issue eight pages long, but they didn't have time to prepare that much copy for No. 1, which came out on Friday, October 22, 1920, as a four-page newspaper, tabloid-size (12¼″ × 18″) with six columns to a page. A two-column box on page 1 of No. 1 promised growth (opposite page).

This promise was almost fulfilled. One further issue — December 17, 1920 — came out with only four pages, explained on the editorial page as follows:

Why Four?

The news at this season of the year did not warrant an eight-page issue this week. For that reason we are cutting our size to four pages, and charging but three cents for the issue. You may expect us back strong next month, however, with the same eight pages as always.

---

*In 1921 Pearson took a job as textbook salesman with Lyons & Carnahan, later moved to Harper, and then to Macmillan as vice president. He died March 24, 1957. A nephew, John Pearson Spaulding, joined Scholastic in 1954 and became president in 1971.

The
Western Pennsylvania Scholastic

Volume 1. No. 1 OCTOBER 22, 1920 Price, 5c. Per Copy

Start of W. P. I. A. L. Was Back in 1906

Three Teams in First League

The first agitation for a league such as the Western Pennsylvania Interscholastic Athletic League dates back as far as 1903, when a movement was started by the faculties of Pittsburgh High School, Allegheny Prep, and Shadyside Academy for stated eligibility rules, and generally cleaner sport. Other schools were approached on the proposition, but little sentiment in favor of the plan was found at that time.

In 1903, indeed, it was an extraordinary institution which was represented solely by pupils of that school. With no scolastic requirements in force, the usual thing was to go out and hire the best players in the vicinity, outfit them in high school uniforms, and stack them up against one another in grim battles. This was not peculiar to high schools alone, preparatory and college teams doing their full share in this line.

But the more far-sighted members of high school athletic boards were aware that this loose style of thing was killing the interest of high school athletics. At the time when the representatives of the three schools were meeting together, planning what is now the W. P. I. A. L., the eligibility idea was still a decided novelty, so much so that the new organization found it extremely difficult to secure any data on methods used elsewhere. So the W. P. I. A. L. not only deserves credit for its work here in this state; it may also be called one of the pioneers in the general movement to elevate the standard of school athletics.

So many difficulties and setbacks were met with that it was not until 1906 that the league finally took shape. Two representatives from each of the schools interested, of whom E. W. Rynearson, of the Fifth Avenue High School, is the sole member remaining in the league, drew up the first set of eligibility rules for inter-scholastic sport that were known in greater Pittsburgh. The plan followed was much like that already in force at Allegheny Prep, noted even then as one of the foremost boosters of better athletics in school circles.

The work of the league was not finished, however, when the set of rules had been approved; the big job came in their enforcement. Some of Pittsburgh's largest dailies took up the cudgel against the new movement, characterized its sponsers as fathers.

Only Four Pages?

No!

Next week and every other week thereafter the Scholastic will have eight pages

Scholastic Makes First Appearance

New Paper for W. P. I. A. L. to Come Out Weekly.

With this issue, the Western Pennsylvania Scholastic, believed to be the only one of its size and kind in the country, makes its first appearance. The new paper will be published weekly, will circulate throughout the schools which are members of the W. P. I. A. L., and will devote its columns to topics particularly interesting to those schools.

Every effort will be made to keep up-to-date as possible in the matter of news, and for this reason, representatives have been, or are being appointed in all the schools of the league. Inasmuch as it is impossible for these representatives to learn about everything that is going on, the Scholastic makes an especial appeal to each and every student that he see that his representative is advised of all happenings.

The following men have thus far been appointed as news and sales representatives for their schools:

Donora	Clement Sawvel
Washington	John Pa
Tarentum	George All
Union	Ti Geo H ...
Charleroi	Frank L. S...
Coraopolis	Lawrence Irwin
Woodlawn	Edgar Porter
Beaver Falls	Paul Slater
New Castle	Thaddeus Beck
Butler	Charles Nicholas
New Brighton	Charles Boren
Sewickley	Holton Bull
New Kensington	Richard Cooper
Wilkinsburg	Ted Toner
Norwin of Irwin	William Hershey
Latrobe	George Conrad
Shady Side Academy	Wm. B. Wolfe
Fifth Avenue	Frank Kohne
Canonsburg	W. A. Dickson, Jr.

TARENTUM WILL PUBLISH MONTHLY.

Tarentum High School is to have a school monthly this year. A meeting of 11 students from each class was held recently, under the direction of Principal W. S. McCullough, and discussion favored a monthly over a quarterly. Steps are to be taken soon in regarding to publishing the first issue, and choosing editors.

Dr. Walker and Miss Howe of the English department, together with Mr. McCullough will oversee the work.

SINGERS ORGANIZED.

Both the boys' and the girls' glee clubs of Canonsburg High School are already rehearsing for the Christmas concert, while the high school orchestra is also rehearsing weekly. Miss Violet Mayer is instructor.

BEAVER HIGH TO GET FIELD

Officials of the Borough plan to get together soon to discuss plans for a new athletic field for Beaver High. Dravo Field, the school's former field, has been closed.

TONER WILKINSBURG CHAMP.

The annual fall tennis championship at Wilkinsburg High was won by Ted Toner.

Fast Games Promised Today and Tomorrow

Mid-Season Finds Many Unbeaten

With the football season about half over, and the schedules rapidly nearing those contests commonly known as "big," those in the know are already looking forward to the Syracuse Cup, and picking their choices for victory in the annual race. Upsets have been so frequent during the past fortnight, that it is practically impossible to forecast the final outcome with any assurance, but just now half-a-dozen likely comers have begun to draw away from the herd.

Schenley High, by upsetting Allegheny 7–0 a week ago, not only effectively put the 1919 champs out of the running, but also made itself one of the real contenders of the present season. Schenley was credited with having an average eleven, which, barring its tilts with one or two first-class teams, such as Allegheny, would enjoy a highly successful season. Now, however, Schenley is up among the elite in scholastic football, and must certainly be taken into account when the outcome of the race is being forecasted.

Schenley's team deserved its victory every bit. Not only did Coach Forth's men shone over the lone touchdown of the contest by sheer athletic on the team, on the defensive displayed that it was an eleven of the highest calibre. Allegheny more than once threatened to score, and it is to the credit of the Schenley line particularly that these threats remained threats only, and not deeds.

M'Candless One of Season's Best

When the dopesters sit them down at the close of the 1920 season, and seek to evolve from the long lists of high school football stars an all-Western Pennsylvania eleven that will be worthy of the name, they will halt long at the name of one Howard McCandless, captain of the eleven which represents Beaver Falls High School, and one of the speediest and smoothest little quarterbacks that ever known.

Not alone is McCandless a remarkable individual star; he also pilots his eleven with the skill of a veteran of twice his experience. In running back punts, he has few equals, and on a broken field, he reminds some of the wisest of one Eddie Casey whose name is writ large in the Yale blackbook.

It is uncertain at what college McCandless will continue his scholastic work, but it is an assured fact that the college he attends will not lack first-class quarterback material.

HOWARD McCANDLESS, Beaver Falls' Captain and Pilot.

While the city schools are being accounted for, Peabody and Fifth Avenue must also be mentioned, since this pair have also a good chance to climbing up to the pedastal marked "champion." The Peabody team demonstrated that it was more than a mere eleven, and that it was an excellent scoring machine when it trampled all over South Hills for 44 points last Friday. One of their noteworthy achievements was a four-minute march to a touchdown the length of the field, an accomplishment that few elevens of any type have ever equalled.

Beaver Falls High School looks like the leading out-of-the-city eleven. Heralded as a combination of average power, the Beaver Falls outfit invaded Wilkinsburg last Saturday, and took that school, for which great prophecies had been made, into camp by a 19-point shutout. Attention centered on this game for more than one reason, the McCandless - Riley followers being more interested in the showing of their respective candidates for all-Western Pennsylvania quarterback than in the game itself. It is not detracting from McCandless' wonderful exhibition in the least to say that Riley was in no condition to undergo comparison in this game, every step he took being torture.

Fighting Beaver Falls down in its own district saw Rochester a league newcomer, and New Brighton, both of whom have yet to receive a setback. It is unlikely that either team will lose this week, consequently fans in the Valley district are proclaiming the fact that there are some mighty tough tilts coming down that way, when the season begins to wane. Rochester is credited with being a heavy, experienced team, while the

(Continued on Page 4.)

MANY FEATURES ON LECTURE SERIES PROGRAM.

The annual lecture course at Wilkinsburg High School, which opened last Tuesday with a concert by the Leiter Light Opera Company, will continue throughout the winter season. Coming attractions are the Rondoliers, Nov. 8, "The Mikado," by members of the high school, Dec. 9, Ralph Bingham, called one of America's greatest funmakers, Jan. 7, the Tyrolean Yodlers, Jan. 20, and the College Singing Girls, Feb. 24. Arrangements for the series are in the hands of Principal W. C. Graham and Elmer Milligan '21.

Though it was designated the official weekly newspaper of the WPI *Athletic* Association, *The Scholastic** published news of all school activities submitted by the local student representatives. Keenly aware that the success of the paper, which students would pay for out of their own pockets, depended on a concentration on non-curriculum content, Robinson peppered the paper with articles on everything from personal appearance to advice for those both going and not going to college. He promoted oratorical and declamation competitions, encouraged students to form press, radio, drama, and music clubs, and urged them to read extensively: "If you do not go further with your school work in a college or university, remember that there are mountains of books on the shelves of libraries to which you are welcome. Ask your English teacher to prepare a list of good books for you."

He explained "Why It Pays to Study Music"; encouraged girls to go into sports, and schools to schedule interscholastic contests for girls in tennis, swimming, track and field, golf, and basketball; and published the pro and con of girls playing basketball under boys' rules. "Use the columns of *The Scholastic* to challenge one another, girls, and we promise our cooperation in making your games as popular as those of boys."

A headline in the first issue signified the rise of girls in an activity long considered the reserve of boys:

Girl Cheerleaders
New Idea This Season

*In this chapter, the title *The Scholastic* is used to refer to *The Western Pennsylvania Scholastic*.

The "new idea" came from the female student correspondent who reported: "General feeling among the boys is that a girl has the 'pep' and leading powers necessary to carry a mob along behind the school team, and, to a man, they back their fair leaders to the limit of their vocal powers."

The beginnings of what would in a few years become the Scholastic Writing Awards were seen in the announcements of essay- or article-writing competitions, including one for girls on what they think of boys, and vice versa.

Robinson's purpose in holding these competitions was twofold: They provided an activity in which *The Scholastic* was directly involved and its usefulness to students enhanced; they also stimulated students to put their thoughts in writing beyond what schools were asking in their English classes. Participation was voluntary, the deadline allowed plenty of time, and the prizes were nominal: $7.50 for first prize in the "What Boys and Girls Think of Each Other" contest, with a second prize of $2.50. It turned out that the $2.50 had to be shared by two girls who tied for it, one of whom, said the report, "does not wish her name used."

When the first Pittsburgh Radio Exhibition was to be held in April 1922 at the William Penn Hotel, attended by radio clubs from the high schools of western Pennsylvania, southeast Ohio, and West Virginia, *The Scholastic* announced the program and carried a coupon entitling any bearer of high school age to 10 cents off the regular admission price of 25 cents. *The Scholastic* published the radio programs of station KDKA, East Pittsburgh, the nation's pioneer

THE WESTERN PENNSYLVANIA
SCHOLASTIC

VOL. II. NO. 5   THURSDAY, OCTOBER 27, 1921   Price To Subscribers, - - 5c / To Non-Subscribers, 7c

Dope Upset; Seven Teams Remain in League Cup Race

Monongahela, Rochester, Schenley, Shadyside, Tarentum, Washington and Westinghouse seem to be the chief remaining contenders for the Syracuse Trophy. Sewickley, upsetting the dope last week, eliminated Beaver Falls, but Sewickley's schedule does not call for the required number of five league games, so that they cannot be considered among the possibilities.

Westinghouse and Schenley meet this week in one of the most important of the league games, for it means the elimination of one of the strongest teams in the league.

Monongahela City, hitherto not considered among the leaders in the race, showed their strength last week by defeating Coach "Pep" Clyde's strong Tube City team. Tarentum High, although still undefeated, has not met many strong teams, but will meet a real test this week in the McKeesport gridders.

Washington has continued its winning streak and has an easy game this week, but Shadyside will have to show its metal on Saturday to keep in the running after meeting Wilkinsburg. New Brighton again showed its strength by defeating one of the contenders for the cup. It is unfortunate that New Brighton's record was marred with a tie.

Rochester, a contender that must be reckoned with at every count, will meet the Beaver Falls aggregation this week. The game will have a bearing on both the Beaver Valley championship and the league title. The (Continued on Page Three.)

MUNHALL HI WINS OVER BEN AVON 14-0

Munhall again took over its opponent when they defeated Ben Avon High 14-0. The game was featured by long runs and long plunges, but fumbles were profuse throughout. Only once was Munhall's goal in danger and here the line held and threw its opponent. Jackson recovered a fumble and ran forty yards for Munhall's first touchdown. The second touchdown resulted when Ferguson intercepted a pass and ran thirty-five yards. Miller, the Munhall fullack, showed up well.

Munhall—14.   Ben Avon—0.

Munhall—14		Ben Avon—0
Moore	L.E.	Monroe
Culosson	L.T.	Skillen
Evans	L.G.	Peterson
Boyer	C.	Toy
Sano	R.G.	Frazier
Black	R.T.	Sterling
Stires	R.E.	Bates
Ferguson	Q.B.	G. McCabe
Treff	R.H.	D. McCabe
Jamison	L.H.	Rhodes
Miller	F.B.	Boggs

Substitutions: Price for Bates, Bates for G. McCabe, Thompson for Stires, Ulrich for Jackson, Giffor for Moore. Touchdowns: Ferguson 1, Jackson 1. Referee: McCague. Umpire: Crolius.

W. P. I. A. L. MEETING TO BE HELD THIS SAT.

The first meeting of the members of the W. P. I. A. L. will be held this Saturday morning at the Fifth Avenue High School, Pittsburgh. Notices have been sent out to the various principals in the league by the Secretary, C. C. Marshall of Homestead High.

The business that will be brought up at the meeting includes the question of the manner in which basketball will be handled during the coming year, as well as the conduct of the remainder of the year's football schedules. There are several applications on file from high schools in the district who wish to become members of the league, and these applications will be voted upon. Several other matters of less importance will be acted upon.

MONONGAHELA UNDEFEATED; SCORES WIN AT M'KEESPORT

(William Gilbert)

McKeesport High met defeat at the hands of Monongahela City in a well played game at Cycler Park last Friday, by a score of 17-13. Each team scored two touchdowns, but Monongahela City also added a field goal.

In the first quarter McVickers kicked a field goal from the 20-yard line, which ended the scoring in this period. The next quarter Hayes carried the ball over the line for McKeesport. Ward missed the goal and the quarter ended 6-3, with McKeesport ahead. It was in the third quarter that McVickers intercepted a forward pass and made a touchdown on a 60-yard run. McVickers kicked the goal and the quarter ended 10-6 in Monongahela City's favor. Each team made a touchdown in the last quarter. Cain carrying the ball over the line for Monongahela City and Ward for McKeesport. Elder kicked goal for McKeesport, the game ending 17-13, with Monongahela City the victor. The line-up:

McKeesport—13		Monongahela—17
Parker	L.E.	Tustin
Boax	L.T.	Daniels
Ivey	L.G.	Gillingham
Butler	C.	Woodward
Berger	R.G.	Tennent
Ruby	R.T.	Myers
McAllister	R.E.	Cauldwell
Sharpe	Q.B.	Taylor
Hayes	L.H.	Cain
Fleming	R.H.	McVickers
Ward	F.B.	Farragh

Substitutions: Harold for Ruby, P. McAllister for Berger, Elder for Fleming, Smith for Cain, Ceurrutto for Daniels, Cain for Smith, Hoffman for Taylor. Touchdowns: McVickers, Cain, Ward and Hayes. Officials: R. Allshours and J. Egan.

League High Schools Will Take Action on Disarmament

BOND ISSUE PROPOSED FOR M'KEESPORT HIGH

(By William Gilbert)

In order to relieve the overcrowded conditions in the schools of McKeesport, Superintendent Richey has proposed a bond issue, the proceeds of which are to be used to enlarge the Technical High School and so bring all of the high school students into one building. The Junior High School, which is at present used for the freshmen class, will probably be used to relieve the overcrowded condition of the grade schools.

This proposed bond issue will not increase the rate of taxation; on the other hand, the rate will be increased if the majority of the voters of McKeesport do not approve of the bond issue, for money will have to be raised in some way to build the addition to the high school. It is, therefore, to the benefit of all the people to get behind this movement and help make it a success.

NEW BRIGHTON ELIMINATES TURTLE CREEK UNION 29-6

(Lloyd A. M. Corkan)

Saturday afternoon New Brighton High School defeated Turtle Creek Union High on their new field on Oak Hill to the tune of 29 to 6.

Turtle Creek won the toss and New Brighton kicked off. By a series of delayed and double passes Turtle Creek worked the ball down the field. The locals held them for downs and registered two first downs themselves before losing the ball. Turtle Creek again employed their delayed pass to good effect until finally Captain Botti went over for a touchdown; he later failed at goal. This score by Turtle Creek seemed to arouse the locals, as they went to work and delivered their opponents a decisive trimming.

New Brighton's first touchdown came in the second quarter, when after receiving the kick-off they worked their way down the field by end runs and line plunges, Garver finally throwing a pass to Riddle for a touchdown, Garver kicking goal. At the end of the half the score stood 7-6 in favor of the local team.

Turtle Creek kicked off to Boren who returned to midfield. This time the locals marched down the field chiefly by punching Turtle Creek's famous line for long gains. Their opponents braced on their goal line and stopped the locals twice, but the third attempt was successful and Garver went over. He missed goal.

Seiple then kicked off for New Brighton. Turtle Creek opened up a passing attack, which was terminated shortly when Garver intercepted a pass and returned it to Turtle Creek's 30-yard line. A pass, Garver to Riddle, added 15 more and Harris went through the line for eight more. Here Turtle Creek braced and took the ball. On the next play the New Brighton forwards smeared Turtle Creek's play (Continued on Page Three.)

A plan has just been completed by the SCHOLASTIC by which an attempt will be made to start a movement for the high schools of the W. P. I. A. League to take the leadership among the high schools of the country in adopting resolutions in favor of naval disarmament insofar as it is possible within the keeping of the nation's policy.

A letter with the approval of J. M. McLaughlin, president of the league, has been sent by the SCHOLASTIC to the principals of all the league high schools asking that the question of disarmament and the coming disarmament conference be brought to the attention of the students and that resolutions be presented and adopted calling upon the President of the United States to do all in his power at the coming conference to limit armaments. This step is only part of a great movement to assist in moulding public opinion on this great subject.

A student's disarmament conference is being held in Princeton during the present week under the auspices of the students of Princeton University, which is being attended by representatives of more than two hundred colleges throughout the country. The SCHOLASTIC has requested the committee in charge of this conference to accept the co-operation of the high school students in Western Pennsylvania, and permit the resolutions adopted by league high schools to be handled through the organization which will be effected at that conference.

AVALON SENIORS PLAN 'HOPING VICTORY' PARTY

(A. M. Bechler)

The Seniors of Avalon High are going to give a party for the entire high school on Saturday evening, October 29th, the evening of the Bellevue-Avalon game, to celebrate its long looked for VICTORY. Very elaborate preparations are being formulated by the Seniors. A number of contests have been arranged and points will be awarded to the contestants. The ones receiving the most number of points will receive prizes. Dancing will be a feature of the evening, the music being rendered by the High School Orchestra. Refreshments will conclude the evening's program.

LATROBE LECTURE COURSE

In a highly auspicious manner the Latrobe High School entertainment course was ushered in Thursday evening by the Ernest Gamble Concert Company. The company established a high standard for the course. Mr. Gamble, well known basso, was the feature of the evening, and he was ably assisted by Miss Clara Stadelman, soprano, and Miss Verna Page, violinist.

A large audience was in attendance and showed its appreciation of the performance by applauding each number very enthusiastically.

For the second year the page size was reduced to 10" X 15" and better paper was used.

public station with a daily schedule — Monday through Friday, running from noon to 9 p.m. Programs consisted mainly of talks and music and, on Sundays, church services.

A cartoon strip, "The Weekly Twang" by Dave Scott, appeared frequently, but not every week, during the second year. These were commentaries in five or six panels per issue on school life, dating, students' fancies and fantasies, including several on the workings of *The Scholastic* editorial office.

Editor Robinson seized many opportunities to involve *The Scholastic* in the education process, short of actual classroom lecturing or teaching. But he came close at times. For instance, he sent a letter, with the approval of the WPIAL president, to all high school principals asking "that the question of disarmament be brought to the attention of the students and that resolutions be presented and adopted calling upon the President of the United States to do all in his power at the coming conference to limit armaments." This was featured on page one of the October 27, 1921, issue.

The editorial page on page two of the first issue carried three editorials: "Our Bow," followed by "A Fight Against Odds" (a tribute to the WPIAL), and "Your Paper." As typographic decorations, a pair of small American flags was centered between the editorials.

Our Bow

Starting a paper of this type is much like taking an afternoon's stroll along a cliff, blindfolded — you never know when you're going to step off into nothing. But we have a great deal of faith in the high school students of the WPIAL

Circuit, enough to make us believe that they will welcome a publication such as this.

So far as we know, *The Scholastic* is the only paper of its kind and size in the world. Intercollegiate magazines are not unknown, interscholastic papers have even been tried, but, to our knowledge, there is no paper published for a group of high schools as frequently or as large as this is to be.

Despite this fact, that we are blazing a trail never before trodden by the foot of man, we have met with the greatest spirit of helpfulness on the part of principals that could be imagined. And at this time, we wish to extend to them our thanks for the invaluable aid they have given us in these first few weeks.

Another group of men who have rallied to our support is the group of advertisers whose statements you will find here and there through the paper. We wish to impress upon each and every one of our readers that if it were not for our advertisers, this paper would never have come into being. Therefore, every person who regards this paper with any friendliness at all may best show that friendliness by using *The Scholastic* as a medium through which to choose the stores to which he will give his patronage.

As to ourselves. The editorial columns of *The Scholastic* will be as non-editorial as possible, but they will be at all times devoted to the best interests of the greater number. The news columns will carry as detailed as possible accounts of all high school doings among the members of the league and their nearest neighbors.

Your Paper

The success of *The Western Pennsylvania Scholastic* hinges upon the support it receives at the hands of some 25,000 or more students of the high schools in the WPIAL. In no way does it wish to appeal to these students for philanthropy; on the contrary, it wishes at all times to be deserving of their support. For that reason, *The Scholastic* does ask aid in one particular way — that each student consider himself a representative of this organization, and that he or she do everything possible to keep the reporter for the paper in his school advised of every happening, social or scholastic. Only by the utmost cooperation on the part of every individual can this paper be made what its editors want it to be, a newspaper.

The masthead below was to stand through the first semester until January 1921, when McPartlin departed and Maurice R. Robinson appointed himself managing editor. McPartlin left to satisfy a longing to work on a daily newspaper, and the opportunity came at the *Manchester* (NH) *Union and Leader* while he was at home during Christmas vacation. Being the keeper of *The Scholastic*'s income/expense journal, he was well aware of the delicate balance there, and his decision to move may have been

The Western Pennsylvania Scholastic

Official Weekly Newspaper of the Western Pennsylvania Interscholastic Athletic League

Published every Friday of the school year

Office at 715 Wallace Ave., Wilkinsburg, Pa.

Address all contributions and other mail matter to Box 207, Wilkinsburg, Pa. Telephone Bell Franklin 4457.

R. F. McPARTLIN	-	-	-	Managing Editor
M. R. ROBINSON	-	-	-	Business Manager
L. H. RECTOR -	-	-	-	Advertising Manager

FRIDAY, OCTOBER 22, 1920

influenced by his concern over the future of the enterprise. It had been a congenial and informal partnership between friends, and Robinson was sorry to see it end. But, as was characteristic of his reaction to the many disappointments he would face in the years ahead, he lost no time in adjusting to the situation and getting on with the work.

McPartlin left the *Union and Leader* in 1923 to join the *Boston Globe*, where he remained as writer and editor of special features until his death in 1951 at the age of 52. In its obituary, the *Dartmouth Alumni Magazine* called him "the best Dartmouth newspaperman of his time."

L. H. (Louis) Rector, who had a full-time job with the Western Electric Company in Pittsburgh, stayed on as advertising manager through the school year and was paid a percentage of the ad revenue. He sold space mainly by mail and telephone in the evenings and on Saturdays which, even in advertising departments and agencies, was at least a half-workday in the 1920's. The space rate was 20 cents per column inch. Among the advertisers during the first year were Browning, King & Company, West Penn Fuel, Post & Flagg (stocks and bonds), Frank & Seder (a department store), the Bank of Pittsburgh, and the R. B. Robinson & Son Department Stores (in Wilkinsburg and Verona). R. B. was the father of Maurice R. and five other children. Ralph — two years older than Maurice — was the son in the department store title.*

Robinson recalls that his father's department store ads were not on a cash basis, but were paid for with a couple of neckties. After the first year the ads of the

---

*Maurice, the youngest son, was born in 1895. The youngest child, Rachel, was born seven years later. Besides Ralph, Maurice's brothers were Clarence (1884), Hugh (1886), and William (1888).

Robinson home in Wilkinsburg, PA, where first 10 issues were written in sewing room (second floor, double window).

Robinson stores disappeared from *The Scholastic*, but another Wilkinsburg department store, Caldwell & Graham, came in for a small insertion in December 1921, presumably on a cash basis.

By having *The Scholastic* office in his mother's sewing room for the first six months, Robinson had no rent to pay, but there was a telephone expense. An early journal entry shows that Robinson's parents were reimbursed for telephone calls beyond the Wilkinsburg area. Income from advertising at 20 cents per column inch and from subscriptions fell short of the unavoidable expenses — the printer, the post office, $25 per week for McPartlin, gasoline for the Model T Ford, and some train travel up and down the three river valleys in which most of the high schools were located. Robinson's salary from the Pittsburgh Chamber of Commerce, where he was assistant to the editor of *Pittsburgh First*, made up the difference between income and expenses. Circulation income varied between $120 and $130 per issue, after student agents kept two of the five cents per copy. When the price rose to seven cents, they kept three.

15

Norman MacLeod
and Robinson,
1917.

With McPartlin gone, Robinson became the sole proprietor — or survivor, as it must have seemed to some — of the infant enterprise. Yet from the masthead, letterheads, or anything in print, one could not determine who owned *The Western Pennsylvania Scholastic*, but one could guess. Some guessed that it was the Western Pennsylvania Interscholastic Athletic League, but that body made no financial commitment to the paper and was not asked to. The masthead directed that all mail be sent to Box 207, Wilkinsburg, PA, and gave the office address as the nameless family home, 715 Wallace Avenue. It gave the telephone number as Bell Franklin 4457, which meant that callers should use the Bell System, not the rival P&A (Pittsburgh & Allegheny Telephone Company).

In January 1921 Robinson arranged with his boyhood and high school friend Norman MacLeod and his associate George Ketchum to take desk space in the office of Ketchum & MacLeod, a fund-raising and advertising agency, in the Keenan Building in downtown Pittsburgh. He also hired a young woman to be assistant editor and office manager. The Keenan Building was only a few blocks from the Chamber of Commerce, so he could readily shuttle between the two stations to do his work five evenings a week, all day Saturday, and sometimes on Sunday — though Sunday had to be carefully planned, as he was still resident in that staunch United Presbyterian household on Wallace Avenue.

Through the early months of 1921, still operating from that desk in Ketchum & MacLeod's office and continuing with his Chamber of Commerce job, Robinson pondered the problem of what do with *The Scholastic* — and what to do with himself. Should he resign from the

16

Chamber of Commerce job and concentrate on *The Scholastic*? Or should he drop *The Scholastic* and stay with the Chamber of Commerce to move from there to a career in publicity or journalism? He consulted with friends, including his closest, Norman MacLeod, who — reflecting his interest in young people — made it clear that he would like to see *The Scholastic* continued. Robinson decided to stay with it; he resigned from his $150 per month job at the Chamber of Commerce and rented office space (Room 1121) in the Bessemer Building in downtown Pittsburgh. That $150 per month had helped to pay the printing and postage bill, which would now have to be paid for in increased circulation or advertising, or by some stroke of luck. It came with a call from John Cowan, his former boss at the Chamber, who said that part-time publicity work was available with the Salvation Army. "Ask for $75 a week," Cowan advised, which would be more than Robinson had earned with the Chamber of Commerce. "If you ask for too little," Cowan said, "they will question your ability." Robinson followed this advice and held the job from September 1921 until the summer of 1922. In recalling this, Robinson said that getting publicity for the Salvation Army required no genius at that time; it was basking in goodwill from its performance in comforting Allied troops on the Western Front. The American public opened its pocketbooks wide for the organization famed for its doughnuts and hot coffee in the trenches.

With this good catch Robinson had enough cash to pay the rent, utilities, and a full-time secretary (the going rate for an experienced one was $15 per week). This was Anya Freedel, who had been Robinson's assistant at the Chamber. With an office and a secretary he was ready for the opening of the school year 1921–22. He switched printers, leaving the Journal Publishing Company and going to the Western Newspaper Union in the building next to his Bessemer Building office. The page size of *The Western Pennsylvania Scholastic* was reduced slightly to 10″ × 15″ and a better quality of paper was used, newspaper format prevailing. Robinson received two more offers for part-time publishing work, which he accepted: *The Presbyterian Banner* took him on for circulation promotion; the Pittsburgh Athletic Club, as editor of its membership journal, *The Winged Head*. Now he had the finances to publish *The Western Pennsylvania Scholastic* for school year 1921–22 even if he could get no gains in circulation or advertising. However, it did have a circulation gain from 3,000 to 4,000. This amounted to about $840 additional circulation revenue for the year. (There were 28 issues.)

It appears that this windfall of publicity jobs raised Robinson's level of entrepreneurism, as he had his printer produce the following letterhead:

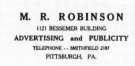

M. R. ROBINSON
1121 BESSEMER BUILDING
ADVERTISING and PUBLICITY
TELEPHONE ·· SMITHFIELD 2187
PITTSBURGH, PA.

It could be that he saw this branch of his business growing to staff proportions and producing the finances necessary for expansion of *The Western Pennsylvania Scholastic*. Expansion? Such as what? He recalls some of his thoughts as he paused between deadlines during the early months of 1922: "I came to the realization that the scope of *The Western Pennsylvania Scholastic*, no matter how successfully it served the high schools of the area, was limited by the number of them in the area — about 50. It occurred to me to duplicate the idea in Cleveland, Detroit, Chicago, etc., for the high schools in and around those and other cities. I got advice on the problems of trying to operate a chain of regional *Scholastics* and was warned of the difficulty of financing such an enterprise or of finding editor-publishers who could succeed in this new field."

Since a chain of *Scholastics* seemed impractical, what could be done with the one in hand to achieve the scope and income needed to satisfy an enterprising publisher? Perhaps it could be made into a tri-state *Scholastic* for all of Pennsylvania, West Virginia, and Ohio. . . . Why stop there? "After days and days of soul-searching," Robinson recalls, "I decided I would never know whether I could make a go of *The Scholastic* unless I kept on trying. So I decided to reach for all 48 states."

The big decision brought on a multitude of tasks to be tackled at once, the most pressing being the raising of capital (Robinson would form a corporation), devising a format and editorial formula for the national periodical and a plan for building circulation, and hiring some new personnel. There was also the matter of the franchise he had from the Western Pennsylvania Interscholastic Athletic League as its official publication. He was loath to lose that.

He had to move fast. In late April he was writing to the Library of Congress: "I desire some information concerning copyrights. I wish to copyright the name of a magazine, *The Scholastic*, devoted to high school students. . . ." The Library wrote back, saying: "The copyright law has no provision under which registration can be made of a name or title," and advised him to "address the Commissioner of Patents, Washington, D.C." In the future Robinson would refer all matters of copyright and trademark registration to his Dartmouth classmate, Nichol M. Sandoe, a New York attorney and specialist in patent law.

He signed on G. Herbert McCracken to promote circulation and join him in business management of the newly organized Scholastic Publishing Company (next chapter). Then he did what he liked to do best — work up ideas for editorial content. These he presented in a four-page brochure, with page one showing the cover design and other pages announcing editorial plans and subscription prices with an order form. He took this brochure to the annual convention of the National Education Association (NEA) in Boston in July 1922. This was the first Scholastic presence at a national convention.* Hundreds were to follow.

*Assisting Robinson at the booth at the NEA convention was his friend, Barbara French, who was en route from Pittsburgh to vacation on Cape Cod. Miss French, who later became Mrs. J. Campbell Burton, was and is a lifelong friend of Robinson and his family, as was her late husband. Campbell Burton was a senior partner of the public accounting firm of Arthur Young & Company, first auditors of Scholastic for fiscal year 1939–40 and the company's auditors ever since. Campbell Burton bought Scholastic stock in 1925, which became worthless with the dissolution of the Scholastic Publishing Company in 1936.

John (Sandy) Burton, son of Mr. and Mrs. J. Campbell Burton, served as a director of Scholastic Magazines, Inc., from 1968 through 1972, when he resigned to become chief accountant of the Securities and Exchange Commission, and later deputy mayor (finance) of New York City. He rejoined the Scholastic board in December 1977.

CHAPTER II

The Scholastic

Now Playing
in the National League

IT would be a busy summer of planning and reconstruction in 1922. The "Robinson property" would become the Scholastic Publishing Company, a Pennsylvania corporation. Guiding Robinson through the legal ramifications and preparing the papers of incorporation was Paul E. Hutchinson, a recent University of Pittsburgh Law School graduate who had just hung out his shingle with a Pittsburgh law firm. "Maybe he never *was* paid for some of that early legal work," said Robinson, "but what other young lawyer ever had his own guinea pig corporation on which to practice what he read in his textbooks?" In a letter some years ago, after Scholastic had gone through a variety of incorporations, consolidations, reorganizations, and mergers, Hutchinson plaintively wrote: "There have been so many corporate changes, I'm confused." Hutchinson served as the company's leading legal light until his death 48 years later in 1970. He was elected a Scholastic director in 1933 and later became a partner in the prestigious Pittsburgh law firm of Reed, Smith, Shaw & McClay.

Going national and going corporate were momentous events. There was yet another: the employment of George Herbert McCracken as circulation manager. This proved

Paul E. Hutchinson, 1895–1970.

to be as enduring and auspicious as the decision to go national. Robinson had met McCracken through their mutual friend Norman MacLeod, a fraternity brother of both (Delta Tau Delta) and a partner in the Ketchum & MacLeod agency. The coming of McCracken was announced in the May 11 issue, next-to-the-last of the school year, of *The Western Pennsylvania Scholastic*, as follows:

'HERB' M'CRACKEN, FORMER PITT STAR, JOINS SCHOLASTIC STAFF

"Herb" McCracken, former popular and prominent Pitt athlete is to enter the journalistic field, and readers and friends of The SCHOLASTIC will be delighted to learn that he has been signed for the staff of The

G. HERBERT McCRACKEN

SCHOLASTIC for next year. He will not give up coaching, however, as he has expressed the desire to continue at his coaching work for a few more years, but during the football season he will write for the League paper from Meadville and at the close of the season will take up full-time duty on this publication. McCracken has arranged to be given leave of absence during any fall season when he desires to coach.

McCracken was born in Sewickley and received his grade and high school education in the schools of that borough, graduating from Sewickley High School in June, 1917. While in high school he participated in practically all branches of high school athletics.

He entered the University of Pittsburgh in the fall of 1917, and won positions on both the football and basketball teams of the freshman class. He played varsity half-back on "Pop" Warner's teams at Pitt during the seasons of 1918, '19 and '20, and was considered by "Pop" Warner the most valuable and all-round man on the 1920 eleven. It is an interesting achievement worthy of note that McCracken played through the entire 1919 season of football with a broken nose.

"Herb" was also a member of the varsity basketball teams at Pitt for three years, being captain in his senior year 1920-21. He was a three-letter man, having won his letter in swimming.

While at Pitt, McCracken did not confine his activities to athletics as he was prominent in other student activities: chairman of the Junior Prom committee, on the cabinet of the Y. M. C. A. and president of his class during his senior year. With all his activities, he ranked high in academic achievement, having been elected to Beta Gamma Sigma, honorary scholarship fraternity in schools of commerce, and to Omicron Delta Kappa, honorary activity fraternity.

Early during his college career, McCracken took an active interest in Y. M. C. A. work and was in demand as a speaker before high school clubs.

After graduation from Pitt, McCracken accepted the coaching position at Allegheny College, where with mediocre material he brought the season to a successful close with a victory over Allegheny's rival, Geneva. In addition to his coaching work, he was instrumental in placing the athletic association at Allegheny on a firmer and more business-like basis. Since last December he has been assistant director of the University of Pittsburgh Y. M.

During the coming summer, McCracken will be the athletic and physical director of Camp Porter which will be conducted from July 2nd to September 2nd at Conneaut, Ohio, on Lake Erie by the Pittsburgh Y. M. C. A. An enrollment of 150 boys is expected. McCracken has announced a football training period at this camp during the last two weeks of August when preliminary training will be given to high school football aspirants. "Red" Byers of Pitt will be assistant coach. There will be no scrimmage, the work being devoted mainly to fundamentals, with special training for men who aspiire to certain positions on an eleven.

Earl Bothwell, secretary of the

There was no reference in the McCracken article to the metamorphosis that would take place. When Robinson wrote the article, around May 1, he had already made the decision to go national and had told McCracken of the plan. It was probably early in April when he came to the decision. His letter to the Library of Congress inquiring about copyright for the title *The Scholastic* was dated April 26, 1922. The April 27 issue of *The Western Pennsylvania Scholastic* gave promise of a change:

> Next Year's
> *Scholastic*
> Will Contain
> 16 Pages Every Week.
> It will be composed of the type of material which 12,500 students indicated they desired in answering questionnaires.
> The subscription price for thirty issues if paid during the month of May will be $1.25. Send your name and money now.

What actually happened "next year" would be not 30 issues but 19, and not 16 pages every week but 24 pages every other week. The subscription price would be $2, with "special rates for more than ten copies to same address."

The last issue of *The Western Pennsylvania Scholastic* (May 25, 1922) carried a thank-you note to "the forty schools that have stood by us in these first two hard years," which merits quoting in full:

Another Milestone

The Scholastic has completed its second year of existence as the only publication of its kind in this country. We are still keeping back the jeers of those who laughed at such an undertaking, and what's more, we have announced expansion for the coming year and we promise to stand by that announcement: 16 pages every week, and instead of thirty issues during the year, thirty-five issues.

We wish to take this opportunity to thank the forty schools that have stood by us in these first two hard years of an uphill struggle. As we progress, we shall not forget the schools that were our constant help in troublous times. We wish the seniors who are graduating a prosperous and happy life, and as for the other classes, we merely remind them of their responsibilities.

It was a strong implication to subscribers that next year they would be getting something bigger, better, and more often, but there was nothing to suggest that it would be in magazine style and no longer a fountain of news about western Pennsylvania's high schools. Explaining this years later, Robinson said that he wasn't sure in the month of May just what he would put into a September national *Scholastic*.

The thank-you note in the final issue of *The Western Pennsylvania Scholastic* promised "the schools that were our constant help" that they would not be forgotten. Robinson surely could not forget those 4,000 paid subscribers, as they and their western Pennsylvania successors formed a sorely needed subscription base. But they wouldn't be served with what they had become accustomed to. Gone would be the reports of school activities in Homestead, Duquesne, Swissvale, Beaver Falls, Sewickley, Wilkinsburg, Mars, and all the other school systems of the area, not to mention Pittsburgh's seven high schools.

The single-copy price was increased from seven cents to 15 cents. The format was switched to the page trim-size of many of the magazines of the day (8¾″ × 11¾″). The paper stock was as good as, if not better than, that used by most of the general magazines. The cover logo declared *The Scholastic* "A Magazine for High School Students," with the line "Published Bi-Weekly during the School Year" paneled at the bottom of the cover. Editorial content was designed to arouse students' interest in literature, writing, the arts, foreign languages, national and world news. Page 2 announced *The Scholastic* as "The National High School Bi-Weekly." A local high school history and civics teacher and University of

Page two of the first issue of *The Scholastic* after two years of *The Western Pennsylvania Scholastic*.

Announcing

That With This Issue

The Scholastic Begins Its

Third Year

And Enters the Publication Field as

The National High School Bi-Weekly

The Scholastic will be devoted entirely and exclusively
to the interests of high school students

Humor	Athletics	Clubs	Vacations	True Stories	Fiction	World Events
		Student Publications		Literature	Art	

21 ISSUES DURING THE SCHOOL YEAR   SINGLE COPIES 15 CENTS $2.00 A YEAR
SPECIAL RATES FOR MORE THAN TEN COPIES TO THE SAME ADDRESS

Readers:
We want you to make THE SCHOLASTIC *your* magazine and to feel at liberty to make suggestions and send in material to be considered for publication. Our Club Department is designed exclusively for the use of our readers. Tell us what clever plans your clubs have developed to make your meetings interesting or to finance some school project.

English Teachers:
Help us to discover and give encouragement to high school students who write. Send THE SCHOLASTIC the really exceptional stories, humorous or worthy essays, and poems your students prepare. We shall publish the best material received and give credit to school, teacher, and pupil.

Student Editors:
Make THE SCHOLASTIC a clearing house for your publications. Put us on your mailing list at once, and watch our exchange columns for criticisms of *your* publication. Our exchange department will be filled with ideas for you to use in your magazine. Send your unique ideas along to us and let us pass them on to other schools, giving you the credit.

THE SCHOLASTIC

Bessemer Building   Pittsburgh, Pa.

The SCHOLASTIC

a magazine for high school students

INTERNATIONAL NEWSREEL

CAMELIA SABIE BREAKS RECORD AT PARIS MEET

Published Bi-weekly during the School Year

VOL. 3, No. 1   PRICE, 15 CENTS   SEPTEMBER 16, 1922

First issue of the national *Scholastic*.

Pittsburgh professors wrote the news in an interpretative manner, but with no apparent effort to reach whatever slow learners there were in the academic-centered high schools of the day. Sports would be included in every issue.

And what about the tie-in with the Western Pennsylvania Interscholastic Athletic League? That too was gone, or — as it turned out — shelved for a year. Dated September 16, 1922, the front cover of the new 24-page magazine featured a photograph of a girl hurdler at a Paris meet.

The lead article, "Enter Business as a Partner," was by Alba B. Johnson, president of the Philadelphia and the Pennsylvania Chambers of Commerce, former president of the Baldwin Locomotive Works. This was followed by a photograph of "The Oldest High School in the United States" (the John Eliot School, Roxbury, MA*); a short story, "Ball—Foul—Strike," by Howard Philip Rhoades; two pages on the Passion Play at Oberammergau; a two-page news review ("The News Caldron," by Louis K. Manley, professor of political science, University of Pittsburgh); and an article entitled "1959" by Edward Rynearson, Pittsburgh's Fifth Avenue High School principal who gave encouragement and guidance to Robinson on *The Western Pennsylvania Scholastic*. Another Pittsburgh-centered feature, an article entitled "The Secrets of Football Fundamentals" by the celebrated coach "Pop" Warner, under whom McCracken had played at Pitt, would have some mollifying effect on those readers of the former *Western Pennsylvania Scholastic* now miffed or mystified by the metamorphosis.

*Ten years earlier the Boston Latin School opened, which is generally considered to be the forerunner of the American high school.

Two foreign-language clubs were announced, *The Scholastic* French Club and *The Scholastic* Spanish Club — "a new departure in the field of language associations; [the club] has no membership fee, no officers, and no constitution, but every high school student of French [or Spanish] who is a reader of *The Scholastic* is eligible for membership." Later a Latin club was introduced, offering a crossword puzzle under the heading "Here's One in Latin. It's Easy!"

The first issue of *The Scholastic* carried no masthead, but did run two agate lines of type at the bottom of page three, as follows: "The Scholastic Publishing Company, Bessemer Building, Pittsburgh, Pennsylvania. Contents fully copyrighted, 1922. Single copies 15 cents, yearly subscription $2.00. Special rates on quantities to one address."

In the next issue (September 30, 1922) two names were included in the notice at the bottom of page three: "M. R. Robinson, publisher; Jane Pine, editor." A recent University of Wisconsin graduate, Jane Pine had majored in journalism and applied for the job as the result of a letter Robinson had sent to a number of colleges and schools of journalism to recruit someone to assist him in copy editing and proofreading. Robinson interviewed her in Pittsburgh and hired her, giving her the title of editor. Never again was that title to be so cavalierly handed out. Jane Pine stayed only two months, the November 11 issue being the last to list her name. The next issue listed no one as editor. M. R. Robinson was listed as president, and A. E. Freedel, secretary and treasurer. (She was Anya who had worked with Robinson at the Chamber of Commerce. She was made a director of Scholastic Publishing Company in 1923.)

Up until the March 3 (1923) issue the notice remained unchanged, but in that issue a noteworthy addition appeared: "G. H. McCracken, vice president." McCracken had been on full-time Scholastic duty as circulation manager since the close of the 1922 football season. He would remain until the 1923 season opened, when he would be coaching the football team at Allegheny College through November.

Anya E. Freedel, first corporate secretary.

One editorial feature was carried over from *The Western Pennsylvania Scholastic*. That was Dave Scott's cartoon strip on the universal boy-dates-girl theme. The University of Pittsburgh and Pittsburgh Academy (a business school) each bought one-page ads, and the Standard Life Insurance Company, Doubleday-Hill Electric Company, and L. E. Balfour Company (class rings and pins) bought smaller spaces.

The 1920 Dartmouth graduate who wanted to be a publisher was now in it up to his national neck — circulation, editorial, capital, and advertising all demanding priority during this difficult transition from regional paper to national magazine. "Transition" may be the wrong word, as it could be taken to mean gradual change. That it was not. It was a jolt, followed by an adjustment by Robinson and his few associates to the new circumstances. McCracken, with his prior commitment as athletic director at Camp Porter for the summer of 1922 — to be followed by three months as football coach at Allegheny College — would not be available for full-time duty until December.

With Jane Pine's departure two months after the opening of the 1922–23 school year, Robinson probed among the seven Pittsburgh newspaper offices for someone to assist him in editorial work. He found his editor —

though she was not to bear the title — on the staff of the morning *Post* and the evening *Sun*, both under the same ownership. As art and drama critic on both papers, Penelope Redd had enough free time during the day to write, edit, and read proof for *The Scholastic*. The masthead at the time gave no titles, but listed the personnel under departmental headings, thus:

Editorial
    Maurice R. Robinson
    Penelope Redd
Circulation
    Herbert O. Shaffer

Business
    G. Herbert McCracken*
Advertising
    Harry C. Gow, Jr.

With her art and writing background, Penelope Redd was of invaluable help to Robinson in conducting the Scholastic Awards program during its early years. In 1928 she married and moved to Harrisburg with her husband, Edward W. Jones of the Pennsylvania State Highway Department.

Herbert Shaffer, a high school classmate of Robinson's, and Harry Gow worked on a freelance basis, preparing circulars, letters, order forms, etc. Gow ran a lettershop in the building across the street from the Scholastic office in the Bessemer Building, and he regularly made the rounds of local merchants to solicit direct-mail work for his shop. While at it, he made the pitch for ads in *The Scholastic* strictly on a commission basis.

The early editorial mix included articles on careers, personal guidance ("Progress Is Measured by Your Habits" by Nicholas Murray Butler, president of Columbia University), art, literature, drama, sports ("Girls Are

*By December 1923 Gow had resigned and the affiliation for McCracken became "Business and Advertising."

30

Stealing the Limelight in Athletics"), and personal finance ("Tax-Exempt Securities: What and Why?"). The "what" explained municipal and state bonds; the "why," the recent Congressional action exempting these securities from the federal income tax. Subject matter of articles ran the gamut of curriculum, careers, and world affairs: "Putting Humor Into the Study of Latin," "How Girls Can Market Their Talents," and "Can the Soviets Hold Out?" Every issue carried "The News Caldron," a biweekly news review, in addition to articles on national and world affairs. The umbrella term "social studies," covering history, civics, economics, etc., was not yet generally applied to the high school curriculum, although the National Council for the Social Studies was formed in 1920. Not until 1926 did *The Scholastic* begin to use the term in the lesson plan. Prior to that the lesson plan divisions were headed: "For the English Class," "For the Current Events Class," "For Current History: Around the Globe," "For the Art Classes or Literary Society," "For the Dramatic Club," "For the Home Economics Club or the Girls Club." There was something for every interest, except mathematics. A science club column offered science and engineering news and simple experiments in chemistry and physics, *viz.*, from the February 23, 1924, issue:

A "Patriotic" Experiment

Dissolve 3 to 4 grams of agar in 100 cc. of hot water, and a few crystals of potassium ferrocyanide in 10 cc. of water. Add the latter to the hot agar solution. Then add 5 to 10 drops of phenolphthalein solution and 10% sodium hydroxide solution, drop by drop (about 5 drops) until a pink color develops. Fill an eight-inch test tube about two-thirds full of this mixture and place in ice water. After the agar has set to a solid, carefully pour a dilute solution (5%) of ferric chloride on top (about 15 cc.). The iron forms with the ferrocyanide a slowly advancing band of blue (Prussian blue), before which the more rapidly diffusing hydrochloric acid (from ferric chloride and water) spreads a white band as it discharges the pink of the phenolphthalein indicator. Watch the development of the colored layers. In a few days the tube is about equally banded in *red, white* and *blue*.

In developing circulation, Robinson and McCracken had to take into account the presence in thousands of classrooms of a weekly magazine, the *Literary Digest*. Each student paid for his or her own copy, which was ordered by the teacher (usually the English teacher). A major attraction of the *Literary Digest* was its pro and con presentation of public issues; it did this by reprinting editorials and cartoons from newspapers around the country. Credit the *Literary Digest*, which was not expressly edited for school use, for its role in fostering the discussion of controversial topics as a weekly exercise in the high school classroom.*

---

*After the presidential election of 1932, the *Literary Digest* began a decline in circulation, ending with its folding in 1938. To what extent the Depression and the election figured in its demise is a matter of speculation among the historians of journalism, but the *Digest*'s prestige did suffer considerably as a result of the presidential poll it conducted in the fall of 1932, which predicted Hoover the winner. The *Digest* made the mistake of polling only persons listed in telephone directories, which — in Depression year 1932 — could not be considered a cross-section of the voting public. Another factor was probably the growing popularity of *Time* magazine (founded in 1923) and *Newsweek* (1933).

As for the *Digest*'s circulation in the high schools, the weeklies of Civic Education Service, American Education Press, and Scholastic—edited expressly for classroom use—were undoubtedly cutting into it.

Robinson seized every opportunity, which occasionally proved illusory, to tailor part of the magazine and its services to the personal nonacademic interests of its readers. Far from the curriculum was his offer to help solve any problems his 22,000 subscribers might wish to present to "The Scholastic Question Box." This announcement appeared in the October 27, 1923, issue:

Are You?

Are you using any of the free services offered to its readers by *The Scholastic*? If not, bring your problems to us and we shall help you solve them: Your school dramatics, your personal problems about your vocation — how to go about entering it and what to study, your choice of a future specialized school or college — your school paper, and other problems that you feel we could assist you to solve.

The Scholastic Question Box

Bessemer Bldg.   Pittsburgh, Pa.

Whatever questions came to the Question Box have been lost in moving over the past 55 years. As none was published or answered in the magazine, it is to be assumed that any readers who wrote received answers in letters from the one-woman-one-man editorial staff (Penelope Redd and M. R. Robinson).

Before the end of school year 1924–25 another name had been added to the editorial staff — that of Harry Stanley. And with the first issue of the next school year, two others were added under "editorial": Ruth Fuller Sergel and Kenneth M. Gould.

Harry Stanley, one of Ketchum & MacLeod's star writers, possessed the gifts of versatility and speed. Robinson had him on a freelance string, swinging between editorial and promotion writing. Stanley stayed with Scholastic for several years and worked part of the time on the magazine *Better Busses* after it was taken over by McCracken-Robinson, Inc., in 1925 (pp. 41–42).

Sergel, whose writing appeared in nearly every issue over a three-year period, had been on the staff of the *Fargo* (ND) *Forum* and wrote a book column for that paper. She and her husband Roger, assistant professor of English at the University of Pittsburgh, left Pittsburgh to take over the management of the Dramatic Publishing Company in Chicago. Now, as Mrs. Charner Perry, she continues to write plays for the Dramatic Publishing Company.

The name of Kenneth M. Gould first appeared in *The Scholastic* in the January 24, 1925, issue as the author of a piece entitled "Iowa as a Literary Nursery." At the time he was university editor at the University of Pittsburgh and, shortly after the publication of his article, he agreed to serve as one of Scholastic's 11 advisory and contribution editors. Among them were Horace Liveright, the publisher; Richard Bach, director of the Metropolitan Museum of Art; Guillaume Lerolle, foreign representative of the Carnegie Fine Art Galleries; Orton Lowe, director of English instruction for the Pennsylvania State Department of Education; Rufus Daniel Smith, professor of government, New York University; and Edward Rynearson, executive secretary of the National Association of Vocational Guidance, who had been helping Scholastic from the beginning in 1920, when he was principal of

Pittsburgh's Fifth Avenue High School. Gould was the most frequent contributor of the group and was signed on as a full-time staff member starting with the first issue in September 1925. He was named managing editor the following year, went on to become editor, and in 1942 became editor-in-chief. Throughout his 35-year Scholastic career, he reported directly to Robinson, who held the title of editor until he transferred it to Gould. Upon his retirement in 1960, Gould was named Scholastic's first editor-emeritus and continued to work on Scholastic's Multi-Text Series (world history in paperbacks) until a few years before his death in 1969.

Thora Larsen (secretary to Robinson 1938 – 47, assistant corporate secretary 1947–55, corporate secretary 1955–76) in her work, *The First Forty Years of Scholastic Magazines*, published by the company in 1960, ably described the situation Robinson faced after his decision to go national:

> In trying to hit upon an editorial formula that would make the magazine an effective and successful supplement to the high school curriculum, *The Scholastic* scattered its shot all over the field in its first years. Robinson recognized that the few courses taken on Saturday mornings at the University of Pittsburgh were far from giving him an adequate knowledge of high school education. But if he knew little about it, there were plenty of people who did and he quickly learned to ask the right questions in the right places. A teacher is a teacher is a teacher, generous alike to pupils or publishers who want to learn. *The Scholastic* had an Advisory Board in its very first year. Every other Scholastic magazine can make the same statement.

The question of the editorial content of the new magazine was, however, a joyous problem for the publisher. The real headache was money. How could the magazine be financed until it could pay its own way? A circulation of 10,000 couldn't begin to pay expenses. Teachers were bombarded — even as now — with sales letters and sample copies. There were small cash prizes for the best letter on "Why I Use *The Scholastic*." And there was Herb McCracken making speeches during a school's chapel exercises. "If you do not desire it, he will not choose *The Scholastic* as the subject of his talk," said the letter offering a school his services.

But sales letters, sample copies, local circulation agents, talks to students in chapel about moral qualities — sneaking in maybe just one quick reference to *The Scholastic* — none of these was building the circulation fast enough to keep pace with the mounting expenses. Not even second cousins twice removed were safe from importunate pleas to buy a few shares of stock in the struggling company. The two young men were learning painfully that it takes capital to build a self-sustaining enterprise. . . .

Thirty years had to pass before Robinson and McCracken could recall with a laugh a typical day when a creditor was pressing particularly hard: the frantic search for funds, borrowing, selling stock; the breathless rendezvous at the bank just before closing time; the anxious comparison of results; the rush into the bank to deposit the money so a check could be written for the dunning creditor. Or McCracken asking for a small payment on his past-due salary and Robinson suggesting sympathetically that he go out and sell some more stock to raise the money for it.

Larsen referred to sending out "sales letters, sample copies" and other actions intended to build circulation.

Many of these were individually typed, with personal salutations, and signed by Robinson or McCracken. Some, even to school principals, were solicitations intended to sell stock. An example of the former follows; an example of the latter appears on p. 45 in Chapter III, "Stockholders Ahoy!"

August 22, 1922

Mr. F. L. Orth, Principal,
New Castle High School,
New Castle, Pa.

Dear Mr. Orth:

As you already know, next year *The Scholastic* will be changed from a newspaper to a magazine. It will be an educational magazine prepared expressly for high school students, with enough general material such as stories, material on athletics, humor, etc., to interest the high school boy and girl. Our world events department will be designed to be sufficiently complete to replace any magazines which are being used in the high schools for such things as oral English, current events, etc. Combined with those, our columns for Science, French, Spanish, and Radio Clubs will make it possible to use *The Scholastic* in other classrooms. Another of our features will be a complete exchange department with ideas for improving the school publications and promoting the work of press clubs.

Of course you do not think of *The Scholastic* as a publication which you could have your students buy to replace such magazines as the *Literary Digest, Independent, Outlook, Pathfinder,* etc., but our complete change of policy makes our magazine thoroughly desirable for this purpose. Consider, if you will, the advantage of having a magazine prepared exclusively — not one department, but in its entirety — for the use of the high school student. *The Scholastic* will be a magazine the students will enjoy reading and will never resent buying.

Our regular subscription price per year is $2.00, mailed to any address, but by selling in quantities to a school, and having a teacher in that school act as an agent, we can sell for much less than $2.00 a subscription. At Latrobe it is planned to sell *The Scholastic* to the students at $1.25 each per year and as they will use more than 100 copies our price to them will be $1.00, the profit thus made of 25 cents on each subscription will be turned over to their own school paper to assist in the financing. You might be interested in this plan, which many schools have considered a good one.

Another plan which might appeal to you is the joint subscription campaign which you could run with your own school publication. By this plan, if your subscription price were $1.00 for your own paper, you could put on a campaign for both magazines to be sold at $2.00. The regular subscription price of our magazine being $2.00, it would not only help sell your magazine, but give the students a good, substantial magazine to read. This latter plan will be used at Bellevue.

Would you be kind enough to use the enclosed postal card? Let me know whether you have your students buy a magazine for current events work, and if so whether you will be willing to hold up your order of subscriptions for the coming school year until we have an opportunity to show the new *SCHOLASTIC*, which will be about September 12th. Will you also state when it would be possible, either before or soon after school opens, for me to call on you?

Very truly yours,

M. R. Robinson

All through the 1922–23 school year Robinson and McCracken were to hear complaints about the disappearance of western Pennsylvania high school news from the national *Scholastic*. After consultation with some of the high school principals, they decided to restore the regional sports and activities features by inserting an eight-page supplement in all copies of *The Scholastic* going to the western Pennsylvania high schools, starting in September 1923. They signed on Jack K. Lippert, then a sportswriter for *The Pittsburgh Press*, to produce the supplement on a freelance basis. He suggested the title, *The High School Blue Sheet*, to be printed, of course, on blue paper. (It was his first lesson in reading legibility: Black on blue is taboo.) McCracken had signed up a leading Pittsburgh department store — Boggs & Buhl — to pay the cost of publication. The masthead, reproduced below, gives further details.

The High School Blue Sheet

The Scholastic's Activity Supplement
For Western Pennsylvania

Issued by The Scholastic Publishing Co. through the
courtesy of Boggs & Buhl

JACK K. LIPPERT—Editor

Offices—815 Bessemer Building, Pittsburgh
Phone Smithfield 2187

The Blue Sheet cannot be purchased separate from the
magazine

Address all communications to the Editor

OFFICIAL ORGAN AND STATISTICS
BUREAU OF THE W. P. I. A. L.

Note: W.P.I.A.L. stands for Western Pennsylvania Interscholastic Athletic League.

The eight pages of *The Blue Sheet*, the same size as the parent periodical (8¾″ × 11¾″), included reports from Scholastic representatives in the high schools of western Pennsylvania, with a heavy application of photographs of sports activities. The sponsor and only advertiser, Boggs & Buhl, carried two or three ads in every issue, prepared especially for area high school students; for example, for boys: "Society Brand Clothes priced as low as $40"; for girls: "Plenty of the Newer Sweaters at Attractive Prices — $5.75–$7.50." Although Boggs & Buhl had a monopoly on advertising space in *The Blue Sheet*, there was no attempt on their part to influence the editorial or circulation promotion activities. A notice carried in *The Blue Sheet* announced: "*Scholastic*, including *The Blue Sheet*, is on sale at Boggs & Buhl, Joseph Horne Co., Kaufmann's, and Harris & Hays, East Liberty" (department stores). The press run of *The Blue Sheet* for its first year was 10,000 and for the parent periodical, 22,000 — as it had acquired about 12,000 subscribers beyond western Pennsylvania. McCracken recalls that the first out-of-state order came from Bisbee, ND (22 copies), and the second from Flemington, NJ (11 copies). About 90 percent of the increase outside Pennsylvania came from Ohio and West Virginia. A year later another 7,000 "national" subscriptions from more states coast to coast would swell the circulation to 29,000.

The Blue Sheet would continue for two years through school year 1924–25, when *The Scholastic* had reached a national circulation of about 33,000 on a slow climb to 67,300 during the next five years.

Bus Stop, 1924. Early in that year Robinson and McCracken became the instigators and principal stockholders of another publishing enterprise which bore the name, appropriately enough, of McCracken-Robinson, Inc. Its purpose was to acquire and operate a trade magazine called *Better Busses* ("Devoted to Motor Coach Transportation") with "a guaranteed distribution of not less than 15,000 copies monthly," as the corporate letterhead declared. The nominal president of McCracken-Robinson was F. C. Andresen, a Pittsburgh attorney, with Edward B. Smith as vice president and general manager.

McCracken-Robinson purchased the publication from Brian J. Boshier, who continued his association with the magazine as owner of 25 of the 100 outstanding shares of stock, and as advertising space salesman on a commission basis. Conflicts and misunderstandings with Boshier so distracted Robinson and McCracken from their main Scholastic interest that, after a year, they decided to turn over to Andresen most of their stock and full

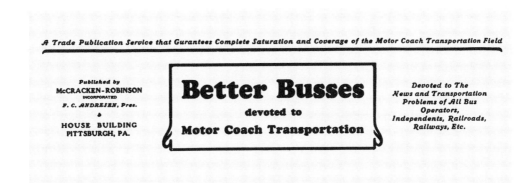

41

responsibility for operating the magazine. They so notified interested parties in a letter dated October 28, 1925, from which this paragraph is drawn:

> *The Scholastic* was growing so rapidly and was requiring so much of our attention that we decided it was impossible to do justice to *Better Busses* without making a large increase in the size of our staff and without causing too much attention to be taken away from our main job, that of building *The Scholastic*. Consequently, when an offer came, we made an arrangement with Mr. F. C. Andresen to carry on the magazine *Better Busses*. Mr. Andresen has been in the trade journal publishing business for years and is far better equipped than we are to conduct the magazine.

Robinson still feels that, had he and McCracken been able to give *Better Busses* more of their time and had dealing with Boshier been less of a nuisance, the magazine might have served its purpose, as they saw it: to provide financing for the Scholastic Publishing Company, since conditions at the time were propitious for growth of the bus transportation industry.

CHAPTER III

Stockholders Ahoy!

T HERE was nothing "incorporated" about *The Western Pennsylvania Scholastic*. It started and ended
two years later as the personal property of M. R. Robinson.
Although designated "The Official Weekly Newspaper
of the Western Pennsylvania Interscholastic Athletic
League," that organization had no proprietary responsibility whatsoever. The paper required no registration, no
license, no directors, no officers. In the 44 issues published during its two-year existence (1920–22), the proprietor was never identified. Robinson was listed as business manager and later as managing editor. No one was
listed as editor or publisher. McPartlin was there during
the first five months of the first year as managing editor.
He and Robinson were on the books for the same pay, $25
per week, but did not always get it. Robinson considered
him a partner rather than an employee, but a partnership
was not the kind of ship McPartlin wished to sail on, so he
took off for his first love — the newspaper business, as
explained in Chapter I.

The lemonade-stand informality of *The Western
Pennsylvania Scholastic* was bound to end when the big
move took place, changing the periodical from a regional
newspaper of student activities to a national magazine
supplementing classroom work in English, social studies,

science, and foreign languages.* The anonymous proprietorship became a readily identifiable Pennsylvania corporation. Now there would be stockholders, directors, and officers. The certificate of incorporation, dated June 7, 1922, issued by the Secretary of the Commonwealth of Pennsylvania to Scholastic Publishing Company, declared: "The amount of the capital stock of said corporation is (50) fifty shares of preferred stock at a par value of $100.00 per share and 50 shares of common stock without nominal or par value. Said Corporation will begin business with a capital amounting to $3,000.00. $500.00 in cash has been paid into the Treasurer [sic], W. R. Robinson [sic], 715 Wallace Avenue, Wilkinsburg, Pa." (In the four other places where Robinson's name was listed on this certificate, his first initial was typed correctly.)

The certificate also stated: "The number of directors of said corporation is fixed at three and the names and residences of the directors who are chosen as directors for the first year as follows: W.R. Jarvis, South Graham St., Pittsburgh, Pa.; N.E. Degan, King Edward Apts., Pittsburgh, Pa.; M. R. Robinson, 715 Wallace Ave., Wilkinsburg, Pa." Each name was repeated with shares subscribed as follows: Jarvis, 1 share common; Degan, 1 share common; Robinson, 46 shares common and 5 preferred. Jarvis and Degan, personal friends of Robinson, were Pittsburgh businessmen who agreed to serve as qualifying shareholders and went with Robinson to the

*From the first issue of *The Scholastic* (Sept. 16, 1922) on through 1926, Robinson promoted interest in Latin, Spanish, French, and science in the columns of the magazine. For more on this see Chapter II.

office of Paul E. Hutchinson, attorney (who would be counselor to Scholastic until his death in 1970), to sign this document. Hutchinson also had one share of common stock in the original allocation.

Throughout the 1920's the need for cash was acute, as there was not a year in that decade when the company turned a profit. The summer months were without an income-producing product, as the publishing year ran from September into May. Unlike general magazines, *The Scholastic* subscriptions all expired at the same time in May, and the income had been received long before that. There was simply not enough bread to feed the company through the summer as salaries, rent, and other expenses ran on.

The postwar depression of the early 1920's was not an auspicious time for raising capital, especially for an enterprise as unfamiliar to possible investors and nearly everyone else as a national high school magazine. In his probe for money Robinson even included the principals of four western Pennsylvania high schools in his attempts.

November 21, 1922.

Mr. J.C. Amon, Principal,
Bellevue High School,
Bellevue, Penna.

Dear Mr. Amon:

We are planning to increase the capitalization of the Scholastic Publishing Company co-incident with our plans for expansion which will begin on December 1st when Herb McCracken begins full time work with *The Scholastic*.

Our plans for expansion in addition to McCracken's active work in the circulation department will include a direct mail advertising campaign to every library and high school in a number of the adjacent states and the employment of a man to work full time selling advertising space. The returns from this planned expansion will not be evident for two or, perhaps, three months, but the commendation we have received from a large number of schools in which we circulate and the fact that we have recently received the endorsement of The Carnegie Library of Pittsburgh, substantiated by a check for ten subscriptions — one for each of its branches — gives us confidence in our campaign to have a copy of *The Scholastic* in every public library and in every high school library in the United States.

The reason for this letter: in order to keep within the laws of the State in increasing our capitalization we must sell ten additional shares of stock. Due to the fact that *The Scholastic* is only known among persons interested in the school game it is necessary to make an effort to sell this stock among school men. That is why I am writing to ask if you would be interested in purchasing one or, perhaps, two shares of this stock. Preferred stock in the Scholastic Publishing Company, bearing a six-percent cumulative dividend, sells at $100.00 a share and with each share purchased we give one-half share of common stock with no par value. The stock may be paid for in installments arranged according to desire. It will be of interest to you to know that *The Scholastic* was started on a borrowed capital of $170.00 and that the total amount of borrowed money ever outstanding against *The Scholastic* was less than $1200.00, $400.00 of which has already been paid back, our total borrowed indebtedness now being approximately $800.00. At the present time

The Scholastic is almost breaking even financially. If we break even over the period of this year it will be nothing short of marvelous, and we feel confident that we will break even and be making money prior to the end of the year 1923.

You will pardon the length of this letter; it is necessary in order for you to understand the situation. I am writing this letter only to four school men — you and three others. I am doing so because you four men have always shown deep sympathy in my work and have believed in the purpose and ideals of *The Scholastic*.

If you are not interested in purchasing one or, perhaps, two shares of Scholastic stock do not think that I shall feel hurt. I feel confident in *The Scholastic*'s success and that your investment will pay not only the six percent cumulative dividend from the time of the first deposit, but that the common stock will not only take value but will pay dividend.

Sincerely yours,

M. R. Robinson

Recalling those letters, Robinson admits that in his innocence of hard economics he probably believed what he said when he told friendly high school principals that "break even" would occur within a year. This was not said out of intent to mislead the principals but out of sheer naiveté over the economics of publishing on a national scale and over what he was asking a school administrator to do. One of the high school principals, a personal friend, to whom Robinson wrote, explained that it would not be proper for a school administrator to own stock in a company supplying his school with instructional materials. This friendly advice gave Robinson his first awareness of the principle of conflict of interest. Another lesson came a few years later when, as a premium for teachers who ordered 20 or more copies of the magazine, he sent them each a high-quality leather briefcase, a large quantity of which he had picked up at a distress sale. But the gift boomeranged as letters of complaint implying bribery overloaded Scholastic's incoming mail for several weeks. Henceforth the only premiums to be offered by Scholastic would be materials for classroom use or book dividends on book club offers.

Robinson lost no time in turning to a greener pasture in his campaign to sell Scholastic stock by mail. He compiled a list of 35 of Pittsburgh's captains of industry and wrote each:

March 13, 1923

Mr. Homer Williams
President, Carnegie Steel Co.
Carnegie Building
Pittsburgh, Pa.

Dear Mr. Williams:

You are one of a selected group of persons in the Pittsburgh district to whom this letter is being written. Because we know of your interest in education, we believe that you will be interested in what we are doing, and will grant us the courtesy of reading this letter.

Less than three years ago a small four-page newspaper was established in Pittsburgh known as *The Scholastic*. Today this publication has expanded into a high class educational magazine carrying a minimum of twenty-four pages and having a national circulation of more than 5,000.

The Scholastic has an enviable field to cover. There are 17,000 high schools in the United States with a total enrollment of more than 2,500,000 students, yet no magazine expressly and exclusively makes an effort to cover this field except *The Scholastic*.

As *The Scholastic* was established in Pittsburgh, a large part of its circulation is in Western Pennsylvania and almost every high school principal in this district, the Secretary of the Pennsylvania State Education Association, the Director of English Instruction and the Director of History Instruction in the Pennsylvania Schools, the President of the National Association of High School Principals, and the officials of the University of Pittsburgh have endorsed this publication.

Why are we writing to you? Because we wish to conduct a nation-wide concentrated drive to reach and obtain a circulation in every high school in the United States. Our plans are made but we require capital. We want certain men and women in the Pittsburgh district who are interested in education and who will permit us to show by letters and by endorsements that we are giving a splendid education service to buy one share of preferred stock in the Scholastic Publishing Company at $100.00 a share. Will you not help us to the extent of purchasing one share?

The Scholastic Publishing Company is regularly incorporated under the Laws of Pennsylvania and is a going concern conducted on a strictly business basis by men interested in the high schools and their problems. Will you not grant us the privilege of showing you why we believe you will be interested in becoming a stockholder in this concern? We are not seeking contributions on a charity basis. This is a business proposition.

Thank you for your courtesy in reading this letter. If you are interested, please write your name on the enclosed postal card and we shall call for an appointment.

Very truly yours,

M. R. Robinson
President

49

Results from this mail campaign were minimal, although at least two on the list later became stockholders.

The drive for capital took a somewhat more sophisticated turn with the decision to put McCracken on the trail of wealthy Pittsburgh men. (In those days, the women of wealth were not on easily accessible lists of prospects.) Early in 1924 McCracken made the connection that proved fateful to the course of Scholastic for many years. He went to see George Hubbard Clapp, Pittsburgh philanthropist and a founder of the Aluminum Company of America. He lived in Sewickley, a suburb of Pittsburgh where the McCrackens lived. Clapp had been a trustee of Carnegie Institute from the year it was founded in 1896 and was a charter member of the Academy of Science and Art of Pittsburgh, organized in 1890.

As a young chemist, Clapp organized the Pittsburgh Testing Laboratory with his partner, Alfred E. Hunt. They worked with the inventor Charles Martin Hall on his electrolytic process for the commercial production of aluminum, organizing the Pittsburgh Reduction Company in 1899, which became the Aluminum Company of America. Clapp was retired and was devoting himself to his many philanthropies and civic interests, including the boards of trustees of the University of Pittsburgh and of Carnegie Institute (the Carnegie Library, the Carnegie Museum* and Art Galleries).

Presumably Clapp had never heard of the Scholastic Publishing Company until one spring morning in 1924 when McCracken dropped in on him, unannounced, at

*The museum houses Clapp's vast collection of mollusks, numbering over 15,000 lots.

George H. Clapp, 1858–1949.

his office. McCracken left with Clapp's check for $500 (two and a half blocks of Scholastic stock) and the suggestion that McCracken might wish to call on a friend "who knows much more about the publishing business than I do." The friend was Augustus K. Oliver, publisher of two of Pittsburgh's seven daily newspapers — the morning and Sunday *Gazette Times* and the evening *Chronicle Telegraph*. He received Robinson and McCracken, and bought two blocks of stock with his check for $400.

Both Oliver and Clapp were in for far more than they ever could have imagined in the beginning. After the sale of the two newspapers in 1928 in a consolidation that reduced the seven Pittsburgh newspapers to three, Oliver became chairman of the board of the Pittsburgh Consolidation Coal Company and, following a merger, chairman of the finance committee of the Consolidation Coal Company. Throughout his entire career much of his time was spent in the public interest. He was on the boards of trustees of several Pittsburgh educational institutions, was a founder of Allegheny County's Community Chest, and was chairman of the Pittsburgh Chapter of the American Red Cross for more than 30 years.*

In retirement Clapp would amuse himself by turning up unexpectedly at stockholder meetings, sometimes to the dismay of officers of the companies in which he had invested. After becoming a Scholastic stockholder, he dropped in at the company's annual meeting in 1924—and Robinson immediately placed his name in nomination as a director. If they could persuade Oliver and William Penn Snyder, Jr., to serve on the board, Clapp said, he would be willing to serve. He did so when both Oliver and Snyder, a Pittsburgh businessman prominent in the iron ore, shipping, and steel industries, accepted the invitation and became directors in 1925. (Snyder was a former Yale athlete and lived in Sewickley.) For the next six years, until the crisis of 1931, it was largely the financial support of these three men that kept Scholastic afloat.

A score of other Pittsburgh businessmen and professional leaders bought small amounts of stock to help keep the enterprise going, among them C. McK. Lynch, A. Rex Flinn, B. F. Jones, C. W. Ridinger, John C. Hill, William L. Clause, Wilbur Hockensmith, H. Lee Mason, Ralph W. Harbison, and Arthur E. Braun as well as McCracken's father-in-law, his dentist, and other personal friends. Braun was president of the Farmers Deposit National Bank, which would soon become Scholastic's source of cash on the word of Oliver or Clapp.

After the close of its second school year in the summer of 1924, the Scholastic Publishing Company issued a four-page prospectus "offering the remaining $20,000

*Some of these activities had to be curtailed in the early thirties when a serious throat operation resulted in his inability to speak above a whisper.

unsold portion of its seven percent Cumulative Preferred Stock and the remaining $8,000 unsold portion of its Common Stock." The prospectus also explained the purpose of the magazine and its prospects for success under such subheadings as "Its Field for Circulation," "Its Field for Advertising," "Its History," "Its Professional Associations," "The Management," "The Possibilities for Financial Return," "The Stockholder's Returns," and "A Few Endorsements."

Order for stock from Campbell Burton, partner in Arthur Young & Co. (1924).

Scholastic Publishing Company
Bessemer Building, Pittsburgh, Pa.

Common Stock Authorized......$20,000		Preferred Stock Authorized.....$30,000	
Common Stock Sold........... 12,000		Preferred Stock Sold........... 10,000	
Common Stock now offered.....$ 8,000		Preferred Stock now offered....$20,000	

To The Scholastic Publishing Co.

I hereby subscribe for _*one*_ units of stock in your company and attach check for $_*200*_. It is understood that each unit consists of three shares of preferred ($50 *par value each*) and two shares of common ($25 *par value each*) and that the cost to me is two hundred ($200) per unit.

(*If installment plan is desired fill in here:*) I shall pay the remainder in monthly installments of $............ each. (*Note: If payment is made in installments the purchaser will be paid 7% interest on installments until the entire amount is paid, when the stock will be delivered.*)

Name _Campbell Burton_

Address _87 Beaver St_
_n.y._

The "field for circulation" was represented by a heavy line from margin to margin of the eight-inch-wide page under which was printed: "This line represents 20,000 high schools in the U.S. with a total daily attendance of 4,000,000 students." Below this was a line, no more than a dash, about one-eighth of an inch in length, under which was printed: "This line represents the 364 high schools that have adopted *The Scholastic*. Yet this scratch

53

on the surface has brought 16,200 paid subscribers. The circulation possibilities are unlimited."

Under the subheading, "The Stockholder's Returns," the prospectus held out the carrot, quite legally in that decade before the arrival of the Securities and Exchange Commission: "If finances permit us to carry out our present promotion plans, within the next school year the circulation should reach between 50,000 and 60,000 — at which point the profit per issue will amount to about $1,000. On this basis, the return to the holder of each block of stock — three shares of preferred and two of common (an investment of $200) — will be something over $50 annually."

The circulation did reach between 50,000 and 60,000, but not the very next year. On gains of about 5,000 paid subscriptions per year, it reached the 56,000 mark in the school year 1928–29. Through the 1920's *The Scholastic* was published every other week — 18 issues during the school year.

Once a stockholder, you were in an even more select group to receive a letter affording you the opportunity to purchase more stock, and such a letter might well come from major holders, such as this signed by George H. Clapp and William P. Snyder, Jr., dated June 25, 1925:

To Stockholders of the Scholastic Publishing Co.:

Upon the invitation of Mr. A. K. Oliver, about a dozen of the stockholders of the Scholastic Publishing Company met at luncheon in the Duquesne Club on Tuesday, June 23rd to give the officers of the company an opportunity to tell the story of its progress, the plans for future development, and to discuss the question of the need for additional working capital.

All the men present were satisfied with the progress made and with the work that was being done and planned; it was decided that additional capital to the extent of $40,000 would be needed during the next fifteen months. After listening to the report of the officers, each man present more than doubled his present holding of stock and agreed to speak to other stockholders and other friends who might become interested in the venture in an effort to raise at least $25,000 of the needed capital immediately.

This memorandum is written in order that the stockholders who were not present at the luncheon might have information from a source other than the officers themselves to indicate the enthusiasm shown by those who were present. It is hoped that the other stockholders will make the problem of raising the additional capital a comparatively easy task by at least doubling their present holdings of stock in the Scholastic Publishing Company.

Very truly yours,

George H. Clapp
Wm. P. Snyder Jr.

Snyder resigned as a director in 1931. Clapp and Oliver continued their association with Scholastic as major stockholders and directors through its ups and downs during the thirties and forties, eventually having the satisfaction of seeing fewer and fewer red figures in the financial statements and then seeing the company completely in the black.

George Clapp lived to a hale 90 years old. Just four

Augustus K. Oliver,
1881–1954.

months before his death in 1949, Scholastic repaid the final $25,000 it owed him. In 1943 arrangements were completed for the settlement of Clapp's stock. He sold his stock back to the company, and those shares were then sold to employees.

Augustus K. Oliver was on the board of directors from 1925, serving as chairman from 1932 until his death in 1954. He was also the company's treasurer from 1932 until 1947, personally signing all company checks for the first 10 of those years. At his death in 1954 his Scholastic stock was left to his six children. The oldest, Joseph Wood Oliver, at the time vice president in charge of Public Relations and Personnel of the Consolidation Coal Company, succeeded his father as Scholastic chairman. He has been on Scholastic's board from 1946 to the present.

The $28,000 capital raised by the 1924 offer eased the financial crunch for two years, but in 1927 another offering, in the same blocks of three preferred and two common shares for $200, was authorized. Oliver, Snyder, and Robinson — spearheaded as usual by McCracken — again went to work on their friends and acquaintances to get pledges for the new issue. One such pledge came from

Charles D. Armstrong, president of the Armstrong Cork Company, already a stockholder, who told Snyder on the telephone to put him down for another $500 worth of stock. Snyder immediately phoned the good news to McCracken who dashed off this letter to Armstrong asking him to make it $600:

June 1, 1927.

My dear Mr. Armstrong:

I just had word from Mr. W. P. Snyder, Jr., that you have agreed to make an additional subscription to the stock of our Company. Mr. Snyder informs me that you have suggested another $500.00 subscription, and we assure you that your interest in the work we are doing is greatly appreciated.

I am taking the liberty to ask you if you will raise this subscription to $600.00 inasmuch as our stock is being sold in blocks of $200.00, covering three shares of $50.00 Preferred and two shares of $25.00 Common. We hope you will be willing to make this increase.

We are very anxious to bring to a successful close as soon as possible our efforts to raise the additional money needed at this time. We will therefore consider it a favor if you will send your money to us at your earliest convenience, and we will immediately deliver to you your certificate of stock. I hope this arrangement will be satisfactory to you.

We have just closed our fifth year in business, and feel more confident than ever that *The Scholastic* will eventually be a very big thing.

With kindest regards,

Faithfully yours,

G. Herbert McCracken
Business Manager

Armstrong's check for $600 arrived in the next mail.

Fifty years later, in looking over these letters and documents, Robinson remarked: "It is hard to believe that we could have been so naive." Perhaps it was the naiveté, the entrepreneurism, and the optimism that charmed some 82 buyers into putting up a few hundred dollars each. Surely it was something besides the prospect for earnings that held Oliver and Clapp steadfast.

The doors of the offices of many other captains of industry in the Pittsburgh area were wide open to McCracken, as he was well known for his all-around athletic prowess at Pitt — notably in football — and as a successful head coach of football at Allegheny and Lafayette colleges. The doors were opened even wider if the captain happened to be a Pitt alumnus or, better yet, a Pitt trustee, as was George Clapp. While Robinson "minded the store," McCracken moved in and out of the offices of wealthy Pittsburghers, seeking and getting the necessary capital to keep the enterprise alive during its infancy

McCracken carried his message of "investment opportunity in Scholastic" far beyond the Pitt trustees and alumni. In demand as a speaker at Hi-Y Club dinners, football banquets, and school assemblies, he would arrive at the high school early and meet with teachers to sell subscriptions or find someone who might buy a $200 block of stock. Following a football banquet for the Norwin High School team, a Dr. McCormack came forward to congratulate McCracken on a rousing speech. After a gracious response, McCracken went into his pitch for a sale of Scholastic stock. The good doctor declined to buy any, but did write out a check for $22 to pay for 20 subscriptions to *The Scholastic* for Norwin High School ($1.10 per school year per subscription for 10 or more to one address).

McCracken had left his coaching job at Allegheny College in 1924 to succeed Jock Sutherland as head football coach at Lafayette College in Easton, PA. When Scholastic moved its advertising "desk" to New York

After *The Scholastic* became a national magazine in 1922, much of its advertising for the next eight years was Pittsburgh-centered, even though subscriptions came in increasing numbers from points beyond. This Rosenbaum's ad is from the April 28, 1928, issue. Rosenbaum's, Pittsburgh Plate Glass Co., Duquesne Light Co., and the University of Pittsburgh were regular large-space advertisers through the 1920's. Among other local advertisers were People's Natural Gas Co., Rieck McJunkin Milk, Reymers Candies, Reliance Life Insurance, and a half-dozen area banks—but not the one that held Scholastic's fluctuating account (Farmers Deposit National Bank).

ROSENBAUM'S
SIXTH, LIBERTY AND PENN   "THE STORE AHEAD"   PHONE ATLANTIC 4800

Headquarters for the Younger Folks

Smart
Appareling
for All Ages
of Youth

Splendid Assortments
Reasonably Priced

Located Right in the Heart of the Pittsburgh business district—convenient to all cars and busses—Your Store, Today, Tomorrow, Always.

A MOST satisfactory place for outfitting the young people of the family, because we have the things that the smartly dressed boys and girls are wearing . . . well made, smartly fashioned garments that appeal to youth . . . priced in a way that mothers appreciate. New spring assortments of great interest are ready now,—see them before making selections.

Girls' and Junior Misses' Shops—Seventh Floor   Boys' Shop—Fourth Floor

(into the offices of the Educational Advertising Company at 1133 Broadway—later at 55 West 42nd Street) McCracken, joined by his wife Helen, soon followed and took up residence in Mt. Vernon, and later in Scarsdale.

With McCracken out of Pittsburgh after 1928, it remained for Robinson to take care of the financing and to maintain contact with the Farmers Bank, with the stockholders, and with the three directors (Messrs. Clapp, Oliver, and Snyder) who were the chief financial backers. Three years later Scholastic had its own offices in New York, at 155 East 44th Street, to house the Editorial and Advertising Departments and the *St. Nicholas* editorial staff (see Chapter IV, "Premature Expansion"). The Circulation Department remained in Pittsburgh for a few more years. Two or three times a month Robinson was on the train or in his REO* on the Lincoln Highway rolling between New York and Pittsburgh to check on the operations of the Circulation Department (then in the Chamber of Commerce Building) and often to take the elevator upstairs to Oliver's office for some support for the sagging bank balance.

---

*The REO was one of 68 different makes of automobiles in its heyday — 1908–38. "REO" is an acronym for the pioneer auto builder, R. E. Olds.

In one instance Robinson borrowed a Pierce-Arrow rumble-seated roadster from Jack Lippert, which was stopped by the Pennsylvania State Police for a faulty muffler.

CHAPTER IV

Premature Expansion

E ARLY in the summer of 1929, when Wall Street was flying high and it looked as though an entrepreneur could sell anything, the Scholastic Publishing Company acquired a weekly social studies periodical for upper elementary and junior high school students, paying for it in Scholastic stock — $15,000 in preferred, $5,000 in common.

The periodical was *The World Review*, published for some six years by the W. F. Quarrie Company of Chicago and printed by Kable Brothers of Mt. Morris, IL. An eight-pager, it had a circulation of 20,000, at 70 cents per pupil for a school-year subscription. *The Scholastic* at that time was $1.10 per school year, published fortnightly, with 36 pages per issue.

The purchase was actually from the printer, Kable Brothers, not the publishing house, W. F. Quarrie. J. A. Watt, Kable vice president, had called on Robinson in Pittsburgh to say that he was authorized to sell this property in settlement of a printing bill. Part of the understanding between Watt and Robinson — oral and not included in the bill of sale — was that Robinson would shift the printing of *The Scholastic* from the McMillan Printing Company in Pittsburgh to Kable Brothers, and that Kable would continue to print *The World Review*. Robinson saw this as a fast "no cash" way to move into the upper elementary and junior high field in which American Education Press of Columbus, OH, had a virtual monopoly. He notified McMillan that he was moving the work to Kable and announced to the schools that Scholastic now

MAURICE R. ROBINSON — *Editor*
KENNETH M. GOULD — *Managing Editor*
H. C. COURTENAY — *Associate Editor*
DONALD B. BROWN — *Assistant Editor*
G. H. McCRACKEN — *Advertising Manager*
A. L. SAVAGE — *Circulation Manager*

BOARD OF SUPERVISING EDITORS

RANDALL J. CONDON, *Former Superintendent of Schools, Cincinnati, Ohio;* FRANK CODY, *Superintendent of Schools, Detroit, Michigan;* WILLIAM M. DAVIDSON, *Superintendent of Schools, Pittsburgh, Pennsylvania;* HERBERT S. WEET, *Superintendent of Schools, Rochester, New York;* JOHN W. WITHERS, *Dean, School of Education, New York University.*

ADVISORY BOARD

FRANK W. BALLOU, *Supt. Public Schools, Washington, D. C.;* LYNN BARNARD, *Director Social Studies, Ursinus College, Pa.,* JOHN H. BEVERIDGE, *Supt. of Schools, Omaha;* HAROLD CAMPBELL, *Supt. of High Schools, New York;* M. G. CLARK, *Supt. of Schools, Sioux City;* JAMES M. GLASS, *Secondary Education, Rollins College, Winter Park, Florida;* HOWARD C. HILL, *University High School, Chicago;* ARTHUR J. JONES, *Professor of Secondary Education, Univ. of Pennsylvania;* MARY McSKIMMON, *Principal Pierce School, Brookline;* A. B. MEREDITH, *Commissioner of Education, Connecticut;* M. V. O'SHEA, *Professor of Education, Univ. of Wisconsin;* FRANK REXFORD, *Supervisor of Civics, New York Schools;* HAROLD RUGG, *Teachers' College, Columbia Univ.;* PAYSON SMITH, *Commissioner of Education, Massachusetts;* WILLIS A. SUTTON, *Supt. of Schools, Atlanta;* HENDRIK VAN LOON, *Author;* ESTALINE WILSON, *Asst. Supt. of Schools, Toledo.*

Editorial and Circulation Office, 923 Wabash Building, Pittsburgh, Pa. Advertising Office 55 West 42d Street, New York. Publication Office, Mount Morris, Illinois.

Published weekly during the school year from September to May inclusive, except Thanksgiving, Christmas, and Easter holidays, at Mount Morris, Illinois, by The Scholastic Publishing Company. Entered as second class matter Sept. 28, 1926, at the post office at Mount Morris, Ill., under Act of March 3, 1879. Contents full copyrighted, 1929.

had a magazine for the "younger student." The attractive brochure, featuring photographs of its special editorial board of distinguished educators (the superintendents of schools of Cincinnati, Detroit, Pittsburgh, Rochester, and the dean of the School of Education of New York University) heralded the acquisition as follows:

For Younger Students

The Scholastic Publishing Company takes pleasure in announcing that it has acquired ownership of *The World Review*, long favorably known as a school periodical.

The World Review will be continued, beginning with *September, 1929*, as an inexpensive, high-quality, eight-page weekly paper for the upper elementary grades and junior high school, with special emphasis on the social studies and current public affairs.

The Special Editorial Board of distinguished school men announced on the front of this folder will have direct oversight of the editorial program of *The World Review* as well as of *The Scholastic*.

Teachers, Principals, and Superintendents who have found *The Scholastic* the one indispensable magazine for the senior high school may order *The World Review* in full confidence that it will reflect the stirring pageant of modern life and society with the same standards of integrity, simplicity, teachableness, and luminous style, adapted to the younger age group.

When Preston Davis, president of American Education Press, in the business of publishing school periodicals, saw *The World Review* coming out under the Scholastic banner, he pondered the possible effect on the circulation of *Current Events*, AEP's flagship paper which his father had founded in 1902. Davis's uneasiness over the Scholastic acquisition prompted him to put in a phone call to Robinson to express interest in buying *The World Review*. Robinson relayed this to his fellow directors — Augustus K. Oliver, George H. Clapp, William P. Snyder, Jr., and G. Herbert McCracken — who decided to invite Davis to attend the next directors' meeting on January 2, 1930. It had been agreed by the directors in advance that they would sell if Davis would pay $20,000 in cash — the claimed value of the Scholastic stock that was assigned to Kable Brothers in the acquisition of *The World Review* just six months earlier.

Between sales — that is, between the Scholastic purchase from Kable Brothers in July 1929 and the American Education Press purchase from Scholastic in January 1930 — the stock market had crashed, sinking the country and the world into the deepest economic depression of the industrial era. This climate persuaded Robinson that the prospect for circulation growth of *The World Review* was not what it had seemed before the crash on October 29, 1929. At the meeting Davis agreed to the $20,000 price, and then and there wrote out a check for the full amount. It was the same amount as the "paper price" Scholastic paid to Kable Brothers in stock, so the whole double transaction turned out to be a much-needed cash harvest for Scholastic at a time when it was nigh impossible to raise capital by issuing new stock.*

*American Education Press did not continue the publication of *The World Review*, nor was it ever its intention to do so. Its interest lay in switching *The World Review* subscribers to one of its own social studies weeklies, either *World News* or *Current Events*, and this was done for the remaining weeks of the school year.

The Scholastic Publishing Company again faced the uncertain future with only one periodical. But not for long. George Bryson, head of the Educational Advertising Company, where McCracken had desk space at 55 West 42nd Street, got word that *St. Nicholas* magazine was up for sale at $50,000. This most-beloved of all children's magazines had seen better days, but it made up in prestige what it lacked in profit. Robinson beamed over the prospect of having it. Fifty thousand was out of the question, but as the Century Company could find no buyer at anywhere near this price, the figure came down to what Robinson had offered — $10,000. To raise capital to operate the magazine, a new corporation was formed — the St. Nicholas Publishing Company, with M. R. Robinson, president; G. Herbert McCracken, vice president; Paul E. Hutchinson, secretary-treasurer; and Ida Schein, assistant secretary-treasurer. Augustus K. Oliver was chairman of the board of directors, which included Charles McK. Lynch, William P. Snyder, Jr., F. G. Blackburn, Robinson, and McCracken. The June 1930 issue (96 pages and cover) was the first under Scholastic's imprint.

At the time Scholastic took over *St. Nicholas*, Albert G. Lanier was editor. He stayed on as managing editor after May Lamberton Becker was named editor. She retained her job as children's book editor at the *New York Herald-Tribune* and was paid on a fee basis per issue for her work on *St. Nicholas*. In the spring of 1931 the *St. Nicholas* staff of six moved into Scholastic's offices in Jacob Ruppert's new Commerce Building at 155 East 44th Street, built by the beer baron soon after the stock-market crash of 1929. (Though prohibition was still on, it was waning. Ruppert, sole owner of the New York Yankees baseball club during the reign of Babe Ruth, explained that he built the Commerce Building to relieve unemployment.) Scholastic's 10 employees and St. Nicholas's six occupied only a fraction of the space on one floor; the rest went unrented for several years, some of which was used by the Scholastic staff for table tennis, and by Owen Reed for photography.

Started by Scribner's in 1873 and sold to the Century Company in 1881, *St. Nicholas* won fame and following under the editorship of the noted children's author, Mary Mapes Dodge (*Hans Brinker*, or *The Silver Skates*). Upon her retirement 30 years later William Fayal Clarke, who had served on the editorial staff from the beginning, became editor. Never a barometer of the magazine's influence and prestige, circulation in its heyday ranged between 60,000 and 65,000, at $5 per annual subscription of 12 issues — a premium price in those days. With the onset of the Depression in 1930, it was reduced to $4. Some of the lost circulation was regained, but at its peak — before Scholastic sold it in 1932 to Kable Brothers — it was about 50,000 (Chapter VI, "From Cash Slow to Cash Flow").

CHAPTER V

Scholastic Coach

Sport of the Family

*S*CHOLASTIC *Coach* evolved from an advertising promotion idea developed by Herb McCracken in 1929 in order to sell ad space in *The Scholastic* to the manufacturers of sporting goods equipment. As football coach — first at Allegheny College and later at Lafayette, with winning records at both — McCracken had become nationally known in college and high school athletic circles and in the sporting goods industry. Doors were open to him at all the leading houses — Spalding, Draper-Maynard, Wilson, Reach, Riddell, Goodrich, Hood, Converse, U.S. Rubber, Dubow, Becton Dickinson and scores of others. A few had bought space in *The Scholastic*, and to lure more of them McCracken came up with a plan to give advertisers in *Scholastic** space on a sports-picture poster at no extra cost.

This poster featured news photographs of sports events, and a new one was mailed every month to the athletic directors of the high schools throughout the country, thus reaching "the point of purchase" for team quantities of athletic equipment. Athletic directors and coaches welcomed these posters and displayed them on school bulletin boards.

*Starting with the September 1931 issue the title was changed from *The Scholastic* to *Scholastic*.

McCracken realized that the small space assigned to advertisers on the photo-posters left much to be desired. It occurred to him that they could have all the space they were willing to buy in a Scholastic magazine for athletic coaches. After the football season of 1930 he presented this idea to his many contacts in the sporting goods industry and their advertising agencies. He would call the new magazine *Scholastic Coach*.

Despite the deepening Depression, he sold enough ads to assure a profit on the first issue without any income from subscriptions, as *Scholastic Coach* would be distributed free to every high school in the United States with an enrollment of 100 or more students. With the approach of summer, McCracken had insertion orders for ads from Spalding, Wilson, Riddell Athletic Shoes, Absorbine Jr., Benjamin Electric (night lighting of playing fields was blazing a trail), Draper-Maynard, Reach, Jules Racine (stopwatches), Greyhound, O'Shea Knitting Mills, and some 16 others, large and small.

A long-delayed step was to arrange for the editorial work needed to fill up the rest of the issue! McCracken thought he had Robert Harron, a sportswriter for the *New York Post*, lined up to edit the magazine, which Harron had expected to do.* But the spring and summer months were the busiest part of the year for sportswriters, and Harron could not find the time to work on *Scholastic Coach*. McCracken wondered if he could interest Jack Lippert, who had been a sportswriter on the *New York World* (folded in February 1931), and who was, at that July moment of urgency, directing a boys' camp at Con-

---

*Harron was also sports editor of *The Scholastic* magazine.

neaut, OH, on Lake Erie.* Robinson telephoned Lippert at the camp, and a deal was made that Lippert would resign his school-year job at Avon Old Farms, a boys' school in Connecticut, and at the close of camp in late August take up the editorship of *Scholastic Coach*.

Since a September issue could not wait until Labor Day to be worked on, Lippert took some time out from camp duties to line up material. It came off the press late that month and was mailed free to 13,000 high schools at the third-class "controlled circulation" postage rate (considerably higher than second-class, which required paid subscriptions). It was a 32-page, self-cover first issue, on good-quality paper, with articles by Andy Kerr (Colgate), Harry Kipke (Michigan), Ray Conger (national one-mile champion), two physicians (on physical fitness programs), and coaches of several minor sports. A women's department would be started in the November issue, which would also contain an article on dancing by Eugene C. Kelly, a recent Pitt graduate, who within a few years would become Gene Kelly of movie fame.

McCracken was well aware that he was entering a publishing field in which one of the country's athletic notables had a virtual monopoly. For more than 10 years Major John L. Griffith, athletic commissioner of the Intercollegiate "Big Ten" Conference, had been publishing *The Athletic Journal* on a paid-subscription basis for high school and college coaches. McCracken, accustomed to engagements with bigtimers, was not overawed by the prospect of stiff competition. But it did get

---

*Lippert had edited *The Scholastic* supplement, *The Blue Sheet* (Chapter II).

SCHOLASTIC COACH

Much of Yale Football This Year Will Go Back to the Days When the Ball Was Round"—Dr. Stevens, Yale Coach

FOOT BALL

Courtesy Ackermann Galleries, New York

OCTOBER · 1931 · · · 25c

Cover of the second issue. The first was not fit to reprint.

very rough at one time in 1937 when Griffith, perhaps feeling the effects of the free-circulating *Scholastic Coach*, sent a letter to the heads of sporting goods manufacturers that advertised in Scholastic's two magazines, calling their attention to the notorious "Report on *Scholastic Magazine*" issued in 1935 by an organization called the Civic Council of Defense of California, and enclosing a copy of the report. It accused *Scholastic* magazine of being "un-American in principle, filled with subversive literature, advertising and propaganda. . . .

70

There is not a copy of the magazine issued that does not look with favor upon the teachings of Communism."

Scholastic had, two years before, established to the satisfaction of inquiring schools the falsity and absurdity of this report, but Griffith accepted it as the truth. Scholastic demanded a retraction from Griffith, and had to threaten legal action to get it. Again, A. K. Oliver would leap to Scholastic's rescue by arranging through his friend and Yale classmate, Colonel Robert R. McCormick, publisher of the *Chicago Tribune*, for the prestigious Chicago law firm of Kirkland, Fleming, Green, Martin & Ellis to represent Scholastic. Oliver's "Dear Bert" letter of April 5, 1938, to McCormick was a masterpiece of denunciation of the Civic Council's report and of Major Griffith's use of it.

Owen Reed.

The five-headed Chicago law firm moved quickly into action and soon had Griffith's signature on a letter stating he found the charges of the Civic Council to be untrue and that he would "make amends for any harm, injury, or damage I may have caused Scholastic Corporation or its publications."

When in the spring of 1936 Robinson tapped Lippert to be editor of *Junior Scholastic* (to be launched in September 1937), an arrangement had to be made for his successor on *Coach*. Owen Reed, who had been manag-

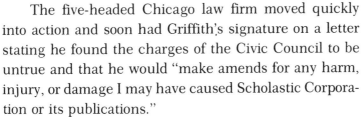

One of Owen Reed's "continuous action" sequences of the hundreds of top-flight athletes he photographed. This one is Fred Perry, U.S. National Singles Champion, 1936.

ing editor of *Coach* with responsibility for art, photography, and production, was named editor. At the same time a search was begun for an assistant editor to be groomed for the editorship in order to free Lippert completely for *Junior Scholastic* and to allow Reed to concentrate on art and photography. Reed's action-sequence photographs, taken with a French motion-picture camera he had altered for fast film speed, gave *Scholastic Coach* what was then a distinctive method for illustrating the fundamental movements of all sports, and a jump on *The Athletic Journal.* In 1947 Reed became advertising manager.

The search for a potential editor ended in the fall of 1936 at New York University with a telephone call to Jay Nash, head of the Department of Physical Education. He and his associate, Floyd Eastwood, recommended Herman L. Masin, a recent graduate, as one who combined a knowledge of athletic techniques with writing ability. Evidence of the latter was apparent in his lively column in the school's official journal, *Education Sun.* It was a fortunate choice for the company and the *Coach,* as Masin

Herman Masin at his favorite occupation — telling people what to do. Here he is instructing St. John's University players in a maneuver to illustrate a *Scholastic Coach* article and his book, *How To Star in Basketball.*

quickly developed mastery of the job and proved perfect for the long run — now going into his 41st year at Scholastic with the writing of these words. During his first 20 years as editor Masin performed without an assistant editor. He planned issues, lined up contributors, rewrote their copy as required, wrote the heads and captions, marked up copy for the printer, and saw it to press. The design of the magazine has been in the hands of Art Directors Mary Jane Dunton (1947–60), Charles Hurley (1960–66), and Howard Katz (1966—). It was not until 1965 that Masin consented to take on an apprentice editor, and he has never had a secretary. (He types his own letters.) He has never missed the supervision of any issue of the more than 400 that have moved through his office, where for the past 13 years he has had the assistance of Bruce Weber (now associate editor), and Madelaine Schwendeman and Gay Siccardi in advertising production.

The circulation pattern of *Scholastic Coach* has, in recent years, been changing at a fast rate from a "controlled" base to a "paid" base. Launched in 1931 as a controlled circulation monthly and distributed free, one copy to each of the 13,000 high schools that had an enrollment of 100 or more students, *Scholastic Coach* had over its first 30 years picked up a modicum of paid circulation without trying. About 1970 a serious effort was made to develop the paid percentage, and it was so successful that by December 1977, 73 percent of *Coach's* 41,000 circulation had become paid-for by subscribers. ("Controlled" means that the recipients of the magazine are selected by the publisher and they receive it free. This assures advertisers that their message is reaching only those in a position to purchase their goods — in this case, high school coaches and athletic directors.) The record shows that the paid circulation also consists mainly of professional coaches — though some may be coaching other than high school teams — and that a growing number are women.

"WomenScene," a special section on coaching and physical education for girls, was launched in 1976 in recognition of the tremendous upswing in girls' athletics generated mainly by Title IX of the Federal Education Act. A department for women coaches had appeared in the earliest issues of *Scholastic Coach* (1930–31), languished, was briefly resuscitated in the late thirties, and then faded off to become an occasional article.

A collateral program in sports is the Scholastic Coach Athletic Services (SCAS). Since his arrival at Scholastic in 1969 Neil Farber has been in charge of the SCAS programs, which include coaching clinics in football, basketball, tennis, soccer, and track, and films, books, and other instructional materials for the school sports and physical education market. The clinics, usually of two days' duration, are attended by coaches and athletic directors, mainly from high schools.

Scholastic Coach and SCAS are under the jurisdiction of Vice President M. Arthur Neiman.

CHAPTER VI

From Cash Slow
to Cash Flow

THE ravages of the Depression drove the Scholastic Publishing Company to the crisis stage despite an increase in circulation of 19,000 during school year 1929–30* and a nominal increase of 1,500 the following year. Nothing else was up, except Robinson's determination to protect his 10-year-old enterprise, even if it meant a marriage of convenience. Financial backers Oliver and Clapp, their losses substantial in the fallen market with no relief in sight in the spring of 1931, were loath to invest more money in the company, yet they did not wish to see it cast adrift.

What could be done? Could an arrangement be made with another publishing house for a joint venture? A merger? A marriage? For a marriage, the parties are usually on cordial terms before the ceremony, getting to know each other through dating, etc. Whom in the publishing community had Scholastic been dating? Robinson was on friendly terms with many publishing executives and

---

The Scholastic magazine was the company's only publishing property at the time. The first issue of *St. Nicholas*, under Scholastic's control through the St. Nicholas Publishing Company (Chapter IV, "Premature Expansion"), was the June 1930 issue; *Scholastic Coach* would not be launched until September 1931 (Chapter V, "*Scholastic Coach*").

counted as personal friends Horace Liveright, president of Boni and Liveright, and Richard Pearson of Harper's, his Dartmouth classmate and partner in planning a college magazine during their senior year. Scholastic and Harper & Brothers shared a sales representative on the West Coast — Blanche Montgomery, a former teacher who many years later joined the Scholastic staff in New York.*

Then there was that highly successful publisher of *Current Events, My Weekly Reader*, and other school papers — Preston Davis, principal owner of American Education Press in Columbus, OH. The sales and circulation manager was William Blakey, with whom Robinson was on cordial terms. Robinson had met Davis and Blakey and had gotten to know the latter quite well at educational conventions. In May of 1929 Davis and Blakey had tried to buy Scholastic for AEP, offering $150,000 for all rights. The Scholastic directors turned this down.

Before the summer ended, a proposal came from J. A. Watt, vice president of the Kable Brothers printing house in Mt. Morris, IL, for a merger of three publishing houses: the one he represented, W. F. Quarrie Company of Chicago, publishers of *The World Book*, for which Kable did some printing; Scholastic; and AEP. Robinson and

*To extend this connection a bit further, let it be noted that: Blanche Montgomery had taught English at Avalon (PA) High School, just outside Pittsburgh. A star pupil of hers had been Florence Liddell. That star pupil had won first prize in the literary article competition for the student-written number of *The Scholastic* in 1925. Florence Liddell got a job with Scholastic in Pittsburgh in 1930 and in New York in 1931, and she married the boss in 1934 to become Mrs. M. R. Robinson. They have five children: Richard (1937), Mary Sue (1939), Barbara Anne (1942), Florence Liddell (1944), and William Walker (1950).

Watt knew each other, as they had just recently (in July) arranged for Scholastic to purchase the weekly social studies periodical *The World Review* for $20,000 in Scholastic stock (Chapter IV, "Premature Expansion"). Watt's proposal for a three-way merger appealed to the Scholastic and AEP principals to the point where they were willing to talk, and to the further point of scheduling a meeting with the Harris Trust Company in Chicago to discuss underwriting and financing the proposed triumvirate. After all, these were high times; anything goes. It was easy to envision big earnings from a merger of these three reputable publishing houses.

The meeting at the Harris Trust Company was scheduled for late October. Robinson arrived, representing Scholastic; Davis arrived, representing AEP; and Watt arrived, representing Quarrie. Where were the bankers? After some delay, word came that they were preoccupied elsewhere in the bank, tangled in tickertape and in the mayhem caused by plunging stock prices. It was the afternoon of Tuesday, October 29, 1929. The meeting was canceled, never to be rescheduled.

Blakey and Robinson continued to meet perchance at educational conventions and on trains during the early months of 1930, their conversation turning inevitably to the future of the business of school periodicals, not to mention the future of the American free-enterprise system. A new entry into the school magazine field concerned them: George Brett, president of the Macmillan Company, had made a deal with *The New York Times* to adapt its "News Review of the Week" section of the Sunday paper into a tabloid paper for classroom use.

Macmillan had a large force of "bookmen" in the field

calling on schools, whereas Scholastic had two or three and AEP not many more. Most of their circulation was obtained by direct mail. Macmillan was doing very well with its adapted and adopted *The New York Times* "News Review," and this circumstance, more than anything else at the time, gave Robinson and Davis a common target for talk.

Their talks led to correspondence—just between the two—and in a letter of November 21, 1930, Robinson suggested some approaches to a "consolidation," but not one that "involved a loss to our stockholders." The suggestions were along the lines of the purchase of Scholastic common stock by AEP and settlement with Oliver and Clapp of the notes held by the Farmers Bank in Pittsburgh bearing their endorsements. "If you think we ought to talk this over any further," Robinson wrote in closing, "let me know and we can arrange to get together sometime soon."

In that letter, one paragraph reveals the frustration Robinson felt in the fall of 1930:

> I think you understand my personal feeling. I'm being turned into a businessman, which is what I shall never be successful at doing; and if this keeps up, my reasons for being in the publishing business will soon no longer exist. Of course, if I must, I shall, and I'm getting so now that costs and balance sheets and operating statements are occupying a great deal of my time and, who knows, perhaps I shall become proficient in that direction and shall actually be carrying on the good fight with profits instead of capital.

Five weeks later on January 2, 1931, Davis wrote, apologizing for the delay because "I did not know what to say." Now he said, "I agree with your main premises and yet to be frank I doubt whether anything can be done." But further on in the letter he left the door open with:

> I have no doubt that the two properties [*The Scholastic* and *St. Nicholas**] will some day be worth more than the investment, but in order to convince the rest of our people, it would be necessary for me to show them something pretty definite in the way of a prospectus. If you want to take the time to get this up, I shall be very glad to go over it and submit it to our directors. I agree that the definite proposal will have to come from this end, but it should not come until you and I are in accord on a very definite set-up. Thanks for the Christmas card, which Mrs. Davis and I agree is about the most artistic one we received; also Happy New Year.

Robinson answered this letter, making no copy, but he wrote in the margin of Davis's letter for filing: "Answered 1/5/31 — telling him to forget it — no carbon. R."

Davis would not forget it. He discussed with his directors whether the matter should be pursued further. It was. Telephone calls, correspondence, and meetings between principals of the two companies culminated in an agreement to form a new company: Scholastic–St. Nicholas Corporation — 50 percent of the voting stock was held by AEP; 49 percent, by the Scholastic Publishing Company; and one percent, by M. R. Robinson. For the 49 percent, the new company took over *The Scholastic* and *Scholastic Coach* from Scholastic Publishing Company. In return for $25,000 of preferred stock, it took over

*See Chapter IV, "Premature Expansion."

St. Nicholas magazine from the St. Nicholas Publishing Company. And in return for 50 percent of the voting stock and 468 shares of preferred stock, it obtained four periodicals from American Education Press: *The Magazine World* (which AEP had bought from *The Atlantic Monthly*), *World News, Current Literature,* and *Loose-leaf Current Topics.* It was agreed that M. R. Robinson would be president; Preston Davis, William C. Blakey, and C. E. Richards (all of AEP) would be vice president, secretary, and treasurer, respectively. The September 1931 issues were published by the new corporation.

What happened to Macmillan's school paper? Macmillan gave up on it after about two years because its sales staff had been spending too much time selling subscriptions to the neglect of selling textbooks. Yet its appearance had a considerable bearing on bringing about the joint venture of Scholastic and AEP in 1931. Had Macmillan succeeded with it, the competition would have been tough, and perhaps other prestigious and well-financed book publishers might have attempted a foray into the burgeoning field of classroom periodicals.

The Magazine World had already been merged into *Scholastic,* according to the agreement made the preceding summer in setting up the Scholastic–St. Nicholas Corporation. The November 28, 1931, issue of *Scholastic* appeared with the logo reading, "*Scholastic* and *The Magazine World.*" The inside front cover proclaimed:

A Momentous Announcement

With this issue, *Scholastic* takes on a new significance in the educational world. The publishers of *Scholastic,* looking toward the best pos-

sible service to high schools, have assumed ownership and publication of four other high school
periodicals. These are: *The Magazine World,
Current Literature, World News,* and *Looseleaf
Current Topics.*

There followed some 300 more words before the final
paragraph:

It is the sincere belief of the publishers that
with this new alliance the interests of the high
schools of the country can be served in a manner
never before attainable. And with the cooperation
of the thousands of teachers who have made possible the growth of these publications, the contribution of this united organization to the educational advance of the country can be and will be
momentous.

It was signed: "Scholastic–St. Nicholas Corporation.
Columbus . . . Pittsburgh . . . New York."

After only two months into the new school year, the
corporate marriage began showing strains characteristic
of marriages of convenience. The AEP half in Columbus,
where the treasury lay, started sending distress signals to
Robinson as early as November 5, 1931, such as the one
by Harrison Sayre, AEP editor, saying, "the sensible thing
to do would be to ship Gould out here — if you feel he is
indispensable — and roll up your sleeves to bail ship."
(Gould, as Scholastic managing editor, had just recently
moved from the Pittsburgh office to the newly opened
office in New York.) Then there was the letter of December 31, 1931, to Robinson from AEP's William Blakey,
officer and board member of the Scholastic–St. Nicholas
Corporation, expressing extreme alarm over the imbal-

Who would Ever Believe that Pants Could Be So Captivating !

THE BEACHCOMBER — White mesh or plain broadcloth shirt. Regimental stripe pants with hat to match. Color combinations: (Navy, Copen, Orange, and White) — (Navy, Red, Orange and White) — (Light Green, Dark Green, White and Red). Age sizes 8-22. Bust 32-40.

Hat, Shirt and Pants.............. **$2.95**
Pants and Hat only.............. **$1.95**

THE FISHER BOY — Broadcloth shirt — White, Copen, Green, Maize or Rose. "Fisher Boy" slacks of white or natural color duck — worn high water or rolled to knee. Age sizes 8-22. Bust 32-40.

Complete Costume.............. **$1.95**

Who said pants belong exclusively to the boys!

Surely not the girl of this enlightened day.

For here are pants for girls, designed by Man O' War — so essentially feminine, so utterly devastating and styled with so smooth a swing and rhythm that they put those prosaic masculine slacks completely to shame.

What a summer you'll have, girls, reveling in these smart Paris designed costumes so perfectly adapted to strenuous vacation activities — in camp, on the beach, in the country.

And how fortunate that Man O' War has produced them for you at such amazingly low prices — for you'll never in the world be satisfied with one — or even two of the many becoming models shown you.

If you cannot secure the styles you like send the name of your dealer and we will see that you are supplied through him.

B R A N I G A N ,   G R E E N   &   C O .
7 1   W e s t   3 5 t h   S t r e e t ,   N e w   Y o r k

MAN O' WAR
SCHOOL, GYM, CAMP AND DANCE TOGS

Camp and Gym Suits of Man O'War Good Game suiting in Green, Copen and other colors. Absolutely fast color.

Price
$1 $1.50 $2

© 1932 B. G. & Co.

THE OUTBOARDER — One piece pajama sports costume in soft and alluring color combinations. Green and white, Red and White, Blue and White, Brown and White. Age sizes 8-22. Bust 32-40.
Complete with Hat.............. $3.95   Without Hat.............. $2.95

Advertisement in the April 16, 1932, issue of *Scholastic*.

ance of expenses and income and enclosing a "report" recommending action to be taken. Blakey wrote:

Dear Robbie:

When I received the financial statement and outlook from Mr. Davis on December 29, I was actually stunned. Although I felt for two months that we were skating on thin ice, I didn't have the actual picture until these figures were presented to me. I consider it my duty as a Director to give each Director my best thoughts on this situation. I think time is too precious to wait for a Directors' Meeting; therefore, I am submitting the attached report to each of the three other Directors.

Blakey's report ran some 3,300 words and listed points or options he would have the board consider and act upon at its January 8 meeting. In addition to these options Blakey made several definite recommendations, explained on p. 84. In the accompanying letter to Robinson, Blakey said he would be in New York within a few days and would telegraph the date of his arrival, which was Sunday, January 3. They met and went through the 26-page, single-spaced, typewritten report point by point, recommendation by recommendation. After the meeting Robinson said he would respond by preparing a memorandum to the directors and posting it in time to reach the Columbus directors before the January 8 meeting. (In the year 1932 you could depend on a letter posted in New York on January 6 being delivered to the addressee in Columbus on January 7.)

In his report Blakey observed: "A continuance of the present policy is business suicide. Action should be taken immediately. Nothing is of more importance than an immediate decision on the emergency which now exists and the policy that is to be followed in the future." Among his recommendations were the following:

> Decrease the expenses in the next six months to a point that will bring these expenses within the estimated receipts for the year. A balancing of the budget to bring expenses within receipts seems to be the only procedure that is open to us. This cannot be done by small percentage cuts in salaries or eliminating small expenses. It must be done by drastic readjustments without regard for any one except the company.

The preceding paragraph served as a preamble to specifics that followed, among them being:

> Reduce *Scholastic* to 32 pages and cover. [It had been running 40 and cover, issued every other week.]
> Reduce *Scholastic Coach* to 24 pages and cover for the January issue, and to 16 pages for three remaining issues, February, March, April. . . . The services of the present editor [should] be concluded on Jan. 31, 1932. It should be possible for him to get together enough material for these [three remaining] issues during that month. [The editor was Jack Lippert, who had been on the job since launching the first issue in September 1931.]
> Eliminate the Pittsburgh office entirely and transfer the work to Columbus.
> Limit the Scholastic Awards expenses to $800 (at once).
> Move the entire New York editorial office to Columbus, operating *Scholastic* and *St. Nicholas* on reduced editorial salaries and freelance fees.

JUNE, 1930

ST NICHOLAS

Cover of the first issue
of *St. Nicholas*
published under the
auspices of Scholastic.

Robinson's response — the "Memorandum for the Directors of Scholastic–St. Nicholas" — posted on January 6, opened as follows.:

> The honest and outspoken report which Mr. Blakey prepared and submitted to the Directors prompts me to address you prior to the meeting scheduled for Friday on the same subject. In doing so, although I disagree with Mr. Blakey on numerous points, I wish to express my thanks to him for bringing to our attention the necessity for immediate decision on a number of major points. The thoroughness with which he worked up the details of his recommendations deserves, I am sure, the thanks of all of us.

Robinson's goal was to save Scholastic and then to strengthen it. In this he had the full support of his fellow director, A. K. Oliver. One of Blakey's seven options served this purpose, and in his memorandum Robinson wrote:

> Of those seven possibilities, I think the first one, namely the idea of having one magazine, the *Scholastic*, and merging all of the papers into it, is the most desirable of his suggestions, and I would like to set forth a few reasons why I think this is true.

This he did, in considerable detail, concluding with:

> In the light of the above expression of my personal opinion, I should like to make a suggestion to the Board of Directors that we discontinue immediately *Current Literature, World News,* and *Looseleaf Current Topics,* and that we merge them into one super magazine, *Scholastic,* to consist of 48 pages plus cover, completely departmentalized, with a heading at the beginning of the English section with sixteen consecutive pages of straight English classroom material, followed by sixteen successive pages of straight social studies material and news with a departmental head. We shall thus substitute for the sixteen pages of *World News* and the eight pages of *Current Literature* eight additional pages in the *Scholastic.* I recommend the forty-eight pages and cover for the *Scholastic* because, to begin with, I think it essential to publish a sort of super magazine so that we can show what the merging of all these magazines into one has been able to do for the high schools of the country.

He went on to recommend "that in the course of the coming semester and next year we add other departments . . . which would help us get circulation and advertising." Two departments he mentioned were one "devoted to art instruction that would permit us to take advantage from a circulation standpoint of the tremendous interest in the *Scholastic* which has been built up among art students and teachers because of our art exhibit" and "a regularly established vocational and personal guidance department. . . . An examination of the courses of study throughout the United States indicates that vocational civics and the teaching of vocational and personal problems has increased as a required subject more than any other single course of study."

In his reference to "merging all of these magazines into one" (*Scholastic*), Robinson did not mean to include *St. Nicholas* and, of course, not *Scholastic Coach*. Concerning *St. Nicholas* he said, "There are a number of good reasons why we should continue *St. Nicholas* as one of the periodicals of the organization, provided it doesn't lose money."

Concerning *Scholastic Coach* he wrote:

> To follow any restrictive policy in connection with the *Coach* would make it necessary to discontinue its publication at the close of this first year. So that if we are to decide to cut it to 16 pages, in making that decision we shall have to decide definitely to discontinue it as of April, 1932. In discussing this subject with Mr. McCracken, who, after all, is completely responsible for the establishing of the *Coach*, he has asked me to tell the Board of Directors that he will make a standing offer of $5,000 for the *Coach* at any time we wish to discontinue its publication.

The Scholastic–St. Nicholas directors met in Columbus on January 8 as scheduled, and after prolonged discussion reached a decision to support Robinson in his recommendation to combine *Current Literature*, *World News*, and *Looseleaf Current Topics* into *Scholastic*. The announcement of this appeared in the February 6, 1932, issue:

> HERE is an announcement which SCHO-LASTIC proudly makes and which we believe will be enthusiastically welcomed by all the high school students and teachers of the United States.
>
> Last fall, the Scholastic–St. Nicholas Corporation published five separate periodicals for high school classrooms: *Scholastic*, *Magazine World*, *Current Literature*, *World News*, and *Looseleaf Current Topics*. This issue marks the culmination of a plan to merge all five of these papers into one enlarged quality magazine—*Scholastic*.
>
> Thus the publishers of *Scholastic* further demonstrate their determination to issue for the high schools of America a magazine which will continue to broaden its scope, improve its quality, and add to its distinction. It is the hope of the publishers that *Scholastic*, through this merger, will be able to make a constantly greater contribution to the intellectual life of American high school students.
>
> An important aspect from the standpoint of students, teachers, principals, and parents is this: ONE periodical instead of two or more now COMPLETELY fulfills the needs of English, history, civics, and art classes and saves money for pupil and school alike. And finally, unification of the editorial boards of all five periodicals makes available an eminent array of talent to serve the needs of high school students.

That issue, and six of the remaining eight of the school year, carried the 48 pages and covers that Robinson considered proper for the consolidation of the other periodicals into *Scholastic*. One issue had 40 pages and one 32 pages, plus covers.

As to the future of *Scholastic Coach* and *St. Nicholas*, the board accepted Robinson's position that these be continued with the frequency and editorial program planned for the remaining issues of the school year on the condition that the tightest possible economies be put into effect in producing them. The AEP members of the board stated that they were making no commitment beyond the current school year and that the future program would depend on the financial statements of the remaining months.

Whatever economies Robinson made in 1932 did not include firing Gould, *Scholastic* managing editor; or Lippert, *Coach* editor; or May Lamberton Becker, *St. Nicholas* editor. Mabel Bessey,* head of the English department of Bay Ridge High School, Brooklyn, who had been editing *Current Literature* on a freelance basis, became associate editor of *Scholastic* to handle its English features. Harrison Sayre of the Columbus office, who edited *World News* and *Looseleaf Current Topics*, was reassigned to other AEP publications.

---

*It was Mabel Bessey who, some six years later, wrote Robinson to recommend one of her brightest former pupils for a job at Scholastic and asked if he would interview her. He did and hired Thora Larsen as combination receptionist/switchboard operator/ stenographer. She would become his secretary, a member of the board of directors for a short period, and corporate secretary during the next 38 years, with two years' absence on an illness leave. In 1960 she wrote *The First Forty Years of Scholastic Magazines*. She retired on February 27, 1976, and continued to assist in the research on this book.

Operating statements of the "new alliance" for the first three months of 1932 dissipated whatever hope the half-owners in Columbus held for an improvement in the "bottom line." Fears of worse deficits persisted. The condition of the patient, so unsettling in January, became critical by April; as witness, this letter from Preston Davis to A. K. Oliver:

April 8, 1932

My dear Mr. Oliver:

I'm sorry my telegram wasn't self-explanatory. Perhaps I shouldn't have sent it, but I intended it just as a reminder of our judgment of the situation as outlined at the conference in Pittsburgh.

You will remember that I said at the outset that it was our judgment that the future prospects did not warrant investing more money. In the end, I said that, inasmuch as you would have to await Mr. Clapp's return before making a decision on your side, I would take the matter back to our directors again to see if they wanted to reconsider — a final decision to be made just as soon as we heard from you.

As I see it, there are four possibilities —

1. To put in an additional $90,000 to carry through to September on the hope of breaking even next year.

2. To drop the whole thing, let it go to bankruptcy, lose what we have put in, and forget it. In this case we would have to decide what to do with the accounts payable, as a matter of ethics.

3. You advance money to pay the American Education Press bill and we will give you all

our common stock and you can do what you want with company.

4. We will assume all of the obligations in exchange for all of the assets.

I am proposing the latter two alternatives because, in case the American Education Press directors should decide not to change their first decision, I don't want to appear to be arbitrarily blocking progress. Robinson thinks, and with much justification, that we are working under a psychology of defeat — that if we don't believe it can be done, we probably can't do it. Therefore we offer to get out.

If the third suggestion above were adopted, Robbie would have accomplished two things during the year — getting the circulation of our four publications, which he very much wanted, and getting our $25,000 to help on the deficit.

Honestly, I don't know what we ought to do about it, but I don't think we are getting anywhere as it is. I don't think Robbie ought to go back to New York till we get it definitely settled.

The accounts payable April 1 are

American Education Press	$37,816.39
Others	32,816.61

This does not include the April 1 bills from New York, which have not come yet.

Sincerely,

Preston Davis

The telegram to which Davis referred stated that the funds of the Scholastic–St. Nicholas Corporation were exhausted and an early decision would have to be made about future operations.

In response to this letter, Oliver telephoned Davis to

Scholastic News Examination winning students and their teachers with President Hoover on White House lawn, July 1, 1932. Scholastic Circulation Manager Richard Mathewson in light suit to left of the President.

invite him to come to Pittsburgh to resolve the problem. The meeting was scheduled for early afternoon on April 12 in Oliver's unpretentious office in the Chamber of Commerce Building. That day Oliver, Clapp, and Robinson lunched together in the Duquesne Club to discuss strategy. They believed that Davis would have possibility number four as his goal, and they agreed to go for number three with whatever variation regarding payment they could achieve. Clapp said that he need not attend the meeting and told Oliver to make the decision, adding that he would go "fifty-fifty" with him on whatever he decided. Robinson and Oliver then went to the latter's office to await the arrival of Davis.

Thirty years later, when asked what he considered

92

the most dramatic moment in Scholastic's history, Robinson said it was this meeting with Davis to settle the fate of the company.

Davis arrived and made the opening move. He said he would assume all obligations if Scholastic would yield its 50 percent ownership, and he would give Robinson a job at $25,000 a year with AEP in Columbus. (He was then getting $5,000 a year with Scholastic.) Davis said that he would discontinue *Scholastic*; he said that it would never sell—that only papers like the AEP's would. He was willing to continue *Scholastic Coach*, however; but he would sell *St. Nicholas*.

Oliver, feigning the inclination to yield, asked Davis if he wouldn't pay something for the Scholastic 50 percent stock holdings in addition to assuming all obligations. After some banter over this, Davis said he would. He offered $2 per share for the 500 Scholastic shares. Oliver said: "Would you give a dollar more per share?" All right, Davis agreed, a dollar more. "Would you give another 50 cents?" asked Oliver. Davis said no, that was the limit. All the while Oliver was writing something on a piece of scratch paper, and as Davis closed his offer, passed it across the table to him. It was an offer to buy AEP's stock in the Scholastic–St. Nicholas Corporation at the price Davis said he would pay for Scholastic's. Davis just sat there not saying anything for several minutes. In the meantime Oliver had buzzed his secretary, Miss Grubbs, and asked her to call the garage to send his car in 15 minutes. Then, turning to Davis, Oliver said, "We are not going to sell. Either we both put up more money or we'll have to finance it all ourselves, but we are not going to sell out."

Davis, stymied in his move to get the kit and kaboodle, and convinced that *Scholastic* magazine was not worth saving, agreed to sell at the price he had expected to pay if he bought it.

One can imagine the relief and joy Robinson felt over the disappearance of the $25,000-a-year job.

When the car came and they rose to leave, Oliver made no further reference to the deal they had made. He just said, "You play golf, Preston?" When Davis said he did, Oliver suggested he bring his clubs the next time he came to Pittsburgh. They then drove him to the Pennsylvania Station for the train to Columbus, and Oliver drove Robinson to his hotel.

"Mr. Clapp is going to be awfully mad at me when I tell him about this tomorrow," said Oliver.

However Clapp felt about this development, there was abundant joy, but little money, in Scholastic's office on East 44th Street; the joy was somewhat modified by the realization that the company had been "liberated into" what would soon become the deepest depression in American history. Thousands of companies were failing while Scholastic was experiencing a new lease on life. It would be rough going for Scholastic during the next 10 years, with some of the darkest hours bordering on doomsday.

With the escape from the AEP partnership, Oliver and Clapp again had full control of the Scholastic–St. Nicholas Corporation. Soon — in June 1932 — the Scholastic–St. Nicholas Corporation would change its name to Scholastic Corporation, with M. R. Robinson, president; G. Herbert McCracken, vice president; A. K. Oliver, treasurer and chairman of the board of directors; and Ida Schein (sister of I. Jay Schein, manager of the Subscription Service Department), assistant treasurer.

94

Scholastic Corporation's publishing properties consisted of the magazines *Scholastic, Scholastic Coach, St. Nicholas,* and a few book titles (Chapter XV, "The Book Business"). Before the year 1932 was out, *St. Nicholas* would be sold.*

In 1935 McCracken resigned from his sideline as head football coach at Lafayette College to give full time to Scholastic. He had turned down an offer of a $12,000 annual salary from Lafayette College to become its director of athletics, preferring to go full-time with Scholastic as director of advertising at a salary less than half of that (specifically, $5,400), making him the highest-paid person on the Scholastic payroll.

When stock in the new Scholastic Corporation was offered for sale, the stockholders of the Scholastic Publishing Company and the St. Nicholas Publishing Company were notified that the companies would be dissolved and that they could buy into the Scholastic Corporation if they wished to do so, but that their certificates in the old companies were without value. The Scholastic Corporation stock owned by the defunct companies was offered at public sale on May 19, 1936, and was acquired at a nominal sum by the directors of the corporation, who assumed the bank indebtedness. Many of the 65 stockholders of the defunct companies were persons of means who chose

St. Nicholas was sold to Kable Brothers, printer, of Mt. Morris, IL, in settlement of a printing bill. Kable Brothers, without publishing even one issue, sold it to its recent half-owners — American Education Press. AEP published it for about three years then sold it to Roy Walker, publisher of the *Grade School Teacher* in Darien, CT. At some point in 1942 or 1943, *Grade School Teacher* sold *St. Nicholas* to Julia Lit Stern, wife of the publisher of the *Philadelphia Record*, and after publishing one issue — March 1943 — she discontinued it.

to take their loss for what it was worth as an income tax deduction. (Neither Robinson nor McCracken was so placed.) So the Scholastic Corporation started with Oliver and Clapp owning 2,415 of the 2,500 shares of the voting stock; Robinson, 35 shares; McCracken, 10 shares; and the rest owned by others holding fewer shares. Robinson and McCracken also held a few shares of Class A and Class C stock, both nonvoting. Several other Pittsburghers who held Scholastic Publishing Company stock came in for a few shares of the Class A stock.

All through the Depression and up to 1942, Scholastic zigged and zagged from one financial crisis to another — a period vividly described by Robinson in a statement he issued to members of the staff on April 9, 1938, to help them better to understand the necessity of his announcing "that in addition to the regular half-month vacation with pay, there would be a half-month without pay — for all members of the organization — with no exceptions." The Scholastic unit of the Newspaper Guild contested this action and wrote Robinson: "We cannot accept your offer of a cut as a substitute for the raises we asked for."

Robinson decided to address the whole staff in a 4,200-word review of the history of the company from its beginning, concentrating on the problems of financing it. After explaining the rescue of the company from half-ownership by American Education Press during school year 1931–32, he recounted the vicissitudes of the six Depression years that followed:

> We started anew in the fall of 1932, fully realizing the Depression — everybody in the organization accepted tremendous cuts in salary, we tightened our belts and tried again. By careful management and hard work, we started to make

some progress although the circulation dropped from about 175,000 to 100,000 in the fall of 1932. We were experiencing losses but losses not too frightening. Daily reports were being made to the directors. Mr. Oliver assumed the position of treasurer and accepted greater responsibility for helping us run our finances. By January, 1933, things were not looking so bad. We were getting little money but were able to keep alive. Between February 25 and March 1, 1933, of the second semester, we billed out as is our usual custom a half a year's business. Two weeks later, as you can imagine, we had a safe full of checks back from closed banks (due to the bank holiday) and a file full of cancellations.

I presented a report of the desperate situation to the directors. I said that every member of the staff was ready to forego ¼ of each month's salary for the balance of the fiscal year. We needed money again and quite a lot of it. But I showed the directors that the staff was ready to take the utmost portion of its responsibility to help carry on. We took the cover off the magazine. The directors put up $30,000 in cash to pay the bills and keep the business going. I then determined to attack the job with a new offensive and got the approval of the directors to do so. We announced that in the fall of 1933 *Scholastic* would become a weekly. We continued with the cover off the magazine, cut the quality of paper and started in again to attempt to push this business through. The offensive, aided by gradual improvement in business, was somewhat effective. We gained 25,000 circulation and we pushed through the following year with a loss of about $15,000. Again the problem of financing and again patience on the part of the directors — in fact, congratulations to the staff for this slight improvement.

In 1934–35, we made another gain in circulation but still had to contend with a loss of $25,295.16; the 300th anniversary celebration book,* which we hoped would help — hit us for a loss. Again the request for more money and again the need for funds to carry the business over the summer. Another year — 1935–36 — a loss of $10,000. And finally the fiscal year 1936–37, we showed the first profit that the business had ever shown since it was incorporated in the fall of 1922; a profit extremely slight, as you know, totaling only $2,400, and not nearly sufficient to pay for the purchase we had to make of furniture and fixtures, Addressograph equipment, etc. Again the need for funds to make up for capital outlay for additional equipment of furniture and fixtures, for an expansion of office space, etc., and for starting a new publication, *Junior Scholastic,* which we hoped would make it possible for us to give more important positions and higher pay to those persons on the staff who had been admittedly under-paid and had devoted their energies to attempting to build up this business. In the summer of 1937, the directors approved salary increases for each member of the organization who had been with the company for a year or longer. These salary increases, though fully deserved, were not warranted by the financial record of the company. I said at the time that the salary increases were based on hope — hope that this fiscal year 1937–38 would prove that we could pay these increases. For the first time since the fall of 1932, members of the organization who had been receiving salaries of $200 a month or more were increased. From September 1932, to September 1937, with one exception, no salary increases had been granted to any employee who was receiving $200 a month or more. It was the judgment of the management that any slight increase that could be made during that period

*This 126-page volume was published as the February 23, 1935, issue of *Scholastic* magazine. (See "A Tricentennial Special" in Chapter XXIX, "To Talk of Many Things.")

should be confined to the groups earning less than $50.00 a week.

In the fall of 1937 we made another substantial increase in circulation for *Scholastic. Junior Scholastic* [founded in September 1937] failed to come close to the 75,000 circulation we hoped to get but the management and the owners of the company were quite willing to concede that the new publication would require an investment of some funds and that any losses on this new publication should not be reflected in decreased pay to the staff. Had the circulation of *Scholastic* for the second semester of this fiscal year stayed within 6% of the circulation for the first semester, we would have been able to avoid any loss on *Scholastic* but as I reported to you previously, the circulation of *Scholastic* took the worst nose-dive it has ever taken since the fall of 1932. Reductions and cancellations in orders were worse than anything we had previously experienced. Collections — always excellent in March — dropped off at an alarming rate.

Then came the experience of last week. I returned to Pittsburgh and faced accounts payable of $33,000 and no money to meet the payroll for March 31. A four-hour conference with Mr. Oliver who had previously received detailed reports of the situation, a hurried directors' meeting, a conference with the president of the bank offering guarantees from the directors, and finally funds for the payroll available at 1:30 in the afternoon of March 31.

Meantime, any person who will examine the fiscal affairs of this company now, as at almost any other time in its history, will know that from a financially realistic point of view, the business has no right to exist. Nor does anyone who knows anything about the history of periodicals for young people believe that any periodical in this field that requires support from advertising revenue is likely to be a highly profitable enterprise.

Accordingly, it cannot hope to compete in salaries with adult periodicals that are able to sell a large volume of advertising. It can be kept going harmoniously and can have a reasonable assurance of continuing only by continued exercise of the cooperative spirit which has held it above water for these many years.

During the entire ill-fated history of *Scholastic*, at least there is one thing that no one who really knows the inside bookkeeping facts of this business can deny; and that is this: I have never asked anyone to share low pay, financial worries, and occasional layoffs in order that I might have ease and comfort and a high salary. I have never given a cut in salary without taking a larger proportionate one myself — nor have I ever advanced my personal salary without advancing first the salaries of my associates, beginning always with the lowest paid. Brief periods of prosperity were always shared. That's all the credit I shall take as a manager. My faults, I suspect, are more apparent to me than they are to any of you.

The payless holiday was observed without further word from the Guild.

Although the circulation of *Junior Scholastic* made substantial gains after opening at 40,000 (advanced to 70,000 in 1938 and 101,900 in 1939), although *Scholastic* was holding its own at 199,000, and *Scholastic Coach* turning in a fair profit, these developments did not ease the pressure from Clapp to be relieved of the bank notes he had endorsed. Robinson was urged to continue his quest for a buyer, merger, partner — or whoever might prove to be a source of new capital.

Mindful of these wishes, Robinson listened with dutiful ear when in August 1939 he received a call from an entrepreneur in the publishing field named John Hanrahan requesting an appointment to discuss a publishing venture then in the planning stage. For the meeting with Robinson he brought with him a broker named Edmund D. Sickels, a specialist in publishing properties. Their proposal was to form a consortium of youth magazines into an organization called the Forum of American Youth. This would include, at the outset, *Scholastic, Junior Scholastic, Scholastic Coach,* and *American Boy.* At a second meeting John M. Whitbeck, of the well-known financial house of Blair and Company, made a presentation explaining (1) "The Business Opportunity" and (2) "The Social Opportunity" of the project. The preamble for "The Business Opportunity" stated: "The amalgamation of these four publications in one single publishing house will effect pronounced economies in production . . . in the gathering of editorial contents . . . in broadening the potential of advertising acceptance"; and for "The Social Opportunity": "to prepare the young for their place in life; to implant an understanding of their personal rights and responsibilities; to implant an understanding sense of their relationship to their families, their communities and their State; to prepare them to face the world of work and service and enjoy happiness in self-development."

It is not surprising that, with these noble purposes, the Hanrahan group was able to enlist "full approval and support of the purpose and work of the Forum of Youth" from 30 notables of the times, including William Lyon Phelps, Eduard Benes, Alfred E. Smith, James Rowland Angell, Raymond Gram Swing, Eddie Rickenbacker, Frank Buck, Eleanor Roosevelt, Raymond Massey,

Robert Hutchins, Walter Damrosch, George Sokolsky, James T. Shotwell, Lou Little, Eddie Cantor, J. Edgar Hoover, Wilbur Cross, and Bishop Manning.

The expressed purposes of the Forum and the implied support of these and other celebrities smoothed the path of Blair and Company in its approach to prospective investors. In October 1939 Whitbeck wrote Hanrahan "to advise you of the progress to date in developing the financial angle of the Forum of American Youth. The program has evoked considerable interest in money circles and appears to be a timely enterprise. . . ."

A. K. Oliver and George Clapp, Scholastic's principal owners whom Robinson had kept informed of these developments, gave the signal to explore the possibilities; the following is excerpted from Oliver's "Dear Robbie" letter of August 29, 1939:

> I talked with Mr. Clapp this morning and together we agreed: (1) that, at the proper price and possibly with some reservations regarding you and Herb, we would be willing to sell all of our interest in the Scholastic Corporation, but would not sell less than all; (2) that, unless you see some objection to disclosing the information to Mr. Hanrahan (in view of the fact that in the event of his entering the field in competition with Scholastic such information might be of some value to him), there seems no good reason for not letting him have a Condensed Balance Sheet prepared for the purpose by Young & Company. . . . I know you will keep me advised if it looks as though the nibble might turn into a bite.

Turn it did. Hanrahan and associates examined the condensed balance sheet and other Scholastic data, such as circulation and advertising revenues, and came up with a "tentative offer": $250,000 for everything — $75,000 to be in cash, $75,000 in five-year serial notes, and $100,000 in stock in the new company. "Blair and Company will furnish the capital," wrote Sickels to Robinson on September 14, 1939. "Both you and Mr. Mc-Cracken, as well as your organization, would be expected to carry on, and of course you two gentlemen will have to be 'sold' on the plan of operation that Mr. Hanrahan has in mind, and he feels that you will be enthusiastic about it when it can be divulged."

Robinson and McCracken hoped that developments would not reach the stage where they would be in a position to be "sold," accustomed as they were to being sellers. Regardless of their hopes, they moved matters along expeditiously on signals Robinson got via letters and telephone from Oliver.

To decide what response to make to Hanrahan's tentative offer, Oliver, Clapp, and Robinson met in Pittsburgh on September 21. The Scholastic owners decided on a minimum of $300,000 in cash, "plus assumption of current liabilities including that portion of the summer loans not repaid at the time the transfer is effected," so recorded in the minutes of that meeting. It was decided "in view of Mr. Clapp's desire to get his estate in order,* to have the negotiations confined to cash rather than deferred and unsecured notes or stock, unless those deferred notes or stock are above the minimum."

The owners would be firm on the $300,000 cash feature, four times the amount in the Hanrahan "tentative offer." But when Robinson met with Hanrahan, Sic-

*At the time Clapp was 83 years old.

kels, and Whitbeck on October 3, he did not reveal this minimum cash requirement except to say that it was considerably above their bid. In reporting the meeting to Oliver and Clapp, Robinson mentioned that the Hanrahan group was moving to include two other youth magazines in the Forum of American Youth — *Open Road for Boys* and *Young America* — and already had a tentative option on *American Boy*.

During the meeting Hanrahan, eager to know the minimum figure, asked Robinson if he would telephone Oliver then and there for permission to reveal it. Robinson declined, but said he would put this request in his report to Oliver, which he sent off that same day, October 3. The final paragraph reveals quite a bit about Robinson's state of mind over these developments:

> They know that your minimum price is considerably higher than the price they originally suggested. They know that your first consideration is cash and why. I have given them the best sales talk I could on how valuable a piece of property we have, and I have assured them that if they get it at your minimum figure they will get a bargain. At that point I left off. I really can't say the words that might sell Scholastic at a price below what might be obtainable, nor can I say the words that, by some slight inflection or by placing the figure just too high, might eliminate your getting out from under a financial burden that Herb and I got you into. So, I again say I fear I must ask for instruction, or be relieved of making the next move. I say this knowing that you both know I'm not afraid of responsibility.

In a telephone conversation on the evening of October 4, after Oliver had received Robinson's letter, he gave

Robinson the green light on revealing the minimum cash of $300,000. This disappointed the Hanrahan group, but did not induce them to abandon the quest. Whitbeck, of Blair and Company, intensified his money-raising efforts, reporting that "a number of New York's foremost figures in business and finance have expressed their willingness to investigate this business. W. A. Harriman, Paul Felix Warburg, Leonard Dreyfuss, George E. Sokolsky, Harry F. Guggenheim, and William T. Grant, among others, now have the matter under consideration as a project worthy of their support."

To give them more time to solicit investors, the Hanrahan group asked for an extension to December 31 of the November 30 deadline Oliver had set for a decision. This was granted, but the additional days did little to brighten prospects for the Forum of American Youth. Its chiefs called for a meeting with Robinson and McCracken well ahead of the deadline—on December 13—in New York. Grierson of *American Boy* attended this meeting. The bidders were represented by Hanrahan and Sickels; Blair and Company, by Whitbeck. They announced that the $300,000 minimum probably could not be raised and asked for consideration of a lower figure. The next day Robinson wrote Oliver, summarizing the meeting:

> Whitbeck gave a report on the progress of his activities in raising funds, indicating that he had been unable to supplement to any considerable extent sufficient pledges to make possible the purchase prices agreed upon.
> This seemed to me, and in later discussions it seemed the same to Herb and Grierson, to be a build-up toward what has apparently been coming for several weeks, namely, a proposal that we

accept a nominal cash payment and accept stock for the balance. I decided, after a brief aside conference with Herb, to take the stand that the whole deal was off. They apparently even wanted to bargain over what the "nominal" cash amount would be, and since I knew that the financial status of Scholastic wouldn't permit of any such plan, I said that I saw no reason to continue the discussions and that the entire thing should revert to status quo ante.

This satisfied Oliver and Clapp that further negotiations would be fruitless, but it did nothing to raise money to solve the bank-note problem. Clapp then proposed a *final* deadline "for some sort of settlement before the 31st of December, 1941." Months before the two-year deadline Oliver and Clapp would be commissioning the well-known troubleshooting firm of Booz, Fry, Allen & Hamilton to try to find out why Scholastic wasn't making a profit (Chapter IX, "Incompetence Alleged").

As Robinson was heard to remark when pondering the events of the first quarter-century: "I'll never understand what it was that moved Mr. Oliver and Mr. Clapp to put up the cash, and put up with me, to keep us going." Had Robinson looked in a mirror, he could have seen "what it was."*

---

*Apropos his wonder over why Oliver and Clapp put up the cash and put up with him, Robinson also expressed wonder over his personal durability in the following marginal notation he made on a piece of this manuscript: "How I lived through 1940—the American Legion attack, and on top of that, through Booz, Fry, Allen & Hamilton in 1941—I don't know. No wonder I was in the hospital in 1942." The ailment, requiring surgery, was a perforated abdominal diverticulum.

For some light on the American Legion attack, see Chapter XXI, "Attacks!"

By the summer of 1943 Scholastic Corporation was in debt to the Farmers Deposit National Bank (later a branch of the Mellon Bank) and the Union Trust Company of Pittsburgh in the amount of $245,000 on corporation notes that were guaranteed by Clapp, Oliver, Robinson, and McCracken as individuals. The banks were insisting on payment of the notes. Both Clapp and Oliver wished to be fully free from responsibility for the corporation's liability to the banks. A directors' meeting was held on July 2 of that year to work out a plan for discharging the bank debt. Clapp, Oliver, McCracken, and Robinson undertook personally to pay the banks in full. McCracken and Robinson, through personal loans, together were able to raise only $15,000. Clapp and Oliver agreed to pay the balance in the amount of $115,000 each. The Scholastic Corporation was then authorized to issue promissory notes to these four individuals in the amounts that they had paid to the bank. The promissory notes contained a covenant that 50 percent of the company's profits in each of the five years ending December 31, 1948, would be applied to repay them. Clapp's note was given priority, in return for which Clapp sold his common stock to the others at $1 per share. This agreement was to be formalized by a board meeting held on July 14, 1943.

As the meeting ended, Robinson produced a photograph made from an oil painting of Clapp and asked him to autograph it as a memento of the meeting that proved to be a historic one for the company. That photograph, inscribed "To Robbie, Herb and Scholastic, George H. Clapp, July 2, 1943," has been hanging in Robinson's or Thora Larsen's office ever since.

At the annual stockholders' meeting on December

20, 1943, Clapp reiterated his desire to sell his preferred stock in Scholastic along with a settlement of his note, and withdrew his name for reelection to the board of directors. The stockholders elected John E. Crawford to represent Clapp's interests on the board.*

In order to give further preference to Clapp for payments on his note, on January 31, 1946, Oliver accepted 500 shares of Class A preferred stock as a $50,000 payment on his note. Thus by the fall of 1948 the $115,000 note held by Clapp had been reduced to $50,000 by the payment of $65,000 out of the earnings of the company. Clapp then, as an inducement to having the final $50,000 owed to him repaid before December 3, 1948, offered to sell his remaining stock—320 shares of Class A preferred—at a nominal price. In order to accomplish the settlement of the debt, the company borrowed $25,000 against insurance held on the lives of company officers and $25,000 in loans from a small number of officers and employees. Each of those who made loans was given an option to buy four shares of Clapp's preferred stock at $1 per share for each $1,000 lent to the company. These lenders were Lavinia Dobler, $500; Margaret Hauser, $6,000; Kenneth M. Gould, $500; John Studebaker, $2,000; M. R. Robinson, $5,000; and Paul E. Hutchinson, $500. Ernest H. Earley, a Dartmouth College friend of Robinson, who had helped in arranging the life insurance loans, also advanced money ($2,000) to the company and participated in the stock purchase option.†

*Crawford continued as a director until December 1948.

†As was mentioned previously, Clapp lived to be 90 years old. He died on March 31, 1949, barely four months after the company had fully settled its debt to him.

In December 1951 Robinson signed checks for the first dividend ever paid on any Scholastic stock (while Thora Larsen, blotting signatures, bemoaned the fact that this epochal event of a dividend on its *preferred stock* was taking place without fanfare or camera). In the letter enclosing the dividend check to Mr. Oliver dated December 26, 1951, Robinson wrote:

Dear Mr. Oliver:

Never did I sign or mail a check before that made me so genuinely happy as I was when I signed the enclosed. Now if you will just promise to live as long as Mr. Clapp lived—and I sure as hell hope you do—and. if, by the same sort of happy fortune I also can continue to drive on for twenty more years, perhaps by then some small portion of Scholastic's genuine debt to you can be repaid, if only in a monetary way.

With sincere appreciation from Scholastic to you, I enclose the first dividend check of $2,500. We shall try awfully hard to keep them coming every year and in larger amounts.

Cordially yours,

Robbie

In response, Mr. Oliver wrote:

Just received the preferred dividend check. Disobeying my first impulse, which was to have it framed as a museum piece, I have reluctantly decided to put it through for payment just like any other ordinary piece of business paper—which it most certainly *ain't*. A.K.O.

Six years later in December 1957 the company began to pay dividends on the common stock. On that occasion Robinson enclosed a personal letter with the checks going to each of the Oliver children, saying:

> The event is in part robbed of its joy because Gus Oliver is not present to see it happen. He and I had often talked about how we would celebrate when the day came to spend the first dividend check, for he always had faith that the day would come. So this day I find I'm sad rather than jubilant because Gus is not here in person;* but I know he is here in spirit congratulating Herb and me—yet at the same time ribbing us for taking thirty-seven years to do such a simple thing as earn money to pay a dividend to those who furnished the capital.

At the present writing, there are at least 22 Oliver children and grandchildren holding Scholastic stock.

Since the first dividend on common stock in 1957 Scholastic has not missed a quarterly dividend, the 83rd having been issued in October 1978 (12½ cents per share).

The offer of a stock option to employees who would lend the company money in order to settle the debt to Clapp was the beginning of the movement toward wider participation of employees in Scholastic stock ownership.

The next opportunity came in 1952, when the certificate of incorporation was amended to increase the capitalization of the company, and the stock was reclassified. At that time the employees who had lent money to

*Augustus K. Oliver died on October 15, 1954.

the company to settle the Clapp debt were given an opportunity to convert their notes into shares of the new preferred stock at $80 a share, with an option to purchase at $5 a share four shares of the new common voting stock for each share of preferred purchased. A number of additional employees (as limited by the regulations of the Securities and Exchange Commission) were also given an opportunity at that time to purchase preferred and common stock at the same prices.

When it became necessary in subsequent years to increase the capitalization of the company, the stockholders received the benefit of several stock dividends or stock splits. For instance, one share held in 1958 increased to 100 shares in 1968 by this means.

In 1960 a limited stock offering was made to key employees under a fixed subscription quota. The stock was offered in blocks of one share of Class A common stock and four shares of Class B common stock at a price of $133.50 per block ($26.70 per share). All purchasers signed a restricted stock agreement giving the company an option to repurchase the stock if the employee stockholder left the company. The agreement included a formula for establishing a price on the stock—at first, 10 times average earnings per share for the most recent five-year fiscal period, later amended to 15 times average earnings per share.

The first SEC "Regulation A" offer was made in 1963—4,200 shares of Class A common stock and 16,800 shares of Class B common were offered in blocks of one share of Class A common and four shares of Class B common, for $66.75 per block. All shares were restricted as in the 1960 limited offering; that is, an owner wishing to sell shares had first to offer them to the company at the formula price stated in the restricted stock agreement. If the company declined, the owner could sell to anyone at whatever price he could get.

The second and final "Regulation A" offering was made in 1966. This was an offer of 11,750 shares, sold in blocks of one share of Class A common and four shares of Class B common at $127.50 per block. The offering was made to finance the purchase of two offset printing presses for approximately $2,100,000, to be installed at the McCall plant in Dayton where the company's magazines are printed. As in the 1963 offering, these shares also were offered subject to the terms of a restricted stock agreement.

In December 1967 the stockholders approved the filing of a restated certificate of incorporation providing for an increase in capitalization and the reclassification of the stock into Class A stock and common stock, the Class A to be convertible into common at any time on the option of the stockholder. In January 1968 a four-for-one stock split was declared on both the Class A and on the common stock. In December 1968 all outstanding shares of preferred stock, amounting to 1,619 shares, were called in for redemption at $105 per share. No preferred stock has been issued since that time.

As recorded in Chapter XII, "Merger Talks," the company received many inquiries as to its availability for merger, joint venture, or outright acquisition. Some

Directors' meeting (1964)
Left to right: Agnes
Laurino, Paul Hutchinson,
William Boutwell, Joseph
Oliver, Donald Layman, G.
Herbert McCracken, M. R.
Robinson, Thora Larsen
(secretary), Henry Laughlin
(in partial eclipse),
John Studebaker, Jack
Lippert, John Spaulding.

of these led to negotiations with outstanding firms in the communications field. Scholastic's principal owners, concerned over the problem of inheritance taxes their estates would face were there no ready market for Scholastic stock, gave serious consideration to a number of proposals from companies whose stock was on the public market.

There was yet another way to market, and as detailed in Chapter XII, the directors took it on June 20, 1968, by resolving "that the Company offer for sale to the public through responsible underwriters shares of its common stock . . ." (from a resolution of the board of directors). Since the amount of stock to be offered to the public would not be sufficient to enable any consortium of new owners to seize management of the company, this solution was especially gratifying to those officers and stockholders who put a high premium on independence—foremost among them, the founder. He has transmitted to his colleagues in the present management of the company an unshakable determination that Scholastic must

113

remain independent and do its growing from internal resources.

The board of directors promptly started in motion the wheels for the long ride toward a public offering of Scholastic stock. The executive committee (Oliver, McCracken, Robinson, Layman, and John Spaulding) established procedures and recommended the brokerage house of White, Weld & Company as the principal underwriter. The public offering in January 1969 was for 297,200 shares of common stock at $20 per share. The McCrackens and Olivers were major selling shareholders, along with M. R. Robinson. A number of other employees also participated as selling shareholders to the total of several thousand shares. The company's participation was the sale of 50,000 shares of unissued stock. The stock was offered on January 8, 1969, and oversubscribed at $20 per share. Certain categories of employees—those of five or more years of service, those already Scholastic stockholders, and field representatives—were given an opportunity to indicate whether they wished to purchase shares, and how many, at the opening price with no commission attached. The employee demand far exceeded the number of shares allotted for this purpose and it was necessary to lower the original allotment per employee in order to accommodate all who applied.*

*In 1969 the company initiated, and in 1970 the stockholders approved, a stock option plan reserving 85,000 shares of its common stock for this purpose. Since then the company has, from time to time, granted stock options against these shares at the market price on the day of the grant to certain members of management responsible for the growth and development of the company. Options not exercised by May 20, 1981, will expire.

Traded over the counter, the Scholastic stock rose to a "bid" price of 21½ within a few weeks of its opening and then began a decline. When it was at 17 in 1970, the principal underwriter, White, Weld & Company, had an encouraging word to say about the prospects for the "good defensive growth" of Scholastic stock in its biweekly publication, *The Investment Observer*, from which these excerpts are taken:

INVESTMENT SUGGESTION

Scholastic Magazines, Inc. (17)

This company is a leading, highly respected publisher of supplementary materials for schools—graded student magazines, children's book clubs and classroom learning aids. The company's products augment basic classroom materials and are also used as part of the curriculum in certain subject areas. Supplementary educational materials of this type have found increasing classroom use to enrich and enliven the school curriculum. Such materials allow for differing reading and ability levels and include specialized products adapted to minority group interests. Key product lines are paperback books sold through children's book clubs and graded student magazines. Of total revenues of $46.5 million last year, 57% represented book sales and 28% magazine subscriptions. . . .

Scholastic's magazines have a combined circulation of more than 12 million copies per issue, 5½ million at the elementary school level and 7 million at the secondary school level. *Junior Scholastic*, with a circulation of about 1.5 million, is the largest of the magazines. . . .

Scholastic's editorial ability, the quality of its

Director's meeting (1969). M. R. Robinson (chairman. brushing hair). To his left, clockwise: Joseph W. Oliver, G. Herbert McCracken, John P. Spaulding, John C. Burton, Fred H. Gowen, George H. Milne, Walter J. Heussner (assistant treasurer), Steven Stepanian (corporate counsel, holding pipe), William D. Boutwell, C. Talbott Hiteshew, Jr. (top of head showing), Donald E. Layman, Thora Larsen (corporate secretary). Not in picture: Paul E. Hutchinson, Jack K. Lippert.

products and a strong marketing organization are the company's greatest assets. Over the years Scholastic has responded well and quickly to the needs of professional educators. . . . Since many of the company's newer materials are geared toward the culturally deprived urban school child or aid in developing reading skills or are text-type materials, Scholastic should benefit from any pickup in federal aid to education.

The initial public offering of Scholastic shares was made in January 1969. Prior to the public offering the company had been run as a private small business rather than with the motivation of a publicly owned concern, and profit margins had been low by normal publishing standards. Margins widened somewhat last year. We believe further gradual improvement is likely since the profit motive is greater now, benefits are beginning to be received from improved order processing, sales and inventory control systems

116

put into effect in the past two years, and the mix of the business is shifting somewhat in favor of higher margin products. Scholastic's sales growth has been excellent — a compound annual rate of 16% was achieved in the past five years. Sales growth of 10%–12% seems likely over the next five years. . . .

Scholastic common is selling at a reasonable price earnings ratio of 16 times estimated fiscal 1970 results. We estimate earnings at around $1.05 per share for the fiscal year ending August 31, 1970, up from $0.88 per share in fiscal 1969. . . . It seems realistic to expect an earnings growth rate of better than 10% over the next few years. . . . Thus we feel Scholastic has the attributes of a good defensive growth stock — a reasonably open-ended investment with virtually no exposure to the business cycle at a price earnings ratio which is modest relative to growth expectations and the multiples at which the leading text-book publishers sell. The dividend is $0.20. Since the market for the shares is thin, orders should be placed carefully.

Jean R. Kingsley

Had White, Weld & Company published this several years later, the identification of Scholastic as "publisher of supplementary materials for schools" would be incomplete, as it was to a degree at the time. An increasing amount of the Scholastic product has since qualified as text material for instruction in reading, literature, science, foreign languages, art and humanities, home economics, career guidance, American and world history.

On two occasions in the early 1970's the New York Society of Security Analysts invited Scholastic officers to

117

make presentations on the condition of the company, prospects, etc., and to answer questions. Scholastic was represented at one or both of these meetings by M. R. Robinson, Donald Layman, John Spaulding, George Milne, and Richard Robinson.

Despite the encouraging words, spoken and printed, and despite the company's steady improvement in revenues and earnings per share—sellers, not buyers, initiated what transactions there were in Scholastic stock over the counter, and the bid price in 1973 fell to a low of 4. The market as a whole, especially publishers' stocks, had declined sharply and did not make the upward turn until late 1975. By March 1976 Scholastic stock rose to a bid price of 8, then advanced in stages to 18/19 by August 1978.

The early decline in the price of Scholastic stock put a number of employees into serious financial straits, particularly those who had borrowed money to buy the stock at $20 in the initial public offering with the expectation that they would soon sell it at a higher price, pay their indebtedness, and pocket the difference. But this was not

Stockholders' meeting, December 11, 1969 (first meeting after Scholastic became public) in cafeteria, Englewood Cliffs, NJ. Foreground: left, Edgar Browning, manager/book order; right, Gordon Studebaker, far west regional director, and Associate Director Kenneth Allard.

the case with the large majority of the employee-purchasers, who managed to retain their stock by long-term installment payments on the $20 price. The company continued to pay dividends, starting with 20 cents per share for 1969 (at that time, the highest since dividends had been paid) reaching 37 cents per share in 1976 and 50 cents in 1978.

Who Owns Scholastic?

Scholastic's success is seen in terms of its service to and its status with the schools, its publishing integrity, its corporate independence, and its financial stability. As recounted in Chapter XII, "Merger Talks and a Near Miss," Scholastic's directors have declined the proposals of many corporate suitors seeking major or total ownership. Principal ownership resides with the founding families — the Robinsons, McCrackens, and Olivers — who hold 55 percent of the 1,700,000 shares of voting stock. As of June 1, 1978, 144 full-time employees, 83 retirees, other individuals, and institutional investors held the balance.

The company paid its 83rd consecutive quarterly dividend in October 1978 (12½ cents per share). Over the past 30 years revenues have increased from $1 million in 1947, to $6 million in 1957, to $10 million in 1960, to $111 million in 1978. Net income per share of stock advanced from 16 cents in 1957, to 26 cents in 1960, to $2.43 in 1978.

JUNIOR
Scholastic

THIS ISSUE: DISCOVERY AND INVENTION IN THE MODERN WORLD · SEPTEMBER 18 · 1937 ·

First issue of *Junior Scholastic*.

CHAPTER VII

For Improving Income, Progeny

W HAT moved Robinson to go to Oliver in the summer of 1936 to get his approval for starting a second classroom periodical, this one for the junior high schools? Robinson explains: "Revenues from *Scholastic* and *Scholastic Coach* combined had, for the first time, put us in the black by a very thin margin, but there was the huge company debt — some $200,000 in notes held by Farmers Deposit National Bank and the Union Trust Company in Pittsburgh, countersigned by Oliver and Clapp. I said to Mr. Oliver that if we were to reduce this indebtedness, we would have to improve income, and I saw the growing junior high market as the place to do it with a weekly that combined material for both English and social studies classes. Thus, the one magazine could appeal to both, or to the new core classes where the one teacher combined history, current affairs, and literature into one program."

So the planning for *Junior Scholastic*, under the editorship of Jack Lippert, began with a target date of September 1937 for an opening issue.

Junior was issued weekly, 32 times during the school year, 16 pages, self-cover, on newsprint, and for the first year carried no advertising. (Circulation was 39,500; bulk price, 80 cents per subscription.) During the second year (circulation 70,000) it carried a page or two of advertising in most of the 32 issues (Planters Peanuts, Shredded Wheat, Corona and Royal typewriters, Wearever Fountain Pens, movie and radio program ads).

In 1939, in order to put *Junior Scholastic* in a better competitive position with AEP's *Current Events* and Stuart Sheftel's recently launched *Young America,** the price was reduced to 50 cents, and there followed a gain of 32,000 subscriptions on top of a 30,000 gain the year before. This was one of the rare instances of a Scholastic magazine reducing its subscription price, and it held for three years, rising to 60 cents for school year 1942–43. Each year it gained in circulation — sometimes by a leap of 100,000 — and reached a peak of 1,780,000 after the company acquired the Civic Education Service periodicals in 1969 and the subscription list of the Catholic Messenger papers, which the George Pflaum Company had just discontinued. The CES weekly, *Junior Review*, was merged into *Junior Scholastic* as one magazine with the issue of February 2, 1970. For four years the masthead carried the line "*Junior Scholastic* Combined With *Junior Review*." Like the other CES periodicals, *Junior Review* had been issued in newspaper format, eight pages per issue, and carried no advertising. *Junior Scholastic*, in magazine format with a slick cover and at least 16 pages per issue, had much more variety in content than *Junior Review*. To what extent this switch and merger disenchanted some of the former *Junior Review* subscribers is

*In 1949 Sheftel sold the *Young America* papers to Alfred Gwynne Vanderbilt, and in 1952 Vanderbilt sold them to American Education Press, then owned by Wesleyan University, Middletown, CT (Chapter XIV, "The March of Magazines").

THE COMPANY WILL APPRECIATE SUGGESTIONS FROM ITS PATRONS CONCERNING ITS SERVICE

1201-S

WESTERN UNION

CLASS OF SERVICE

This is a full-rate Telegram or Cablegram unless its deferred character is indicated by a suitable symbol above or preceding the address.

R. B. WHITE PRESIDENT   NEWCOMB CARLTON CHAIRMAN OF THE BOARD   J. C. WILLEVER FIRST VICE-PRESIDENT

SYMBOLS

DL = Day Letter
NM = Night Message
NL = Night Letter
LC = Deferred Cable
NLT = Cable Night Letter
Ship Radiogram

The filing time shown in the date line on telegrams and day letters is STANDARD TIME at point of origin. Time of receipt is STANDARD TIME at point of destination.

Received at 215 East 45th Street, New York

NK171 18=PITTSBURGH PENN 10 247P

M R ROBINSON.SCHOLASTIC=

:250 EAST 43 ST:

:YOU WIN GO AHEAD MR CLAPP AND I WILLING TO GAMBLE TWO
THOUSAND DOLLARS APIECE ON YOUR JUDGMENT:
=A K OLIVER.

Telegram (May 10, 1937) responding to Robinson's appeal for start-up money for *Junior Scholastic*.

not known, but *Junior Scholastic*'s circulation dropped by 275,000 in 1971–72 and by 121,000 more the following year. By 1974–75 it had fallen to 1,060,000 and held at that level in 1975–76.

From time to time the question was raised over the value of the name *Junior Scholastic*. Its readers were in their early teens, and during the post-Sputnik period were said to have become so sophisticated that anything called "junior" would function under a handicap. It was proposed to drop the prefix and call it *Scholastic*, a title available because the parent magazine had added the prefix *Senior* to its title in 1943. An inquiry was made among the field representatives to get their reaction to this proposed change, and nearly all 160 of them pleaded that it not be made. *Junior Scholastic*, they said, was a title so ingrained in use and application to the pre-high school level that to cut it in half would befuddle teachers as to what grade level it was being changed to serve. The change was not made, but some years later Jim Brownell, then editor of *Junior Scholastic*, came up with a logo that featured the initials *JS* in type considerably larger than that of the full title, which it also carried.

There were several magazine title changes over the years: *JAC* (*Junior American Citizen*) became *NewsTime* in 1952; *Young Citizen* became *News Citizen*; *Practical Home Economics* became *Practical/Forecast*, then later *Forecast for Home Economics*; and *Practical English* became *Voice* in 1969.

CHAPTER VIII

20 Years Old

Delayed Adolescence

Entering the 1940's with the three properties —
the flagship magazine *Scholastic, Junior Scholastic,*
and *Scholastic Coach* — the company seemed to be rest-
ing on its laurels, such as they were, after the 1937 start-
up of *Junior Scholastic.* The two student magazines had a
combined circulation gain of only 3,000 during the school
year 1940–41 — the result of a gain of 6,000 by *Junior
Scholastic* and a loss of 3,000 by *Scholastic.* No one in
ownership or management was impressed, least of all
Oliver and Clapp, whose concern over the Scholastic condition prompted them to commission a management-
consultant firm — Booz, Fry, Allen & Hamilton — to
examine the company and make a prognosis. This they
did in the fall of 1941, with results that are explained in
the next chapter, "Incompetence Alleged."

Although the Booz, Fry, Allen & Hamilton medicine
would not be swallowed, their investigation stirred some
action, including the start-up of a new magazine called
World Week, the first issue dated September 14–19,
1942. Intensified interest in world history and geography
brought on by World War II justified launching a magazine to bridge the gap between *Junior Scholastic* and the
senior magazine, both of which were weak in ninth- and

At 1939 Advisory Board meeting: Jane Russell (Fliegel), secretary; Kenneth Gould, managing editor, and Margaret Hauser, associate editor.

10th-grade circulation, where world history was then a required course in most school systems. Promoted as "The New All Social Studies Classroom Magazine Graded to Meet Your Wartime Teaching Requirements," the periodical announced itself in the teacher edition with the following statement (reprinted in part):

Vol. 1, No. 1

The first issue of any publication is an occasion that calls for an editorial pronunciamento. The question naturally asks itself: "Why in these days of crisis and priorities should anyone start a new classroom periodical?" We'll answer as briefly as we can, and hereafter avoid editorializing.

Scholastic Publications, beginning with the original all-purpose magazine for senior high schools, *Scholastic*, now entering its twenty-third year of publication, have over a period of years expanded to publish several special editions, together with *Junior Scholastic*, for junior high school students.

126

In this continuous process of adjustment to classroom needs, it became apparent that there existed a twilight zone not adequately filled by any of our publications. This gap was in the intermediate high school years, where younger pupils just emerging from the upper grades had not yet fully adjusted themselves to the more mature requirements of the senior high school. . . .

World Week will therefore address itself to providing a weekly current events and social studies paper primarily for Grades 9 and 10, in which young people may win their way to a full consciousness of their civic duties and patriotic responsibilities in a period of global war. For these young people we shall do our best to provide a basis for intelligent study and decision in the coming crucial years.

The reference to "crisis and priorities" proved prophetic, for just four months later on January 1, 1943, paper rationing went into effect, with quotas based on tonnage used during calendar year 1942. As *World Week* had less than half a calendar year to use as a basis, it could not make the full-year contribution to the company's total

English Department staff with M. R. Robinson, 1940: John Jamieson, librarian; Ernestine Taggard, literary editor; Gladys Schmitt, associate editor.

127

tonnage that the three other periodicals could.

A publisher's quota was based on total tonnage of all materials that it published or printed, including promotion pieces. This allowed some flexibility in the dispensation of the paper for various uses. It was possible to accept an increase in circulation by trimming page size and reducing the amount and weight of paper used in promotion. Most magazines could reduce the quality (weight) of the paper they used, as could *Scholastic Coach*, but the pages of *Scholastic, Junior Scholastic*, and *World Week*, being printed on lightweight 32-pound newsprint, could not get much thinner. These magazines could and did, however, reduce the trim size, the number of pages per issue, and the number of issues per school year. *World Week*, starting with a circulation of 46,000, gained circulation — as did *Scholastic* and *Junior Scholastic* — throughout the war to the extent that paper conservation allowed. Yet all three had to turn away subscribers who placed orders late in the customary ordering periods.

During those years nearly all high schools observed the two-semester school year and graduated senior classes in mid-year as well as in late spring. Half of the orders for Scholastic magazines were placed on a semester basis; thus the mid-year renewal as well as new-business campaign was essential to the company's economy, less so during the World War II years than in peacetime because of paper rationing. To its subscribers and prospective subscribers, the company emphasized early ordering and used its teacher editions to encourage it, with announcements such as this from a February 1944 issue:

Julian Whitener, production assistant, and Sarah Gorman, production chief and copy editor. She served the company for 35 years (1940 photo).

128

Circulation Department sales staff, 1940. Standing, left to right: F. H. Anspacher, Hugh Robinson, Paul Sarkoff. Sitting: Wendell Lake, A. C. Price, Richard Mathewson (manager), Genevieve Bohland. Price was Scholastic's first full-time subscription salesman.

***Tomorrow May Be
Too Late . . .
Scholastic Magazines
Are Rationed***

During the fall semester, we returned hundreds of classroom orders to teachers who placed their orders late or did not revise in time.

Because of wartime paper restrictions, the total number of copies of all magazines is limited. We can accept only a limited number of additional orders or increases on present orders.

That's why you should mail this coupon today . . . to revise your present order . . . to enter a tentative order . . . to *confirm* your order.

During the World War II years the company had the good fortune to strengthen its ranks by acquiring the services of Donald E. Layman (1944) for the advertising staff, Agnes M. Laurino (1942) for the subscription service and accounting staff, and Eric Berger (1941) for the editorial staff.

Laurino had been in charge of subscription fulfillment for the Hearst organization for many years. When Hearst decided to shift that operation to Ohio, Laurino was invited to go along, but her interests were in New York and there she decided to remain. After training the new staff for Hearst in Ohio, Laurino began job-hunting.

129

Agnes Laurino
(1965 photo).

Scholastic was one of the first places she applied, and Robinson hired her. She joined the company on January 2, 1942, and served for almost 26 years until her death.

Her qualities of leadership, her friendly but firm discipline over a fast-growing staff, her insistence on meeting schedules without sacrificing accuracy, and her close, person-to-person supervision of every branch of business operations made her one of the company's most valuable human assets. She was elected controller and treasurer in 1954 and a member of the board in 1963. After a brief illness, she died of cancer on September 23, 1967. In a tribute to her published in a memorial book, Robinson wrote:

> As we went through all of the necessary changes in our business operations brought about by our rapid expansion, I worked long hours with Mrs. Laurino but I could not keep up with her — nor could anyone else. . . . She absorbed Scholastic; Scholastic absorbed me; Scholastic absorbed her. Since I was likewise dedicated to being a Scholastic slave, our lives became so enmeshed in mutual work that we lived Scholastic together. . . . The way she hurled herself tirelessly into her work, my work, and the work of her associates without concern for personal pleasure, rest, and recreation prompted me time after time to demand that she stop, that she take real vacations. Those were the only times she refused to obey my orders or abide by my requests. Her invariable response was, "But, Mr. Robinson, I love it, this is what I want to do, this is my recreation!"

A portrait of Agnes Laurino by Wayne Blickenstaff was commissioned by Robinson and hangs in the Englewood Cliffs office.

Essential to Scholastic's overall good health is the sale of advertising because it makes possible the enrichment of the magazines' editorial content. As new magazines were created and projected, McCracken's responsibilities as director of advertising expanded beyond the capacity of one man to handle. He found an enterprising and articulate associate in Donald E. Layman, a graduate of the University of Michigan, who had been with the publishing division of the Reuben H. Donnelley Corporation before joining Scholastic in 1944. His experience in both advertising sales and editorial supervision while at Donnelley gave Layman a head start on his Scholastic job. He proved an excellent presenter of the Scholastic story, working in close harmony with McCracken to score successes in what was then and, though perhaps to a lesser degree, still is one of the most difficult markets for selling magazine space—the teenage mixed market (boys *and* girls).

Layman was given executive responsibility for advertising sales, and as the company product line advanced, took on broad administrative and top-management responsibilities. He was elected vice president in 1948, a member of the board in 1957, executive vice president in 1961, and president in 1963—then the only person other than Robinson to hold that office since the company's first incorporation in 1922.* With Richard Holahan as his deputy, Layman led Scholastic through its 1960 period of acquisition of real property and construction of warehouses and order-processing centers in the United States

*When they elected Layman president, the directors elected M.R. Robinson chairman of the board and chief executive officer.

131

and Canada (Chapter XV, "The Book Business"). He retired at the end of 1971. He and his wife Enid live in Buck Hill Falls, PA, part of the year, then move to John's Island, SC, and Fort Myers, FL, with the onset of winter.

Within a year of joining Scholastic as editor of English features, Eric Berger was named editor of *World Week*—its first—while continuing with his *Scholastic* magazine duties. A year later in October 1943, he was in the Army, assigned to Military Intelligence Service. After the war Master Sergeant Berger* returned to *Senior Scholastic* (the *Senior* had been added with the March 8, 1943, issue) as associate editor, and when *Literary Cavalcade* was launched in the fall of 1948, he was named editor—again, as custom seemed to require—continuing his duties on *Senior Scholastic*. These duties had expanded to the point where he was serving as virtual editor of *Senior Scholastic* (and by 1950 was given the title), continuing to report to Editor-in-Chief Gould, and as editor of *Literary Cavalcade* (Chapter XIV, under "Quality at 30 Cents per Subscription"). When Scholastic acquired *Science World* from Street & Smith in 1959, Berger was named editor, and later, editorial director of the newly organized science department (Chapter XIV, under "Plunge into Science").

*Berger's commanding officer was Colonel Sidney P. Marland, who later became superintendent of schools of Darien, CT, and Pittsburgh, PA, and United States Commissioner of Education. He served two terms on Scholastic's National Advisory Council, was elected to the board of directors in 1976, and was appointed chairman of the Editorial Boards and National Advisory Council in 1978.

CHAPTER IX

Incompetence
Alleged

THERE is no instance of the principal owners, Augustus K. Oliver and George H. Clapp, ever attempting to dictate or influence the editorial policy or content of the magazines. Of course, by reason of their financial support during the company's years of dependence, Oliver and Clapp held a life-grip on its survival. However, they doubted whether Scholastic would ever be able to make it on its own. At one point Robinson, presiding at an annual meeting, opened it with the usual "The stockholders will please come to order." In Oliver's light dry whisper came the retort, "Bag-holders, you mean." Again, at a time when the "bottom line" seemed unusually bottomless, he told Robinson: "Pretend I'm dead."

As the company turned into its third decade and Franklin Roosevelt, into his third term, Oliver had the notion that the business might be helped by seeing a "doctor"—one of the management-consultant firms that had come into vogue in corporate circles. Oliver had in mind one that had done a good job for the Pittsburgh Coal Company of which Oliver was then board chairman. He had discussed this notion with Clapp, had mentioned it to Robinson in 1940, and a year later decided to go through with it. Oliver and Clapp contracted with Booz, Fry, Allen

& Hamilton (BFA&H) to give Scholastic a thorough physical and fiscal examination. Late in September 1941 they went to work. Robinson had several weeks to prepare himself and his staff for the survey.

First, on September 3, he met with his department heads and supervisors, including Herb McCracken, Sol Oppenheim, and Marie Kerkmann of the Advertising Department; Kenneth Gould, Owen Reed, and Jack Lippert of Editorial; and Dick Mathewson of Circulation. Robinson asked each of his top staff to "write out a list of your duties and activities and responsibilities. I'm sure the first question the surveyor will ask me about each member of the staff is: What does he do?" Robinson importuned his chiefs to be "frank and complete" in their answers to questions, and said: "We must approach being 'surveyed' without fear of the possible consequences. I alone am the person to be worried. And I am worried . . . but I count on being able to demonstrate to any management consultant that this is an organization which should be approved. Every person in this room and practically every member of the staff has a deep, sincere devotion to the task of building up this business, making it pay its way and gaining for the business the best reputation possible. We all have at heart the same objectives, and in spite of occasional lapses which are a corollary of spirited drive, we have a spirit which will be apparent to anyone spending any time in this office. I count on that enthusiastic devotion to our objectives to offset some of our lack of efficiency which might disturb the efficiency expert mind."

Three weeks later Robinson received word that BFA&H would start its investigation. Robinson sent out a general office memo announcing the purpose of the survey: "to help management find a solution to some of our business problems. There is no other motive. . . . I wish you to feel perfectly free to give [the investigator] whatever information he requests and to answer frankly the questions he may ask. . . . I shall appreciate your cooperation."

In preparation for the survey, Robinson made notes over a two-week period between September 26 and October 9, and organized them in a 4,000-word statement to Oliver, Clapp, and George A. Fry, a partner in the management-consulting firm. This basically was a statement of Robinson's belief in the future profitable operation of Scholastic, and what he would do to bring this about. He set forth his convictions in the opening four paragraphs:

> I believe there are no basic reasons why the Scholastic Magazines cannot be operated as a profitable business enterprise, paying 6% interest on an investment of from $300,000 to $500,000 and permitting the paying of fair—but not large—salaries to the management and staff—salaries comparable to those of a fairly successful text-book publishing house (which in a primary sense is what Scholastic Corporation is). Furthermore, I am confident that in addition to paying the 6% return, above indicated, by careful expansion of certain phases of the business, there could be built up an increase in earnings, which in addition to paying fixed charges of interest would pay fairly substantial dividends on the common stock. I admit this involves a faith in the future of our country and its institution of private enterprise; a faith I happen to have in spite of evidence to the contrary, and in spite of the prognostications of many prominent contemporaries.

If I did not believe what I have set down in the preceding paragraph, my obligation to my family would have prompted me to chuck the entire enterprise and accept one of the several opportunities for financial advancement and comparative security which happened to have been offered to me in recent years. I say "my obligation to my family" rather than my personal ambition and personal wishes would have prompted that decision. Personally I have never been motivated either by a wish for personal security or a desire for financial reward. Perhaps that is a personal weakness which has been partially responsible for the failure of Scholastic Corporation to show a financial return comparable to its educational and cultural influence or in ratio to its prestige in the educational world.

Then, too, did I not believe what I have set down in the first paragraph above, I would long ago have reported my doubts to Mr. Oliver and Mr. Clapp, because, above all else, the motivating force which has driven me in recent years to attempt to solve Scholastic's problems and pull it out of the financial dumps has been the fact that I did not want to let them down, did not want to have to lose the large investment they have made in this business and in me.

Of course, I am perfectly aware that "personal vanity," hating to admit that I may have been wrong about this enterprise all these years, and the fact that Scholastic was my "baby" may have been stronger influences in some of my decisions than I realized; but I'm not quite weak-minded enough to have permitted those emotions to blind me completely. Often, in the course of my analyses of the business problems of Scholastic, I doubly challenged my own logic because of my awareness of these emotions which might be affecting my thinking.

Robinson then sketched the financial history of Scholastic, focusing on the lack of capital and the "unusual relationship" between the owners (Oliver/Clapp) and management (Robinson/McCracken):

Mr. Oliver and Mr. Clapp didn't want to engage in the publishing business.* They went into Scholastic in 1925 because they considered it deserving of their support and encouragement. . . . In later years, the point was reached where they feared they were sending good money after bad, where it was doubtful if the business should be carried through the Depression; consequently each year — as we failed to turn the corner — decisions were made on the basis of whether the business should be given another year to see what might happen; and instead of being financed in terms of a long-range program, arrangements were made with creditors, and funds borrowed at the bank, to permit us to get by another summer's drought and into a new school year. And each time the decision to continue was accompanied by instructions to the management to be on the lookout for a prospective buyer, to institute if possible a plan which would lead to the sale of the business. As a result, there was no plan made to have the business reach a certain goal one year, a further goal the next year, etc. Decisions had to be made on the basis of how to keep the loss for the next fiscal year to a minimum. . . . Because of that condition, the Company has always had a faulty financial structure, heavy debts, bad credit standing; expansion took place without funds, losses led to more debts and funds had to be raised to pay back losses.

*Oliver had gotten out of the newspaper business 14 years earlier.

Thus Robinson described the predicament the company faced through the Depression years. But he was writing this in 1941, at the start of a new school year, after having completed a year (1940–41) in which — as he noted further on in his memo — there was "a $40,000 increase in gross sales and a year of bigger increases coming up; and with 17 of the country's leading department stores joining us in an activity which is the envy of all our competitors."*

In a section headed "Possible Company Expansion," Robinson said: "One of my first recommendations would be to start a new periodical to solve the problem of meeting the competition of *Our Times, Weekly News Review, Every Week* and in some areas *American Observer*" (periodicals of American Education Press and Civic Education Service for high school social studies classes).

"Another direction in which we might consider moving," Robinson continued, "is the field of high school textbooks. . . . Our prominent place in the field of art might make a magazine for art classes a good field for us to enter. Science is another field . . . and home economics . . . and a periodical devoted to commercial education . . . and for industries."†

George Fry spent several hours interviewing Robinson and his department heads and thereafter turned over

*The Scholastic Art Awards.
†Scholastic would publish magazines in all these fields. Quite soon came *World Week* in 1942, followed by *Practical English* and *Prep* (Preparation for Practical Living) in 1946, by *Science World* in 1959, and *Art & Man* in 1970. Scholastic moved into the textbook field with the Literature Units in 1960, followed by the World Affairs Multi-Texts and Arithmetic Practice Books in 1962 (Chapter XIV, "The March of Magazines," and Chapter XV, "The Book Business").

all interviewing and on-the-premises investigating to a young business school graduate who will be referred to here as Mr. X, "a boy sent to handle a man's job," as Robinson described him at the time. As for Fry, Robinson considered him "extremely experienced and a smart businessman, highly capable."* Fry had once done yeoman's work on a survey of the *Washington Post*.

Completing their survey in about four weeks, BFA&H prepared a report and sent it to Oliver and Clapp in late November. After they read it, Oliver telephoned Robinson to set a date for a meeting in his office in Pittsburgh to hear Fry report on the report. Clapp also would attend the meeting. It was set for Wednesday, December 3, to accommodate Robinson's schedule.† Fry's oral presentation of the report was the first inkling Robinson had of what it contained, and what he heard was more than an inkling. He made copious notes as Fry talked, and returned to New York with him on the train. In their conversation then and the next day at lunch, Fry advised Robinson to act promptly "in quietly learning if

*In 1942 Fry left BFA&H to form Fry, Lawson & Company, then later, George Fry & Associates. Booz, Allen and Hamilton is still a prominent management-consultant firm.

†The December date was chosen so that Robinson could attend the annual meeting of the National Council of Teachers of English in Atlanta over the Thanksgiving holiday weekend (Chapter XXIV, "Never Home for Thanksgiving"). In consideration of Scholastic's straitened circumstances, he rode the train to Atlanta by coach, sitting up all night. Ernestine Taggard, Scholastic's literary editor, did likewise. Once in Atlanta, the standard of living improved, as quarters had been taken in the Atlanta Biltmore Hotel. That's where Scholastic, with its typical hospitality toward customers and guests, served cocktails and dinner for a hundred or so teachers and administrators, including Willis Sutton, the Atlanta superintendent of schools.

certain organizations might be interested in the purchase of Scholastic; he suggested *Readers' Digest*."*

On Friday evening, December 5, at the Hotel Lexington in New York, Robinson met with his department heads to give them the bad news. McCracken, Oppenheim, Gould, Reed, and Lippert attended. Mathewson was absent but was briefed later.†

To this group Robinson said: "This discussion is the most serious one we have ever faced. It is the most difficult position in which I have ever been placed." Robinson described the meeting he had just attended in Pittsburgh and the oral presentation of the report by Fry. "With the exception of a small segment of the 300-page report, I have no copy, and doubt if I ever shall see a copy." (Clapp later mailed his copy to Robinson.)

Robinson continued to talk to his associates from the notes he took during Fry's oral presentation in Pittsburgh:

> Starting with the good news — of which there was very little — one complimentary comment, that the morale of Scholastic employees is high; that they are exceptionally loyal, with no undercurrent of office politics discernible and no signs of employees' knifing one another. Fry made one other comment that could be construed as a compliment: that a survey made by his firm showed that Scholastic had a high reputation among educators.

*Quotation from a letter Robinson wrote Oliver on Saturday, December 6, reporting his meeting with Fry.

†McCracken was director of advertising; S. Z. Oppenheim, advertising manager; Gould, editor of *Scholastic;* Reed, editor of *Scholastic Coach;* Lippert, editor of *Junior Scholastic;* R. D. Mathewson, circulation manager.

Robinson then said, "Let's get to the bad news," the thrust of which was:

> The general attitude [of the staff] is one of complacency created in part by management's soft treatment. Business and editorial department personnel show little evidence of aggressiveness and drive.
>
> The company has an impaired capital working position; runs expenses too high in view of its profit possibilities; circulation policies are weak and ineffectual; advertising sales effort, poorly planned and directed; budget control, sloppy and lax; accounting records, inadequate and submitted too infrequently to be of any value to the management.

Robinson continued:

> Although I have been perfectly willing to tell you what was said about me and my ability, I shall not say to this group as a whole what was said about each of you. I want to do this privately with you.

This he did, then called the group together again and said:

> Now you have heard the worst about yourselves — as seen by [Mr. X]. The question, as I see it, is: "Can we take it?" Which brings me to the major recommendation of the report: that M. R. Robinson be replaced as head of the company by a more efficient businessman. Mr. Fry stated that they had hoped there might be someone in the organization now who would be competent to undertake my job, but after considering four of those here present, saw no one who was capable of furnishing the leadership and business drive to

handle the job, and recommended that the owners go outside to find the right man for the position.

I wish to strike one mild note of optimism before we proceed . . . neither [Mr. X] nor Mr. Fry even remotely intimated that the business was improving this year — they don't know what we are doing this year, nor what prospect we have for early growth.* The new man who would come in would be in a position to turn this business into an immediate profit-making situation. I have figures up to October 31st — comparative with last year.† If I have to leave this job, I'd like to turn in a profitable year. . . .

I think all of you can appreciate fully the situation which now confronts me, and indirectly — but to a lesser degree — all of you. . . . I should add that the owners have not adopted this report as yet. . . . Neither Mr. Oliver nor Mr. Clapp commented on the report in my presence.

What I would like to do:

    a. Ask the owners to give us six months to disprove the contentions of Messrs. Booz, Fry, *et al.*

    b. Institute some of the economy measures mentioned as possibilities by [them].

    c. Give the organization, especially this

---

*When Robinson said this, he had not seen the report and had only his notes to go by. In the actual report, BFA&H briefly referred to the blue in the sky as follows: "Subscription sales and advertising revenues are now at their peak." The date of the report was November 14, 1941. Its official title: "Business Survey SCHOLASTIC CORPORATION."

†The figures Robinson referred to showed a loss of $34,190 for school year 1940–41. A loss of $6,000 was projected for 1941–42. (It turned out to be $6,934.) And as it turned out a year later, a profit of $40,888 was produced, the second profit in the 22 years of Scholastic's life. (The first was in 1935–36, and it amounted to $2,325.)

group here, a sample of the kind of management I am confident they would have to face as soon as I am replaced by a person whose sole interest in the job would be to prove to the owners that he is their man — that he is the man to turn losses into profits, a sour business into a sweet one.

The next morning, Saturday, December 6, Robinson went to the office as usual, but the routine of going there was the only thing usual about it: His mind was seething over the problem of rescuing Scholastic from the clutches of some other publishing house, or perhaps a fate even worse. He wrote a letter to Oliver, suggesting dates for the meeting with him and Clapp in Pittsburgh. (It was later set for December 17.) Determined to persuade Oliver and Clapp to retain the existing management, he began typing out drafts of points he wished to make when he met with them. Tomorrow would be a fateful Sunday.

After dissecting *The New York Times* in the Robinson apartment on 79th Street in Jackson Heights, he and his wife Florence left for a midday dinner with friends at the Union Theological Seminary, and while there heard the news of the Japanese attack on Pearl Harbor. He and Mrs. Robinson went to the Scholastic office in the Daily News Building, the place throbbing with the comings and goings of that newspaper's staff. He telephoned Kenneth Gould and Jack Lippert about catching the next issue of *Scholastic* and *Junior Scholastic* with the Pearl Harbor story, the former going to press on Tuesday, December 9, the latter the day after, for the issue dated December 15.

On Monday Robinson arrived at the office at his customary 8 o'clock, after breakfasting at Schrafft's in the

Chrysler Building. In the mail he received Clapp's copy of the BFA&H report, and was grateful to have for the first time the document to which he would respond. Although Robinson had taken as many notes as his pen could record while Fry talked at the meeting with Oliver and Clapp in Pittsburgh, he was aghast at seeing, in cold type, specifically what Oliver and Clapp were advised to do:

> In view of the present unsatisfactory condition of the business and the urgent need for improvement in results, there are three possible alternatives to be considered. These are:
> 1. Rehabilitate the company for permanent operation.
> 2. Immediate and complete liquidation.
> 3. Take certain remedial measures and then sell the company as a going concern.
>
> Considering the acute financial condition of the company, the highly competitive nature of the school publishing field, and the lack of competent management, the interests of the stockholders will best be served by following [plan 3]. Of the alternative plans considered this is the one most likely to succeed.

The report itemized "certain remedial measures," which included:

> Bring in an outside executive capable of providing sound business leadership. This individual could act in the capacity of a business manager representing the interests of the company's stockholders.
>
> Budget all departments of the business and set up strict expense controls. Drastic reductions should be made, particularly in those departments not producing revenue.

Circulation policies, the field sales program, and subscription revenue procedures should be reorganized. . . . The emphasis should be placed on contraction rather than further expansion of activities. Circulation objectives would be aimed at holding to present levels.

Editorial content should be cut down, the number of pages reduced, the use of color minimized, and some editorial personnel eliminated. *Scholastic*'s editor could be eliminated and the job taken over by the present publisher. The staff of part-time contributors should be contracted.

The circulation and advertising functions should be realigned under a business manager. This will be the major responsibility of the new executive to be brought in from outside.

An assistant should be employed for the accounting department. This will expedite the release of current reports needed for management control purposes.

The responsibility for the Scholastic Awards should be placed under the advertising department. . . . The associate editor now handling this function should be released.

More supervision should be exercised over the personnel. The present easy-going and indifferent work habits should be corrected.

The accounting function should be placed under the direction of the new business manager. This will expedite the preparation and use of control reports.

The librarian should be eliminated and her duties taken over by others. Editorial staff writers should be responsible for their own research activities. Responsibility for clipping newspaper items could be given to the receptionist who frequently is idle. Photographic filing could be done by the production department.

Present salaries should be reviewed and adjusted downward wherever feasible.*

Effecting these changes should correct many of the weaknesses in organization and operating methods brought out in the survey. While possibilities for profitable operation are slight, the company's activities can, at least, be carried on at a break-even basis until such a time as an acceptable offer is received to purchase the company.

During the time this modified improvement program is going on the directors should make every effort to find a purchaser. This should not be done by anyone now actively engaged in the company.

For the December 17 meeting in Pittsburgh, Robinson took the Pennsylvania Railroad's all-Pullman "Pittsburgher," departing New York at 11 p.m. and arriving in Pittsburgh at nine the next morning. He went directly to Oliver's office.

*Of the 39 employees in the New York office on the regular payroll, only one was recommended for an increase in salary: the bookkeeper who pilfered petty cash and forged checks but had not yet been detected. There were 14 on the payroll in Dayton, OH, where the magazines were printed and mailed. All salaries at that time were on a monthly basis and were paid on the 15th and last day of each month. Samples of salaries expressed in a week's pay: McCracken, vice president and advertising director, $126.92; Robinson, president and publisher, $92.30; Gould, editor of *Scholastic*, $88.85; Lippert, editor of *Junior Scholastic*, $88.85; Owen Reed, editor of *Scholastic Coach*, $54.23; Berger, production manager, $46.15; Marie Kerkmann, advertising salesperson, $46.15; Gladys Schmitt, Ernestine Taggard, and Margaret Hauser, writers, $40.38; Herman Masin, assistant editor, *Scholastic Coach*, $33.46; Sarah Gorman, production assistant, $30; Mary Jane Dunton, art assistant, $28.84; Jane Russell (Fliegel), secretary to Gould, $23.07. Other secretaries' salaries ranged from $16 to $20.

He opened his prepared statement by saying:

> I have studied the report in detail, and appreciate your giving me the opportunity to discuss it with you. You have taken no action on it, as yet, and before you do, I wish to give my reaction to it. . . . If the report is an accurate appraisal of the business, if the appraiser is correct in his conclusion, then it seems to me there is nothing to do except to toss me out, rue the day you ever saw me as well as Herb, and liquidate or sell at a distress price. Before you make such a decision, I feel it is my duty to question the validity of the report. I shall not comment on the phases of the report which concern me as an operator. This is not to be a personal defense.

Robinson mentioned that Mr. X, having had no experience in the publishing business, was "utterly incapable of handling this survey. When interviewing the staff, [Mr. X] mistook modesty for weakness, and frankness about our shortcomings as an indication of mediocre talent."

Robinson gave some examples of Mr. X's inability to make intelligent appraisals of the competence of the staff, including his mistaken assessment of the new bookkeeper, the only person on the staff for whom he recommended an increase in salary. The bookkeeper had been with the company less than two months when the survey started. After Mr. X had finished his week of interrogations, Robinson had cause to examine more closely the work of the bookkeeper and found "the most incompetent, careless worker it was ever my mistake to hire."

The bookkeeper will be referred to here as BX, an anonymity preferred in order to protect that individual from exposure of deeds committed 37 years ago. Robinson gave Oliver and Clapp examples of the bookkeeping errors BX had made plus some hanky-panky with the petty cash and forgery of Editor Kenneth M. Gould's name to a paycheck. Faced with this evidence, BX promptly and involuntarily resigned, and the bonding company made good on the identifiable losses. (The discovery of BX's malfeasance was made with the help of an Arthur Young & Company accountant.)

Robinson then gave Oliver and Clapp some 20 examples of outright errors in the report and its failure to mention that the so-called "hodge-podge *Junior Scholastic*" had in one year jumped from 107,584 circulation to 192,771 at the very time BFA&H was making the survey.

In conclusion Robinson said:

> Now I'm not fool enough to think or say that because there are numerous errors in the report that it did not have plenty of truth in it, too. I also realize that showing up the errors does not prove that the present management has been high grade. . . . [Mr. X] saw nothing except what he wanted to see of a situation that most certainly is and has been unsatisfactory. But he didn't look for nor did he apparently discover the basic causes of our predicament, causes which I set forth in a memorandum to him with a carbon to Mr. Oliver . . . who will recall that the chief point in that private memo pertained to the fact that each year it was a question of whether we could find the wherewithal to keep going for another year—and if so, how little money could we scrape through on to tide us over the summer; and could I possibly find a prospective purchaser before the next year was out?

Robinson then proposed to the owners that they give him a year to "turn losses into profits," and outlined steps he would take to accomplish this, including some economy measures proposed by BFA&H.

Oliver and Clapp asked Robinson to prepare a revised budget for the remainder of that school year and an organization chart that would list all personnel and their functions. They approved Robinson's choice of Raymond Black for controller (official title: assistant treasurer) and the employment of a bookkeeper to assist him. This turned out to be Agnes M. Laurino, who reported for duty the same day Black did—January 2, 1942.

Returning to New York, Robinson met with his management group on Saturday, December 20, 1941, to report the outcome of his meeting with Oliver and Clapp and to repeat Oliver's admonition to him at the close of that meeting: "Get away forever from the idea of leaning on the owners. It rubs off on the staff and they become leaners. Turn losses into profits and a spirit of achievement will permeate the organization."

A few days after the meeting with his management group on December 20, Robinson met with all employees to quash rumors they may have heard about the viability of the company. "Not one that I heard is true," he told them. "The strongest criticism in the report was of management—of me, as that's my job." He asked for their cooperation, saying that if everyone worked up to his or her capacity, there would be no sign of softness in his administration of the business. "I ask you to help me to avoid instituting rules, rules, rules, as I hate to treat adults as children. Let's all remember that this is a business office—that we are here for a purpose; each one knows his job. Your continued deep interest in doing your job well is all that I ask for." He then wished them a Merry Christmas, as it was 4:30 p.m., December 24, 1941. And it was also his 46th birthday.

When Raymond Black announced early in 1942 that he was leaving Scholastic for a better-paying job, Robinson asked him if he would participate in interviewing candidates for his replacement as controller. Black said, "You have her right here—Mrs. Laurino." How right he was. She became indispensable to the management of the company through the war years and during two decades of its extraordinary growth until her death in 1967 at age 65 (Chapter VIII).

None of the BFA&H recommendations for the firing of certain employees was carried out by Robinson.

In the warmth of retrospection and success some 30 years later, M. R. Robinson said that the BFA&H report proved to be of vital importance to the future of Scholastic. "I admit to my shortcomings as a hard-nosed businessman," he said, "and that my primary skills and main interest were in the editorial and promotion aspects of the publishing business." He pointed to the financial figures of the years preceding and immediately following the report, saying: "These attest to the BFA&H influence not only on me, but on Messrs. Oliver and Clapp, who saw that I needed some assurance that the hand-to-mouth financing would be replaced by a measure of financial stability and available working capital. The engagement of the auditing firm of Arthur Young & Company in 1940—followed by the BFA&H report and the arrival of a strong accounting team in Black and Laurino in January 1942—started the company on a swing upward for the next 30 years to grow to 100 times its then-revenues."

CHAPTER X

"Look around the place and tell me what needs to be improved."

–M.R.R. to J.W.S.

IT came as no surprise to those close to him that Robinson, near the end of World War II, had been talking with John W. Studebaker, U.S. Commissioner of Education, about a future with Scholastic. Studebaker was then approaching 60 years of age, looking and acting like a man in his forties. Robinson had never before tried to lure into the Scholastic fold the nation's ranking education official, but he had an excellent track record in getting the highest city and state educators to serve on the National Advisory Council and in other consultant capacities. Remember, it was the Pittsburgh superintendent of schools and an assembly of 42 high school principals in western Pennsylvania that gave a vote of confidence to the would-be publisher before he had a publication to show.

Studebaker was superintendent of schools of Des Moines, IA, when Robinson first met him. It was in May 1926, and Robinson went to Des Moines to present prizes to two East High School students, winners in the poetry competition for Scholastic's student-written issue, which was the forerunner of the Scholastic Writing Awards. Studebaker attended the ceremony.

It would be almost 10 years before their paths crossed again, as happened several times before and during World War II on Robinson's frequent trips to Washington (Chapter XXI, "Attacks!"). Studebaker, then United States Commissioner of Education, had organized the Victory Corps among the nation's high school youth during World War II, and Scholastic lent editorial support to this project. There was yet another reason for Robinson to call at the Office of Education: his friend William D. Boutwell was on Studebaker's staff as information director and editor of the magazine *School Life*. By January 1945 Boutwell would be on the Scholastic staff and Robinson would be pondering how to lead Studebaker down, or up, the same path. It would be a fateful spring and summer on the world scene: President Roosevelt would die on April 12; Hitler would commit suicide 12 days later; and the United States would drop "the Bomb" on Hiroshima and Nagasaki in August.

At President Truman's request, Studebaker continued as Commissioner of Education, but he was thinking of a change. Robinson, aware of this, stepped up the pace of his suit to win Studebaker for Scholastic. Robinson invited him to Scholastic's 25th anniversary party to be held in the Scholastic offices on October 19. It was a jolly party, and Studebaker doubtless was left with a good impression of one attribute of life among the Scholastic crowd, all 82 of whom were there plus some spouses and offspring. For two years Robinson pressed his suit, gently, persistently. Studebaker wasn't playing hard to get. He was weighing his options, some from our most estimable centers of learning. Why he chose Scholastic is explained in a statement in the Sept. 22, 1948, *Scholastic Teacher:*

WHY I DECIDED TO JOIN SCHOLASTIC

By JOHN W. STUDEBAKER

Vice-President and Chairman of Editorial Board, Scholastic Magazines. U. S. Commissioner of Education, 1934-1948.

WHEN I became U.S. Commissioner of Education in 1934, it was on "leave of absence" from the Superintendency of the Des Moines Public Schools. I had fully expected to remain in Washington only a year or two at most. That "year or two" stretched out into nearly fourteen years, full of challenge and accomplishment.

Why did I resign as United States Commissioner of Education to accept the position of Vice-President and Chairman of the Editorial Board of *Scholastic Magazines?* An answer to that question involves a number of considerations which I studied carefully before making a final desision. These considerations I share with you here.

I had for some time felt that the major aims for which I went to the U. S. Office of Education in 1934 had been achieved. There were other reasons, too. But primarily, I had been weighing various opportunities to serve young learners in the classroom as directly as possible. Of these opportunities, I considered the one offered by the *Scholastic* organization to hold the greatest possibilities for direct service to the largest number of young people in our elementary and secondary schools.

MY WHOLE professional life has been devoted to education as the one best hope of men and women to achieve a better world for themselves and for their children. With *Scholastic* I expect to be of practical service to teachers and school administrators in thousands of school systems of every state of the Union. My years of experience in education have convinced me that the best method of keeping the curriculum up-to-date and pointed at problems students must face is the use of that uniquely American instructional service, the classroom magazine.

In the classrooms of the United States are millions of American youth preparing for careers as useful citizens of this great republic. On the insights they gain and the wisdom they develop under the guidance of teachers will depend the future of this nation and indeed, of the world. The school system which encourages the regular use of instructional materials that bring today's facts and tomorrow's problems directly to the attion of the pupils is providing a much-needed vitality and reality to learning. When pupils read and discuss current information about contemporary affairs, they are developing understanding and attitudes essential to the American way of life.

History and English have long been educational staples. In the junior and senior high school curricula it has become standard practice to employ classroom magazines to tie the past and present together. First introduced several decades ago, the classroom magazine is a well-established aid to the teacher and pupil. *Scholastic Magazine,* founded in 1920, has now expanded to five classroom magazines for different grade levels and purposes.

With the aid of classroom magazines the teacher can show history and literature as a record of events and ideas, not of the past alone but as part of everyday life. The orentation must be always toward the present, since we seek to develop citizens for modern life rather than cloistered scholars. That orientation to the present cannot be achieved by textbooks alone, basically important as they are and however recent their adoption. The tempo of modern events is too swift. The best and most recent textbooks should be used, of course; but they need to be supplemented by a more flexible means of recording and reporting the current scene.

The mythical teacher with time to spare could conceivably assemble clippings, bring in magazines and newspapers from the newsstand, assign radio listening, and by other means bring the current of contemporary life into the classroom. But let us be realistic. Teachers now do as much as possible within the limits of time and human endurance. So, to the conscientious and busy teacher, *Scholastic Magazines* offer a means by which fugitive but significant materials of contemporary life are selected and put in teachable form. The materials are edited to the reading abilities of pupils in different grades by especially trained editors and writers.

If you knew the members of the staff, you would be deeply impressed with their skill in putting together words and pictures that help teachers teach. They, too, are educators. One of our advisors said to me after a recent meeting of the Advisory Council with the staff, "I have never seen before so fine a professional attitude in any commercial organization. I am genuinely impressed."

In *Scholastic Magazines,* the historical roots and parallels of current events are noted. Personalities in the news; the *pros* and *cons* of great issues; modern examples of literary skill; the practical, everyday uses of the English language; the best in motion pictures and books; persuasive advice on healthful living — all are brought within the purview of the pupils.

There is another consideration — cost. For the small sum of 3¢ to 5¢ a copy the student has his own personal periodical, designed according to his needs and those of his teacher.

These magazines find their way to the reading table in many homes. That means that *Scholastic Magazines* also help to carry the influence of the school to the entire family.

In the teacher edition—*Scholastic Teacher* — are testing devices and suggestions for stimulating pupils' interest.

THE POLICIES and editorial content of *Scholastic Magazines* have the professional guidance of well-known educators who serve on *Scholastic's* advisory boards. I look forward to working with these distinguished associates.

What these *Scholastic Magazines* offer is well-nigh indispensable to the teacher who takes seriously his responsibility for the development of good citizens who have learned to use sound judgment and who have acquired the language skills they need for communicating their thoughts.

At least that's how it seems to me. And that's why I decided to join *Scholastic Magazines!*

Studebaker arrived as the company was on the threshold of expansion in magazine circulation, new titles, and diversification of product. Warmly welcomed by fellow executives and staff, he was seen by no one as a threat to anyone's job. All were soon to recognize his rare talent for organization, his analytical approach to problems, and his systematic attack on them.

Robinson, having no specific duties for Studebaker, said to him: "Look around the place and tell me what needs to be improved." At the time, "the place" was a rather jammed-up array of desks, typewriter tables, and filing cabinets on an open floor of the Fairchild Publications Building on East 12th Street. (Scholastic had been unceremoniously dispatched from its spacious quarters in the Daily News Building because the management of the newspaper wanted the space for a television station soon to be launched: Station WPIX.) None of the Scholastic staff had a private office on 12th Street. Thora Larsen built a stockade out of bookcases and file cabinets to protect the president from the multitude.

In "looking around the place" Studebaker pondered the effectiveness of the methods used for selling the product, then consisting of the magazines *Senior Scholastic, World Week, Practical English, Junior Scholastic, Literary Cavalcade,* and the newly acquired Teen Age Book Club. The magazine *Scholastic Coach* did not require "marketing attention" for subscriptions, as its distribution to high schools was mostly on a free basis, known in the trade as "controlled circulation." Studebaker was particularly interested in what the company hoped to accomplish with a staff of four full-time salaried salesmen calling on the schools to sell subscriptions to the classroom magazines and Teen Age Book Club sponsorships. He noted one for the Pacific Coast states; one for Chicagoland plus Indiana; one for the city and state of New York; and one for New Jersey, Maryland, the District of Columbia, and Pennsylvania.

"I looked at this setup," he recalled, "and came to the conclusion that it was impossible to make substantial gains in circulation by personal selling if the salesman's territory was so large that he could cover only a small segment of it in a given year. So I said to myself, how can we correct this? We can change over to part-time people, so that each one will have a district small enough to enable him to visit most of the schools at least once a year, working 20 to 25 weeks a year, paying his own expenses strictly against a commission—a small commission on the business already in existence, plus a much larger commission for annual increases in business over the preceding year's base."

Robinson gave him the go-ahead and Studebaker proceeded to polish his plan for carving up the country into "Scholastic districts," with the idea of having a commission salesperson in each. It was known as the Resident Representative Plan,* and getting it started required financing to a degree that strained the exchequer, if not the conscience. Robinson wondered if some way could be found to launch the plan without so much start-up money—mainly the dollars that would have to be paid the representatives on business they inherited. He hazarded

*Later the terminology would be changed from Resident Representative to Scholastic Representative.

the thought that some other publishing house selling to the school market and Scholastic might share sales representatives. Scholastic and *Harper's* had done this for a few years in California with Blanche Montgomery. Studebaker mentioned that he was well-acquainted with Fred Murphy, head of the Grolier Society—successful publishers of *The Book of Knowledge* and other encyclopedic works—and the director of its education division, Leonard Power. At Robinson's suggestion, Studebaker broached the subject to Murphy, and there soon followed intensive discussions of a plan for sharing sales representatives. Travel time and expense money could be saved, and a representative would have the opportunity to earn more money on a given call to a school,

M. R. Robinson (left) welcoming John W. Studebaker to Scholastic, 1948. Center: Herold C. Hunt, general superintendent of schools, Chicago.

156

as he would have noncompeting products to sell. Studebaker and Power worked up the plan to the last detail and presented it to Robinson for final consideration. "Final" is used advisedly, for Robinson had been in constant touch with Studebaker during the five or six months of meetings with Grolier. Now it was up to Robinson to decide whether to "go it with Grolier" or "go it alone." It was a difficult decision to make, because the cost figures showed a considerable saving over going it alone.

Skittish over joint ventures since the 1931–32 experience with American Education Press, Robinson could not satisfy himself that the problem of direction and supervision of a salesman representing two houses could be handled to the satisfaction of both. Also, would the salesmen call on a school if that school had recently purchased its full complement of encyclopedias and so be unlikely to order replacements for some time to come? Would not the salesman pass that school by and concentrate his calls on schools without Grolier products so that he could make his pitch for both Scholastic magazines and Grolier reference books in the one visit? Scholastic would get the short end if the salesman followed this line, for the Scholastic magazines were consumable and subject to annual renewal by the schools. In any given high school there was the opportunity to make a new sale of magazines at any time, since in every school there were teachers of social studies and English who were not subscribing. Finally Robinson said to Studebaker, "I don't want to lend-lease you or any part of you to anyone. We'll go it alone." As events have proved, that was the right decision.

Studebaker's Scholastic plan as mapped out in 1949 indicated a total of some 180 districts in the United States, each district to be small enough to enable the sales representative to reach any school in the district and return home the same day. There would be a peak of 180 sales districts administered from regional offices (at present, six), each headed by a director to whom the representatives of that region would report.

Thus began Scholastic's first systematic nationwide effort in personal selling and service to the schools. The number and perimeters of regions and districts and commission arrangements have been changed over the years, but not the concept on which the plan was built — to reach as many of the schools as economically as possible by personal representation.

In organizing the headquarters staff to assist him in managing what was then known as the Department of Field Service, Studebaker called upon a school administrator he had worked with in Des Moines to be his associate director. This was C. Elwood Drake, who had been dean of boys and vice principal of Roosevelt High School in Des Moines from 1932 to 1935. At the time Studebaker waved the Scholastic flag at him (in the spring of 1951) Drake was director of the Newton Junior College, Newton, MA. Studebaker put him in charge of communications between the home office and the 150-plus "Resident Representatives." During his 20 years with Scholastic, Drake served in other key posts related to sales and the field staff. He was named director of Field Service in 1960 and in 1962 headed all phases of sales administration within the department. He retired in 1971 and lives with his wife Adelaide in Heritage Village, Southbury, CT.

Other departments, especially editorial, direct-mail promotion, and professional/public relations, benefited from Studebaker's ideas and energy. His suggestions to editors on the handling of controversial issues contributed substantially to the teachability quotient of the articles they prepared. He played a major role in planning material on the differences in government systems, in particular between dictatorship (fascist and Communist) and constitutional democracy. He ably represented the company in cooperating with school officials to help them respond to the not infrequent attacks on Scholastic during the late 1940's and into the 1950's during the McCarthy fright. That ill-starred senator attempted with considerable success to panic the nation with his accusations that schools, publishers, churches, and government agencies were harboring Communist spies in their organizations (Chapter XXI, "Attacks").

Studebaker retired in 1967 at the age of 80 to live in Walnut Creek, CA, near his son Gordon, Scholastic regional director for the Far West until his retirement in 1974. Father and son co-authored a five-volume Arithmetic Practice series published by Scholastic in 1963. They, with Gordon's children, celebrated John Studebaker's 90th birthday on June 10, 1977.

SCHOLASTIC

Volume 26 Number 15   *The National High School Weekly*   *May 18, 1935*

To Americans Who Love Their Country

An Editorial

IN the issue of April 13, devoted to the United States Constitution, the editors of *Scholastic* presented five planks in an editorial platform of ten points recently adopted by the staff in an effort to state clearly, briefly, and honestly our stand upon important issues of the day. To the students of American high schools, to their teachers and administrators, to their parents and the great body of citizens interested in education, it is no more than fair that the policies of the magazine used for supplementary study in their classrooms should be an open book.

Today, then, we publish below the complete platform. The first five points, as previously explained, deal with questions of Constitutionality, civil liberties, social change, tolerance, and educational method in the present emergency. The last five, here set forth for the first time, take up problems of economics, technology, culture, war, and the hopes of American youth. In our judgment the principles here enunciated constitute a program on which all forward-looking citizens who love their country and wish to see its people happy and prosperous can and should unite. We do not assume that these points alone will furnish a solution for every problem. There may be other aims and emphases equally important. We do not propose definite methods by which these ends can be given a more living reality than they have at present or may have had in the past. On such questions we have as many doubts and uncertainties as other average plain men. Nor are we willing to commit ourselves to a program so rigid that it cannot adapt itself to changing conditions. We expect to learn many a new idea in future and to adopt additional objectives whenever and wherever common sense may lead the way.

But what we are concerned with here is a spirit, a point of view with which American schools should attack the vast and troublous unsolved questions of our time. This program is not conceived from any political bias. But the stubborn facts of life in the fourth decade of the Twentieth Century insistently demand that a democratic society look at its problems in the light of their relations to and their pressure upon whole populations of human beings. No civilization, we believe, can be called great which does not place in the forefront of its attention the kind of values we have attempted to bring together in this platform. Nor can these values be realized in America or anywhere else without the free play of critical intelligence which we have tried to epitomize in Point 3, and which we hope is implicit on every page of *Scholastic* every week. To this common effort and fellowship we invite the students and teachers of the American high school.

★★

Scholastic's Editorial Platform

1. American freedom, fought for by our Revolutionary fathers, and embodied in the Constitution and the Bill of Rights, including freedom of speech, of the press, and of assemblage, for all persons of every class, minority, or opinion.

2. American methods of effecting social change, by peaceful persuasion, education, the ballot-box, democratically controlled legislation, and revision of the Constitution by the methods prescribed therein. These imply uncompromising opposition to all systems of dictatorship, whether from the extreme right or the extreme left.

3. A scientific approach to social and intellectual problems, freely stating all sides of controversial issues, fostering critical thinking, attacking superstition, and exposing propaganda by any medium for selfish interests or pressure groups.

4. Free public education, tax-supported, with first-class equipment, trained teachers, and a modern curriculum, for every child capable of assimilating it, from kindergarten to college; schools and welfare services must not be allowed to suffer through economic distress.

5. Tolerance of every sincere religious creed without domination by any; justice and protection against oppression for every racial group within our gates.

6. Economic security for the masses of the people, including a job at an adequate living wage for every one able and willing to work, universal maximum distribution of consumers' goods, good housing, health protection, and insurance against the hazards of unemployment and old age.

7. Vocational and personal study, training in craftsmanship, guidance, and placement for every child, correlated with a systematic occupational survey and expansion of the nation's employment resources, and the abolition of child labor in industry.

8. A just balance between the rights of individual personality and the necessarily enlarging social functions of government in a rapidly changing mechanical and industrial world.

9. Enriched leisure for every child and adult, through free outdoor recreation, creative handicrafts and hobbies, better regulated commercial entertainment, and widespread personal appreciation of beauty in music, literature, and the arts.

10. Prevention of war and advancement of peace by persistent international cooperation, civilian control of national defense, strictly limited armaments, voluntary military training, government ownership of munitions manufacture, restraint of imperialistic policies abroad, realistic education on the costs of war, and encouragement of a national popular will against war.

CHAPTER XI

Editorial Policy, Credo, and Platform

THE company survived its first 15 years without issuing a formal statement of editorial policy — no "platform" or "credo" had been put down in so many words until 1935 (page opposite), although the magazine had for several years included editorials on the issues of the times, including peace and war (Chapter XXI, "Attacks").

As part of Scholastic's 25th anniversary celebration in 1945, a policy statement was published in a 20-page booklet titled *An Editorial Credo*. This was an adaptation of a speech by Editor-in-Chief Kenneth M. Gould, with an introduction by President and Publisher Maurice R. Robinson.

Gould, in adapting his speech for the booklet, explained the purpose and content of the then-existing Scholastic classroom magazines *Senior Scholastic, World Week,* and *Junior Scholastic:*

> We conceive it to be our function to present the best of living thought and writing and the clearest explanation of important current events, problems, and trends, within the understanding and interests of modern young people. We have

no contempt for the classics nor for the lessons of history. We believe thoroughly in building in the minds of children a vital link with the past. But the textbooks and anthologies have pretty well taken care of this phase. And aside from frequent features aiming to show the relationship between the literatures of the past and present, or the historical background of the world today, we feel that our best contribution lies in the field of contemporary writing, where the classroom magazine, for many schools, supplies the only reliable source and guide.

Taking *Senior Scholastic* as a specific example of our content, from ten to twelve pages in every issue are prepared for the special needs of English classes. A similar section is set aside for Social Studies classes. These classroom sections are supplemented by other material planned to appeal to the general interests of all students, including personal and vocational guidance, motion picture and radio criticism, aviation, sports, manners and conduct, and entertainment. In the Combined Edition, to which an increasing number of teachers are subscribing, the student has access not only to the English and general sections, but to all material on public affairs and social problems.

In contrast to the Social Studies material, which is largely staff-written, approximately two-thirds of the English material is derived from reprint sources, including published books and adult magazines. This consists of specimens of all the standard literary forms, short stories, poetry, drama (including radio scripts, one-act plays, and condensations from longer plays), narratives from biographical and autobiographical works, familiar essays, excerpts from novels, works of literary criticism, etc.

Magazines for Youth

I am often asked what are the criteria of selection for our literary material. In many respects they are similar to those of any good quality magazine. But with a difference—a difference dictated by the nature and interests of our youthful audience. The line between adolescence and adulthood is almost non-existent today in reading tastes. Young people read most of the adult best-sellers, and if there is anything they shy away from, it is the implication of babyhood.

But, to sharpen the point, I will say that our criteria are: *first, human interest:* in other words, the high-level vital appeal which any widely read book or magazine must have; *second, craftsmanship:* the literary values which distinguish the first-rate from the shoddy; *third, social significance:* the choice of themes which treat life and human problems as something more than a superficially romantic joyride; and *fourth, youthfulness:* the use, whenever possible, of young people as characters, and of young people's activities, recreations, and idioms.

. . . These criteria, to us, imply that vocabulary for young people must be relatively simple, non-academic, graphic, concrete, and Anglo-Saxon. But *Scholastic* style must not be patronizing, preachy, or juvenile. . . .

Within these limitations, I think I may safely claim that we have published the best available work in short compass of virtually every significant American or English writer of recent years. A sampling covering only a small fraction of our volumes through the past two decades might include the names of Stephen Vincent Benet, Pearl Buck, Willa Cather, Joseph Conrad, Edna Ferber, Dorothy Canfield Fisher, John Galsworthy,

Ernest Hemingway, Sinclair Lewis, Thomas Mann, Katherine Mansfield, Somerset Maugham, Christopher Morley, Marjorie Kinnan Rawlings, John Steinbeck, Jesse Stuart, Thomas Wolfe, Maxwell Anderson, Eugene O'Neill, Thornton Wilder, Norman Corwin, Van Wyck Brooks, Henry Seidel Canby, A. E. Housman, Carl Sandburg, Franz Werfel, Carl Van Doren, Donald Peattie, Robert Frost, Langston Hughes, Edna St. Vincent Millay, Archibald MacLeish, Edwin Arlington Robinson, Vachel Lindsay, and John Masefield. I should not wish you to assume from this list that we make a fetish of great names. We search always for fresh new talent. . . .

The Mother Tongue

Apart from literature, we devote a substantial portion of each issue to the best methods we can find for training students to speak, read, and write their mother tongue effectively. Persuasive and practical articles on troublesome problems of composition, reading, diction, spelling, punctuation, and grammar help students to learn the mechanics of language skills. Challenging tests, quizzes, exercises, and book reviews increase the speed, accuracy, and retentiveness of backward readers. Classroom activities, lesson plans, and bibliographies prepared by experienced classroom teachers furnish timely help when needed by overburdened teachers. . . .

Good English is not only a profoundly necessary and functional tool for successful living, but the chief medium for our leisure-time enjoyment and the source of most of our higher values throughout adult life. It is one of our objectives to convince students that these things are worth their time and effort.

The Social Studies

It is here that we come face to face with ends, rather than means. What is the aim of all this highly geared literacy? Why teach young citizens in a democracy to read, write, and speak skillfully? What freight of social ideals and critical thinking should the vehicle of language be expected to bear?

The chief efforts of a classroom magazine in turning young people into good citizens must obviously be concentrated in its Social Studies pages. Here we present, week by week, two major articles, one in the field of national or domestic affairs, one in international or foreign affairs. These subjects, chosen in weekly editorial conferences on the basis of recent events, are not primarily summaries of the news. They discuss significant trends and problems growing out of the news, explained with all the clarity and objectivity we can muster, visualized as fully as possible in pictures, maps, charts, and cartoons, and interpreted in the light of the historical, geographical, political, social, and economic facts that lie at their roots.

In addition, the Social Studies section contains background articles by distinguished historians; comment on the behind-the-scenes phases of government by our Washington correspondent; graphic map studies of every section of the world at war; biographical picture pages on the lives of great Americans; debates and panel discussions on timely controversial issues; object-lesson descriptions of successful projects of many kinds demonstrating democracy in action; pictorial treatments of basic American industries and their vocational opportunities; outlines of every aspect of the postwar world and of the United

Nations organization; human interest sketches of leading personalities of the day; weekly round-ups of "The March of Events."

These are the raw materials of civic understanding. Out of them young people learn to live in "one world."

There followed a brief description of *Junior Scholastic* "for younger students of the upper elementary and junior high school grades. . . . Broadly speaking, its content is essentially similar to that of *Senior*, but naturally on a simpler, briefer, and less mature level"; and of *World Week,* "the third and youngest member of the Scholastic team . . . for the 9th and 10th grade levels [for] advanced geography and world history courses."

The 1945 credo concluded with a section headed "Fairness and Balance," from which the following paragraphs are drawn:

. . . We are ready and willing at all times to discuss any controversial issue in the political, social, and economic life of our times. We do not seek to avoid them. We could not evade them if we wanted to. Life is full of controversy, and in the senior high school we believe these questions must be faced fully and frankly.

But controversial questions are relative to time and place and the climate of opinion of the community. Wartime conscription is controversial today in Canada, not in the United States. Peacetime conscription will be controversial tomorrow in America. The poll tax is controversial in Texas. It should not be in New York. . . .

But we believe the educational approach to these subjects demands that the points of view of all responsible groups concerned, whether of labor or management, Administration or opposi-

Kenneth M. Gould in 1945, when he
wrote "An Editorial Credo."
Gould joined Scholastic as managing
editor in 1926, was named editor
in 1940, editor-in-chief in 1942.
Upon his retirement in 1960 he
became Scholastic's first
editor emeritus.

tion, Soviet Russia or capitalist America, be fully
expressed and given a balanced treatment. We
believe, too, that young people should know the
sources of these points of view, and be equipped
to examine them impartially, to detect special
pleading, and to make up their own minds on the
basis of evidence, not of emotion.

We have our procedures for such matters.
Within our own editorial staff, by constant conference and discussion, by research, checking,
re-checking, and careful editing, we select our
topics and work out our articles, our debates, or
panel discussions to give full representation to all
the relevant facts and opposing points of view.

But sometimes we come to issues so hot that
we do not trust our own judgment. We do not
then accept the conventional attitudes of the public press. We go out and get the various sides to
tell us their own arguments. When the Petrillo
case came up, for example, we submitted our text
for criticism to both the Radio Corporation of
America and the American Federation of Musi-
cians, and considered their suggestions. When
we were preparing our quadrennial election
handbook, *America Votes,* we submitted the

manuscript to both the Democratic and Republican National Committees. They approved it with only the most minor changes. And we defy any critical reader to deduce from the finished product whether its writers and editors voted for Roosevelt or Dewey.

We sometimes find ourselves in competition with general magazines which seek to enter the school field. I do not contend that adult magazines are *ipso facto* unfit for classroom use. Occasionally I have heard a teacher say that she preferred to introduce her students early to the type of magazines she hoped that they would read throughout their adult lives. We have no quarrel with that. General magazines should be part of the mental furniture of all young people, just as should much of the literature, art, movies, and radio fare that adults enjoy. . . . The classroom magazine, specifically designed and edited for high school students by experts who devote their lives to the study of this field, should be the backbone of any modern school program in English or the Social Studies. Selection of material and methods for the classroom is a highly specialized art. Young people deserve the best, adjusted to their needs, comprehension, and interests, and prepared in the spirit of public stewardship. That is the editorial policy of *Scholastic Magazines*.

Three years after the issuance of *An Editorial Credo*, John W. Studebaker joined the company, with instructions from Robinson to "look around the place and tell me what needs to be improved" (Chapter X). He came upon the 3,200-word credo, and although he did not say that it could be improved, he did say that it could be reduced. As with all reducing programs, this took time. By April 2, 1952, a streamlined, 200-word "Editorial Platform" appeared in *Scholastic Teacher*, with this introduction:

Avowed Objectives

Several years ago Scholastic published its *Editorial Credo*. It was a solid, scholarly, clear statement of the basic educational purposes of Scholastic Magazines together with an explanation of effective ways in which the magazines may be used in classrooms country-wide.

The Credo set forth the avowed objectives of Scholastic which are as pertinent now, in these troublous times, as they were when first announced. But it was a lengthy treatise quite characteristic of the painstaking and conscientious care with which our organization has always dealt with the schools and subscribers. The Credo had all the advantages of thoroughness but the disadvantage of such length as to burden the reader, even if space could be made available for its frequent publication.

Two or three months ago we decided to try to produce our Editorial Platform in a sufficiently condensed form to render feasible its appearance several times each year *in the student editions*. That means space—millions of lines each school year. Since a magazine is always fighting for space to meet innumerable demands, we naturally wanted to compress into the fewest lines the most significant, representative, and intelligible planks in our platform.

Obviously we sought the advantages of brevity even at the risk of not being fully understood.

Fortunately, in any such undertaking, we have the invaluable assistance of many exceedingly competent people on our various Advisory

Boards and our Council. The members of all of these groups have been consulted and have given us the benefit of their ideas and detailed editorial comment. The result is the 200-word Editorial Platform appearing on this page. From time to time it will be printed in the student editions of all Scholastic Magazines beginning April 23.

We hope the Platform will be read and discussed in all classes and in the homes of all students using Scholastic Magazines.

J. W. Studebaker
Chairman, Editorial Boards
Scholastic Magazines

Our Editorial Platform

SCHOLASTIC MAGAZINES are published to promote the education for enlightened citizenship of students in the schools of the United States.

We believe profoundly in, and strive to inspire faith in:

. . . the worth and dignity of the individual;

. . . high moral and spiritual values;

. . . the democratic way of life, with its basic liberties and responsibilities for all;

. . . the American system of constitutional, representative government;

. . . free competitive enterprise and free labor working for abundant production;

. . . cooperation and understanding among all peoples for the peace of the world.

We are unalterably opposed to communism, fascism, or any other system in which men become the slaves of a master state.

We aim to present the clearest explanation of current affairs, the best contemporary thought and creative expression, and the most helpful guidance for adjustment to life, adapted to the understanding and interests of youth. Good citi-

170

zens honestly differ on important public questions, and the young people of today need training under wise teachers to participate in solving these problems of tomorrow. We therefore believe that all sides of these problems should be impartially discussed in the schools and in classroom magazines, with deep respect for facts and for logical thinking.*

This version held until 1970, when a revision appeared under the title "Scholastic's Credo & Editorial Platform," having undergone the scrutiny of top management, editors, and members of the National Advisory Council. In the revised version the very first sentence identifies the credo with all material that Scholastic publishes. There are other significant changes the reader will readily note:

Scholastic's Credo & Editorial Platform

We publish Scholastic educational materials to:
   . . . inspire and assist students to cultivate their minds to their utmost capacity;
   . . . seek the most effective ways to live a satisfying life;
   . . . work tirelessly to build a society free of prejudice and hate, a social order worthy of being called civilized.

We strive to present the clearest explanation of current affairs, contemporary thought, and creative expression, adapted to the understanding and interests of young people at all levels of learning.

We believe in:
   . . . the worth and dignity of the individual;
   . . . his right to live in a wholesome envi-

*As published in the April 2, 1952, issue of *Scholastic Teacher*.

ronment and, equally, his personal responsibility to help gain and preserve a decent and healthful environment, beginning with the care of his own body and mind;

. . . high moral and spiritual values;

. . . a democratic way of life, with basic liberties and responsibilities for all;

. . . constitutional, representative government;

. . . responsible competitive enterprise and responsible labor with opportunities for all;

. . . cooperation and understanding among all peoples for the peace of the world.

We pledge ourselves to uphold the basic freedoms of all individuals; we are unalterably opposed to any system of government which denies these freedoms to its people. We are equally opposed to any discrimination on the basis of race, creed, color, sex, or national origin.

Good citizens may honestly differ on important public questions. To become responsible citizens, young people need to learn how to analyze and evaluate public questions on the basis of facts. We therefore believe that all sides of public issues should be fairly discussed — with deep respect for facts and logical thinking — in classroom magazines, books, and other educational materials used in the schools.*

*As published in the October 19, 1970, issue of *Junior Scholastic*.

Merger Talks and a Near Miss

DURING the boom years of the 1960's there was hardly a publishing house that did not get involved in merger talks or an actual merger. It was a popular subject of conversation and gossip at publishers' conventions. During the cocktail hour in a room filled with representatives of publishing houses large and small, speculation ran rife as to who was buying whom. One could amuse oneself by trying to identify a publisher who sought or wished to escape courtship. One good-natured publisher sported a large lapel button lettered "WANNA MERGE?"

Many of them did. Xerox — which in 1965 had acquired Scholastic's principal competitor, American Education Press (Chapter XIII, "Tax-Free Competitor")— now bought Ginn & Company. American Book Company was bought by Litton Industries; Bobbs-Merrill, by ITT; Holt, Rinehart & Winston, by Columbia Broadcasting (for $260 million, by far the costliest of publishing acquisitions during the merger fever of the sixties); Science Research Associates, by IBM; Silver Burdett, by Time, which—with General Electric—folded it into their jointly held General Learning Corporation.*

---

*The assets of the General Learning Corporation were acquired by Scott, Foresman & Company in 1976.

These sub-mergings of long-established publishing houses by giants of the communications industry were undertaken in the expectation that technology would revolutionize learning—big industry wedded to the suppliers of instructional materials would produce, so it was predicted, a much more efficient and beneficial system of learning than had ever been imagined. A profusion of teaching machines flooded the school market, as if somehow teachers had lost the art. (Teachers *were* in short supply.)

Education proved to be not so readily machined. The process of learning was not a thing of gears and gadgets, but of people whose thought processes could not be manipulated by technology to the extent its proponents had hoped.

Scholastic, caught up in this merger fever, was susceptible on two counts: (1) It needed capital to maintain a safe pace with Xerox—principal competitor in the school magazine and book club field—and to provide for expansion into film and text products. (2) Scholastic's principal owners, two of whom were approaching 70, needed to convert their stock in Scholastic Magazines, Inc., for which there was no public market, into marketable stock (such as the stock of whatever public company acquired Scholastic or by changing Scholastic from a private to a public company so that its stock would become marketable). Thus, in case of the death of a major stockholder, cash would be available through the sale of stock to settle estate taxes (Chapter III, "Stockholders Ahoy!").

Scholastic had a score or more of suitors interested in union of one kind or another—merger, outright purchase of all stock or a sizable portion of it, joint venture, or some other variation of shared ownership. The roster of suitors included some of the giants, among them McGraw-Hill; Newsweek; Holt, Rinehart & Winston; Columbia Broadcasting System; Doubleday; Book-of-the-Month Club; (Crowell-Collier) Macmillan; Grolier; Times-Mirror; Westinghouse; Cox Broadcasting; Litton Industries; Harcourt, Brace; and ITT.

As inquiries about Scholastic's "availability" and requests for meetings came to Robinson, he would discuss each with his colleagues on the board of directors before deciding how to respond. After a few months of this the board decided that Robinson need report only those approaches he believed to be worthy of consideration.

One such was a call in the spring of 1966 from Michael Burke, vice president for Development with the Columbia Broadcasting System, suggesting a meeting to talk about their mutual interest in education. (CBS was known to have attempted earlier to acquire Allyn & Bacon, a Boston publisher of schoolbooks.) Talks and luncheons with Burke were followed by several meetings with Frank Stanton, president of CBS, and a luncheon meeting with William Paley, chairman, all initiated by CBS. Robinson saw in the resources of *CBS News* an opportunity to develop special features in the classroom periodicals. Robinson perceived the prospect of having firsthand news resources from around the world and other tie-ins with *CBS News* that could add prestige to Scholastic periodicals. He envisioned Cronkite and Sevareid being regular contributors to Scholastic's social studies periodicals, and further—even acknowledging the problems of being a small fish in the CBS bowl—he envisioned a happy collaboration between Scholastic's educational abilities and the instructional potential of television. Would that have happened? It is doubtful. It appears that neither Holt, Rinehart & Winston nor Random House received such benefits from their relationships with CBS and NBC, respectively. However, those houses were not producing topical material in periodicals for the schools, and Scholastic's access to the output of highly respected TV commentators could have been a decided asset.

A warm relationship had developed between Robinson and Stanton. Robinson felt that the CBS president shared his vision of beneficial collaboration and that Stanton understood and believed in Scholastic's educational philosophy, as expressed in its Credo. Their talks continued through the summer of 1966 as they explored ways in which CBS and Scholastic might work together. At one of these meetings in late summer, Stanton told Robinson that a block of Holt, Rinehart & Winston stock owned by the Murchisons of Texas was available and CBS was considering buying it. The block amounted to 11 percent of the total shares. Stanton asked Robinson what effect this purchase might have on CBS-Scholastic discussions. He replied that the 11 percent was not a problem, but if CBS were to acquire full ownership of Holt, he would be reluctant to see Scholastic enter into that situation. Shortly after, Stanton told Robinson that CBS had bought the Murchisons' 11 percent of Holt, Rinehart & Winston.

In recalling these events Robinson said: "Despite my personal feeling that the Holt acquisition was a definite negative toward continued discussion with CBS, our talks with them did continue. One private meeting of Joe Oliver, Herb McCracken, and me with Stanton was held. We exchanged much information. We gave their accounting department our figures, and early in December [1966] six of our officers dined with Stanton and his top staff in their executive dining room to talk freely about the situation."

The talks continued but the officers of Scholastic were reluctant to agree to start serious negotiations. At the end of February Robinson got a call from Stanton to say that CBS had proposed a merger with Holt, Rinehart & Winston. The announcement was made and the actual acquisition took place a few weeks later. At this point Robinson lost what interest he had had in a merger with CBS.

Nevertheless there were some members of the Scholastic board who wished to continue considering the CBS possibility, but this interest waned as the weeks passed. By August 1967 Robinson would record for the board: "The final discussions have been held with CBS. In view of their decision to establish a CBS-Holt Group, which would in our view make a merger uninviting, we have agreed to drop any further discussion."

After the CBS talks were dropped, some board members felt that Robinson was not being "receptive enough" to some of the callers, and asked that he listen to each and get as many exploratory details as possible, which usually required one or more meetings with spokesmen for the companies.

To help him in his thinking about the numerous offers for merger or acquisition, Robinson sought the counsel of some of his close friends in education, many of whom had served on Scholastic's National Advisory Council. One whose comment reflected the thinking of several others wrote Robinson as follows:

> I've been doing some additional thinking about the merger question. The mergers appear to me to have produced some technically exciting but intellectually inadequate educational materials. It appears to me that if you were in the textbook marketing field, there might be some limited advantage in having hardware available to supplement the textbook usage through workbooks and other programmed materials that could be utilized with the hardware. I do feel that we have a plethora of teaching machines, programmed learning devices, and other computer-based equipment that has considerable appeal, but none of the suppliers has really given full-time attention to the application of the "software" and the development of meaningful programs to make their products effective in learning situations.
>
> I do recognize the fact that for the first time in educational history we have increased federal support for educational research and development and that it is now possible that this work may proceed under private auspices. This fact undoubtedly encourages the merger concept. At least it has produced several weddings between publishers and electronic firms. The fact remains, however, that within educational circles bitter disagreement over the value of this equipment exists. The large majority of opinion that I sampled suggests to me that educators see the result of the merger as being inordinately expensive and very dehumanizing. Many teachers are not yet ready to accept reinforcement theory as an adequate basis for their teaching programs. They

see real teaching as involving a direct relationship between the teacher and the learner. My assessment would be that while some will come to accept the hardware components for what they are, the vast majority of teachers will see them only as classroom supplements and they will continue to place greater value upon those educational materials that can be used directly in the human relationship that exists between a child and his teacher.*

To widen the "listening" range in response to the board's request, Robinson appointed an ad hoc committee consisting of Donald Layman and John Spaulding to study each inquiry, decide on which to look into further, and report back to the board at their discretion.

One of the strongest suitors was the Westinghouse Learning Corporation, a subsidiary of Westinghouse Electric Corporation. Two of its officers—Donald H. McGannon and Peter Schruth—met several times with Scholastic officers. Following these meetings an offer to acquire Scholastic came from Westinghouse through the brokerage house of White, Weld & Company. This was made in a letter of May 26, 1967, to Scholastic's ad hoc committee. The letter said that White, Weld was authorized to make "a tentative offer to acquire your company, subject of course to a detailed investigation of Scholastic Magazines. The tentative offer is at a price of 30 times audited net operating income of Scholastic Magazines for the most recent 12-month period, and the consideration would be common stock of Westinghouse Learning."

*Excerpt from letter dated April 28, 1967, from George B. Brain, dean, College of Education, Washington State University.

Following receipt of this letter McGannon and Schruth appeared before the Scholastic board on June 8, 1967, for further discussion and to answer questions. Some members of the board were inclined to favor the Westinghouse proposal. Net operating income of Scholastic for its previous fiscal year was $1,081,754, thus putting the proposed price at more than $32 million in Westinghouse common stock. A flattering offer it was, and quite tempting.

Twelve days later on June 20 the board would meet again, determined to resolve the critical question: to sell or not to sell. Each member had an opportunity to express his or her position, and the discussion went on for more than two hours. Robinson, as was his custom in presiding over controversy, kept his silence—until Paul Hutchinson broke in to say: "Mose, we haven't heard from you."* Then they heard a most eloquent but low-keyed appeal for the continuation of Scholastic as an independent company. There was no mistaking the depth of his feeling over the prospect of losing, after 47 years of rearing and raising, the child of his creation. He said he would support "going public" in order to solve the estate problem and would take the lead in arranging for it. The sentiment of the board then swung toward this solution, and the members unanimously adopted the following resolution:

*The nickname "Mose" had its origin in Robinson's elementary school days in Wilkinsburg. There, as elsewhere surely, the name Maurice was pronounced Morris, even by teachers. Had it not been for one Wilkinsburg classmate—Ben Wylie—who went on to Dartmouth with Robinson, that nickname might not have survived the transplant. At any rate, today when "Robbie" is called "Mose," the speaker is either a Pittsburgher or an "Indian" from Dartmouth.

180

RESOLVED, That for the purpose of secur-
ing additional working capital to meet the needs
of the Company, the Company offer for sale to the
public through responsible underwriters shares
of its Common Stock, such offer to be made in
conjunction with secondary offers by certain
shareholders of the Company who have expressed a desire to participate therein; and
FURTHER RESOLVED, That the Chair-
man of the Board, acting with a Committee to be
named by him, shall promptly select a responsible
investment brokerage company and thereafter
negotiate and submit to the Board for its approval
at a Special Meeting to be called prior to the time
of the next Regular Meeting a plan detailing the
requirements and costs of such public offering,
together with their recommendations.*

From the foregoing narrative concerning suitors who
came with cash or stock in hand for the purpose of buying
Scholastic, it could be inferred that all of the courtship
took place during the 1960's. Nearly all of it did, but the
closest Scholastic came to losing its corporate independence and individual identity† occurred between 1954

---

*For more on the public offer see Chapter III, "Stockholders Ahoy!"

†In the joint venture between Scholastic Publishing Company and
American Education Press in 1931, Scholastic did not lose its
corporate identity. One could say that it gained half a corporation
on this reasoning: The company that was formed to operate
Scholastic magazine, *St. Nicholas* magazine, and *Scholastic Coach*
magazine was the new Scholastic–St. Nicholas Corporation,
50 percent of the voting stock held by American Education Press,
49 percent by Scholastic Publishing Company (Oliver and Clapp
holding it), and 1 percent by M. R. Robinson. Robinson was
president of both the Scholastic–St. Nicholas Corporation and the
Scholastic Publishing Company.

and March 1957, the years following the death of Augustus K. Oliver in October 1953. The party of the other part was Houghton Mifflin Company of Boston, as prestigious as they come. In December 1955 after Robinson had had some exploratory talks with Henry A. Laughlin, Houghton Mifflin president, and William F. Spaulding, vice president, he received letters from both expressing interest in pursuing the matter of an affiliation. Robinson and Spaulding had been friends for many years, and now a warm relationship would soon develop between Robinson and Laughlin.

Neither Houghton Mifflin nor Scholastic moved very quickly toward the affiliation both seemed interested in developing, and five months passed before anything significant happened. This came during conversations Robinson had with Laughlin and Spaulding at the annual meeting of the American Textbook Publishers Institute at Absecon, NJ, in May 1956. During those talks Laughlin and Spaulding expressed definite interest in acquiring a substantial block—up to as much as 45 percent—of Scholastic stock, buying it from any of the stockholders willing to sell. Only some combination of any two of Robinson, Joseph Oliver, and McCracken could provide that much. In a letter to Joseph Oliver reporting the Absecon meeting, Robinson observed: "I think they would pay a fairly good price. . . . No figures were mentioned, but my guess is that an area between $60 and $80 a share for the common stock would be a starting point which would lead either to an offer from them or acceptance by them of an offer from any present shareholders. . . . Please bear in mind that I am not recommending that we take any action at all. Nor am I opposing it. If

Houghton Mifflin becomes a minority stockholder in Scholastic Magazines, Inc., there would be a market—i.e., an available purchaser—for any or all of the stock of McCracken and/or Robinson and/or the Olivers at any time it might become necessary to sell it."

The original idea on the part of both parties was that Houghton would buy a minority interest—25 percent or so—depending on the disposition of those willing to sell, and pay for it in cash. This, the Scholastic owners soon realized, would create a capital-gains tax problem for them, and in the discussions thereafter it was understood that payment would be in Houghton Mifflin stock. Houghton Mifflin's interest now turned to acquiring all or a majority of Scholastic shares, and thus control of the company. In effect it would be a merger in which Scholastic would become a subsidiary under the direction of Robinson, McCracken, and their management team. Many telephone calls and meetings followed as the parties approached the "show and tell" stage of agreeing on what Scholastic's stock was worth in terms of Houghton Mifflin's.

The principals tried to decide this at a meeting in the Houghton office in Boston on November 1, 1956, attended by their board members and by Oliver, Robinson, and McCracken. It became clear during the meeting that the parties were far apart on this critical question. They agreed to select an outside appraiser to give full consideration to the relative values of Scholastic and Houghton Mifflin stock, and that whatever the appraiser recommended would not be binding on either party. It was agreed that Laughlin would confer with the dean of the Harvard Graduate School of Business to get nominees for this task. The dean suggested three people. Laughlin eliminated one because he was a personal friend. The Scholastic side asked Houghton Mifflin to make the choice between the other two, and Professor Pearson Hunt of the Harvard Graduate School faculty was chosen. He studied the financial and sales records of both companies, interviewed all principals in their offices, and issued his report before the February 1 deadline. He put the relative worth of the stocks of the two companies at two to one — two shares of Scholastic stock for one share of Houghton Mifflin, a ratio that closely corresponded with what Scholastic would settle for. Houghton Mifflin thought otherwise, and held to a three-to-one ratio.

Faced with this stalemate, the parties agreed to adjourn without closing the door to further consideration of the matter. Robinson, Laughlin, and Spaulding met again on February 13, but there was no change in their positions. The saga reached denouement with a letter from Robinson to Laughlin, dated March 11, 1957, from which the following paragraphs are taken:

> After our meeting in Boston on February 13, I gave a report of our discussions to Joe Oliver and Herb McCracken. Then Bill Spaulding and I talked some more in Atlantic City. At my request Joe Oliver came to New York and we spent most of a day discussing the pros and cons and whether we should make counter-proposals or in any way suggest continuing the negotiations. At the close of the day, we concluded that all the possibilities had been sufficiently explored and that the wisest course for all concerned would be for us to express our genuine regret, our personal respect for you and your associates, and to table the subject until sometime in the indefinite future.

Accordingly, I telephoned you and since you weren't in, I talked with Bill, briefly conveyed that sentiment to him, and said I hoped we could work together in many ways to our mutual benefit. The hours devoted to discussions and correspondence were amply rewarded by the friendships we gained, but I knew there were many other opportunities for joint activity which we should not fail to pursue.

Henry, you said you knew of no other organization you would so much like to see joined with Houghton Mifflin Company. I too feel that Houghton Mifflin is the only organization with which I could happily work.

In recalling this episode some years later, Robinson said: "One of the nicest things to come out of the meetings with Houghton Mifflin was the response of Mrs. Augustus K. Oliver upon hearing that an agreement could not be reached. She urged me to prevail upon Henry Laughlin, a childhood friend, to join Scholastic's board of directors as the best possible successor to her late husband." Laughlin became a director, attending his first meeting in December 1958, and served until June 1965. In retirement Laughlin divided his time between his Castle Hyde in County Cork, Ireland, and his stateside home in Concord, MA. In October 1976, after reading a draft of this account, he wrote the author to say: "I have read with great interest your account of the negotiations between Scholastic and HM Co. and could find nothing to condemn and much to praise—only regretting that it came to a fruitless end except for my having the great pleasure of serving on the Scholastic board for a number of years."

Laughlin died on August 10, 1977, at the age of 85, in his summer home in Ireland.

William Spaulding retired as Houghton Mifflin president in 1967. Although it was not in the cards for him to preside over a Scholastic branch of Houghton Mifflin, he continued his interest in Scholastic through his friendship with Robinson and through his sons John (president of Scholastic from 1971 until his death in 1974) and Richard, elected vice president in 1971 and elected to the board and executive vice presidency in 1974.

Scholastic itself was not immune to the spell of acquisitiveness, of buying properties for the sake of expansion, diversification, or elimination — all but one within the school or youth field. The exception was the magazine *Better Busses* in 1924, long before busing became controversial. There was nary a decade in all six when Scholastic did not acquire some publishing property. See "Scholastic Acquisitions" in the Appendices, which shows the periodicals acquired plus the Teen Age Book Club and Enrichment Records. (*Headline Focus Wall Map* is considered a periodical, since it is published on a regular frequency of 18 issues per school year and has second-class postal entry.) Scholastic's agreements with Mary Glasgow Publications, Ltd., for rights to its foreign-language periodicals; with Moe Asch for Folkways Records; and agreements with other organizations are also included in the Appendices.

CHAPTER XIII

Tax-Free Competitor

AMERICAN Education Press (AEP) and Scholastic went their separate and happier ways after the divorce of 1932, each to do a little expanding despite the deepening Depression. AEP had, in 1928, moved lower into the elementary grades with the introduction of its first *My Weekly Reader* paper for grade four, soon to be followed by *My Weekly Reader*s for all elementary grades and kindergarten, under the general editorship of Eleanor Johnson. It would be several more years (1937) before Scholastic would produce a second classroom magazine, *Junior Scholastic,* although there was that brief proprietorship in 1929 of *The World Review,* a weekly paper for the upper elementary grades and junior high (Chapter IV, "Premature Expansion").

For the first 47 years of its successful operation, AEP had been owned and managed by its founder, Charles Palmer Davis, and upon his death, by his son Preston (with whom Robinson had dealt in the sale of *The World Review* in 1929 and in the Scholastic-AEP joint venture of 1931.)

Early in 1949 the first of a number of "coincidences" occurred that will help in an understanding of events that led in October of that year to the sale of AEP to Wesleyan University of Middletown, CT. A broker named Allen

Kander called on Robinson in his New York office to propose that Scholastic sell its stock to a nonprofit institution such as a university to become a tax-free business, managed by Scholastic executives, under long-term contracts as employees of the institution. Kander would not reveal the name unless Robinson showed a serious interest in the proposition. After several meetings with Kander and discussions of the idea with Oliver, Robinson and McCracken decided not to pursue it.

The reason Robinson and McCracken took the time even to discuss Kander's proposal with him was their disposition to listen to any voice that might offer relief from the pressing need for capital and higher income. The next day, after Kander had been told that Scholastic preferred to go its own way, Robinson and McCracken discussed prospects for the year ahead (school year 1950–51), following which Robinson wrote a long memo to McCracken "to clarify my thoughts, some of which you may not agree with. But since we've lived together for most of our adult lives and have been through so many crises together in 26 years, I think we can continue to meet whatever new problems may arise, no matter how critical they may be." An additional paragraph of the memo is quoted in order to further convey the spirit that sustained Robinson in the struggle for survival: "I'm glad you don't wish *now* to have us take steps to get rid of the business and get out of it for whatever we can salvage. We both, I know, feel that we may have to do that sometime if we can't get and maintain a stronger financial position, or if AKO* insists on getting out. But I think we still have the joint courage to make the final push up

*A. K. Oliver.

the tough road to a higher level before we agree to let someone else take over."

Sometime later Robinson learned from Kander that both Civic Education Service and American Education Press had declined his offer to enter into negotiations with the still unidentified nonprofit institution. This was not the last of Kander's phone calls to Robinson that year. One bearing news of the utmost importance came from him late in September. He called to report that AEP had been sold to Wesleyan University, adding that he was not involved in the transaction. Robinson immediately wrote to Preston Davis of AEP, saying he had heard "fantastic stories" about AEP being sold to Wesleyan, and was this a rumor or what? Back came a "Dear Robbie" letter from Davis saying:

> In reply to yours of October 29 [1949] I don't know what fantastic stories you have heard about the sale of the AEP. If there was anything in the *Times*, I didn't see it. One paper in Columbus carried a couple of paragraphs; that is all. The whole thing is really very simple. All of the stock of our companies was sold by the stockholders to the Wesleyan University Press, Inc. The old corporations were later dissolved so that the whole thing is now Wesleyan University Press. However, we shall continue to operate under the trade name of American Education Press and Charles E. Merrill Co.

AEP, a highly profitable operation and what had been up to that point in 1949 a tax-paying enterprise, was sold to Wesleyan for $8,625,000. The agreement provided employment and management contracts for certain AEP executives and department heads.

"The stroke that brought Wesleyan into the field of classroom publications," explained the *Wesleyan University Alumnus* magazine, "to the substantial benefit of both Press and University, is attributed to Stuart Hedden '19. Harrison M. Sayre '17 was then president of AEP and advised Hedden that it was about to be sold. Hedden saw the possibilities, made a presentation to the Board of Trustees, and negotiated the purchase. The trustees accepted it as a worthwhile educational program after receiving assurances from Hedden and Stuart Silloway '29 (the only two who knew anything of its financial operations) that the investment would be no drain on the University's resources."

How right they were! It was no drain or gamble whatsoever, but a sure thing—as the operating statements and balance sheets over the years showed. AEP's *My Weekly Reader* papers had nine-tenths of the market, the *Young America* papers being the only competitor in the public elementary schools and Scholastic not yet having ventured into the schools below the junior high level (*Junior Scholastic*, 1937).

The magazine *Connecticut Life*, in an article on Wesleyan's growth-minded president, Victor L. Butterfield, said: "The college has a unique asset in its Press, which owns the lucrative *My Weekly Reader, Current Events,* and other school publications. They are estimated to bring in more than one million profit a year, largely tax free."

It was undoubtedly the tax-free status that appealed to the trustees when presented with the opportunity to acquire AEP. The privately held publishing company that had been paying 52 percent of its profits in federal and local taxes was, at the stroke of a few pens, to become a department of a prestigious university expecting to retain 100 percent of the profits. The word "expecting" alludes to a precaution taken by the university trustees in setting aside in an escrow fund the dollars that would be required if the university's applications for tax exemption were not to be approved by the Internal Revenue Service. Thanks to an amendment to a bill sponsored by Senator Brien McMahon of Connecticut that was passed by Congress, the IRS was given a basis on which to rule in favor of Wesleyan. The business of publishing periodicals for the schools was thus declared "substantially related to the educational purposes of the University."

This eventuality was foreseen by Robinson, McCracken, Studebaker, Layman, and Spaulding—often joined by Clay Coss of Civic Education Service—who put in hundreds of hours trying to convince the Wesleyan and AEP chiefs, legislators, and IRS decision-makers of the unfairness of such an exemption. To have the most profitable of a trio of publishers serving the schools with similar materials operate on a tax-exempt basis while the other two—Scholastic and Civic Education Service—paid Uncle Sam to the tune of half their profits, seemed palpably unfair. The Wesleyan trustees thought not, and one trustee even recommended to Robinson that he go out to find a university as a tax-sheltered partner rather than continue the campaign to get Internal Revenue to reverse its ruling. Scholastic and Civic Education Service were not trying to drive Wesleyan out of the magazine business; they wanted only to get Wesleyan to pay taxes on the profits of a company that had been paying them for 47 years. If it had paid taxes on AEP, Wesleyan would still have had a big annual profit on the business.

Well, after 16 years Wesleyan shook itself free from AEP and was paid handsomely by the buyer—the Xerox Corporation. It paid Wesleyan $56 million (400,000 shares of Xerox stock, then at $140 per share) for the package: publications, land, and buildings. Some years earlier AEP had changed its name from American Education Press to American Education Publications. A few years after Xerox took over, the name was changed to Xerox Education Publications.

In an article, "The University and the Power of 'the Press,'" the *Wesleyan University Alumnus* magazine in its August 1965 issue reviewed Wesleyan's 16 years of ownership of what it referred to as "the Press" (meaning Wesleyan University Press, the entity that held title to AEP), referring to its tax-free status and achievements in these paragraphs:

> Good men have testified for years to the educational aims behind Wesleyan's acquisition and operation of the Press. The Internal Revenue Service conducted a long and exhaustive investigation and concluded that the activities of the Press were substantially related to the educational purposes of the University and were therefore largely tax-exempt. Yet the questions were often asked rhetorically as if the financial success of the Press arose from a lack of concern for educational values.
>
> The Press was very clearly a money-maker. For most of the 16 years, operating within the restrictions imposed by tax exemption, it provided more than $1 million for the general purposes of the University. Overall it made available $28.5 million, a sum that cannot be regarded casually.

However, this success was itself the proof of the acceptance of the Wesleyan publications as educational materials. They are read and used so widely because thousands of schools all over the country choose to include them in their curricula. The Press is the largest publisher of educational periodicals because professional educators respond to them.

This is not to say that the relationship between the Press and the University was always a glorious one. Confusions and criticisms persisted from start to finish and it was easy to get the impression that nobody was happy with the arrangement. Yet, when it was all over, there was no mistaking the fact that the Press had taken some long strides forward in those 16 years. The quality of the publications had improved very substantially; they had also increased in number and size. Moreover, the potential of the Press had greatly increased because its staff was better and larger and the production facilities had been expanded. Those 16,500,000 school children were the unwitting beneficiaries of the improvements.

In an editorial, "A Welcome to Xerox," the *Middletown Press* of May 21, 1965, referred to Middletown's advantage in having the property go on the tax rolls:

For Middletown, the acquisition by Xerox of the publishing enterprise is an excellent development for a variety of reasons. The chances are greater under Xerox that the Wesleyan Press will grow because the new owners will not be at any point inhibited by the fear of a violation of the tax rulings under which the college operated the publishing division. Moreover, the Wesleyan Press building, built at a cost of $1,500,000 will go on the local tax rolls.

News of the sale of AEP to Xerox set Scholastic staff members to wondering how developments would affect the relative competitive postures now that a company noted for its financial resources was in charge. Would Xerox be pouring so much money into promotion and AEP products that Scholastic would be under great strain to hold its place? The nontaxpaying Wesleyan University Press did not use its profits in that way, but turned them into buildings, curriculum and staff expansion. To let Scholastic employees know what Scholastic officially thought of the transfer, Robinson issued a fighting message to the staff on May 28, 1965, from which the following is excerpted:

> Who's afraid of Xerox? Not I—and I am confident that none of my management associates is, either, and I have a secure feeling that all other members of our organization will rise to this challenge with the zest, energy and imagination that has brought to Scholastic a reputation of the highest level in educational circles. This prestige and professional reputation among educators have been painstakingly built up over a period of 45 years. The excellence of our products and our service, in which we have had the guidance of our Advisory Council and our Editorial Advisory Boards, an editorial staff dedicated to the best principles of education, the professional character of our field organization, and the furnishing of such services as the Scholastic Awards program, have been the major factors in creating this enviable reputation.
>
> We are determined to preserve this reputation and enhance it, with a staff equal to the task. True, we shall be competing with an aggressive, strongly financed and highly publicized competi-

tor, but that competitor will have to pay the same rate of taxes that we have to pay. That competitor will have to prove itself in the field of education. Our products are and have been superior to the products of Wesleyan University Press. Although *My Weekly Reader* elementary papers, Grade 1 through Grade 6, have larger circulations than our elementary school publications, we have been far ahead of their periodicals in the junior-senior high school field and our book clubs far outdistance in sales the book clubs that now become the property of Xerox.

Our *Co-ed* magazine and *Practical/Forecast* and *Scope* have no counterpart at Xerox, nor does *Scholastic Coach* nor *Scholastic Teacher*.

Also, our nine foreign language periodicals in French, Spanish, German, and Russian, with accompanying records, etc., are unique and exclusive with Scholastic. Our franchise for U.S. and Canadian rights to the publishing properties of the famous London house of Mary Glasgow & Baker, Ltd., has made it possible to move rapidly into the foreign language field with spectacular gains this past year. Other unique Scholastic educational properties not on Xerox lists are our Multi-Texts and SLU, our patented Self-Teaching Arithmetic series, our Readers' Choice Catalog sales, and the recently acquired distribution contract with Folkways Records. Also, our Canadian affiliate [Scholastic-Tab Publications, Ltd.] has made remarkable progress in establishing our four book clubs in Canada and in September will launch an exclusive periodical for the Canadian elementary schools called *Canadian Newstime*.

The only area in which Xerox is represented and Scholastic is not is in the kindergarten field, where they have a weekly periodical called *Surprise*. We may surprise them by producing something even better for children in kindergarten.*

In short, I merely wish to tell all members of our organization that Scholastic will meet the challenge of Xerox aggressively and creatively. This is a challenge which I welcome and which I am confident all of my fellow executives welcome. I hope you will roll up your sleeves and join in the fray. It's going to be *hard work AND fun*!

M. R. Robinson

In the 10-year period between school year 1966–67 and 1975–76 inclusive, Scholastic's elementary line of periodicals registered a circulation gain from 4,534,826 to 5,781,879—a 22-percent increase. At the same time, the Xerox elementary periodicals, including their kindergarten *Surprise,* declined from 13,018,799 to 7,898,844 (39 percent). The steepest decline among the Xerox group was in their sixth-grade periodical called *Senior* (formerly *My Weekly Reader No. 6*), which fell from 1,301,979 to 665,785 (49 percent). The Xerox periodical *Current Events,* serving approximately the same grades as *Junior Scholastic,* declined from 974,093 to 679,475 (30 percent). *Junior Scholastic* had a less precipitous decline of 22 percent, from 1,380,763 to 1,074,179. *Read,* the Xerox periodical for upper elementary and junior high school language arts classes, climbed from 387,913 to 720,436 during the same period (46 percent). Comment on the Xerox social studies periodicals at the high school level appears in Chapter XIV, "The March of Magazines."

*The "something even better" Robinson prophesied appeared in the fall of 1968 under the title *Let's Find Out.* Issued monthly for kindergarten classes, it consists of four periodicals for the child, including a "Read to Me" story to take home, and teacher materials that include posters, a monthly calendar, and guides for classroom use of the children's periodicals.

CHAPTER XIV

The March
of Magazines

SOON after the end of World War II two more student weeklies, *Prep* and *Practical English,* were launched in September 1946, expanding the Scholastic magazine family to six. *Prep,* subtitled *Preparation for Practical Living,* was folded at the end of its first year because it lacked practical application to the school market. It acquired only 30,000 subscriptions, half the number expected as a starter. Such optimism was based partially on (1) the return of tens of thousands of young war veterans to complete their high school education and (2) on the company's expectation that its working connection with the American Vocational Association would produce orders for *Prep.* The connection was made in 1944 under a contract whereby Scholastic provided publishing services for the Association's official monthly, *American Vocational Journal,* starting with the January 1945 issue. The 26,000 members of the Association were considered prime prospects for subscriptions to *Prep,* as they were mainly teachers and administrators in vocational schools and in the vocational departments of general high schools (Chapter XXIX, under "Vocational Sideline").

Prep and
Practical English

Each issue of *Prep* concentrated on an industry or major field of work or service (teaching, farming, cosmetics, steel, rubber, coal, lumber, airlines, railroads, automotive, utilities, forestry, etc.). In the high schools there was no identifiable class or teacher assigned to the general subject of careers, a formidable hurdle when it came to addressing promotion material. Most of the mail promotion for *Prep* was addressed to the school principal. In the specialized vocational high schools, manual skills were the "majors," and the teachers showed little interest in subscribing to classroom sets of a magazine that dealt with the broad field of careers. The school library could use a subscription, but the economics of Scholastic publishing required bulk classroom subscriptions.

Some 25 years later, leaders in education, responding to the call of Sidney P. Marland, U.S. Commissioner of Education, provided for greater emphasis on career education to serve the throngs of students arriving in the high schools ill-equipped for academic work.

Practical English, directed to English classes, the largest subject-matter body of students in U.S. high schools, was designed to serve many of those classes in a way that *Senior Scholastic* could not. This opportunity for a new English skills magazine developed with the increase in the number of students in the high schools and the higher percentage staying the whole four years. Many were enrolled in the "business English" course as a concomitant to their courses in bookkeeping, typing, stenography, and other secretarial skills.

In planning the editorial content of *Practical En-*

glish, Editor Margaret Hauser sought the counsel of hundreds of English teachers and received the encouraging word: Yes, they could use a magazine that would make the basics of English more appealing than the traditional textbook and workbook.

Hauser and her staff developed in *Practical English* an easy-to-read, humorously illustrated approach to articles and exercises on all facets of verbal expression. "How-to" pieces dealt with how to use the dictionary, the library, the telephone; how to write a sentence, a paragraph, a letter, a check, an outline, notes, a job application; how to get along socially (conversation, introductions, courtesy); how to study, cultivate a good speaking voice, take a test, and make travel reservations. It was a functional approach with a difference, the emphasis being on human relations and the lifelong advantage of being a good communicator.

At the time *Practical English* was launched, *Senior Scholastic* was being published in three editions: English, social studies, and the combined edition, and this would continue until September 1948 when *Literary Cavalcade* would be launched. The emphasis in the discontinued English edition of *Senior Scholastic* had been on literature (short stories, plays, biographies) and student writing in the forms of short story, poetry, essay, etc. A regular department was "Young Voices," consisting of contributions by student writers, which then became entries in the Scholastic Writing Awards competitions. A similar feature was continued in *Literary Cavalcade.*

With the January 26, 1970, issue *Practical English*

Marjorie Burns, book editor (former editor of *Voice*), and Abraham Lass, former high school principal and long-time contributor to *Practical English.*

Niel Glixon, editor of *Voice*.

underwent a change of title. It became Scholastic *Voice*, and the reasons for the change were explained by the then Editor Marjorie Burns as follows:

1. It's human and active.
2. It means language and everything connected with it.
3. Today, more than ever, language means not only the printed word but the spoken word—in plays, records, radio, television, films.
4. It's short and easy to remember.

Niel Glixon, who had been with Scholastic since 1966, became the acting editor of *Voice* in 1976 and the designated editor in 1977, succeeding Marjorie Burns, editor from 1962 to 1976, when she moved into the Text Division to work on books.

Quality at 30 Cents per Subscription *Literary Cavalcade* made its bow at the start of school year 1948–49. A monthly issued eight times during the school year, it was a bargain at one dollar, and a steal at 30 cents (for all eight issues) if the teacher ordered five or more annual subscriptions along with *Practical English* or *Senior Scholastic*. The frequency of *Literary Cavalcade* has remained constant throughout the years, starting each year with an October issue distributed with the opening of school in September, and ending with a May issue. The price has risen to $2.25 as of the October 1977 issue, a modest increase compared to what has happened in recent years to the price of other nutrients of mind and body. The cut-rate combination price, long since discontinued, was offered to entice teachers to subscribe to *Practical English* or to mollify those teachers who had been using the Advanced English Edition of *Senior Scholastic* and could no longer get it.* Now they could get the regular edition of *Senior Scholastic* or *Practical English* plus *Literary Cavalcade* for a rather inviting combination price. All three magazines had substantial gains over the next five years.

Eric Berger, the first editor of *Literary Cavalcade*, held that job while continuing as editor of *Senior Scholastic*'s English department, where he presided over such features as the short story, "Speaking of Books" column, "Young Voices: Student Writers' Own Weekly Page," and "Reading Comprehension and Vocabulary Quiz." When in 1950 he was promoted to editor of *Senior Scholastic*, Berger shifted much of the *Cavalcade* workload to his managing editor, Mary Alice Cullen, who—five years later—was named editor on a sharing basis; the masthead

*For four years until May 1948 *Senior Scholastic* was issued in three editions: Social Studies, Advanced English, and Combination (which contained everything in the other two). With the launching of *Literary Cavalcade*, these editions were discontinued, and once again *Senior Scholastic* basked in singular bliss. Gradually it shifted its curriculum orientation from the English/social studies core to all social studies. Still, many English teachers continued to subscribe in order to have its pro and con presentation of national and world issues for class discussion and debate. In deference to these teachers, a short story was included in each issue for a few more years.

Michael Spring, editor of *Literary Cavalcade*.

read: "Eric Berger, Mary Alice Cullen, editors." A year later Cullen ruled the roost and Berger became consulting editor, to serve in that capacity through the next two editors after Cullen resigned to be married. She was succeeded by Jean F. Merrill* for school year 1956–57 and William Kehoe for 1957–58. The next editor—Jerome Brondfield—would be with it for the long run—14 years. During his term *Literary Cavalcade* passed the 300,000 circulation mark and has swung between 325,000 to 375,000 ever since. In 1972 Brondfield switched to editing Scholastic books, and Associate Editor Michael Spring became editor of *Literary Cavalcade*.

Literary Cavalcade ran in the red for the first 20 years of its bright and useful life, and began turning into a profit center during Brondfield's editorship. If ever there were thoughts of sacrificing it for the sake of the company's bottom line, they were quickly dismissed by a management dedicated to the encouragement of good reading and the cultivation of teenagers' literary taste.

Tiptoeing into the Elementary Field

Scholastic's decision to enter the elementary periodical field, long preempted by American Education Press with its *Current Events* and *My Weekly Reader* and by the *Young America* papers, was not the culmination of a plan that had long been in the making. It was rather an intuitive response by Robinson when he heard, early in 1952, that the *Young America* papers had been acquired by American Education Press (AEP), owned by Wesleyan

*Jean Merrill, who became a distinguished writer of books for children, had been writing for *Senior Scholastic*, *Practical English*, and *Junior Scholastic* and had served as movie reviewer for all three.

University of Middletown, CT. Robinson surmised that AEP would discontinue the *Young America* papers and merge them into *My Weekly Reader.* So it happened. This meant that AEP would hold a monopoly on periodical business in the elementary grades in the public schools.*

News of the *Young America* sale did not come as a complete surprise to Robinson because Alfred Gwynne Vanderbilt, who had acquired the *Young America* papers from Stuart Sheftel, had informed Robinson of their availability, presumably to the highest bidder. The two had lunch together to talk about it, and the upshot was a rejection of Robinson's offer of $10,000 because it was not enough to feed the Vanderbilt horses for the fall season.

Back in his office Robinson moved among his colleagues, declaring: "We can't let them have the elementary field to themselves for even one year." He, Studebaker, and a few others on the staff had been itching to get into the elementary schools. Studebaker had advised the company to go in with six periodicials, one for each grade, to match Wesleyan's *My Weekly Reader*s. He had a sound and persuasive reason for this advice, but not persuasive enough to move the Scholastic directors to approve launching the whole fleet for grades one through six. They approved the launching of one only, and this would become *NewsTime*, editorially stretched to cover grades five and six. As Studebaker pointed out, *NewsTime* would have to buck the elementary school practice of ordering periodicals for all its grades K–6 from the same publishing house; now only one house, AEP, offered the whole line. Much as many school principals were

*The George A. Pflaum Company of Dayton, OH, published weeklies for the Catholic elementary schools.

impressed with the quality of *NewsTime*, they might be reluctant to split an order just to get one out of six. Despite the marketing handicap, *NewsTime*—starting with 84,000 circulation—moved up each year, and when in 1957 the company launched another elementary periodical (again just one, *Explorer*, for grade four), *NewsTime* had soared past the 600,000 mark. The quality and the promotion of *NewsTime* were excellent, thanks to the dedication and energies of some 120 magazine-centered sales representatives and to the creativity of three outstanding editors: first, Beryl Parker, who had been associated with her sister Lockie in the publication of *Story Parade*; second, Edna Mitchell Preston, a children's writer of exceptional skill; and from 1959 to 1969 Tony Simon, who had been with Scholastic since 1948 on the staff of *Junior Scholastic*, and under whose editorship

New Year's party, 1950, Hotel Brevoort. Left to right: Patricia Lauber, Lee Learner Gray, Lucy Evankow, Sturges Cary, Tony Simon,

NewsTime passed the one million mark in circulation (1964).

NewsTime was not the original title of the periodical. The first and subsequent 15 issues appeared under the title *Junior American Citizen* with the three initial letters *JAC* prominently enlarged. A few weeks after the launching a teacher-subscriber wrote the editor to ask whether *Junior American Citizen* had any connection with the Daughters of the American Revolution, which had been conducting a youth activities program bearing the title. No one at Scholastic had been aware of this, but the chiefs now had to decide what to do about *JAC*. Studebaker telephoned the DAR president-general, whom he knew, to explain the situation. A few days later she called back to say that the Daughters of the American Revolution had no objection to Scholastic's use of the title and thoughtfully added, "Perhaps you would prefer to avoid possible confusion by changing it." Scholastic did prefer to change it and conducted a contest among subscribing classrooms to get suggestions for a new title. Thousands were received. The announced $500 prize money was divided among the 36 classroom groups that suggested titles including either the word *News* or the word *Time*. That came to $13.89 for each winning class. True to the Scholastic spirit, each check was made out for $15. Starting with the issue of January 7, 1953, *Junior American Citizen* became *NewsTime: A Scholastic Magazine for Junior American Citizens*. The subtitle was discontinued after the 1952–53 school year and replaced with *A Scholastic Magazine for Middle Grades*. Several years later the title underwent a typographical change, from *NewsTime* to *Newstime*.

To launch and edit *Explorer*, Scholastic employed

Mary Harbage who had been director of Elementary Education for the city of Akron, OH. By 1960, when the company at last did extend its elementary periodical line into the primary grades, the third-grade magazine *News Trails* was also assigned to Harbage. At the same time Kathryn Jackson was lured from the Silver Burdett Company to launch *News Pilot* for grade one and *News Ranger* for grade two. Six years later the monthly box of learning materials for kindergarten called *Let's Find Out* would be ready to go, and this was also assigned to Jackson.

Until 1965 there were five Scholastic magazines for grades one through six. The leading competitor, American Education Press (then owned by Wesleyan University), had six. The gap in the Scholastic line appeared in grades five and six, where *NewsTime* attempted to serve both grades with a great deal of success at five and less at six — where *Junior Scholastic* had acquired considerable circulation. The five-through-six gap in Scholastic's line would soon be filled following word from Clay Coss of Civic Education Service, Washington, DC, to his long-

Explorer magazine group, 1971. Left to right: Peg Horsburgh, Linda Beech (editor), Lynn Thomas, Ann Weiss.

206

time friend and competitor, M. R. Robinson of Scholastic, that the CES fifth-grade periodical *Young Citizen* was for sale. Coss offered Scholastic first refusal rights. Scholastic declined to refuse, acquired the periodical, and published it under the Scholastic banner starting with the September 17, 1965, issue. Tony Simon was named editor, which made him a double editor, as he was also responsible for *NewsTime*.

When Coss and Robinson agreed on the transfer of *Young Citizen*, they also agreed that in the event CES decided to sell its junior and senior high school periodicals—*Junior Review*, *American Observer*, *Civic Leader*, and *Headline Focus Wall Map* — Scholastic would have first refusal rights on any or all of them. Within four years all would be in the Scholastic family. (pp. 216–22, "Socrates Summoned in Vain").

Sturges F. Cary, emeritus editor-in-chief.

EDITORS OF ELEMENTARY MAGAZINES SINCE THEIR FOUNDING TO 1978, IN THE ORDER OF THEIR APPEARANCE

Let's Find Out	Kathryn Jackson (Schneider), Helen Myers, Jean Marzollo
Pilot & Ranger	Kathryn Jackson (Schneider), Lee Hopkins, Joseph Bielawski, Della Cohen
Trails	Mary Harbage, Sturges Cary, Rebecca Kalusky
Explorer	Mary Harbage, Tony Simon, Linda Beech, Jonathan Rosenbloom
*News Citizen**	Tony Simon, Carol Drisko, Maureen Hunter-Bone
Newstime	Beryl Parker, Edna Preston, Tony Simon, Terry Perkins, Carol Drisko

*The title was *Young Citizen* when purchased from Civic Education Service in 1965. All other periodicals listed above were Scholastic originals. (See pp. 513–17 for a complete list of originals.)

**In Home Ec:
A Student Edition
to the Rescue**

The idea for a magazine for home economics classes occurred to Robinson while he was having lunch with Jo T. Emery at the Advertising Club in New York some four years before idea became reality as *Co-ed* magazine in February 1956. Emery was founder, publisher, and part-owner of the magazine *Practical Home Economics* (*PHE*), for teachers and other professionals in the field, and his company, Lakeside Publishing, had it up for sale. It had slipped from first to third place among the three commercial magazines serving the home economics field, and it was available at a price requiring little cash.* Robinson saw it as a means of entering a new (to Scholastic) curriculum area that would broaden the company's market in the schools. Along with the magazine, Scholastic acquired its staff, including Emery, Editor Ruthanna Russell, Assistant Editor Florence Stassen, and Lulu Wilson, Emery's secretary for 30 years.

Robinson held the idea for a student home economics magazine in the back of his mind in the hope that *PHE* would start to turn a profit, thus paving the way for an easier approach to his directors to get approval for a student magazine. After four years of no profit but manageable deficits, Robinson decided that the way to put the faltering home economics enterprise on its feet was to start a student magazine and let *PHE* serve as its teacher edition. Every teacher who ordered 10 or more subscriptions of the student magazine, which was named *Co-ed*,

*In 1952 Scholastic acquired 100 percent of the stock of Lakeside Publishing Company in exchange for 225 shares of Scholastic preferred stock and 450 shares of common stock. Scholastic also undertook any liabilities of Lakeside not exceeding $15,000 and contracted with Jo T. Emery as a consultant for a period of five years at $5,000 per year. Emery died on November 13, 1960.

208

would receive a free copy of *PHE*. Something of a precedent was set by launching *Co-ed* in the middle of the school year; the first issue appeared in February 1956 with Margaret Hauser as editor while she continued as editor of *Practical English* (pp. 198–200). Hauser edited *Co-ed* until her retirement in 1974 after 38 years with the company. She originated and wrote for many years the popular "Boy Dates Girl" articles under the *nom de plume* of Gay Head (after the colorful cliffs of Martha's Vineyard). She had many other "firsts" in her string of accomplishments for Scholastic, among them: first director of the Scholastic Institute of Student Opinion, first editor of *Practical English,* first editor of *Co-ed*, first editorial director of the Language Arts Division and of the Home Economics and Guidance Division—holding both editorial directorships simultaneously for several years.

Margaret Ronan, movie reviewer and writer-at-large, joined Scholastic as receptionist/switchboard operator in 1937. When she was a junior at East High School, Denver, CO, in 1935, she won second prize in poetry, Scholastic Writing Awards.

Co-ed was an instant success, opening with a circulation of 151,518 and climbing each year, surpassing one million in 1966. This had the desired healthy effect on its teacher edition, *Practical Home Economics*, which returned to ascendancy in its field, surpassing in revenue its principal competitors, *What's New in Home Economics* and *Forecast for Home Economists*. The latter had been acquired from founder Charles H. Goudiss, Jr., by the McCall Corporation, which at the time printed most of the Scholastic magazines. In 1963 Scholastic acquired *Forecast* from McCall,* merged it into *PHE*, and renamed the survivor *Practical/Forecast for Home Economics*, a difficult title to live with. In 1966 *Practical* was dropped, and

---

*Scholastic paid the McCall Corporation $25,000 for *Forecast* and granted a special rate for McCall Patterns advertising in Scholastic magazines for a period of five years.

209

the title became *Forecast for Home Economics* and remains so to this day, with the first word featured in the logo. The editor is Gloria Spitz, fifth in the line that followed Ruthanna Russell and included Irene Parrott, Eleanor Adams, and Edie McConnell.

Co-ed continues as the dominant magazine in its field under the editorship of Kathy Gogick. Both *Co-ed* and *Forecast* are complements of the recently formed Home Economics Division, headed by Vice President Carolyn Bishop as publisher and editorial director. She has had the unusual, if not unprecedented, experience of being employed three times by Scholastic, first as Carolyn Benkert in July 1962 to be a writer-in-training on *Co-ed*. On the confidential performance review form 90 days later, her editor, Margaret Hauser, wrote: "She's wonderful! Hope we can keep her." By the end of the school year in June 1963 she was gone: to be married to Lloyd F. Bishop and live in Arlington, VA. She came back to *Co-ed* in March 1965 as home furnishings and merchandise editor. She left in July 1968 to become editor-in-chief of *Budget Decorating*, and after a year there, joined *Family Circle* as home furnishings and equipment editor. The resignation in 1975 of Midge Turk Richardson, after a year with Scholastic as editorial director for *Forecast* and *Co-ed*, renewed interest in Carolyn Bishop on the part of Scholas-

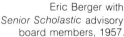

Eric Berger with *Senior Scholastic* advisory board members, 1957.

tic's new chief executive officer, Richard Robinson, and she returned to Scholastic in December 1975 as head of the Home Economics Division.

Street & Smith, the venerable book and periodical house that had its printing plant and offices in Greenwich Village for 75 years, came out in February 1957 with a magazine for high school science classes called *Science World*. This was Street & Smith's first venture into classroom periodicals, but it was not such for the editor they signed up: Patricia Lauber, who had been editor of *Junior Scholastic* during several years of its greatest growth. Street & Smith lured Lauber out of freelance (writing children's books) to launch the new magazine with a February 5, 1957, opener. Issued fortnightly 16 times during the school year, *Science World* started with about 110,000 circulation, and after two-and-a-half years had not exceeded 150,000. The editorial product was excellent, but the company lacked the organization for selling to schools—this was its only school product to bear the full cost of direct mail promotion.

In March 1958 Robinson got a signal from C.C. Westland of McCall's (where *Science World* was printed, as was the Scholastic line) that Street & Smith, after one year, had decided to sell or discontinue *Science World*. A phone call came from Arthur Z. Gray, president of Street & Smith, inviting Robinson to lunch at the Racquet Club. The next day Robinson reported to the Scholastic board and its management committee that Gray "suggested the possibility of a cooperative venture, but I said I could not see how any split responsibility or ownership would work. However, I said that I would be glad to take the subject up with our directors."

In his report to the board management committee Robinson listed the arguments for and against "pursuing the subject and going into the field of science" (in which there was a tremendous public upsurge of interest, the Soviet Union having launched Sputnik 1 and 2 in 1957). Most of the Scholastic board and management committee recommended that Robinson talk further with Gray, for if Scholastic were to take over and promote subscriptions for the school year 1958–59, a quick decision was necessary. The matter became academic for the time being by Street & Smith's decision to continue *Science World*.

Another year with *Science World* did nothing to fortify Street & Smith's faith in its future, and by April 1959, Gray was again in touch with Robinson. Within a month they had signed letters of agreement that would transfer ownership of *Science World* and its teacher edition, *Science Teacher's World*, to Scholastic on payment of $1. The first figure agreed upon had been $1,000, but as Robinson wrote Gray on May 13, 1959, this "is revised from the original $1,000 to $1 through your generous gesture of today." A little more dough was required to knead the bread. So, "in order to give Street & Smith an opportunity to recover some of its investment in *Science World*," as Robinson wrote in a memorandum to Gray, "Scholastic agrees to pay a royalty of 2 percent of the cash subscription receipts each school year for four years." This was expensed annually for a total of $24,483.34 for the four years.

Scholastic assigned the versatile Eric Berger, who had successfully edited *Senior Scholastic, World Week,* and *Literary Cavalcade,* to the editorship of *Science World*. It was continued on a fortnightly schedule, but after the first year Scholastic split it into two editions called Edition 1 (for grades seven through nine) and Edition 2 (for senior high school grades). In September 1965 they became weeklies, Edition 1 carrying the same advertising as *Junior Scholastic;* Edition 2, the same as *Senior Scholastic, World Week,* and *Practical English.* At that time the titles were changed to *Senior Science* for Edition 2 and just *Science World* for Edition 1.

The editor, Eric Berger, concerned over the viability of the two editions as he saw *Science World* galloping ahead in circulation while *Senior Science* stood still, took the position that a return to one edition would turn deficit into profit. He put the question to his 18-member editorial advisory board, which included Watson Davis, head of Science Service, and Robert Carleton, executive secretary of the National Science Teachers Association, and encountered strong opposition to the one-edition idea. Nevertheless Berger persisted in his belief that—in view of the four-to-one ratio of students taking general science in grades seven, eight, and nine and those at the high school level taking chemistry and physics—the senior edition could not pay its way and would jeopardize the growth and profitability of the junior edition. He recommended that the "merged" magazine emphasize general science as the junior edition had done, with emphasis on the life sciences, the earth sciences, astronomy, and health. It emerged in September 1968 as *Science World Combined With Senior Science,* and by November the circulation reports showed that loss had been turned into profit. Berger was named editorial director of the Science Department and Managing Editor Carl Proujan became editor of the magazine. When in 1972 Proujan was promoted to editorial director of the Science Department, Edmund H. (Tad) Harvey was named editor of *Science World*. Harvey had been an assistant editor when *Science World* was published by Street & Smith and worked for awhile under Eric Berger after Scholastic acquired it. Upon Harvey's promotion to the post of editorial director of the combined Science and Social Studies Departments in 1976, Associate Editor Michael Cusack became editor of *Science World*.

High Maturity, Easy To Read   The purpose of Scholastic's new magazine *Scope* was well-stated in an announcement by M. R. Robinson in the pilot issue dated April 24, 1964. He wrote, in part:

> The special mission of *Scope* grows from forces now reshaping American education: the shift of population into the cities; the urgency to keep teenagers in school beyond school-leaving age; and the crucial importance of reading skills.
>
> The need has become so acute that the Great Cities Program for School Improvement has officially asked the cooperation of all school materials publishers. The Research Council committee, chaired by Superintendent George B. Brain of Baltimore, asks for new materials "to represent the special conditions inherent in life as it is now lived in great cities by many minority peoples." Others echo this.
>
> With *Scope*, Scholastic takes up this challenge. A perceptive educator, speaking recently at the School Administrators Convention in Atlantic City, pointed out that children, too, are among the curriculum makers. By accepting or resisting courses and text materials, students influence change. In our cities today, students make their

214

wishes known by apathy or hostility or enthusiasm. They want materials that say something pertinent to their world—a world of imposed maturity and vanishing jobs for youth.

In preparation for the pilot issue of *Scope*, Scholastic invited superintendents representing schools of the 15 cities belonging to the Great Cities Council to a meeting in the Scholastic offices in New York to discuss the venture and to preview the content of the pilot issue. The pages of the 24-page-plus-cover issue were projected for them on a screen, and discussion followed each page. Detroit, Chicago, Los Angeles, Boston, Buffalo, Milwaukee, San Francisco, Baltimore, St. Louis, Washington, Cleveland, Houston, Philadelphia, and New York were each represented by a top-level administrator. Buffalo sent two—the superintendent and the associate superintendent for curriculum.

That turnout represented much more than professional curiosity as to what Scholastic was up to. There was a palpable eagerness to lend support to the production of materials that could help the public high schools with the most serious problem of their existence. At first the Scholastic planners saw *Scope* as appealing primarily to city high schools, especially those in the then-overcrowded "inner city." This direction was plain to see on the front cover of the pilot issue, the title of which was *City Scope*. However, the title was changed to *Scholastic Scope* for the first subscription issue, Vol. 1, No. 1, September 16, 1964.

This was done on the advice of educators and Scholastic representatives in the field who responded to

Jim Brownell, editorial director/ administrator and former editor of *Junior Scholastic*, with the author at left.

the pilot issue. They approved of its contents and extolled its promise for the future, but they asked that the prefix *City* be removed, as it implied that only the city schools were faced with the problem of upgrading reading levels.

Richard Robinson, who with Bill Boutwell directed the prepublication planning of *Scope*, was named editor, and in 1967 he was succeeded by Managing Editor Katherine Woodroofe.* *Scope* passed the half-million mark in 1967; the million mark, in 1971; and by 1977 reached 1,400,000.

Socrates Summoned in Vain

Scholastic acquired the four remaining CES periodicals (*American Observer, Junior Review, Civic Leader,* and *Headline Focus Wall Map*) in 1969 after negotiations with the owners — Clay Coss, operating head of the company, and Ruth Myer, widow of founder Walter Myer. As agreed at the time of the *Young Citizen* acquisition, they notified Robinson of their intent to sell and told him that several prominent newspapers, magazines, and American Education Press (Xerox) were showing serious interest in these periodicals. Robinson, not wishing to have them go to big-name corporations—several already strong competitors in the school market—told Coss that Scholastic would exercise its "right of first refusal" by entering the bidding. Although there was strong indication that Civic Education Service, by awaiting the outcome of negotiations then underway, might have received a substantially higher price than that offered by Scholastic, Myer and Coss concluded that the Scholastic offer was a fair one, and they preferred to have their periodicals

*Katherine Woodroofe and Richard Robinson were married in 1968.

216

go to their long-time friend Robinson and Scholastic. So it happened.

The transfer of operations from Washington, DC, to New York was made in several stages. For one year the CES high school periodical, *American Observer*, its teacher's edition, *Civic Leader*, and the *Headline Focus Wall Map* (issued periodically) continued to be edited and produced in Washington. Scholastic paid CES on a cost-plus basis. *Junior Review* was discontinued as a separate publication, its subscriptions filled by *Junior Scholastic*, starting with the February 2, 1970, issue, which carried a bull's-eye on the front cover stating "*Junior Review* is now combined with *Junior Scholastic*." Thus *Junior Scholastic*'s circulation had an instant increase of 268,427 for a total of 1,733,570. It went still higher the next year (to 1,786,726) after Scholastic had purchased the subscription lists of the George A. Pflaum Company's *Catholic Messenger* periodicals, which would soon be discontinued.

Toward the end of school year 1969–70 *American Observer*, being edited by the CES team in Washington, underwent a radical change in format and frequency for the last four issues of the term. The purpose of the change at this particular time was to give subscribers a preview of the magazine as it would appear under the full control of Scholastic. It was changed from a weekly to a fortnightly, from eight pages to 32 or 24 per issue, and from the tabloid newspaper format of 11½″ × 15½″ to the 8¼″ × 11″ page of most other Scholastic periodicals.

Scholastic named LeRoy Hayman, who had been editor of *Junior Scholastic*, to edit *American Observer* and its separately bound teacher edition, *Civic Leader*.

Senior Scholastic/World Week editorial staff, 1967. Left to right: Ed Sparn, Charles Hurley, Maury Kurtz, John Nickerson, Roy Hemming (hands on desk, center), Steve Lewin (directly behind Hemming), Diana Reische, Jim Brownell (head only), Frank Coakley, Dan Chu, Joel Anastase, Anne Hennehan, William Johnson, Norman Lunger (hands on desk, right).

Hayman reported to Social Studies Editorial Director Roy Hemming, who reported to Publisher Jack Lippert. *American Observer*, having undergone format and frequency change, would now be reconstructed editorially to become "a new inquiry training approach to current affairs." An aggressive promotion department promised "a magazine where young people learn through the give-and-take of debate and discussion; where they learn to recognize prejudice and bias; weigh alternatives; then reach their own reasoned conclusions based on all the facts." You might say that *AO* used the Socratic method—except that now it was called the "inquiry method." Three major articles in the issues of September 1970 were: "Indochina: What Did We Win—or Lose—in Cambodia?"; "USA—Is the Law the Same for Everybody?"; and "Youth—Which Student Protests Are Effective?"

The brave, updated Socratic approach did not catch on. *American Observer* lost 100,000 in circulation the first year and 110,000 in the second. *World Week* too was losing ground, and by school year 1971–72 had lost 40 percent of its 1966–67 peak of 501,473. The company was offering three social studies magazines at the senior high school level, all of them on a sharp decline in circulation. *Senior Scholastic* and *American Observer* required the reading ability of the competent ninth-to-twelfth-grade student; *World Week*'s reading level was at about grade seven. Faced with these declines, the Management Operations Committee decided on some consolidation of the high school social studies magazines.

World Week was the first to go, ending its 30-year life with the issue of February 28, 1972. The farewell message in the teacher edition, signed by M. R. Robinson, chairman of the board, stated: "Profound changes have taken place in the teaching of Social Studies—and are continuing....The Social Studies classroom now needs material and perspectives different from that of the present *World Week*...." Subscribers would see some of these changes in the reorganized *Senior Scholastic,* whose logo was modified to read *Senior Scholastic: Now Including World Week*. In a welcome message in the teacher edition of *Senior,* Richard Robinson, publisher of the School Division, said: "In recent years, *Senior* has focused mainly on national affairs, and *World Week* on world cultures and international affairs. But it has become increasingly clear that the themes and topics of both magazines were overlapping. By bringing the two magazines together, we believe we will better serve the whole range of today's social studies."

One month after the folding of *World Week,* the final issue of the 41-year-old *American Observer,* dated April 3, 1972, would be put to bed, with M. R. Robinson facing up to the challenge of explaining the reason for its discontinuance and incorporation into *Senior Scholastic.* He referred to a survey of teachers the company had recently made:

> Teachers told us that, in this changing climate, a periodical for the upper high school grades could be more valuable than ever if it did certain important jobs. Such a periodical should include world affairs with cultural emphasis . . . inquiry-oriented treatment . . . U.S. problems and government . . . theme-related approaches to people and events . . . and a concentration of values.
>
> Scholastic's three social studies periodicals—*World Week, American Observer,* and *Senior Scholastic*—were thus each doing part of the total job a social studies periodical should do. Was there a reason to have one periodical focusing on world cultures? Another periodical focusing on American values and issues? And a third designed for inquiry and discovery teaching? One periodical *could* serve all these needs. Furthermore, none of these three periodicals separately had enough circulation to be economically viable. In addition we are faced with steep increases in all costs and an exorbitant increase in magazine postage costs. We are determined to keep subscription prices low. As one periodical, the combined circulation could be delivered at the current price of less than 7¢ per copy.

In discussing this experience in retrospect, M. R. Robinson said: "Label it for what it was — a management failure. I see this as one of my major errors." He attributed it to not assessing the impact of changes occurring in the social studies movement as a result of the influx into the high schools of students ill-equipped to do the work required by the traditional courses of study. Many of them couldn't read at the level of the material offered, and those who could decipher some of the words and sentences were unresponsive to them. The Scholastic magazine *Scope* had successfully met this challenge by addressing English teachers (language arts) and the specialist teachers assigned to help the untrained readers. The success of *Scope* and its offspring skills materials led to the development of many new programs, including new periodicals especially prepared for junior and senior high school students reading at as low as the second-grade level.

The new combined *Senior/World Week/American Observer* posted a circulation of 550,045 for school year 1972–73, an increase of 82,040 over what *Senior* had had by itself but 416,883 fewer than what all three had had just before they became one. But *Senior* couldn't hold its profitable 550,045 and dropped 100,000 in each of the following two years, then for 1975–76 fell to 279,641. The new *Scholastic Search*, for high school students reading at fifth- and sixth-grade levels, may have had some influence on the declining *Senior* circulation.

In the spring of 1978 a completely restructured *Senior Scholastic* appeared—presaging the quality of the magazine to come—on a high-grade coated paper instead of newsprint, replete with multiple-color illustrations. In introducing it to teachers Tad Harvey, social studies editorial director, wrote, in part: "We propose to become a place where students can look to America's history for insights about today's problems, explore social issues that touch their lives, meet the people running our institutions, and perhaps most important, learn to develop their own ideas and insights."

Of the four periodicals acquired from Civic Education Service, one has survived: *Headline Focus Wall Map*, considered a periodical because it is issued on a regular schedule, 18 times during the school year. It has had its ups and downs in circulation—up to 8,852 in 1972–73 when the subscription price was $9, down to 4,754 in 1975–76 when the price was $36, upping income to the point of profit.

Social Studies in Transition   There is no simple explanation of the decline and fall of Scholastic's once-successful *World Week* and of *American Observer*, which Civic Education Service had raised to a peak circulation of 539,475 after merging it with their *Weekly News Review* the year before the sale to Scholastic. *Weekly News Review* had had a circulation of 248,100, and *American Observer*, 370,200, for a total of 618,300, but the surviving periodical was not able to hold it all.

During *American Observer*'s three years as a Scholastic periodical, its decline was precipitous, falling to 202,252 when the sponge was finally thrown in. Two of the American Education Press (AEP) high school social studies papers, *Every Week* and *Our Times*, were also in decline and were folded in 1968 (*Every Week* at a circulation of 261,251 and *Our Times* at 164,125). AEP then launched two new papers in the social studies, *Urban World* and *Issues Today*, which were folded in 1973 and 1974, respectively, at a combined circulation of 370,107. *Issues Today* became *OPT* (*On People and Things*), which was folded in 1975.

222

In addition to the periodicals of AEP, Civic Education Service, and Scholastic, there were several others in the high school social studies field during the 1960's and early 1970's, principally *Synopsis*, published by Bernard Berkin in Chicago, and *Student Weekly*, published by *The New York Times*. The former changed its title to *Current Viewpoints* in 1974.

In 1965* the circulation of the high school social studies periodicals published by AEP, Civic Education Service, and Scholastic totaled 2,269,708.† By 1973, with Civic Education Service out of the field and *American Observer* and *World Week* merged into *Senior Scholastic*, the high school social studies periodicals of AEP and Scholastic posted a total circulation of 965,427. This was just before AEP folded *Urban World* and *Issues Today*.

Where had 1,304,281 subscribers gone? The students were there in greater numbers than ever (up from 12,681,000 to 15,337,000 in grades nine through twelve from 1964 to 1975). Among them were hundreds of thousands ill-prepared to read the usual textbooks and magazines. Many schools set up special remedial reading classes to help these students. Scholastic's response to this mounting problem was to launch the weekly magazine *Scope* (this chapter, p. 214), the first high-interest, easy-reading classroom periodical to be published. (Xerox

---

*This was the year Wesleyan University sold AEP to Xerox Corporation, which later changed the name of its publishing arm to Xerox Education Publications.

†*Junior Scholastic*, AEP's *Current Events*, and Civic Education Service's *Junior Review*—all social studies periodicals—are not included, as they were published for upper elementary and junior high grades six to nine.

made this claim for its *Know Your World*, but *Scope* was launched in 1964, *Know Your World*, in 1967.)

Many factors influenced the decline in circulation of *Senior Scholastic* and the folding of *World Week* and *American Observer*. A summary:

Publishing factors (changes, decisions):

1. A radical change in the content and format of *American Observer* from what it had been before Scholastic acquired it from Civic Education Service — a change that alienated many old subscribers and failed to attract replacements.

2. The introduction of other Scholastic products, thus affording a school a wider choice of instructional materials on which to spend its budgeted dollar. (The self-competition factor: *viz.*, reference to *Scope* above.)

3. A change in the marketing strategies of the Scholastic representatives who, with a proliferation of products to sell, understandably could not give magazines the priority they did when magazines and book clubs comprised their whole bag of goods. To validate this factor, it must be assumed that it is more difficult—at the high school level—to sell magazines prepared for social studies classes than those prepared for language arts, science, and home economics classes, since this latter group had a much better circulation record than the social studies group during the decade 1965–75.

Librarians Lavinia Dobler and Lucy Evankow in the process of moving from 33 West 42nd Street to 50 West 44th Street, 1962.

224

School and societal factors (changes, decisions):

1. Changes in social studies curricula as a consequence of the Vietnam War, student unrest, population migration, social stresses on the cities.

2. Pressures on the high schools to extend social studies courses to include subjects that did not call for the use of the available classroom magazines—such as sociology, anthropology, archaeology, economics—thus drawing students from classes where the classroom magazine had been established. The disappearance of world history as a separate subject from many schedules.

3. The use of the local newspaper in the classroom. The Newspaper Publishers Association vigorously campaigned to achieve this, and some newspapers provided copies to the schools free of charge.

4. The practice in some schools of using television for the one-period-a-week discussion of current affairs instead of using reading materials and discussing articles in magazines.

A *Search* for Lost Circulation

The success of *Scope* encouraged the planners of the School Division to look to the social studies field to see if a new magazine could be floated to compensate for the failing circulation of *Senior Scholastic* and the folding of *World Week* and *American Observer*.

A preview issue of 450,000 copies of *Search*, dated March 6, 1972, was distributed to social studies teachers and department heads, inviting them to request classroom sets of that issue for test use. This and the August–September promotion campaign (direct mail and school calls by Scholastic representatives) brought in a confirmed, paid circulation of 211,116.

In preparing for the launching of *Search*, the company followed its practice of convening a group of educators to assist in formulating editorial policy and content. Representatives from 15 major city school systems and state education departments met with Scholastic executives and editors to evaluate the tentative contents of a preview issue and assist in setting the guidelines for a magazine that would motivate "the less able reader who sat uninterested, uncaring, unchallenged by the traditional materials of instruction in the social studies," as stated by Richard Robinson, then publisher of the School Division, in the preview issue. A staff under the editorship of Robert Stine,* who had been associate editor of *Junior Scholastic*, was recruited from within the organization, and Vol. 1, No. 1 appeared on September 18, 1972, with the following message to its readers:

You're the First!

You're the first ever to read *Search*. Because this is our first issue.

Since we're a brand-new magazine, you probably have some questions about us. Like, who are we? And what do we want?

---

*Stine left *Search* to start *Bananas* in 1976, and was succeeded by Eric Oatman, who had been on the *Senior Scholastic* staff.

Maybe we can answer those questions by telling you the things we'd like to do in *Search:*

1. We'd like to help you understand more about you, your community, your country, and your world.

2. We'd like to help you understand how American government really works. And how you can make government work for you.

3. We'd like to show you how other people live around the world.

4. We'd like to tell you about other young people—what they're doing, what they're thinking, how they're solving their problems.

5. We'd like to help you understand more about how you fit into things—how you fit in with your neighborhood . . . your town or city . . . with jobs and careers . . . with money and buying . . . how you fit in with the American past . . . and the world's future.

6. Finally, we'd like to be fun to read, interesting, and to the point.

That's a lot to ask from a new magazine. But we think we can do it. After you've read a few issues of *Search*, why not write to us. Let us know how well you think we're doing. Write to: *Scholastic Search*, 50 W. 44th St., New York, NY 10036. What you think is important to us. Because you're the first readers we've ever had.

In its first 50 years Scholastic published magazines to serve a wide range of the curriculum—social studies, language arts, science, home economics, foreign languages, athletics. But, for one branch of that curriculum in which it was most active otherwise—art—the company had no magazine. Once a year, usually in the last issue of the school year, Scholastic magazines would fea-

Art for Education's Sake

ture the prizewinning works of the annual Scholastic Awards. Although Robinson, whose personal interest had been the moving force behind the success of the Art Awards, had often thought of having an art magazine, the chance of its becoming a source of revenue at least equal to expense seemed dim.

But in 1970 its chances brightened with the appearance of a publishing consultant named Edward A. Hamilton in M. R. Robinson's office with the proposal that Scholastic and the National Gallery of Art collaborate in publishing an art magazine for the schools. Hamilton knew of the National Gallery's interest in such a project, as he had participated in discussions between the National Gallery and the Zacharias group at Massachusetts Institute of Technology on a plan for the advancement of art education. Nothing came of it except a bee in Hamilton's bonnet that buzzed him toward Robinson at Scholastic.

Robinson expressed interest in Hamilton's proposal, and—with the consent of the Scholastic directors—entered into negotiations with the National Gallery of Art in the spring of 1970. The National Gallery was represented by its new director, J. Carter Brown, and Assistant Administrator W. Howard Adams. It was agreed that a periodical, *Art & Man*, developed from an outline and dummy prepared by Hamilton, would be published by Scholastic under the direction of the National Gallery of Art. Scholastic would pay the National Gallery an annual royalty on all subscription receipts. The National Gallery would have a decisive voice—if they wished to exercise it—over plans and content of each issue as submitted by

> **"Art is the only thing that can save us from the apocalypse."**
> *Jacob Landau, distinguished artist, first-prize winner, Scholastic Art Awards, 1934, 1935.*

228

Scholastic. The National Gallery temporarily engaged Richard McLanathan as a consultant for *Art & Man,* and Gray Williams of Scholastic held the title of project director for three years. In preparing for the first year's run of eight issues, he enlisted the help of the company's field representatives in getting evaluations of the pilot issue from high school art department heads and teachers. At the time, stimulated by the availability of federal funds, a strong movement for humanities studies was developing in high schools. To make the Scholastic offering more appealing to these classes as well as to art classes, sets of filmstrips and slides were offered to subscribers. They were related to the themes of *Art & Man* — one theme per issue, such as "The American Wilderness," "Rembrandt and His Holland," "African Heritage," "Florence and the Early Renaissance," "Art and War," "The City," and others. The teacher edition of the first issue of *Art & Man* was given the title *Art & Humanities.*

Margaret Howlett, editor of *Art & Man.*

In preparing for the start-up of *Art & Man,* Scholastic purchased from Ian Mininberg and his sister Rachel Baker their school magazine *Artist Jr.,* published in New Haven, CT. Mininberg and Baker understood that Scholastic would discontinue *Artist Jr.* and use its mailing list of 2,700 teachers to promote subscriptions for *Art & Man,* and this was done.

Its circulation opened at 156,640 for school year 1970–71, rose to 170,819 the next year, then declined to 110,000 in 1976 when the supplementary filmstrips and slides had to be discontinued because they were too costly to produce at a marketable price. In addition, school budgets were tightened, and the cry of "back-to-basics" came from the citizenry in many communities. Many educators, however, concerned over what the public includes and excludes in its conception of what is "basic," have made it clear that they consider art, music, and health education among others as being basic to the high school curriculum. The company, with the National Gallery, convinced that art education is here to stay, is concentrating its sales efforts for *Art & Man* on art classes in the junior and senior high schools, with encouraging results.

Scholastic artist Margaret Howlett, who has been on the staff of *Art & Man* since the first issue was published, was named editor in 1973. She works closely on editorial planning and the selection of illustrations with W. Howard Adams, assistant administrator of the National Gallery of Art, and with Joseph Reis, director of Extension Services.

More Magazines for the Less Able Reader

It was not only at the high school level that school authorities were faced with the problem of reading deficiency. Many school systems found it becoming an increasing problem in the elementary schools. Observing the widespread practice of keeping students within their age groups, many schools were moving them up grade by grade regardless of academic achievement. In 1975 with the magazine *Sprint* and in 1977 with *Action*, Scholastic provided material for reading-deficient students not served by either *Scope* or *Search*. Both *Sprint* and *Action* are written at the second-grade reading level, but for different age groups: *Sprint* is edited by Victoria Chapman for students in grades four, five, and six; *Action* is

Covers of preview, or pilot, issues of several Scholastic magazines—*Scope*, 1964; *Search*, 1972; *Wheels*, 1978; and one in search of a title, 1978. Intended for classes in business and career education, it was without a title as of early 1979, and without a future, since it was decided not to publish it.

A pilot issue of a magazine for math classes was being tested in the spring of 1979, entitled *Tally*.

The word "city" in *Scope*'s preview-issue title was dropped for the regular issues.

231

edited by Jack Roberts for students in grades seven, eight, and nine. Issued biweekly, *Sprint* developed a circulation of 447,000; *Action*, 316,000 (1977 figures).

Wow! Here Come _Dynamite_ and _Bananas_

The parade of Scholastic magazines reviewed in this chapter closes with the entrance of three high-steppers by the names of *Dynamite* (1974), *Bananas* (1975), and *Wow* (1976). Their titles signify a content oriented to the contemporary world of young people—their fads and fancies, heroes, humor, wonders, and worries—with a heavy emphasis on media personalities. It makes for lively recreational reading that sharpens children's cognitive skills without their realizing it. There was some question as to whether to call these publications magazines or monthly books. For a comment on this, see "How Many Scholastic Magazines Are There?" (next page).

Around the office a few executive eyebrows were raised when the title "Dynamite" was proposed by freelance editor Jenette Kahn. Would this be a fitting title for a periodical to be sold through the schools? How would school administrators and teachers feel about it? In the jargon of juveniles, the word *dynamite* packed a joyful burst of life. In February 1974 about 700,000 copies of the first issue were sold through the Arrow Book Club at 50 cents and 75 cents (just testing). Sales soared to a million and a half for some of the later offerings. There were no discernible objections to the title from outside the office.

The success of *Dynamite* signaled a likely success for magazines of similar hilarity for children in age groups above and below that served by *Dynamite*. In 1975 *Bananas* was launched for teenagers and a year later *Wow*, for children in kindergarten and the primary

Sonia Levinthal, director of public relations, (left) and Claudia Cohl, editor-in-chief, Educational Periodicals Division.

grades. Eyebrow-raisers didn't object to the title *Wow* when they realized that it spelled *Mom* upside down.

Wow sales have ranged between 85,000 and 150,000 per issue; *Bananas*, between 150,000 and 350,000. *Dynamite* and *Bananas* are sold and delivered as single copies through Arrow, TAB and Campus Book Clubs as well as via continuing subscriptions to the home. *Wow* is offered by the See-Saw and Lucky Book Clubs for subscriptions only to the home.

Jane Stine is editor of *Dynamite*; her husband, Robert Stine, is editor of *Bananas*.

The creative work on *Wow* is done under contract with the editor/illustrator team of Richard Hefter and Phillip Johnson. Sheldon Sturges, who joined Scholastic in 1973 as director of marketing, Book Club Division, had a leading role in the launching of these periodicals and serves as their publisher.

How Many Scholastic Magazines Are There?

It is not unusual for persons outside the office and school circles to think of Scholastic in the singular—Scholastic Magazine—and be surprised to learn that there are more than one. "Oh, yes," someone will say at a cocktail party, "you have *Junior Scholastic*. So there must be two." The company's public relations department is on a never-ending mission to get the press and other media to comprehend the pluralization of the title.

Even within the office someone will ask "How many Scholastic magazines are there?" and get several answers. A top officer phoned down the line to say, "My count shows 31. What does yours show?" "Yours" showed 32 as of September 1, 1977, counting *Dynamite*, *Bananas*, and *Wow*, but not counting *Headline Focus*

233

Scholastic Periodicals as of December 1978[1]

Title	Grade Level	First Issue

───────────────────ART AND HUMANITIES───────────────────

Title	Grade Level	First Issue
Art & Man	7–12	Oct. 1970

─────────────────────────ELEMENTARY─────────────────────────

Title	Grade Level	First Issue
Let's Find Out	kindergarten	Oct. 1966
News Pilot	1	Sept. 21, 1960
News Ranger	2	"
News Trails	3	"
News Explorer	4	Sept. 20, 1957
News Citizen	5	1965[2]
Newstime	6	Sept. 15, 1972
Sprint	4–6 (written at 2–3)	Sept. 23, 1975

──────────────────FOREIGN LANGUAGES[3]──────────────────

Title	Grade Level	First Issue
Bonjour	first-year French	1963[4]
Ça va	second-year French	"
Chez nous	third-year French	"
¿Que tal?	first-year Spanish	"
El sol	second-year Spanish	"
Hoy dia	third-year Spanish	"
Das Rad	first-year German	"
Schuss	second-year German	"
Der Roller	third-year German	"

─────────────────────HOME ECONOMICS─────────────────────

Title	Grade Level	First Issue
Co-ed	7–12	Feb. 1956
Forecast for Home Economics	professional	June 1952[2]

---

[1]Not included in this table are publications in magazine format not issued on stated frequency and usually part of a merchandising project in support of an advertiser or other client. *Note:* The prefix "Scholastic" is part of the title of some of the English-language periodicals listed above.

Title	Grade Level	First Issue

——————————LANGUAGE ARTS——————————

Title	Grade Level	First Issue
Action	7–9 (written at 2–4)	Sept. 22, 1977
Literary Cavalcade	9–12	Oct. 1948
Scope	8–12 (written at 4–6)	Sept. 16, 1964
Voice	8–12	Sept. 16, 1946

——————————SCIENCE——————————

Science World	7–10	Sept. 9, 1959[2]

——————————SOCIAL STUDIES——————————

Headline Focus Wall Map	7–12	1969[2]
Junior Scholastic	6–8	Sept. 18, 1937
Search	8–12 (written at 4–6)	Sept. 18, 1972
Senior Scholastic	8–12	Oct. 22, 1920

——————————SPORTS AND PHYSICAL EDUCATION——————————

Scholastic Coach	professional	Sept. 1931

——————————OTHER——————————

Bananas	ages 13–18 (through TAB Book Club)	Sept. 1975
Dynamite	ages 5–13 (through Arrow Book Club)	Mar. 1974
Wheels	driver education	Fall 1978
Wow	ages 4–9	Sept. 1976

[2]First issue after Scholastic acquisition. See Appendices, "Acquisitions," for more information.

[3]Chapter XVII, "Going International," gives an account of the nine foreign-language papers distributed by Scholastic under a licensing agreement with Mary Glasgow Publications, Ltd.

[4]Distribution rights acquired from Mary Glasgow & Baker, Ltd. See Appendices, "Agreements."

Wall Map, which is a periodical but not a magazine, being issued 18 times a year for display on the classroom wall. *Wheels*, which appeared in September 1978, would make the count 33.

Dynamite is a regular listing with the Arrow Book Club (nine times a year), and *Bananas*, with the Teen Age Book Club (nine times per year), and both as well as *Wow* (nine times per year) are promoted for single subscriptions to homes. They are not related to a curriculum as are *Scope, Search*, and other Scholastic magazines. Someone suggested calling them "mag-a-books"; another suggested "book-a-zines." In due course they were decreed to be monthly books. They, the latest entry— *Wheels*—and *Headline Focus Wall Map* are included in the list of 34 periodicals.

EDITORIAL DIRECTORS,
EDUCATIONAL PERIODICALS DIVISION (1978—)

Administration:	Jim Brownell
Social Studies:	Tad Harvey
Language Arts:	Richard Maynard
Elementary:	Terry Perkins

CHAPTER XV

The Book Business

S CHOLASTIC was six years old when it first flirted with the book business, issuing two titles in 1926: *Saplings*, a 78-page, 5½" × 8" cardboard-covered collection of verse, short stories, and essays from the entries submitted for the 1925 student-written numbers of *The Scholastic;* and *Enjoying the Arts,* a 32-page, 8½" × 11" paperback reprint of articles from *The Scholastic* on art and literature. Annually thereafter for 14 years, a new, now-clothbound edition of *Saplings* presented the best of the preceding year's Writing Awards entries, selling for $1.50 and later $2 per copy. The end of *Saplings* was not the end of anthologies of the Writing Awards (Chapter XXII, "A Precious Asset: The Scholastic Awards").

The next title published by the company, in 1930, was the 8½" × 11½" paperbound book *The Glory That Was Greece* by Walter R. Agard, followed by *The Sword of Sergestus — The Grandeur That Was Rome* by Paul L. Anderson, in 1932. These were reprints of serials that had appeared in *The Scholastic*. A series of 25 original radio plays by staff writers Pauline Gibson, Gladys Schmitt, and several freelancers appeared in the early 1940's, among them an adaptation of Maureen Daly's Scholastic Awards prize-winning story, "Sixteen."

Scholastic would publish some 50 or more paperbacks (most of them in a trim size larger than the familiar 5½″ × 8″) before setting up the Scholastic Bookshop in 1947. Among them were: *How To Judge Motion Pictures*, *300th Anniversary of High School Education in America*, *Modern Basketball for Girls*, *How To Use Your Library*, *Handbook for Amateur Broadcasters*, *Problems of America*, *Scholastic Debater*, *The War for Freedom*, *Reading Menus for Young People*, *Plays for Holidays and Other Occasions*, *Land of Liberty: A Regional Study*, *Boy Dates Girl*, *The United Nations in Action*, *World Friendship Stories*, and *Hi There High School!*

Most of the pre-1947 books paid their own way and some turned a profit, as profit was figured in those days of loose applications of "allocations" for office space and overhead. There was no expansion of the payroll because the existing magazine staff did the editorial and production work on the books.

Selling Books of Other Publishers
Scholastic Coach, in its second year (1932–33), set up a service called *Scholastic Coach* Bookshop. Through it, any reader could order books of other publishers by checking a list in *Coach* and mailing it with a check to the bookshop, which at first operated from the editor's desk in the company's office at 155 East 44th Street, New York. The *Coach* Bookshop maintained some stock, but most orders were relayed to the publishing houses and the books sent directly from there to the customer ("drop shipments"). Buyers paid the full list price to the *Coach* Bookshop, which took a 40 percent discount in paying the publishers.

It was only pin money, but in 1932, 40 percent of $3 paid for a photoengraving of a football-play diagram for the magazine. With the easing of the Depression the *Scholastic Coach* Bookshop was discontinued. It cannot be claimed that it was the progenitor of the Scholastic Bookshop that would follow in 1947.

The originators of the Scholastic Bookshop — Ian Ballantine of Bantam Books, Inc.; M. R. Robinson and William D. Boutwell of Scholastic — were thinking of bigger game. They agreed that Scholastic would become "the exclusive distributor of Bantam Books to elementary and secondary schools and teacher training institutions," as the brochure stated. The list of paperback books at 25 cents each offered many of the most popular titles on school reading lists, such as Booth Tarkington's *Seventeen*, Sally Benson's *Meet Me in St. Louis*, Alexander Woollcott's *Long, Long Ago*, Sinclair Lewis's *Babbitt*, C. S. Forester's *Captain from Connecticut*, Richard Tregaskis's *Guadalcanal Diary*, and a host of others. Teachers subscribing to Scholastic magazines (then *Senior Scholastic*, *Practical English*, *World Week*, and *Junior Scholastic*) could obtain discounts on bulk purchases of 50 or more books (23 cents per copy).

To direct this new business, Robinson turned to Boutwell, who had joined the company in January 1945 as managing editor of *American Vocational Journal*. He had left that assignment in 1946 to edit *Scholastic Teacher* and continued editing it while directing the new Scholastic Bookshop (Chapter XIV, "The March of Magazines," and Chapter XIX, "Lesson Plans, Teacher Editions").

Scholastic Bookshop sold some 300,000 books through 7,000 teachers during its first year, bringing an income of $75,000. This was far short of the break-even point, but an encouraging start. Now what could be done to attract more teachers to a program in which *they* figured, essentially, as salespersons? As one of the early bookshop promotion pieces explained, under the heading "Resale Advantages":

> Most teachers order Scholastic-Bantams for resale to students. Books purchased at the discounts shown may be sold to students at the standard newsstand rate of 25 cents per copy. The discounts will cover ordering costs and compensate the teacher, the librarian, or the book fund for any small losses.

Involvement of the teacher and in many instances the school administrator in the ordering process as agents who recommended the material to the students, collected their money, and then paid the publisher by personal check, was nothing new in this business. Scholastic had long depended on that process for selling its magazines. So did American Education Press with its *Current Events* and *My Weekly Reader*s and Civic Education Service with its *American Observer*, *Weekly News Review*, and *Junior Review*. Now would it work with books? There were signs that it would.

Birth of the Classroom Book Club   Robinson, Boutwell, and Ballantine were well aware of another infant paperback book program being promoted in the high schools by one of the early ignitors of the paperback explosion — Pocket Books, Inc. Working

240

out of that office was a personable and persuasive entrepreneur named Martha Huddleston, whom Pocket Books employed in 1945 as director of Reading Development. Prior to that she had been director of Community Activities for the Book and Author War Bond Committee. Her assignment for Pocket Books: to stimulate reading interest among young people. She set about it by organizing a project called the Teen Age Book Show, which featured paperback books of all publishers and — as Freeman Lewis of Pocket Books explained it in his *History of Pocket Books, Inc.* — "making it a vehicle for giving boys and girls in public, private, and parochial schools materials for producing their own community-wide book shows."

At one of these shows in Staples High School, Westport, CT, Huddleston and a teacher in the English department were discussing what could be done to follow through on whatever success the show might have had in stimulating reading interest. Huddleston credited this teacher with the idea for the first high school paperback book club: "If I could receive regularly, once a month or so," the teacher said, "a listing of paperbacks that I could recommend to my students, I feel reasonably sure that they would order a large number." That was enough to speed Huddleston on the next train to New York — a little more than an hour's ride — during which she made notes for her proposal to Lewis. He gave it his blessing and Huddleston a budget.

Huddleston organized a selection committee of English teachers and school librarians headed by Max J. Herzberg, principal of Weequahic High School, Newark, NJ, and former English department head. Herzberg was enchanted with the idea and pitched into the organization and promotion work with a dedication far beyond what his responsibility as chairman of the selection committee called for. He combined the scholarship of the savant in literature and contemporary writing with long experience in teaching and counseling teenagers to provide the practical, school-centered assistance Huddleston needed. The infant Teen Age Book Club enlisted clubs in every state, plus Hawaii, Alaska, and Puerto Rico. But the volume was not sufficient to meet expenses, and Lewis came to the conclusion "that the most effective encouragement of book reading by teenagers could not come about solely through Pocket Books' own efforts."

As it did at Staples High School, coincidence again was about to change the course of events. In November 1947 Huddleston was on a train headed for San Francisco and the annual meeting of the National Council of Teachers of English. On the same train, headed for the same meeting, during which he would give the annual Thanksgiving dinner for Scholastic's teacher-subscribers, rode Robinson. He and Huddleston struck up a conversation, clinked glasses in the club car, and got around to sharing ideas on how to win friends and customers in the English classrooms of the 30,000 U.S. junior and senior high schools.

Scholastic had subscriptions in most of these schools with its three editions of *Senior Scholastic* (English, Social Studies, and Combined editions), with its new *Practical English*, and with the 10-year-old *Junior Scholastic*, then widely used in English as well as social studies classes. Huddleston was well aware of Scholastic's presence in the schools, and before that club-car *tête-à-tête* ended, Robinson, if not Huddleston, realized that Scholastic had what the Teen Age Book Club needed.

Promotion and recruitment of classroom book clubs could ride into the schools at a low, second-class postage rate on the pages of the magazines and not have to depend primarily on the more costly third-class mail. At the time Scholastic had six or seven sales representatives making shotgun efforts to visit schools here and there. It would be only a year before Robinson would sign up John Studebaker, who would start working on a plan to cover all high population centers with 170 or more Scholastic Resident Representatives (Chapter X).

Returning to New York, Huddleston reported the club-car conversation to Lewis, and soon he and Robinson were discussing the involvement of Scholastic in the Teen Age Book Club. Lewis proposed that Scholastic take over the operation of the club under Pocket Books' ownership, with the understanding that if there were losses during the first year, Pocket Books would cover them; if there were profits, they would be split fifty-fifty. From the Scholastic position, this agreement signed by Lewis and Robinson was a heads-I-win, tails-you-lose proposition.

New Year's party, Dec. 29, 1950, Hotel Brevoort. Left to right: Agnes Leahy, Agnes Laurino, Martha Huddleston (founder of Teen Age Book Club), Florence Cuddy.

At the end of the first school year of Scholastic operation (1948–49) the Teen Age Book Club showed a proft of $400, whereupon Agnes Laurino, assistant treasurer, made out a $200 check to Pocket Books and sent it to Lewis. Toward the end of that school year in April 1949 the two parties entered into a new, four-year agreement which canceled the first and (1) made Scholastic fully responsible for financing the operation, (2) granted Scholastic the option to purchase the club on a royalty basis at the end of two years. In March 1951 this was revised to permit Scholastic to purchase the club at any time during the term of the agreement for $20,000, payable in four annual installments of $5,000. Scholastic exercised this option on December 31, 1951; organized a wholly owned corporation, Teen Age Books, Inc.; and paid Pocket Books $1,000 for the title.

None of these agreements required that Scholastic purchase its Teen Age Book Club titles from Pocket Books, although it was assumed that Pocket Books would continue to be a major source of supply. The Pocket Books warehouse in Buffalo would store and ship the books on instructions from Scholastic. The Pocket Books facility would also handle paperbacks of other publishers as required by T-A-B's periodic offerings (at first, five a year, then six, and in time, nine).

Lewis undoubtedly had in mind that, if the Teen Age Book Club caught on in the schools under Scholastic's management, it would require vast quantities of paperbacks and would buy them from Pocket Books. Pocket Books had in inventory large quantities of children's books published under two labels: Comet Books and later

244

Pocket Books Jr., bearing the famous Pocket Books kangaroo on the cover. Most of these titles were intended for children of pre-high school age and were not suitable for inclusion on the Teen Age Book Club lists. But Pocket Books had a formidable list of titles for the general trade, many of them appropriate for distribution through high school English teachers — although not all the covers were appropriate and some had to be changed for the Teen Age Book Club allotment when a new press run was scheduled. A paperback including several of Shakespeare's plays might carry a cover depicting Romeo and Juliet in an arrangement which, back in the less licentious 1940's, was inadmissible in many high school classes.

As soon as Pocket Books decided to put the Teen Age Book Club in the intensive care of Scholastic, Huddleston notified the five members of the selection committee of the change and they agreed to stay on as "reviewers and appraisers" of the books proposed for future lists. Besides Chairman Herzberg, the commitee included Richard J. Hurley, professor of Library Science, University of Michigan; Mark A. Neville, head of the English Department, John Burroughs School, St. Louis, and past president of NCTE; E. Louise Noyes, head of the English Department, Santa Barbara (CA) High School; and Margaret C. Scoggin, New York Public Library.

The Scholastic teacher editions of *Senior Scholastic*, *Junior Scholastic*, *World Week*, and *Practical English* in September 1948 carried a double-page announcement proclaiming Scholastic and Pocket Books, Inc., as cosponsors of the Teen Age Book Club.

Teen Age Book Club

A New Service
Co-sponsored by Scholastic and Pocket Books, Inc.
A Complete Reading Promotion Program

Starting this fall all users of *Scholastic Magazines* can offer the expanded TEEN AGE BOOK CLUB reading promotion project to their students through the pages of the classroom magazines.

The T-A-B CLUB (as it is called), started two years ago by Pocket Books, Inc., is, at the present time, being used successfully by 4,000 teachers and librarians, who extend T-A-B CLUB membership to approximately 250,000 students each month. These student members, to date, have obtained through the T-A-B CLUB 1,275,000 books.

"We are proud, indeed," says M. R. Robinson, publisher of *Scholastic Magazines*, "to become joint sponsors of the TEEN AGE BOOK CLUB, the only project which aims to give teachers and librarians real help in promoting the love of reading and ownership of good books. Now we offer teachers a comprehensive reading program: *Scholastic Magazines* for classroom use and recreational periodical reading; the T-A-B CLUB for extended recreational book reading."

Martha Huddleston, TEEN AGE BOOK CLUB director, sincerely believes that this new arrangement will be a real contribution to all who are concerned with our national reading problem. "Hundreds of teachers tell us," says Miss Huddleston, "that such a *complete* reading promotion program will be welcomed as a gift from Heaven."

The promised heavenly gifts for September were the following books from which the student could

246

choose one or more and give his order to his teacher along with 25 cents for each book. The teacher would write the student's orders on a master form, attach his or her personal check, and send the order to Teen Age Book Club, 7 East 12th Street, New York 3, N.Y. — then Scholastic's office.

Four Comedies of William Shakespeare
Forgive Us Our Trespasses by Lloyd C. Douglas
Bill Stern's Favorite Football Stories
We Took to the Woods by Louise Dickinson Rich
Above Suspicion by Helen MacInnes

The same announcement listed 19 additional books for the months to follow during the full term:

What's Coming!

CLASSICS
Oliver Twist, Charles Dickens
A Connecticut Yankee in King Arthur's Court,
    Mark Twain
The Scarlet Letter, Nathaniel Hawthorne
Silas Marner, George Eliot
Anna Karenina, Leo Tolstoy

MODERN FICTION
High Tension, William Wister Haines
The Good Earth, Pearl Buck

NON-FICTION AND COLLECTIONS
Pocket Book of American Poems,
    Louis Untermeyer, editor
Anything Can Happen, George and
    Helen Papashvily
Pocket Book of O. Henry, Harry Hansen, editor
Here Is Your War, Ernie Pyle
Pocket Book of Great Detectives, Lee Wright, editor

TVA: Democracy on the March, David E. Lilienthal
Autobiography of Benjamin Franklin

HUMOR AND ENTERTAINMENT
The Second Believe It or Not, Robert L. Ripley
Peabody's Mermaid, Guy and Constance Jones

WESTERN AND MYSTERY STORIES
Oh, You Tex, William MacLeod Raine
Greek Coffin Mystery, Ellery Queen
The Border Kid, Max Brand
Trent's Last Case, E. C. Bentley

Despite the apprehension of many school librarians over the "intrusion" — as some library traditionalists saw it — of paperbacks into the schools, an increasing number of teachers were won over to the T-A-B plan for encouraging reading. Students could have "their very own" books at rock-bottom prices. In the student editions of the magazines, Huddleston backed up the promotion copy of the teacher editions by such appeals as:

> Order your T-A-B Club books today. . . . Enlarge your circle of friends, your mental capacities, and your personal enjoyment of leisure hours. T-A-B BOOKS! They're as high in entertainment value as they are low in price — 25¢ a book, and a give-away dividend for every four you purchase.

Acquisition of T-A-B did not mean the dissolution of the Scholastic Bookshop, which Boutwell was directing. Within a year he would expand it by increasing its book sources and call it Scholastic Book Service (SBS). The announcement in the September 28, 1949, issue of *Scholastic Teacher* stated: "Scholastic Book Service is the

248

exclusive distributor to elementary and high schools of all 25-cent and 35-cent pocket-sized books published by Pocket Books, Inc., Bantam Books, New American Library, Inc. (Signet and Mentor labels).... Don't be confused," the message said. "Scholastic's two book programs fill different needs: Scholastic Book Service, for classroom use; Teen Age Book Club, for students."

During the summer of 1951 a difference of opinion arose between Huddleston and Robinson over the relationship between Scholastic Book Service and T-A-B, and over her remuneration. When it could not be resolved, she resigned. She wanted participation in T-A-B profits; she also wanted the dissolution of Scholastic Book Service because she felt it was cutting into T-A-B sales. Her reasoning was that if the schools bought books for classroom libraries from SBS, students would borrow these books rather than buy books through T-A-B. Another complication arose: Schools started to buy books being promoted by SBS from local wholesalers, who could buy these titles directly from the publishers. (Scholastic, in the early years of SBS and T-A-B, had few titles of its own.)

As it turned out, the book clubs and SBS lived happily in relative prosperity, and the local wholesaler could not provide the appurtenances that made the book club so appealing to teacher and pupil. Scholastic started building up a master list of titles and publishing it in a *Readers' Choice Catalog*. This grew to a 98-page listing of more than 1,500 paperbacks for all grade levels, K–12, and it offered a 25 percent educator's discount on every item in it, including posters, cassettes, and record-book combinations.

With the departure of Huddleston, Robinson again turned to Boutwell, who had been moving *Scholastic Teacher* along at high speed into its first profit position, and put him in charge of both T-A-B and SBS. This happened some six months before Scholastic would exercise its option to acquire T-A-B outright. There was never a question in the minds of Robinson and his colleagues on Scholastic's Management Operations Committee about exercising this option. It was done in December 1951, with the first of four $5,000 Scholastic checks going to Pocket Books.

For two years Boutwell held the dual jobs of editor of *Scholastic Teacher* and editorial director of the Teen Age Book Club, and it became apparent with the growth of T-A-B that he should be relieved of the publishing responsibility for one or the other. On March 10, 1954, Robinson wrote Boutwell to say:

> It now looks as if T-A-B, Inc., will do more than a half million dollars worth of business this year; at least, it will come awfully close to a half million. This is now becoming, as we both predicted it would, one of the major operations of Scholastic Corporation. I think T-A-B, Inc.,* will soon, if it does not already, require the undivided attention of Bill Boutwell. Almost two years ago when you took the T-A-B job, I said that you would have to decide which direction, which part of the business, you wanted to make your major and eventually your only area of operations. You

*The company had formed a separate corporation for the T-A-B Club in 1951, Teen-Age Book Clubs, Inc., in New York State. This was shortened to TAB Books, Inc., and in 1960 that corporation was merged into Scholastic Magazines, Inc., as part of the Scholastic Book Services division.

elected to take the path labeled "T-A-B Club." I assume that your decision has not changed. If that is the case, then I feel I should repeat again that we must find a really top level person for the *Teacher* job.

Roy Gallant, who had been associate editor of a trade publication, was chosen for the *Teacher* job. An excellent writer, he quickly learned from Boutwell the vicissitudes of editing a Scholastic magazine. John Spaulding, who had recently left *Reader's Digest* for Scholastic, was put in charge of T-A-B promotion copy. After nine months on that job Spaulding was assigned to assist John Studebaker, who had structured the new and expanding Field Service Department.

Spaulding's T-A-B job was given to a new arrival, Morris Goldberger, "discovered" by Boutwell at Montclair (NJ) High School, where Goldberger taught English and ran the Teen Age Book Club in many of his classes. He had participated in several meetings of the TAB Advisory Board. As a sideline he produced a paper called *Listenables and Lookables*, a listing of television and radio programs of cultural and curriculum relevance. This offbeat periodical had not escaped the attention of Boutwell, who had the sharpest ears and eyes for anything "audiovisual." Boutwell arranged with Goldberger to transform *Listenables and Lookables* into a page in the weekly *Scholastic Teacher*, for which Goldberger received a freelance fee of $40 per issue. Soon Goldberger would leave Montclair High School (with the assurance of the superintendent of schools that he could return whenever he wished) to take up full-time duties at Scholastic, the only member of the staff who had actual teaching experience with TAB. On January 25, 1955, Robinson issued the following announcement to the Scholastic staff:

> In connection with the reorganization of functions and responsibilities in the Field Service Department, John Spaulding will begin this week to spend a part of his time helping Dr. Studebaker with the work of the Field Service Central Office.
>
> We are happy to announce that Morris Goldberger of *Listenables and Lookables* fame will shortly become a full-time member of the staff and gradually take over Mr. Spaulding's duties in the Direct Mail Division. He will report as soon as his replacement in the English Department of the Montclair High School can be found—probably about February 7–14.
>
> After March 15th, Mr. Spaulding will spend time in Field Service. Before the end of this year we hope all of his time will be available to Dr. Studebaker.

As the classroom book club idea caught on and teachers from grade six in elementary school through grade 12 in high school were responding to the Teen Age Book Club offers, it became apparent that the "one-level" book club would have a problem in trying to stretch its offerings over too wide an age span. In September 1949 T-A-B announced in *Scholastic Teacher* a plan to correct this stretch under the heading "T-A-B CLUB EX-PANDS":

> Beginning this fall there are two TEEN AGE BOOK CLUBS! The Junior T-A-B CLUB offers four books a month especially selected for junior high pupils. The Senior T-A-B CLUB offers five books each month for senior high students.
>
> A new list each month, regular arrival of the

books, free dividends for added incentive, the fun
of belonging, and reading what others are reading, all add up to more reading among students.

For a few years this took care of the "overreach" in
the span between grade seven (the beginning junior high
year in most systems) and grade 12. But *Junior Scholastic*'s circulation was growing in the sixth grade at a much
greater rate than in grades seven, eight, and nine, although it wasn't planned that way. The company's subscription sales representatives, especially the two in
California and New York (there were only six altogether
nationally), found their time much more efficiently
applied to calls on the elementary schools than to calls on
the junior high schools (though they did both), as the
former outnumbered the latter by at least four to one in
most districts. Thus the "message" about T-A-B pene-
trated more and more elementary schools through the
pages of *Junior Scholastic*. The company did not have a
periodical of lower grade level at the time, as it was not
until 1952 that *Newstime* would be introduced for grade
five.

With *Junior Scholastic* in an increasing number of
elementary schools through sixth-grade subscriptions
and *Newstime* catching on in grades five and four in
the early 1950's, the market was opening for more book
clubs geared to even lower grade levels. First, in 1957 the
Arrow Book Club was introduced for grades four, five, and
six, with Lilian Moore as editor, succeeded by Phyllis
Braun in 1969. Next came Lucky Book Club for grades
two and three in 1961, Beatrice deRegniers, editor. See-
Saw Book Club was launched in 1966 for grades K–1, Ann
McGovern, editor, succeeded by Bernice Chardiet in
1967.

The design and illustration of books are of the utmost importance in what E. B. White called "this treacherous field" of writing for children, in which he did not trust himself "unless I am running a degree of fever." Scholastic has had from the beginning of its foray into this field a designer of consummate skill and soaring imagination in Mary Jane Dunton. As art director she chose artists who gave the low-priced paperbacks the quality of illustration and design heretofore reserved for the more expensive hardbound books.

In 1958 another club at the high school level was launched called Campus Book Club. Directed by Boutwell, Campus was actually an extension and retitling of the Senior T-A-B Club, which would be discontinued. Mary MacEwen, who had come to Scholastic in 1954 as secretary to Dudley Meek* (later to be secretary to John Spaulding), was named editor of Campus in 1960. Betty Owen, at one time assistant editor of three book clubs (T-A-B, Campus, and Science World Book Club) was named editor of T-A-B in 1959. She retired in 1978 and was succeeded by Daniel Weiss. Mary MacEwen was named editorial director of T-A-B and Campus in 1978, and Betsy Ryan succeeded her as editor of the latter.

Twenty years after Scholastic had eased into the book club field as co-sponsor of the Teen Age Book Club, there

*Dudley Meek, who had been treasurer of Harcourt Brace, joined Scholastic as treasurer in 1954, succeeding A. K. Oliver. Meek and Robinson had known each other for many years through their contacts at educational conventions and meetings of the American Textbook Publishers Institute. After nine months with Scholastic, Meek resigned to give full time to business management responsibilities at Radcliffe College and its course in publishing procedures.

were five Scholastic clubs providing books for elementary and high school students at all grade levels.

The teacher played a principal role in this program, for without his or her cooperation a club could not even be started. It was up to the experience, taste, and ingenuity of the editors and their selection committees to choose titles that would appeal to a range of interests at each age level, satisfy the teacher, and gratify the parent—especially the parents of children at the elementary levels. Of course, not every title on every list satisfied every teacher and every parent. There were and continue to be complaints over titles offered, story incidents, or language used in dialogue.

The policy of the company has always been to answer every complaint, and editors have been assiduous in doing so promptly, with a courteous explanation of the reason for offering the disputed title. There were instances, especially in the early years of T-A-B and Campus, of books raising such a storm of criticism that top management would be drawn into the process of responding to the critics.

Meeting Resistance to the Clubs

Scholastic's paperback book clubs did not meet with instant and universal acceptance in the schools, and after 30 years there were still schools and school districts that did not allow them. Scholastic representatives, book club editors, and others from the home office made frequent excursions into the schools to explain the book club concept and try to overcome the resistance of those teachers and administrators who thought the club would (1) divert students from the required reading mandated by the course of study; (2) encourage reading paperback books

M. R. Robinson and
William Boutwell
(about 1958).

which, as a category, had become identified with off-color fiction between salacious-looking covers; (3) usurp teachers' time to collect money from students, keep records, fill out forms, and write checks.

Scholastic representatives and home-office staff, on their visits to schools, met these objections by (1) citing examples of schools where the clubs were arousing students' interest in reading and converting reluctant readers into eager ones and poor readers into better ones without sacrificing course work; (2) displaying club books to reveal covers and content supportive of school standards; (3) demonstrating the use of the master form to which the students' orders were transferred and pointing out that a student could do this clerical work and be all the better for having had such responsibility.

Even the youngest student could help open the carton when it arrived and distribute the books to classmates. The arrival of the carton and the distribution of books made for an exciting time—better than recess!

In the period between school year 1949–50 and school year 1959–60, the Teen Age Book Club grew from a membership of 5,210 (estimated) classroom clubs that purchased 831,000 books to 22,953 that purchased 6,212,000 books.

GROWTH OF BOOK CLUBS, 1961–71

Book Club	Year Founded	Number of Clubs		Number of Books Purchased	
		1960–61	1970–71	1960–61	1970–71
Lucky	1961	33,316	130,000	2,076,000	13,325,000
See-Saw	1966	40,000*	71,000	4,225,000*	6,726,000
Arrow	1957	64,195	236,000	8,632,000	28,537,000
TAB	1946	30,315	84,000	7,740,000	15,678,000
Campus	1958	4,855	28,000	706,000	4,383,000

*1966 figure (year of founding).

Although there was a healthy growth of the clubs through the 1950's and 1960's, Scholastic representatives in the field continued to report "roadblocks" they encountered in this and that school or school system that barred the introduction of the book clubs. John Studebaker, William Boutwell, and their associates in marketing in the mid-1960's planned some high-level missionary work designed to overcome such obstacles. They decided to conduct a detailed study of the operation of book clubs in the schools of five cities: Tucson, AZ; Atlanta, GA; Rochester, NY; Rockford, IL; and the schools of the Archdiocese of Philadelphia, PA. Studebaker visited the superintendents in each of these school systems to get their cooperation and to set the stage for the study. Fifty-two teachers were involved in the study and each agreed to:

1. Keep a record of the number of books purchased by the classroom book club.
2. Record the number of books acquired by each student.
3. Record the average number of books read.
4. Report activities or practices in the class-

room associated with or stimulated by the operations of the book club.

5. Report briefly the values of the club to the classroom reading development program, parents' reaction to it, relation to parents, and other pertinent observations.

6. Submit one or two case studies of teacher experience with students having reading or personality problems.

Their records and reports were turned in to their respective study coordinators, reviewed by their superintendents, and then forwarded to Studebaker along with comments by each superintendent. This material was organized by Derek Burleson and edited by William Boutwell for publication under the title *They Love To Read: Report on a Study of Paperback Book Clubs in Classrooms in Five Cities*, and it was widely distributed to school principals, reading specialists, curriculum consultants, language arts department-heads, and other educators. Scholastic's 175 representatives throughout the country used it to advantage in their campaign to win over school administrators and teachers to the book club idea. The report in all phases was a formal confirmation of the fact that the book club plan was providing students easy access to inexpensive books and getting them excited about reading. Here are excerpts from what the five educators said about the study in their districts:

> The very fine selection of paperbacks available from Scholastic book clubs, at prices within reach of most of our families, offers a valuable

means for our young people to gain vicarious experiences, pursue many interests, and to explore many types of books.

Thomas A. Shaheen
Superintendent of Schools
Rockford, Illinois

Frankly, when I was first told about the Scholastic book club survey, in spite of the fine reputation of Scholastic magazines I was skeptical. I thought another big-time promotional deal was being cooked up. However, in checking with teachers, parents, curriculum specialists, and other resource people in the Tucson schools, I found them to be most enthusiastic about the clubs. Pride of ownership and subsequent increased interest in reading on the part of many pupils of varied ability were direct results of membership in a Scholastic book club.

Robert D. Morrow
Superintendent of Schools
Tucson, Arizona

The study made by Atlanta teachers supported fully a personal conviction that the Scholastic book club is an excellent program. In the study completed recently, Atlanta teachers reported that the book club materials contributed to improved reading performance.

John W. Letson
Superintendent of Schools
Atlanta, Georgia

More and more of our elementary schools are providing students with paperbound books, including those from Scholastic book clubs, to supplement the curriculum and to provide children with many more books than the school system could otherwise afford. At the high school level, English and social studies classes are emphasizing independent study in programs stimulated by the wide availability of paperbound books. Perhaps the most permanent result of the purchase of paperbound books in the classroom is that they enable nearly every child to begin a personal library at low cost.

I am pleased that the Rochester schools were chosen to participate in this study and that so many teachers found it a rewarding experience.

Herman R. Goldberg
Superintendent of Schools
Rochester, New York

Scholastic book clubs have proven to our teachers that the paperback book, well chosen for reading and interest level, is a strong factor in motivating children to read. Children delight in choosing their own titles and acquiring their own library collection.

The program is especially helpful to the reluctant reader. He, like his classmates, can choose an appealing title from the variety of levels within each club. Wise teachers use the reading experience in a variety of classroom techniques, and books provided by the club as the basis of many classroom lessons.

Scholastic Book Services can be very proud of its accomplishments, particularly in making it possible for all children, of every educational or economic level, to secure good books and to acquire the habit of good reading.

Sister Mary Arthur, I.H.M.
Director, School Libraries
Archdiocese of Philadelphia

In the mid-1950's the mounting book club business brought on a growing pain which the company decided it could no longer bear. After several years of effort to get essential service from the Pocket Books warehouse in Buffalo—which, understandably, was giving Pocket Books' customers priority service over Scholastic's — Scholastic decided to explore alternatives. It would take time. Should the company rent again or build? If it decided to build, then it must decide what to build, find a site, sign on an architect and builder, and get the job done. The decision came quickly: Go! It took just 20 months from the beginning of the site search to the dedication of Scholastic's first building in 1959.

Vice President Donald Layman accepted the responsibility for heading the site search, its purchase, and the manifold building arrangements to follow, assisted by Richard Holahan on leave from his responsibilities as manufacturing manager. They inspected a score of sites east of the Mississippi and settled on 12 acres at Englewood Cliffs, NJ, 13 miles from Scholastic's West 44th Street office in New York and four miles north of the New Jersey end of the George Washington Bridge. The price was $12,500 per acre with a one-year option to buy an adjoining 15-acre site at $15,000 per acre. The option was taken up well before the deadline, and plans were made for construction of a 40,000-square-foot office building on two floors with an adjoining warehouse.

The company had hoped to be able to get financing to build both the warehouse and the office building at the same time, but was turned down by Prudential Insurance Company. Scholastic then applied to John Hancock Insurance Company and got financing for the warehouse

At dedication of the first company-owned building — the warehouse/shipping center, Englewood Cliffs, NJ, 1969. Center: M. R. Robinson and Agnes Laurino. John Spaulding, holding hat. Front right: Paul King, backed by Herb McCracken and Jimmy Caraberis (profile). Front left: Robert Holden, Richard Holahan (handkerchief), Thora Larsen (white bow). Tony Lanza, left behind Holahan. Carmine Montaperto, back row, third from left (necktie).

195

and the 15-acre site, but not for the office building. Since financing was a problem, the decision was made to build the facilities in two stages—the warehouse first (started in 1958) and the office building when practicable. The 15-acre site was chosen, as it would be less costly to prepare for construction than the 12-acre site. (The 12 acres were left to the woods, as they remain as of 1978.) The 15 acres cost $225,000; the warehouse (72,398 square feet) cost $1,105,345.*

Eighteen months later Prudential, with second thoughts about another construction loan going out of its home state, approved a loan for the office building despite its being on land on which Hancock held the mortgage. The office building (53,289 square feet, including a 12,739-square-foot basement), opened in October 1962, cost $1,848,247.† The architect for both buildings was

*A 27,146-square-foot addition to the Englewood Cliffs warehouse was built in 1967 at a cost of $433,464.

†A 22,086-square-foot addition to the Englewood Cliffs office building was built in 1966 at a cost of $1,011,415.

Skidmore, Owings & Merrill and the contractor, Turner Construction Company.

With the Englewood Cliffs warehouse under construction and scheduled for completion in September 1959, Scholastic was faced with the decision on how to operate it efficiently. For advice on this, Robinson went to see the president of Reuben H. Donnelley Corporation, who expressed interest in making a study of what was then almost entirely a book club "pick and pack" operation. Len Schirmer, representing Donnelley, was assigned to make the study. He began with the Scholastic operation at the Buffalo Pocket Books warehouse. Upon approval of his cost estimates, Scholastic and Donnelley entered into an agreement for the latter to operate the new facility, with Schirmer in charge.

Because the company depended almost entirely upon the United States Post Office for distributing its products within the United States, it seemed advisable early in the sixties to decentralize the shipping operation for books and other nonperiodical products so that major regions of the nation could be served as rapidly as possible. Studies of postal facilities and transportation time were made and buildings and sites for possible construction were examined on the West Coast and in the Midwest. It was decided to build first on the West Coast, as the Far Western states were most distant from the Englewood Cliffs warehouse.

The site search was conducted by Layman, John Spaulding, and Holahan. They recommended an 11½-acre site in the town of Pleasanton, CA, 34 miles southeast of San Francisco; the price was $98,734. The area was checked out by Gordon Studebaker, western regional director, and construction of a warehouse and a 12,500-square-foot connecting office building was begun in 1963. It was completed in 1964 at a cost of $744,920.* James Palmer was the architect; Associated Contractors, the builder. Perry Lusby, who had been gaining experience in the management of order fulfillment and the operation of a distribution center at the Englewood Cliffs facility, was put in charge at Pleasanton.

As the nonclub business (texts, audiovisual, and trade books) expanded at a rapid rate, it became obvious that the Englewood Cliffs and Pleasanton centers alone were not enough to provide the best available service to schools throughout the nation. After a search of locations in the Middle West conducted by Clinton Smith, Scholastic's controller, and Edward Louden, manager of Book Distribution, it was decided to purchase a 33-acre site on the outskirts of Jefferson City, MO, at a cost of $40,667. In 1968 a warehouse and shipping center connected to an office building was completed for $1,667,094† and Louden put in charge.‡ The Jefferson City facility would

*An expansion of the Pleasanton warehouse in 1972, costing $300,210, brought the total warehouse square footage to 70,000.

†25,000-square-feet for the office; 140,000 for the warehouse, including an addition built in 1970. Jim Hill designed the building without having visited the site, and Associated Contractors put it up.

‡Louden and Lusby are former Air Force colonels. Scholastic's executive vice president, Donald E. Layman, became acquainted with Louden through calls on him in connection with Air Force advertising in the high school magazines. After Louden joined Scholastic in 1963, he introduced Lusby to Layman and other Scholastic officers, and Lusby was employed to manage the Pleasanton facility, then nearing completion.

handle a share of the book club business and all of the nonclub business.

In 1970 the contract with Donnelley for the Englewood Cliffs operation was terminated and Schirmer joined the Scholastic staff as national manager of the three distribution centers in the United States.

As the inventory and product lines continued to grow, the problem of expediting bookkeeping, inventory, and order processing had to be resolved. The numbers were becoming too great to be handled manually, and computerized operations were introduced. Arthur Young & Company, Scholastic's auditor, headed the task force to develop this phase of operations. Club orders continued to be processed manually at the three centers, but the inventory system for all was centralized at Englewood Cliffs. The order processing system for all of the rapidly growing nonclub business was also computerized and centralized at Englewood Cliffs, with orders being sent to Jefferson City for fulfillment.

In 1978 new advances in data processing allowed the installation of a minicomputer system in Jefferson City to

The burgeoning book business brought forth offices and distribution centers in the U.S. (Englewood Cliffs, NJ; Pleasanton, CA; Jefferson City, MO [left]) and Canada (Richmond Hill, Ontario), New Zealand (Auckland), England (Southam), Australia (Gosford, shown in Chapter XVII, "Going International").

Confronting the computer at IBM headquarters, New York, 1962. Scholastic executives at demonstration of printing unit of 1401 computer, soon to be installed in Englewood Cliffs office building. Left to right: IBM demonstrator, John Spaulding, M. R. Robinson, Clinton Smith, Agnes Laurino, Donald Layman, Richard Holahan, Andrew Eastwick.

eliminate the need for photocopying and mailing club orders to Englewood Cliffs. Now data keyed at Jefferson City directly from the original order are electronically transmitted to Englewood Cliffs, with the customer files updated within a few hours of order-processing time.

The pioneer in a given field of endeavor, if successful in the marketplace, usually does not have the field all to himself for long. Early in the flowering of its elementary paperback books, Scholastic learned that it had produced a competitor from within its ranks. The promotion manager of the Scholastic book clubs, Joseph Archie, had become so impressed with the prospect for success in this new enterprise that he resigned to form his own company, which launched three paperback clubs—Willie Whale, King Cole, and Falcon.

The scramble for a piece of this new market revealed the free-enterprise system at its catch-as-catch-can best. Archie sold his clubs to Ace Publishing Corporation; Ace sold them to Pocket Books, which operated them under the name Young Readers Press (which was eventually discontinued). Archie started a new club—Alley Cat Book Club—and sold it to *Reader's Digest*, to be renamed Firefly. It was purchased by Scholastic in January 1979.

The veteran Grolier Society entered the field for about a year (1966) with the Peter Possum Book Club for the primary grades and the Gold Mine Book Club for the middle grades. These clubs offered full-color paperback editions of children's classics and other titles in the public domain, but the venture failed and the large inventory was sold some years later to the publisher Franklin Watts.

American Education Press, at the time an arm of Wesleyan University,* entered the paperback promised land after many years of operating children's book clubs offering only hardbound books. (Its clubs were named Buddy, Good Time, Discovering Books, Read, and Senior Paperback Books.)

In Rahway, NJ, the Educational Reading Service launched the Troll Book Club for the primary grades, profiting from the counsel of a former Scholastic See-Saw Book Club employee, Nikki Fried. As of early 1978 Educational Reading Service had plans to launch another club at the next-highest level where Scholastic's Arrow Club has been functioning since 1957.

Scholastic announced its first hardbound book club in 1977, Children's Choice Book Club. Books are mailed directly to the child's home on orders bearing a parent's signature.

A strong inducement to an author, especially an established author, is the prospect of getting a contract for

*Later to become Xerox Education Publications (Chapter XIII, "Tax-Free Competitor").

Vice Presidents (left to right) Andrew Bingham, publisher, Text Division; Carol Rafferty, corporate director, Personnel; Morris Goldberger, publisher, General Book Publishing.

royalties on both hardbound and paperback editions. On the initiative of John Spaulding and Morris Goldberger, the company organized a hardbound book publishing unit, naming it Four Winds Press (1965).* With 11 titles published during its first year, Four Winds increased its list annually and by 1977 had 325 titles.

Four Winds Press became the nucleus of a new division of the company—the Library and Trade Division, under the direction of Morris Goldberger—for sales of the company's large stock of books to libraries and through wholesalers to bookstores, department stores, supermarkets, and through Sears catalog sales. The division launched its own list of Starline paperbacks and assumed responsibility for marketing Scholastic/Folkways Records in an arrangement with its founder and owner, Moses Asch.† Another unit, Citation Press (originally called

*There was a strong movement among company executives to name the new publishing unit "The Robinson Press," but when M. R. Robinson heard of it, he came down hard for something else. As he explained, "I knew I would not be guiding its philosophy or its selections and wanted none of someone else's opinions to perpetuate my name."

†In 1965 Donald Layman and William Boutwell negotiated a sales agency contract with Folkways Records for exclusive worldwide representation of the approximately 1,400 titles in its collection. The list was rich in authentic folk music, historical lore, and sounds of nature. In 1970 Scholastic withdrew from the marketing arrangements with Asch and would soon organize the Audiovisual and New Media Department with Russell D'Anna as director. The department issues a 43-page catalog of filmstrips, audio cassettes, and records for marketing by the Text Division. Included in the catalog are American Landmark Enrichment Records, acquired by Scholastic in 1970 from the founder and principal owner, Martha Huddleston, first director of the Teen Age Book Club. Enrichment Records present dramatizations of literary works and episodes from American history.

268

Educators' Service when organized by William Boutwell in 1965), specialized in the publication of paperbacks for the education profession. Citation Press became a unit of the Library and Trade Division in 1970.

The Library and Trade Division became the General Book Publishing Division in the reorganization of 1975, with Goldberger as division publisher, Judith Whipple as publisher of Four Winds Press, and Nathan Garner as division marketing director.

The "one thing leads to another" aphorism applies to a number of phases of Scholastic growth, but to none better than to its book club business, starting with the club-car meeting between Martha Huddleston and M. R. Robinson en route from New York to a teacher's meeting in San Francisco in 1946. That led to Scholastic's acquisition of the Teen Age Book Club, which led to *Readers' Choice Catalog* and four more clubs—Arrow, Campus, Lucky, and See-Saw—which became the source of books for such collections and programs as Reluctant Reader Libraries, Individualized Reading, and many others.

Even before a second book club was launched (Arrow, in 1957) there was an urgent need for Scholastic to get some titles of its own. Until 1952, when the Teen Age Book Club issued its first original (*Boy Dates Girl* by Gay Head, pen name of Margaret Hauser), the Scholastic listings included only the books of other publishers. If the club did not have a sufficient supply of a given title in stock to meet club needs, it would go back to press for the required number (usually 15,000 or more), sometimes with a new cover design in instances where the original cover might be considered in poor taste for school distribution. With the growth of the clubs came increased press runs, reaching the point where it became profitable, on a run of 35,000 or more, for Scholastic to sign up authors and make its own arrangements with printers. The search was now on for authors, with new ones easier to come by than the well-known, who already had their publishing connections.

Perhaps every publishing house has its tale of the author, rejected elsewhere, who has his or her manuscript accepted to become a best-seller. Here is Scholastic's favorite:

During the summer of 1962 Norman Bridwell was calling on New York publishers, trying to sell his art for children's book illustrations without success. At Harper & Row, Susan Hirshman told him that they could not use his art and suggested that he write a book for children. He went home over that weekend, made up a story, "Clifford, the Big Red Dog," illustrated it, and took it to another New York house — Grosset & Dunlap. The next thing he heard came two weeks later — a call from Beatrice deRegniers, editor of Scholastic's Lucky Book Club, saying she was interested in "Clifford."

How did that happen? Lilian Moore, editor of Scholastic's Arrow Book Club, had been serving as a consultant to Grosset & Dunlap on their "Easy Readers" and kept in touch with Doris Duenewald, Grosset's editor of children's books. She knew of Lilian Moore's interest in original manuscripts for the Scholastic clubs — especially for Arrow and the new Lucky club. Duenewald sent the Bridwell manuscript to Moore with a note saying that Grosset couldn't use it. Moore and deRegniers both liked it at once and put in a call to Duenewald to confirm release of the manuscript. That done, deRegniers telephoned

M. R. Robinson attending story hour at Central Park Zoo, New York, to give the zoo 1,000 copies of the Scholastic Book *Gorilla Baby*, the story of Patty Cake, the baby gorilla in residence (1974).

270

Left to right: Lilian Moore (first editor of Arrow Book Club), Clinton Smith, Donald Layman, John Spaulding (1964).

Bridwell. "I was very surprised," said Bridwell. "I didn't even know Scholastic had a book division."

"It was the right book at the right time," recalled Moore, "and Beatrice with her special editorial genius went on to develop Norman Bridwell into a lucky star."

Clifford, the Big Red Dog had eight offspring — *Clifford Takes a Trip; Clifford Gets a Job; Clifford, the Small Red Puppy;* and five others — to become best-sellers for the Lucky Book Club and Scholastic Book Services. Three of the Clifford titles have appeared in hardbound editions through the Four Winds Press.

Scholastic's vast inventory of books, ever-changing with the influx of new titles, was the source of many of the books offered to the schools in special sets, or "libraries," *viz.*: Reluctant Reader Library, Lunchroom Reading Library, Teacher Edition Library, Professional Library. The books were also offered in sets arranged by themes such as mystery and suspense, science fiction, humor and satire, teens in trouble, values, death, black studies, women's studies, sports, crime, and so on.

A significant outgrowth of the paperback explosion at Scholastic — significant for both the schools and the child as well as for the company's sales — was the program called Individualized Reading from Scholastic (IRS), developed under the direction of Priscilla Lynch, former teacher and reading specialist. IRS utilized hundreds of books selected from the basic Scholastic list to give teachers and pupils from grades one through six a

271

choice of titles, activities, and measurements to improve reading skills. The heart of IRS's rationale was that children read best when primarily self-motivated. This indeed was the philosophy of the paperback book clubs. However, IRS selected titles and supplied activities that teachers and pupils could use to improve and measure their reading progress. Although it was not intended to replace the hardcover basal reading programs, IRS did add a dimension to reading instruction that thousands of teachers found new and exciting. Moreover, the price was low — approximately $100 per class unit in its early years — which further enhanced the appeal of the program to budget-conscious school systems.

It is impossible to calculate the total effect of Scholastic's entry into the paperback book business more than 30 years ago. There is no way to determine the number of young people who formed the constructive habit of reading at an early age because of the book clubs. What is known is that the teacher faced with a lack of interest in reading on the part of his or her students found a powerful ally in the quality children's books offered at low cost and sometimes exclusively through these channels. One positive answer to the problem of reading motivation among young people in the age of television was to offer them a choice of good books on subjects in which they were interested and at prices they could afford to pay. Paperback books did this, and in the process have made and are making an inestimable contribution to the total educational process.

Into Texts

TO the Literature Units and World Affairs Multi-Texts go the honors for Scholastic's serious entry into publishing books directly related to courses of study: books to be ordered with school board funds, just as textbooks are, in contrast to book club titles that students themselves choose and pay for. As noted in the preceding chapter, Scholastic started publishing books in 1926 with *Saplings*, a collection of verse, essays, and short stories from entries in the 1925 student-written issue. In the years prior to Scholastic's taking over direction of the Teen Age Book Club (1948), the company had published some 50 titles. Instructional they were, many assembled from articles that had appeared in Scholastic magazines. But they were not intended to serve as principal texts for a whole course of study.

As the decade of the sixties began, Scholastic headed into the two programs that would lead it into non-magazine instructional materials and render out-of-date, if not misleading, the corporate title Scholastic Magazines, Inc. Scholastic Literature Units (SLU) evolved out of an idea Stephen Dunning, a graduate student at Florida State University, and Dwight Burton, professor of English Education there, had for publishing a series of graded anthologies adapted to youth of varying reading abilities. One day in 1958, at Burton's suggestion, Dunning took the idea to a major all-purpose publishing house in New York. He was heard right up to the president, who, at the end of 15 minutes, said that he wasn't a bit interested in a program designed for deficient readers. Dunning then made a phone call to Scholastic and was connected with William Boutwell, whom he would be meeting for the first time at the Columbia University Club on West 43rd Street.

"Mr. Paperback," the title Boutwell had earned by his enthusiasm for the medium and his success with the Teen Age Book Club, saw in the Dunning material an opportunity for extending the use of paperbacks into the text field, and he proceeded to get the company's support in developing the Scholastic Literature Units. At their core were paperback anthologies graded for reading levels. There were to be 12 theme units (*Courage, Frontiers, Moments of Decision, Mirrors, Animals, Survival, Family* and five others) and later 10 genre units (*Poetry, Short Story, Personal Narrative, Drama, Satire,* and four others). A complete SLU Unit consisted of multiple copies of the core anthology, smaller multiples of different titles of the same theme or genre, a student workbook, and a teacher's manual. Burton dropped out of the project in its early years, and Dunning, who had become professor of English and Education at the University of Michigan, continued as supervising editor.

The idea for the World Affairs Multi-Text books also came from the outside, but not on the first bounce. Jay Davis Conner, chief of the Division of Instruction, California State Department of Instruction, and then a member of Scholastic's National Advisory Council, brought up the idea at the annual meeting of the council in 1958. His state's Curriculum Commission was interested in developing a series of paperbacks on world history to replace the monumental textbooks which, besides their girth, included nothing that happened later than the years in which their readers were born. John Studebaker and Kenneth Gould went to Sacramento to discuss the idea of a world history paperback series with the commission, and they were encouraged to prepare a prospectus for a series on the major world regions, with such titles as *The Subcontinent of India, The Two Chinas, Emerging Africa, The Rim of Asia, Latin America*, and six others. The plans were approved, and the books published over a period of four years. Kenneth Gould was general editor until his retirement in 1960, succeeded by Irving Talmadge.

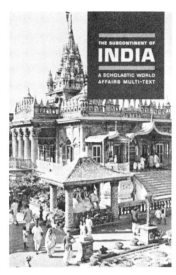

First of the Scholastic Multi-Text series, 1961.

Most of the books ran into four or more printings and were usually updated with each printing—a feature that appealed to schools pleased to have history books that brought the record up to within a year of publication date. Sales, begun in California, spread to schools throughout the country.

The Literature Units prevail into their twentieth year, with frequent improvements and rearrangements, overseen by Dunning. The World Affairs Multi-Texts were phased out after 12 years, to be followed by the company's at first gradual, then rapid, move into programs more closely related to traditional text materials.

Nothing said here is meant to imply that the basal textbook is or was disappearing from the schools. Many of the old-line textbook publishers supplemented their basal

275

textbook offerings with sets or series of paperback and other softbound books and with film and sound appendages. The "back-to-basics" movement of the early 1970's gave heart to those who believed that the textbook is the foundation of a sound instructional program. However, a new definition of the word *textbook* may be in order.

Many of Scholastic's innovative text materials are outgrowths of the magazines' content. Back in the 1920's, as noted above, soon after *Scholastic* had become a national magazine, features of the magazine were reprinted in book form and offered as supplementary text material. This sideline was continued through the decades without claim that the reprints were anything but supplementary to textbooks. The first major spinoff from magazine material into text programs came from *Scope*, starting in the late 1960's: Scope Skills Books, Scope Visuals, Scope Playbooks, Scope Activity Kits, American Adventures, and later Action and Sprint materials. These set the stage for adapting the content of other magazines into text and reading development programs for pupils at all grade levels and reading abilities. In the case of Action and Sprint, magazines of the same titles were created after the success of the text programs.

The need for greater product diversification with nonmagazine instructional materials was becoming increasingly apparent to the company's management. In their 1968 annual report Chairman Robinson and President Layman wrote:

> Although income from books and magazines represents the cornerstone of the Company's sales structure, it is obvious to your management that future progress also depends heavily upon

the Company's ability to produce new units of instruction in the sphere of multimedia, utilizing not only the solidly established periodicals and paperback book clubs, but additional products in the audiovisual field in combination with our print materials. It is also our intention to press forward with the development of basic text materials and our hardcover book department, Four Winds Press.

During the next decade good intentions materialized in a flow of new text products as reorganization of the company and reassignment of personnel had the desired effect of setting new production goals and accountability for quality and profitability of the product. Richard Robinson, elected president in 1974 and chief executive officer in 1975, was especially astute at assessing aptitude and ability in recruiting personnel to augment the limited staff that had been assigned to text products. A new expanded Text Division was established in 1977 and put under the general direction of Vice President and Publisher Andrew Bingham. His domain encompassed editorial, art, production, mail promotion, and field operations. Chapter XX, "Here Come the Divisions," outlines the new organization structure for the Text Division and its counterpart for magazines, the Educational Periodicals Division.

The Text Division moved apace with an excellent backlist and other programs in the developmental stage inherited from its predecessor divisions. Some of these programs combine filmstrips and audio material with print—produced by the Audiovisual and New Media Department headed by Russell D'Anna—and are offered in packages that include teaching guides. The entire list

Vice President Russell D'Anna (Audiovisual and New Media) and Concetta Lamberti Moran (General Books) clink glasses at the annual dinner for employees with five years' or more service (Tammy Brook Country Club, Cresskill, NJ, 1978).

requires a 96-page catalog, *Scholastic Instructional Materials Catalog, K–12,* ranging over nearly all the curriculum areas: language arts, reading, arts and humanities, social studies, science, careers/guidance, and athletics, with the greatest emphasis placed on language arts, reading, and the social studies. In the social studies area, Scholastic published in 1977 its first hardcover text, *American Citizenship.*

A Loyalty Oath by Any Other Name

Upon being elected president of the American Textbook Publishers Institute at its annual meeting in 1962, M. R. Robinson mounted the podium and opened his acceptance speech with these words: "I am not now, and never have been, a textbook publisher. Nor do I intend to become one."

How the magazine house of Scholastic had in 1946 become a member of the American Textbook Publishers Institute is explained in Chapter XXIX, under "Publishers of the Land, Unite!" The election of Robinson as the Institute's president in 1962 was a reflection of the personal esteem in which he was held by the membership. At the time he made his acceptance speech Scholastic had already moved into paperback books but had published nothing that resembled a basic text. As noted in preceding chapters, Scholastic from its earliest days as a curriculum-oriented magazine had been providing the schools with material not obtainable from the textbook publishers — filling in the gaps, so to speak. By the mid-1970's, in response to the "back-to-basics" movement, Scholastic's output would be such that M. R. Robinson could not have taken the "loyalty oath" quoted above.

CHAPTER XVII

Going International

One Thing Leads to Another

SCHOLASTIC'S first products to cross an international boundary on bulk orders from schools were the magazines, starting with *Scholastic* and *Junior Scholastic* in the 1930's. Despite the handicap of the United States orientation of the editorial content of these magazines, several hundred Canadian schools found them sufficiently useful to order classroom quantities. There was neither a Scholastic office nor a salesperson in Canada to promote subscriptions. It was strictly a mail-order operation from New York, garnering several thousand new subscriptions each year as *World Week, Practical English,* and *Literary Cavalcade* started up. In the 1950's the total subscriptions there never exceeded 50,000.

It remained for books to give nourishment to the Canadian side of the business. A Canadian named John Irwin, who operated the Book Society of Canada, Limited, made annual visits to publishers in New York during the early 1950's to buy books for his small book club, and he included William D. Boutwell, director of the Teen Age Book Club, in his rounds. Their talks led to Scholastic's granting a franchise in 1955 to the Book Society for developing TAB clubs in Canada.

After two years of little progress, the Book Society relinquished the franchise and gave Scholastic its list of member schools, representing about 400 clubs. Scholastic then obtained a Dominion Charter for a wholly owned subsidiary, Scholastic-TAB Publications, Ltd., and arranged with the McCall Corporation for clerical and shipping services in their pattern division warehouse in Toronto (Allan Mahaffy, manager). TAB would soon be joined by Arrow, Campus, Lucky, and See-Saw book clubs as they started up in the States.

Within two years the book club business had outgrown its allotted space at McCall's and had to operate at several other rented warehouses. During part of one year three different warehouses were being used. Such diffuse and inefficient operations were making life difficult for the two executives on the scene—Mahaffy, who had left McCall's in 1960 to become business manager, and William C. McMaster, who joined the company in 1961 as managing director with special responsibility for editorial, promotion, and professional relations.

McMaster had been assistant superintendent of Curriculum and Textbooks in the Ontario Department of Education. He had served as head of the English department of a college and a collegiate institute, managing editor of a publishing house, wrote a column, "Know Your Language," for the *Toronto Telegram*, had written an English textbook, and had been co-author of two others. With his many contacts among educators and his knowledge of Canadian schools, McMaster moved with professional finesse in letting them know of the Scholastic approach to getting young people excited about books.

One of McMaster's early moves to add Canadian spice to the repertory of material imported from the United States was to launch a magazine for the upper elementary grades patterned after *Scholastic NewsTime*. Under the title *Canadian NewsTime* it was published weekly for three years, but did not reach more than 40,000 in circulation—about one half of what it needed to break even—and was suspended. But book club memberships of Scholastic-TAB Publications, Ltd., soared throughout the provinces, taxing the capacity of the rented warehouses in Richmond Hill, a suburb of Toronto. McMaster and Mahaffy started a search for land on which to build a warehouse and offices. Eleven-and-a-half acres along Newkirk Road, Richmond Hill, were purchased, and the facility was built in time to serve the schools for the 1968–69 school year. The land cost $47,981; the building, $338,419. In 1974 an addition to the warehouse was built at a cost of $214,535, to make the total area of the warehouse and offices 52,000 square feet.

The current Canadian catalog lists nearly a thousand titles of books and text materials suitable for the programs of Canadian schools. Revenue for 1975 was $3,762,785, an increase of 96.6 percent over 1970, yielding a healthy profit.

The 200,000 copies of each issue of the various Scholastic magazines sold to Canadian schools in the largely English-speaking provinces are not handled in Richmond Hill. They are trucked from U.S. printing points into the post office at Windsor, Ontario, and from there distributed to the schools. Included in the 200,000 are about 40,000 of the Mary Glasgow foreign-language magazines and the Mary Glasgow English-language *BOUM*, a monthly for the primary grades that the Canadian company gets directly from London.

Most Scholastic materials are popular in Canadian schools where English is used as the language of instruction. Where French is the language of instruction, as in the province of Quebec, Scope, Contact, and Action materials are used in many of the schools that teach English as a second language. The province of Quebec, which has 27.8 percent of the total population of Canada, accounts for 8 percent of Scholastic's Canadian book clubs, slightly better than 8 percent of text sales, and slightly less than 8 percent of magazine subscriptions. Schools in Quebec province must place orders for instructional materials with government-accredited bookstores if they are using school board funds for such purchases. It is, therefore, necessary to have a bilingual person call on schools and bookstores.

A Redcoat Comes   The success of the Canadian company in establishing paperback book clubs in schools put Scholastic's management in a receptive frame of mind when the opportunity came to consider paperback book clubs for the schools of Great Britain. Would they respond to the book club idea in sufficient numbers to make it a viable undertaking? There was no doubt about the British children's appetite for reading in that land of bookshops and literary ascendancy. But getting Britain's tradition-bound schools, be they public or government, to be the vehicle for the sale to students of a publisher's "reading for pleasure" products would require very special diplomacy, soft salesmanship, and patience.

An unexpected chance to take a few first steps in this direction came with a visit to Scholastic in early 1961 by A. Eric Baker of the periodical publishing house Mary Glasgow & Baker, Ltd. (MG&B). Baker's purpose in visiting Scholastic was not to propose book clubs for Britain, but to sign up Scholastic as the American distributor of the MG&B foreign-language magazines, monthlies in French, Spanish, and German that MG&B sold to schools throughout the world where these languages were taught as a second language. The papers were graded—beginners, intermediates, and advanced—without using English at all, and were intended to convey a picture of France, Germany, or Spain. One Russian paper was added for a few years after the ascent of Sputnik.

Baker arranged to visit Scholastic at the suggestion of Mrs. Grace Hogarth, an editor with Constable & Company, Ltd. An American and a Vassar graduate, she had worked for Houghton Mifflin in Boston before her marriage to a Britisher. There was no connection between Constable and Glasgow & Baker beyond a long-standing friendship MG&B had with Hogarth.

It was early in his first talks with Robinson and John Spaulding that Baker learned that Scholastic was as much interested in having MG&B as a partner in getting book clubs launched in Britain as he was in getting Scholastic to sell and distribute foreign-language papers in the United States and Canada. (Arrangements were soon made for Baker to visit with McMaster, head of

Scholastic-TAB Publications, Ltd., Ontario.)

Before returning to London early in January 1961, Baker—from his room at the Lexington Hotel—sent a long memorandum summarizing his thoughts to Robinson, quoted below in part:

> Your book club activities not only represent a most remarkable achievement on your part but also a fine contribution to education.
>
> Conditions in Great Britain differ considerably from here. The structure and organization of the book trade make the chances of success along this line far less promising.
>
> The Net Book Agreement to which all publishers and booksellers subscribe makes it almost impossible to sell a net book at less than published price, or to give away free copies, or to supply books carriage paid. These are all difficulties that would have to be examined carefully.
>
> Discounts on books are lower in Britain. Normally a bookseller is only allowed 33⅓% and only under very exceptional circumstances could one hope to get 50% except by large quantity buying with an offer of cash against invoice. To expect as much as 60% would be quite unrealistic at present.
>
> Having said all that my conviction is that there is a need for a book service to schools similar to the one you are offering and that the autumn of 1961 would be a good moment to carry out some conclusive tests.
>
> Before this could be done my firm would have to set up a recognized bookshop for boys and girls in order to get the necessary trade recognition from the publishers in Britain. Our intention would be to place this on the ground floor of our existing premises in Kensington Church Street which is ideally located for the purpose.
>
> Having done that by, say, August 1st we

would be in a position to bargain with the paperback publishers individually for higher discounts for bulk purchase.

The right age-level to appeal to is the 12–15 corresponding to your Grades 7–10. These are to be found in our Secondary Grammar, Secondary Modern and Technical Schools which number some 7,000 in all.

On the matter of sales and distribution of the MG&B foreign-language periodicals in the United States, Baker referred to the 10,000 subscriptions they already had in private schools through mail promotion prepared in London and said that "this could be developed further" with Scholastic's participation. This overture led to an agreement that Scholastic-TAB Publications, Ltd., in Canada would promote sales and distribute the foreign-language periodicals in both Canada and the United States. By 1964 the New York office would take over the U.S. side of this and contract for the printing of all copies needed for Canadian and American schools. The printing is done in Dayton, OH, from press plates produced from film supplied by Mary Glasgow in London.*

Before a preliminary agreement could be reached on a book club venture into British schools, many cables, letters, and telephone calls would warm the wires and airwaves between London and New York. Robinson even brought his good friend and fellow Scholastic director,

---

*The nine Mary Glasgow foreign-language papers distributed by Scholastic in the United States, Canada, Australia, and New Zealand are: In French—*Bonjour, Ça va,* and *Chez nous*; in Spanish—*¿Qué tal?, El sol,* and *Hoy día*; in German—*Das Rad, Schuss,* and *Der Roller.* There are nine monthly issues during the school year.

Henry A. Laughlin,* into the act, telephoning him at his castle in Ireland to ask if he would go to London to "case the place" at 140–142 Kensington Church Street, the office of MG&B, Ltd. Laughlin was pleased to do so, and from his hotel in London on April 25, 1961, sent Robinson a long, handwritten letter:

> I carried out your instructions this morning and saw at their offices Eric Baker, Mary Glasgow, and Grace Hogarth. . . . It is not a fashionable shopping or commercial district, but very accessible just at the end of Bayswater Road, Hyde Park, and Kensington Palace Gardens—not more than 15 minutes from Bond Street, Claridge's, the Connaught, and the American Embassy by taxi. The immediate neighborhood has a large number of unpretentious antique shops with fairly good examples in the windows. It is within a block or so of a fairly high grade shopping center and the Underground.
>
> The building they have is being remodeled extensively, with three floors and a basement—more room than they actually need. Very light and airy. Their ground floor covers the bookshop in front with windows on the front from wall to wall, with a corridor running the length of the building. The rear half, largely lighted artificially, but not wholly, will contain storage of books, assembling of orders, and shipping. The chief drawback lies in the fact that all shipments must be taken out the single corridor, through the bookshop to the front door. There is no rear or side entrance outside although there is a side entrance to the office

Mary Glasgow and M. R. Robinson (about 1965).

*Henry A. Laughlin was president of Houghton Mifflin Company from 1939 to 1957 and had, along with William E. Spaulding, represented Houghton Mifflin in negotiations for the proposed acquisition of Scholastic in 1955–56 (Chapter XII, "Merger Talks and a Near Miss").

upstairs. The present storage, shipping and book-shop is entirely unfinished awaiting decision as to our association.

I talked first with Mr. Baker, then with Miss Glasgow and Mrs. Hogarth. I found all three eager to give me all the information I asked for and desirous of letting me see something of their hopes and problems.

They discussed points raised by your letters and the recent letter of John Spaulding, all of which Baker has answered I believe, but which they wanted to elaborate on in order that I might fully understand their point of view.

I shall attempt to bring up their chief aims, so far as I was concerned, that is, what they wanted to convince me of and have me present favorably to you . . .

A decision must be reached almost im-mediately if they are to proceed with our joint operation in the year 1961–1962—their year being the same as ours. If they are to go ahead they must finish the equipment of the bookshop and shipping and warehouse rooms, including offices for editors and the bookshop manager. They must employ a bookshop manager and cer-tain others and have all this in order by the first of August, otherwise they believe they must wait a full year and start in August, 1962. They have had a number of applications for bookstore manager and would like definitely to hire one of the appli-cants now at a salary of about £1200 a year.

It is vital that we understand that the bookstore is a major factor in their undertaking. It is not a "front" to enable them to secure the coop-eration of the book publishers, but in some ways is the very heart of the enterprise. They expect in the end to make money on it as a bookstore, but beyond that it is to be an educational center where teachers and all persons interested in "second-ary" education can congregate and look at the books in the field published by all publishers. It is to have—probably in the basement—a "Young Books Club" room where boys and girls—members—can meet when in London. This bookshop is not only vital to promotion of the club but to secure the wholehearted interest of all the publishers, particularly "Penguin" and the other paperbacks, and also all the other bookshops who might be antagonistic if this were not *in fact* a bookshop.

Laughlin commented on the problem of the differences in spelling and terminology between the English and American languages (since books from the Scholastic supply in the U.S. would be offered to the British schools), financing the new company, and characteristics of the modern British primary and secondary school systems. He concluded, saying:

> If, as I hope, you decide to go ahead with this project—which I advocate your doing—I recommend your doing it before I return or at least as soon as you can. . . . I am impressed by all I saw of Miss Glasgow and Baker and think in Mrs. Hogarth they have an able and interested associate.

A new corporation, Mary Glasgow & Baker (Books), Ltd., was formed to operate the bookshop and the school book clubs. The new corporation did not replace Mary Glasgow & Baker, Ltd., which held the majority (55 percent) of voting stock in the new corporation. (Scholastic Magazines, Inc., held 40 percent; Grace Hogarth, 5 percent.) Scholastic also held 75 percent of the preferred stock, and thus would have the right to vote this stock if dividends were not paid at the end of two years. They weren't, so by August of 1963 Scholastic could have taken absolute control of MG&B (Books) if it had wished to exercise its vote. Scholastic did not so wish, as both Glasgow and Baker were willing to go along with whatever arrangements Scholastic considered necessary. These included sale of the bookshop to MG&B;* acquisition of 55 percent more of the voting stock in MG&B (Books), giving Scholastic 95 percent; taking over from MG&B (Books) full control of editorial and order processing ("the works"); and acquisition of office and warehouse space.

The reason for this takeover was MG&B's need for additional capital for expansion of the business in foreign-language education. The company wished to add some new periodicals, recordings, workbooks, build a warehouse, and produce magazines in English for children. Its resources were strained just to raise capital for this purpose, and as MG&B (Books) also needed new capital, MG&B could not do both. So MG&B went its own way and Scholastic got undisputed control of MG&B (Books).

The flip-flop in ownership and change in corporate identity were done in a spirit of this-is-a-good-thing-for-all-concerned; and so it developed. The bookshop is still at 140 Kensington Church Street, Eric Baker, proprietor.

---

* How could Scholastic get along without a bookshop, since it had been considered essential in Great Britain for a publishing house to have a bookshop in order to sell to schools? Effective April 1, 1963, the British Publishers Association instituted a number of changes in the regulations governing the operation of book clubs, and as a result the bookshop became less important in sales to schools. The MG&B (Books) bookshop, called Young Books, operated at a loss of £5,258 in its first year and £5,576 in its second; it was budgeted for a total loss of £6,317 for the two years. Sales of MG&B (Books), Ltd., went from £9,909 the first year to £23,578 the second; and of this, £16,260 was from book club operations and £7,318 from the bookshop.

However, he sold his entire interest in Mary Glasgow & Baker, Ltd., to Mary Glasgow, who then formed Mary Glasgow (Holdings), Ltd.

Having obtained full control of MG&B (Books), Scholastic formed a new company—Scholastic Publications, Ltd., and employed Simon Boosey, who had been the American representative of the music publishing house of Boosey & Hawkes, as managing director.

In February 1964 Scholastic Publications, Ltd., (SPL) set up shop in a cluster of small rooms at 64 Bury Walk in Chelsea under a five-year lease. The rooms were over what were, in Victorian times, stables. Here Simon Boosey was joined first by Richard Henwood, then within the next two years by Douglas Brown, Angela Evans, Bryan Rushen, and Carolyn Lloyd.

To venture into the British paperback market Scholastic not only had to convince teachers that there was a need for their students to buy paperback books but that the teachers should actively participate in the enterprise with an American publishing company. Even more challenging was the fact that the British paperback market was the stronghold of Penguin Books, operating on its own turf.

SPL was fortunate during those early days in receiving help from Alec Hay, a member of the board of directors who was also chief inspector of the London schools. Hay made a personal approach to many schools, pointing out the value of having children own their books and introducing them to the services Scholastic had to offer. One of the teachers he wrote to, Arthur Razzell, was eventually to replace Hay on the board of directors.

There was an evangelical zeal in spreading the Scholastic message. At frequent Saturday meetings a team of experienced teachers met at Bury Walk to argue over the respective merits of books to be included in the Scholastic club offerings. They were determined that each list should contain the best selection of books.

At the end of the five-year lease SPL had outgrown Bury Walk and made arrangements to acquire larger, more modern quarters around the corner at 161 Fulham Road. There the SPL team was joined by Mary Bingley, formerly editor of *Child Education*, who led the editorial team until 1977.

On the warehouse side, SPL was fortunate in the continued cooperation of Mary Glasgow & Baker at its facilities in Kineton, Warwickshire, 100 miles north of London at the geographical center of England. By 1972, after a period of hectic growth, SPL was in a position to build its own office and warehouse on two-and-a-half acres in nearby Southam, purchased for $141,204. The 50,000-square-foot facility (5,000 for the office part) cost $634,230 to build and was opened with due ceremony in October 1974.

On the marketing side, in 1964 SPL inherited a nebulous club in the secondary field with the unfortunate name of Paperbacks Unlimited. It was christened "Scoop" (abbreviated from School Paperbacks), and Boosey ordered a general mailing of bound kits, after the American system. It worked, and SPL started to introduce some of the more dynamic American products.

In 1965 SPL ventured into the much-larger British primary market with Chip Club (abbreviated from Children's Paperbacks) and Lucky Club. SPL pioneered books with larger formats and lower reading levels. See-Saw Club, also introduced at that time, did not start to show viable results until 10 years later.

In 1967, when SPL attempted to negotiate a higher discount on books bought from Penguin, the Penguin management decreased the discount instead, causing a year or so of strained relations and no transactions between Britain's largest paperback house and the tyro SPL. However, the significance of the continued growth of the SPL book clubs was not lost on Penguin's management, and soon the two houses were back in communication, working out terms that have proved beneficial to both.

Not until 1970, after almost seven difficult years of deficit budgeting, was SPL nudged into a profitable trading position. At this point John Spaulding felt that he could safely move away from direct involvement in the operation of SPL, so he assigned Ernest Schwehr to be its offshore commander in his capacity as director of Scholastic International Services.

Two years later Simon Boosey resigned. A difference of opinion had developed between him and Schwehr over the balance to be maintained between books originating in the United States and those having their origin in the United Kingdom, with Boosey unwilling to promote a program that was heavily composed of U.S. books. In 1972 he was succeeded by J. Brian Warde, who had teaching and administrative experience and, later, publishing experience in the field of scientific books. Warde introduced several new programs for Scholastic, including Topic Library Sets and Cassette-Book Sets, in the continuing progress of the clubs. After four years as managing director, Warde resigned because of ill health and was succeeded in 1976 by David Kidd, who had been a marketing director of several British publishing houses including Pan; Hodder and Stoughton; and Batsford.

SPL's success brought its inevitable imitators in the book club field. With a national wage freeze and a declining economy there was a slowing down in the speed of SPL's growth in 1975–77. Nevertheless, a large market remains to be tapped.

Before leaving the London scene, this record should show that Scholastic and Mary Glasgow have continued their friendly and beneficial relationship through the sale of her foreign-language periodicals in the U.S., Canada, Australia, and New Zealand, and the film series, *Toute la bande*. This film series was the upshot of Mary Glasgow's desire to expand her repertory of material for the teaching of foreign languages. In 1968 she proposed that Scholastic underwrite a series of 32 color/sound films of 15 minutes each, along with textual materials, that would constitute a complete course of study for first-year French students. This was called the "Et voilà" series. Scholastic agreed to finance, to the tune of £6,000 ($14,400 at the time), a pilot series of four films to be shown to groups of foreign-language specialists and French teachers in the U.S. This was done in October and November of 1968. The outcome was a decision to go no further with this approach, as it would not be accepted by the schools as a complete course. With the encouragement of Scholastic's principal consultants, Elton Hocking of Purdue University and Robert Nelson of the University of Pennsylvania, Scholastic proposed a shorter series that would supplement existing French courses rather than replace them. Approved by the

Scholastic board in March 1969, the *Toute la bande* series of 13 episodes of 14 minutes each was produced, with Mary Glasgow in charge of every step.

Scholastic at one time owned 10 percent of the voting stock of Mary Glasgow (Holdings), and M.R. Robinson owned 22½ percent. Robinson and Spaulding had on numerous occasions discussed a merger with Mary Glasgow but, with each passing year after she reached 65, she seemed more determined than ever to keep the company within the realm. She even had a lady's/gentleman's agreement with Robinson that he would not sell his shares to Scholastic without her permission, which was sought but not granted.

In 1973 Robinson and Spaulding gave up their quest to merge MG&B and Scholastic Publications, Ltd., and at her request agreed—with the approval of the Scholastic directors—to sell Scholastic's 10 percent of Mary Glasgow (Holdings) to Mary Glasgow, and Robinson agreed to sell his 22½ percent. She, in turn, sold this 32½ percent to Stanley Rosten, a British publisher she had brought into her newly named company, Mary Glasgow Publications, Ltd.

Another Continent   Scholastic began to view the entire English-speaking world as a marketplace for its paperbacks and for the introduction of school book clubs. It fell to John Spaulding, then vice president in charge of Foreign Sales and Development, to initiate the corporate action for expansion abroad. In 1964 he assigned a member of his staff, Ernest Schwehr, to embark on a world tour to call on publishers wherever English was either the national language or the second language. Schwehr, who was fluent in Spanish, Portuguese, French, and German, had lived in Argentina, Brazil, and England for 30 years before coming to the United States. A graduate of the London School of Economics, he had worked as a marketing specialist with DuPont affiliates in South America and as an account executive with an international ad agency in New York.

While in Auckland, New Zealand, on his tour for Scholastic, Schwehr met with Derek Price and Terry Hughes, founders and owners of the H. J. Ashton Co., Ltd., a firm that had established a good reputation among educators as agents for Scholastic; Scott, Foresman; and Graflex, Inc. Schwehr suggested that they try the book club approach to sales of the Scholastic paperbacks. It was doing well in the mother country and in Canada— why not New Zealand? A pilot project with a few schools was arranged, using the Scholastic club names—Lucky, Arrow, and Teen Age, followed by a full operation the next year (1965). To provide capital, H. J. Ashton was reorganized, with Scholastic holding 75 percent of the voting stock, Price and Hughes, 12½ percent each. (Incidentally, H. J. Ashton was an invented name, chosen by Price and Hughes because they liked the sound of it.)

In 1965 Schwehr was named director of Scholastic International Services, which by 1972 would become a separate corporation under the title SBS International, Inc., a New York corporation wholly owned by Scholastic. It was thus set up for a tax advantage on exporting books to Scholastic subsidiaries and to others purchasing Scholastic products abroad, such as the "dependent schools" for children of U.S. armed forces personnel and other schools attended by U.S. children living abroad.

The book project was well received in New Zealand, and it was logical that the Australian market should be considered. In 1968 an Australian company was formed as a replica of Ashton New Zealand under the management of Alan and Olive Izod, reporting to Terry Hughes. With a base in both Sydney and Auckland, Ashton was able to penetrate not only the Australian/New Zealand market but also many islands in the South Pacific, including Papua and New Guinea.

The bright prospects for development of the Australian market lured Terry Hughes and colleagues Myra Lee and Jim Reece from New Zealand in 1970 to join the Izods, with the aim of making Ashton a major force in educational publishing in Australia. A "major force" would require more than the minor space out of which this team operated in Sydney. A site of 26 acres was purchased some 35 miles north of Sydney at Somersby/Gosford, on the assumption that it would be rezoned for industry. Unfortunately, it was soon to be "frozen" as part of a possible second international airport, and Ashton had to look elsewhere while holding 26 dormant acres.* About four miles away, at Lisarow/Gosford, five acres were purchased for $55,864 and building commenced. The new facility of 31,500 square feet (10,000 of it for office space) was officially opened in April 1973 in ceremonies attended by a Scholastic delegation from New York including John Spaulding, Herb and Helen McCracken, and Ernest Schwehr.

Derek Price retired in 1973. Scholastic acquired his

---

*The airport was not built. In 1977 the land was rezoned for industry, and at this writing Scholastic still holds title to the 26 acres.

12½ percent of the Ashton shares and, soon after, Hughes' shares, to make Ashton a wholly owned subsidiary. As a result of this move, it was decided to use the name Ashton Scholastic for public exposure, although the corporate names remained The H. J. Ashton Company, Pty. Ltd., in Australia and The H. J. Ashton Company, Ltd., in New Zealand.

After seven exciting years in building the Australian business, Olive and Alan Izod left Ashton Scholastic in 1975 to go with Scott, Foresman's London office. Excerpts from Olive Izod's account of those early years appear below.

H. J. Ashton, which was housed in an old bakehouse in Auckland when Schwehr first called there in 1964, moved to larger, rented quarters the following year, and in 1969 to its present site in separate leased buildings (25,000 square feet, 7,000 of it for offices) at Penrose, a suburb of Auckland. The Penrose facility is now considered inadequate, and another move may be made within two years or so.

Ashton Scholastic in Australia
Early Years from 1968

by Olive Izod*

Anyone who has only known the Ashton Scholastic Company in its present impressive building complex, with packed carparks, busy offices and brim-full warehouse, will find it difficult to believe that only 10 years ago, the H.J. Ashton Company, as it was then known, set out to win all Australia for Scholastic Book Clubs and the Scott, Foresman Basic Readers from a fur-

*Excerpted from her article in the 10-year-celebration issue of *Ashton's Circus*, house organ of Ashton Scholastic, January 1978.

nished flat in Sydney, and with only four people on the payroll.

We had the advantage of enthusiastic support and practical know-how from our already successful New Zealand Company, and generous backing from our parent company in New York. But there were times when, carrying the first samples to arrive in the country, I was greeted by Headmasters with: "Ashtons? Never heard of them. Paperbacks? We never use them! American? And even you're not an Aussie, are you?" and I wondered if we'd ever make our mark.

But these thoughts and fears were soon dispelled. Our fine new warehouse at Brookvale looked immense as we surveyed its pristine emptiness. How could we possibly foresee that this and another similar warehouse across the road would be crammed within the next four years?

Right from the start we were blessed with staff who shared our enthusiasm and confidence in the new venture. Pat and Charlie Smith, secretary and warehouse-manager, completed our team of four. They were the first of the many, many members of staff—young and old, past and present—who have brought skill and energy to the company, have shared hard work, respon-

Australian office building and distribution center, Gosford, New South Wales, opened in 1973.

sibilities and fun, and have helped to build our present fine reputation. . . .

I should explain that before ever the Ashton Company was officially set up or the warehouse rented, we had checked with all the State Directors of Education that the book club operation met with their approval. Only one state—Victoria—declined to allow the book clubs in its schools, so we had the green light to go ahead, and our first activity was to introduce the clubs through a nationwide mailing to all the other states. And that meant addressing envelopes—about eight thousand of them.

Picture, if you will, Pat with her typewriter on our breakfast counter near the telephone and me with a small portable Olivetti on the ironing-board (none of the tables was steady enough) typing the addresses of all the schools except Victoria from all the telephone directories of Australia.

Once the mailing was completed (all four of us having stuffed envelopes for days like automatons), we could hardly wait for the response, so much depended on it. What a thrill that first order was, and how exciting as more and more orders followed. When Charlie discovered that the number of books ordered by one country school

exceeded the town population, we knew book clubs would be a success in Australia.

Now we were in business. We needed more help in the warehouse and in the neat little offices built in a corner of it—Linda Ryan to help with the mailings, Jean Tanner to pick the orders, and Jane Hellyer to be my secretary. We also needed to develop more personal contact with the schools and decided to start by following the successful New Zealand method, employing recently retired headmasters as our consultants. . . .

By March 1970 we had made enough progress for Terry to decide to make the Australian office his headquarters, and to bring Myra Lee and Jimmy Reece to work with him at Brookvale too. This meant we were desperately short of offices while the architect who owned the warehouse redesigned the front to provide a suite of offices on the first floor. . . .

With Terry's arrival, the completion of the new offices, and increases in office, field and warehouse staff, the company seemed suddenly to grow up. We became more professional, more streamlined, more a part of the educational scene. But while we took our work very seriously, we had plenty of fun. Ashtonians then, as now, loved a party and we had plenty of things to celebrate— like the roof-wetting, like the first time we reached our target on Book Club, like the welcome visitors from overseas, like—well, who needs an excuse for a party! Business flourished, the field force was greatly expanded, our first warehouse became quite inadequate and a second had to be rented. Things were going fine. And then catastrophe!

How or why it happened we never found out. We had all left the warehouse as usual one Friday night, with everything in order. Alan and I looked in on Sunday morning and were stunned by what we saw. Apart from a few shelves against one wall there wasn't a single shelf left standing in the whole warehouse, not a single book or carton left in place. We looked across a vast sea of books — six feet deep in places, out of which splinters of wooden shelves stuck at grotesque angles, with burst cartons spewing out hundreds of books. It was as though the warehouse had been in the centre of an earthquake.

We all learnt during the next fortnight what good management and a united team of people can achieve. Terry and Alan seemed supermen; their planning, organization and positive action in face of this calamity inspired everyone.

A third warehouse was rented nearby, as the immediate job was to clear the sea of books from our warehouse to make room for new shelving to be erected — metal shelving this time. A chain of workers started the formidable task of uplifting books, stacking them on the forklift which Terry drove to and from the new warehouse hour after hour. It was amazing how few books were found to be damaged or spoilt.

News of the disaster spread fast and we were never without voluntary help in addition to our own staff and a few workers recruited from the Labour Exchange. Husbands, wives and friends joined in when their own day's work was through. Food was brought in so that work could continue late into the night. Soon the warehouse came into sight, and the new shelves began to go up.

All the while essential office work went on uninterrupted, and within a couple of days orders started to go out again, books being picked from the heaps in which they lay, and few schools suffered delays. . . . It took only two weeks — an unbelievable two weeks — for everything to be back in place and functioning normally, in fact better than before.

Business increased. It became clear to Terry and Alan that a move was inevitable and with the blessing of our parent company they set out to find a site where Ashton Scholastic could grow. Gosford was the answer.

In December 1978, Ashton Scholastic acquired Oldmeadow, a well-known marketer of children's books in Victoria, South Australia.

Scholastic-Japan (limited)

The teaching of English as a second language in many nations of the world was seen as another opportunity for international expansion, with Japan a promising starting-point. Committed to education, Japan had the economic vitality to support ambitious educational programs. In late 1969 and early 1970 Scholastic approved a study, through its International Division, of the feasibility of promoting English-language book clubs for the millions of Japanese students studying English. The result was a decision in 1971 to establish a subsidiary Japanese company in Tokyo under the management of Jack Seward, an American fluent in Japanese and married to a Japanese woman. After two years he resigned and was succeeded by Hugh Henderson, a Canadian, also fluent in Japanese and also married to a Japanese. The company, Scholastic-Japan Ltd., made numerous market studies and surveys, but little progress, in the frustrating task of selling books in English to Japanese schools through the classroom book club format. Early in 1975 the Scholastic directors decided to close the Japanese operation but maintain the corporation with an address in an attorney's office in Tokyo. Whether the dormant corporation will be awakened and put back to work is a matter of speculation.

CHAPTER XVIII

Scholastic International

5 Years of Travel Experience

EACH summer during the 1960's a mounting number of young Americans, many of them high school students, took to the chartered airways for travel abroad. Tens of thousands of them toured in groups conducted by colleges, by high schools, and by firms organized expressly for this purpose. Several of the latter (American Institute for Foreign Study, Greenwich, CT; American Leadership Study Group, Worcester, MA; Foreign Study League, Salt Lake City, UT) advertised their programs in Scholastic magazines, with good results. Here were student tour organizations building their successes from the market Scholastic was reaching week after week.

The implication was not lost on Scholastic's management. Early in 1971 John Spaulding, then executive vice president (soon to be president), took the initiative in exploring this burgeoning and enticing field — enticing in that it could give the company a potentially profitable enterprise much different from its other business, yet within the realm of education. It could also put Scholastic in a person-to-person relationship with students and teachers over a six- or seven-week summer period, an experience that could be beneficial to all.

Spaulding and President Donald Layman engaged in negotiations with two of the above-named leaders in the student travel field for the purpose of acquiring one or the other, but the price of more than $2 million was too high for the Scholastic directors. They believed that Scholastic could start its own travel/study project and invest far less than $2 million before reaching the point of profit. On the basis of a budget and prospectus presented by an ad hoc committee, the directors authorized funding the project — to be called Scholastic International (SI) — in March 1971. John Spaulding agreed to add this to his many other responsibilities, and began organizing a staff for the first tours in the summer of 1972. Scholastic management knew that it would face stiff competition from the established firms in the field. But it counted on bringing to the program the strengths that figured prominently in the company's growth and success: dedication to the goals of education, nationwide acceptance among teachers and students, and an advanced network of communications to its market.

At the outset SI was managed by what Spaulding called a "venturing team," made up of Melvin Barnes, Clayton Westland, and himself. Each had his specific area of responsibility. The venturing team was supported by a headquarters staff in the company's New York office and a European Operations office in London headed by Eric Moonman, a Britisher, and assisted by Barbara Robinson, who had had experience in organizing foreign-travel programs for Finch College in New York.

It was an ambitious undertaking, with the emphasis on quality at all points — staff, housing, food, and instructors for the study periods on the campuses in Great Britain, Spain, France, Germany, and Italy. An advisory board of distinguished educators in the United States was formed, and the members were escorted to the campuses abroad for an appraisal of the programs.

One of the demanding characteristics of conducting student study/travel programs is the need to plan and make commitments more than a year in advance. Months before the groups departed on their first tours (in July 1972), plans for 1973 had to be well along so that the brochures and other promotion material could reach the schools early in the fall of 1972. This meant that major work on the second year of the project had to be done before the staff had had the experience of conducting the first year's tours. Soon Spaulding saw the need for tightening up his organization, and early in 1972 wrote the staff:

> The need for prompt and frequent decision making, the growing complexity of our marketing activities, the problems of interoffice and transatlantic communications — these and other aspects of the daily operations make it imperative that authority and responsibility for the direction of Scholastic International be vested in a single individual. Therefore, effective immediately, and with the approval of the Management Operations Committee, I am nominating myself as that person.

Though enrollments for the first year (1972) fell considerably short of the budgeted levels, the program was expanded for 1973 to include Russia and Africa. The latter had to be canceled due to lack of interest, but enrollments in the other programs increased, and total

If you've never been to Europe . . . if you've ever participated in any educational travel program . . . even if you've been abroad with **Scholastic International** before . . . This year, there's a whole new experience waiting for you in Europe. Because so much is new about **Scholastic International**, the Educational Travel Division of **Scholastic Magazines, Inc.** Not just new. Better. **Scholastic International** responds more to the needs and interest of students—and their teachers. That's what **Scholastic** is all about.

Cover of brochure for 1975 Scholastic educational travel programs.
There were six European tours, ranging from three to five weeks, with fees
from $1,140 to $1,725.

enrollment was triple what it had been the first year. Even so, with the dollar devaluation and inflation in Europe, the operating deficit for 1973 was nearly as large as it was for 1972.

John Spaulding's illness through the spring and summer of 1974* prevented his full participation in directing the affairs of SI through its third year, and it fell to Clayton Westland to take charge of operations as SI director, reporting to the new executive vice president, Richard M. (Dick) Spaulding, John's younger brother. Of SI's third year, Chairman M. R. Robinson said in his 1974 report to the stockholders:

> Our study/travel project which has caused a decline in our earnings for the past three years led me to say last December. "If we can show substantial operating improvement in a year like this, we will be encouraged to go on. If, on the other hand, we fail to do so, we shall bite the bullet and take the consequences." We definitely did improve the operations of Scholastic International and we did somewhat reduce the loss compared with the previous year. We recognize that because of the fuel crisis and the repeated increases in air fares, 1974 was not a representative year on which to base final judgment. We have shifted our strategy for 1975. We have reduced the number of programs to those that have been profitable and whose costs can be carefully controlled."

Despite the change in emphasis from student programs to more teacher programs in 1975 and a still-greater emphasis on teacher programs in 1976, SI did not

*He died on September 4.

produce sufficient revenue to justify further investment, and the project was declared closed as soon as the 1976 tours had returned home. The end was noted by the new chief executive officer, Richard Robinson, in his annual message to the stockholders (for 1976):

> As our long-time shareholders know, we entered the foreign study/travel business in 1971, anticipating that the division we called Scholastic International would be a major addition to the revenue and profits of our company. In the five years of study/travel effort, we were unable to make a profit on Scholastic International. We experienced significant losses in 1972, 1973, and 1974. Although we reduced our losses very substantially in 1975 and 1976, it became clear during our five-year experience that the foreign study/travel market had undergone significant changes, making it unlikely that Scholastic International would ever become a sizable contributor to our company's earnings. In considering how to make SI profitable we were unwilling to cut program quality or to conduct programs that were not basically educational or in keeping with our name in the educational world. We regretfully decided to discontinue Scholastic International as of August 31, 1976. All costs of discontinuance, which were not material, were included in our 1976 results.

CHAPTER XIX

Lesson Plans, Teacher Editions

A teaching guide, or lesson plan, offering suggestions to teachers on ways to use the magazine, made its debut in the first issue of the 1925–26 school year under the headline, "Plans for Using This Issue of *The Scholastic* in the Classroom." This was not an independently printed section inserted in the magazine as a teacher edition, but part of a page in the student magazine itself. Of course, students as well as teachers saw it. The title was changed in the October 17, 1925, issue to "Scholastic Lesson Plan." The opening paragraph of several lesson plans urged students to play the role of teacher:

> As suggested in the previous issue, it is recommended that the class organize itself into a Current Events Club* or Oral English Club and have its own committees and chairmen for conducting the class during the hour in which *The Scholastic* is discussed. Students are urged to ask their teachers to permit them to conduct their own classes for using *The Scholastic*.

*The use of the term *current events* would later fall into disfavor around the halls of Scholastic, as it was the title of the weekly classroom newspaper founded in 1902 by Palmer Davis (American Education Press) and widely used in the upper elementary grades. By 1937 the new *Junior Scholastic* would begin to give it competition. *Current affairs* became the approved Scholastic term, although the usage was not always observed.

Starting with the issue of November 14, 1931, the lesson plan became a separately printed, one-sheet insert for English and social studies classes. With the front imprinted "Teacher's Edition," it was tossed onto the top copy of each bundle of magazines. Robinson and Gould decided to do this in the belief that most teachers did not wish to share the professional advice (teaching suggestions) with their students. But the editors changed their minds 15 issues later and printed the following announcement in the March 5, 1932, issue:

> In response to numerous requests from both teachers and students, the "Suggestions to Teachers" for English and Social Studies Classes, formerly published as a special insert in the Teacher's Edition, have been reincorporated into the magazine itself. They will hereafter be prepared for the benefit of students as well as teachers, and will be found on pages 49 and 50 of this issue.

During the 1933–34 season the section for teachers began a wavering retreat that was to last for two years. Since its appearance was sporadic, it probably made little impact on the teachers. Whatever disappointment teacher-subscribers may have felt over the irregular appearance of lesson-plan material would be overcome by their surprise at what they received at the start of school year 1935–36. If they subscribed to 10 or more copies of *Scholastic*, they received at no extra charge a smartly edited, tabloid-sized, eight-page periodical called *High-school — Fortnightly for Teachers and Principals*. It had been published under the title *The High School Teacher* by Clarence J. Brown and L. W. Reese of Columbus, OH, who sold it to Scholastic for $1,000.

HIGHSCHOOL

FORTNIGHTLY FOR TEACHERS AND PRINCIPALS

Entered as Second Class Matter, Post Office, Pittsburgh, Pa., under the Act of March 3, 1879. Copyright, 1935, Scholastic Corporation.

Vol. 1. No. 1 — Combined with "The High School Teacher" — September 28, 1935

Loyalty Oaths Demanded by 7 More States

Bills squelched in 7 states, vetoed in 2. Twenty in all require teachers to swear to be good.

Civil Liberties Union Asks Test

Loyalty oath laws for teachers, despite opposition of teachers and liberals, were passed in seven states in this year's legislative sessions, says the Committee on Academic Freedom of the American Civil Liberties Union.

Not since 1931 when six states passed these laws has the propaganda behind such bills been so thoroughly organized, the Union said. The drive for the legislation was headed by the Daughters of the American Revolution, and supported by the American Legion, the Hearst newspapers, the Chambers of Commerce, the Elks, and all the allegedly patriotic societies, says the survey. Oath bills were part of a broad program of state gag legislation, which included sedition bills and measures barring left wing parties from the ballot. Blocked on their complete program, the forces described by the American Civil Liberties Union as "the united front of reaction" enjoyed more success in loyalty bills.

Opposing the proposals as an "unnecessary and insulting threat to academic freedom" were such distinguished individuals as James Conant, President of Harvard University; William A. Neilson, President of Smith College; Mary Woolley, President of Mount Holyoke College; Robert Maynard Hutchins, President of Chicago University; Felix Frankfurter, Alexander Meiklejohn and Dr. Charles A. Beard. Joining with them and hundreds of other educators were parent-teacher groups, the American Federation of Teachers, the Progressive Education Association, adult education groups, branches of the National Education Association.

Introduced in sixteen states this year, bills were defeated in seven and vetoed by governors in two. An unsuccessful effort was made to pass in the House of Representatives at Washington a resolution calling on the states to enact loyalty oath laws. In all, twenty states now have laws requiring teachers to take oaths of loyalty, ten of them affecting teachers in private and parochial, as well as public schools, and four of them applying to aliens as well as to citizens.

Cash in Advance for Schools

Nebraska breaks the ice in the "pay-as-you-go" trend for school building with a law permitting school districts to set up a construction fund with taxes collected on the installment plan, at a rate of not more than 3 mills a year. Before building may begin, 70% of the money must be collected. This plan enables the school, instead of paying interest on bonds, to collect interest on the fund.

Youth Gets 20c a Day from N. Y. A.

Roosevelt sets up fund for 7% of needy youth under new Federal agency.

Superintendents to Select 212,000 for Highschool Aid

Several million boys and girls, forced out of highschool by lack of funds for shoes or books, had their answer from the New Deal last summer in the form of the National Youth Administration.

$50,000,000 out of the WPA fund was set aside by Roosevelt for this agency. About 11 million has been allocated to provide 212,192 highschool students with not more than $6 a month. The sum must be earned at a fair rate of pay through services for which money is not ordinarily appropriated by the schools. School superintendents were assured that they would have complete authority in selecting students to receive this aid, but aid may go only to highschool students who were on relief last May.

(See NYA outline, Sept. 21 Scholastic.)

Announcement of the program during the Denver convention of the N.E.A. dismayed educators who felt that the machinery existing in the schools, in the U. S. Office of Education, and in educators associations could have taken care of the work. A new government agency for youth, they charged, was redundant and politically inspired.

Cries of alarm continued from many quarters while the NYA set to its task of appointing national advisers and state directors.

"Assuming an administrative expense of as little as $20,000 per state, we have approximately $1,000,000, enough to aid 7,500 college students, for agencies which duplicate existing agencies . . .

"No greater danger to democracy can be found than in a central control over education which may at any time be used for purposes of propaganda and which is entirely suited to the needs of those who would develop a Fascist state." (George Drayton Strayer, Columbia.)

"I am against control of a youth program by a separate agency in Washington." (Harold G. Campbell, Superintendent of Schools, New York.)

"As the program involves parttime work and apprentice training,

(Continued on Page Four)

Teacher Seeks Post

Progressive teachers have long held that effective classroom work must be substantiated by effective community work. The teacher who is not active in neighborhood affairs, they hold, lives in a dream world.

Ardent champion of this thesis has been Mrs. Johanna M. Lindlof, lobbyist of the Teachers Union, who last month entered the race for the New York state assembly.

Ave atque Vale!

L. W. REESE
President, National State Highschool Supervisors and Directors

"30"

"The High School Teacher" is now the property of the Scholastic Corporation, and is combined with a new fortnightly newspaper for teachers and principals, HIGHSCHOOL. The new journal will be published twice a month and will be Two Dollars for two years. Each subscriber to "The High School Teacher" will receive equal value in the new magazine. Those subscribers who have part of a year to run will receive the new journal instead of "The High School Teacher."

The management of "The High School Teacher" wishes to thank sincerely all of its subscribers, editors, and contributors who helped to make a ten-year period seem like one year—for the magazine is ten years old. It weathered the depression. It held high the ideals of secondary education. It treated all alike. Race, creed, and type of position never influenced its editors. There was only one standard—The Best Possible.

And now as we write "30" may we recommend that you support whole-heartedly the new journal. The new management will be in position to bring to the teachers of the United States an exceptional educational contribution. The fact that it will be published every two weeks will assure the latest, as well as the best, in educational progress.

"The High School Teacher"
L. W. Reese, Editor
Clarence J. Brown, Publisher

Ohio Schools Boom

Three laws, passed at the last session of the Ohio legislature, spell hope for schools of that state next year.

One law provides each school district with a minimum base appropriation of $67.50 for each pupil in highschool out of the state treasury.

The average amount spent on each highschool pupil throughout the U.S. is $100.

Law Two creates a state textbook commission to fix maximum prices and pay out of state school funds for texts selected by local boards.

Law Three whangs Hollywood in the eye. Film censorship fees are upped to $3 from $1 to provide funds for buying films for school.

Other measures pleasing to school people provided means of cutting interest payments on school debts and borrowing against future receipts.

Credit for showing slow-witted legislators the light goes to the redoubtable Exec. Committee of the Ohio Educational Association.

Pennsy Cuts Restored

Schools Wait Court Decision on Income Tax Revenue

Child Labor Restricted

The most important work of the Pennsylvania legislature with regard to education, in the opinion of new State Supt. Lester K. Ade (AH-dee), is something it did not do.

The Wilson law, which sliced a temporary emergency cut from teacher salaries, was not re-enacted.

Now if the pending court decision only upholds the state's new graduated income tax, with funds earmarked for education, the troubles of the schools will shrink along with the real-estate taxes.

Other school laws straightened kinks in the teachers retirement system, prohibited school boards from taking "gifts" from teachers, established an annual Free School Day each April, prohibited child labor during school hours up to the age of 16, required working certificates for children up to 18, required highschool graduation of registered nurses, stepped toward increasing size of rural school districts, handed $50,000 to vocational schools and $3,000,000 to distressed districts.

Govt. Foils Raid On Teacher Purse

An effort "to deal in an irresponsible fashion with the small savings of school teachers" was denounced this month by the U. S. Securities Exchange Commission, blocking a nationwide issue of $750,000 endowment bonds by the National Educators Mutual Assn. of Nashville, Tenn.

Officers of the organization, assailed for "demonstrated untruthfulness and misfeasance," included several school superintendents.

The bonds ostensibly offered $250 in stock as interest on a ten year investment of $750, but the stock had a value to the officers of only fifty cents.

Highschool Housewives Huddle

Three hundred highschool and college girls, representing home makers clubs of the whole U. S. and Canada, gathered last summer at the American Home Economics Association convention in Chicago.

Hostesses whisked them to tea at Mundelein College, breakfast and a style show at Field's, the opera, Lighting Institute and Electric Club, Field Museum, and to the University of Chicago.

Sophia Reed headed the advisory committee. Dr. Sadie Stark, Millican University, was club sponsor.

N. E. A. Votes Academic Freedom

Denver convention passes resolution with teeth in it to defend free learning

Asks More Federal Aid

Five sharp points in the academic freedom resolution, passed by the National Education Association at Denver last summer under pressure by classroom teachers, promise to:

a. Combat repressive legislation

b. Investigate the firing of teachers for presenting truth or opinion.

c. Enlist public support

d. Aid discharged teachers

e. Cooperate with other groups defending academic liberty.

The resolution was called a triumph for teachers and adherents to progressive theory in the association.

Other resolutions asked federal aid to assure schooling to every child, with local control of policy; proposed that the New Deal youth fund be turned over to the U. S. Commissioner of Education; voted $10,000 for job tenure work; opposed compulsory military training; and declared boldly and unequivocally for democracy, recreation, and the end of child labor.

Another aid to independent teaching was formed last summer in the Committee for Academic Freedom at Teachers College, Columbia, promising legal and financial aid to persecuted teachers; Goodwin Watson, Chairman.

Red splashed last month upon the academic freedom resolution passed by the National Education Association at Denver. The Legion of Valor, whose members are all holders of the Distinguished Service Cross or the Congressional Medal of Honor, called it a "sugar-coating of propaganda and a cloak under which to teach atheism in the schools," in a resolution passed at their Bridgeport convention.

Wisconsin Puts Cooperatives On Must List

One-fourth of Great Britain's business is handled by consumer cooperators. In Sweden and Finland, coop concerns control more than half the national economy. Denmark's land is 90% cooperatized. In the U.S.A., more than a million are members of marketing or buying cooperatives.

This month, Wisconsin becomes the first state to require that its schools teach cooperative buying and selling.

Knowledge of cooperation is also required for a certificate to teach economics, social studies, or agriculture, in a bill passed by the last legislature.

Printed on good-quality paper, six columns to a page, the education news it presented reached the schools perhaps more quickly than that of any other national publication. Marc Rosenblum, whose first contact with Scholastic came as the Butler (PA) High School reporter in 1921, served as managing editor while continuing to write for the student magazine.

Although it appeared every other week and *Scholastic* appeared weekly, one of *Highschool*'s eight pages presented "Teaching Helps . . . for *Scholastic*." The suggestions for English teachers were written by Belle McKenzie* of West Seattle (WA) High School. The helps for social studies teachers were prepared by C. Maurice Wieting* of Lennox (SD) High School, and in one issue by Harold Rugg of Teachers College at Columbia University. For a given issue of *Highschool* McKenzie, Wieting, and Rugg had the task of writing teaching suggestions to relate to the contents of two and sometimes three issues of the student magazines, most of the copy for which had not yet been written. (They worked from outlines or rough drafts.)

After one year of an unbearable deficit, it was decided to discontinue *Highschool* and provide the teachers with a four-page section inserted in the student edition, offering "a variety of teaching suggestions, based upon this issue, for significant and progressive instruction." The front cover for this edition was overprinted with the line "High School Teacher Edition." Beginning in September 1936 the student edition, then carrying the title *Scholastic: The American High School Weekly*, was issued in three edi-

*While they were doing graduate work at Teachers College, Columbia University.

tions: social studies, English, and combined (later called "combination"). A lesson plan covering both English and social studies content appeared in the teacher editions.

When *Junior Scholastic* took on a teacher edition in 1940, the editor, looking for anything to distinguish it from the parent magazine, gave it the title "Teacher's Companion to *Junior Scholastic*." As other student magazines and book clubs were started, a teacher edition was considered essential to their viability.* Upon the suggestion of the Roy Eastman research organization, the teacher section for the first issue of the 1944–45 school year was moved from the inside center of the student edition to an outside, or "wraparound," section, thus making it all the more conspicuous for identification when the package was opened.

In addition to lesson plans, the teacher edition carried education "news in brief," announcements of Scholastic Awards, and paid advertising (movie and recording equipment, Compton's and Britannica ency-

*Through the teacher editions of the magazines and of the See-Saw, Lucky, Arrow, TAB, and Campus Book Club *News*, Scholastic, as of school year 1975–76, had a "reach" to 875,000 teachers on a regular schedule (each issue of the teacher editions of the magazines and the book club *News*). This calculation allowed for a 40 percent duplication of elementary school teachers who subscribed to the elementary magazines and thus received the book club *News* in their teacher editions; 60 percent of the teachers conducting Scholastic book clubs did not subscribe to Scholastic's elementary magazines. Included in this 875,000 total are the actual number of copies of the two teacher monthlies — *Scholastic Coach* and *Forecast for Home Economics* — that were sent to 116,000 teachers every month (41,000 to coaches and athletic directors; 75,000 to home economics teachers). Actually, the 875,000 figure does not represent total readership, only copies sent — there is a considerable multiple readership of all the teacher editions, so the "reach" is well beyond a million.

**SCHOLASTIC MAGAZINES'
TEACHERS SERVICE BUREAU
Can Help You To Obtain...**

★ **BOOKS OF ALL PUBLISHERS** from one source. You merely write one letter and send your remittance to us and we'll have the books shipped directly to you. A real time saver.

★ **SUBSCRIPTIONS TO ALL LEADING MAGAZINES** — many at special rates for our subscribers; others at regular rates. You save time and trouble by ordering from one source.

★ **LISTS OF BOOKS AND PAMPHLETS** of special interest. Watch for announcements of Basic English folder and other useful pamphlets soon.

★ **FREE TEACHING MATERIALS** offered by industrial, scientific and other organizations. Watch for *Teaching Aids* column.

★ **INFORMATION AND FREE TRIAL COPIES** of the specialized and graded classroom magazine best suited to your special classroom needs.

★ **INFORMATION AND RULES** for the Annual SCHOLASTIC MAGAZINE Awards Competition for literary material by students, essays, current events, art and photography contests.

★ **VQ. KITS** and classroom suggestions for using them in connection with JUNIOR SCHOLASTIC'S Victory Quiz program.

For a two-year period (1943–45) Scholastic's Subscription Promotion Department, headed by William Steiner, conducted a Teachers Service Bureau, launching it with a full-page announcement in the November 1, 1943, issue of the teacher editions of *Senior Scholastic, Junior Scholastic,* and *World Week*. The above segment is from that announcement. The Bureau, but not all of its services, was discontinued because of the considerable clerk-power it required.

clopedias, art supply houses, travel, typewriters). In 1948 the title was changed to *Scholastic Teacher*, with the word *edition* added in order to meet U.S. Post Office requirements for second-class postage rates.

The September 23, 1946, issue of *Scholastic Teacher* (still printed on newsprint)* announced that future issues would be edited by William D. Boutwell, although he would be listed on the masthead as associate editor under Kenneth M. Gould, editor-in-chief. In effect Boutwell was editor, and within two years he got the title.

Upon the departure of Martha Huddleston as director of the Teen Age Book Club in 1951, Robinson turned to Boutwell to fill the gap there (Chapter XV, "The Book Business") while he continued to edit *Scholastic Teacher*. The burgeoning Teen Age Book Club was requiring more and more of his time, and the need for some backup on *Scholastic Teacher* was apparent. For school year 1954–55 Boutwell got a budget that provided for a managing editor. This was Roy Gallant, who soon would function as editor without the title.

The monthly issues, to which the advertising sales effort was directed, had become so healthy with advertising that Robinson asked Boutwell and Advertising Manager Marie Kerkmann to open up every issue for advertising. They made some inquires along Madison Avenue and reported that they didn't see all that much advertising to be had, but they would try. Starting with school year 1955–56 the masthead announced: *Scholastic Teacher— The Weekly News Review of Education and Teaching Guide for Scholastic Magazines.*

Scholastic Teacher switched from newsprint to a coated paper in 1947.

Convention Comment

By M. R. ROBINSON
Editor, Scholastic

The most amusing comment made about the convention was written by a columnist in a St. Louis newspaper who said that the receipts at the bar in the Convention Hall were larger during the Department of Superintendence convention than they were during the convention of the American Legion. The reason given was that the superintendents attended the meetings and actually got to the Convention Hall whereas most of the Legionnaires didn't even know where the Convention Hall was.

A big sign labeled "Department of Superintendence, N.E.A." hung behind the bar. It was completely surrounded with liquor bottles of every description.

The tremendous applause at the end of Norman Thomas' dynamic rebuttal was headlined in all the St. Louis newspapers. Superintendents should be more careful. Thomas Blanton might read those headlines into the Congressional Record as evidence that everyone associated with an educational institution is a radical.

I hesitate to make critical comment about the High-school Principals' Luncheon because I was a guest at the Speakers' Table and have had many pleasant associations with them. Furthermore, I am happy to report that the organisation has some far-reaching and important plans which they are developing and will announce shortly. Then, too, the Yearbook of the principals was one of the most significant things presented at the convention.

My only grievance is that the resolutions committee could have found more significant things to comment upon than the single resolution devoted to liquor and cigarette advertising in magazines reaching the highschools and their libraries. I say this without disagreeing with the resolution. As a matter of fact, it gives Scholastic an indirect boost. But the principals surely have worries other than advertising.

The organization meeting of the John Dewey Society, held Sunday afternoon, was one of the biggest disappointments of the convention. The birth of a child to Mrs. Phillip LaFollette, apparently three days late, preventing Governor LaFollette from appearing as the main speaker, was probably the chief cause of this disappointment. More than a thousand were on hand to hear him.

The naming of the public enemies of education by Professor George Counts was a poor substitute. It seemed to me unwise and impolitic, insofar as the whole profession is concerned, serving only to attract the spotlight. Without knowing whether Clyde Miller had anything to do with it or not, it was a publicity stunt which only he has the genius and daring to contrive. But legislative bodies, as is well known to every educator, are influenced by votes and not by making faces at people and organizations who will be unimpressed.

M. R. Robinson's observations on the 1936 winter meeting of the Department of Superintendence, National Education Association, held in St. Louis. From the March 21, 1936, issue of *Highschool*.

What liberals need is more hard work with individual members of our legislative bodies. Some of those skilled in the psychology of education need some lessons in the psychology of public opinion as well as in the American method of influencing legislative bodies.

I might add that a group containing leaders as brilliant as the leaders of that organization should have thought of something more original for a program than the proposed publication of a series of year books.

The meeting deserves one rousing cheer, however, for the suggestion of William McAndrew that teachers propose an oath of their own writing.

ſ   ſ   ſ

The demonstration lesson by Roy Hatch and a class of St. Louis highschool pupils must have convinced many superintendents that even the power of the Supreme Court can be freely discussed in classrooms. The comment most often heard afterwards concerned the fact that a skillful teacher is the primary requisite for handling ticklish subjects. School executives should therefore have their most skillful teachers conduct special classes for other less experienced teachers. How to avoid pitfalls and learning how not to lead with the chin would be the chief objectives of such a course of training for teachers.

Some teachers who heard Mr. Hatch's demonstration questioned whether he should have permitted misstatements and illogical discussions without correction when those errors were not caught by the class. Probably in an actual classroom Mr. Hatch would not permit errors of fact to get by. Mr. Benezet of Manchester, N. H., who has a knack of his own for teaching, said that he had learned some things he didn't know before, with regard to the power of the President to pack the Supreme Court. He was calling attention to an uncorrected error but there must have been many Superintendents who left that meeting with a number of erroneous conceptions.

ſ   ſ   ſ

Dr. Beard's telegram to Governor Landon asking if he were proud of Hearst's support of his candidacy added merriment to the hotel lobby talk. It is too bad Dr. Beard did not use the tactics of a Hearst reporter by wording his telegram "DO YOU OBJECT TO HEARST'S SUPPORT OF YOUR CANDIDACY? IF YOU DO NOT REPLY, I SHALL ASSUME THAT YOU DO OBJECT."

ſ   ſ   ſ

The Department of Secondary-School Principals has a real business man as its secretary. The profits of this organization of only 5,000 members for the year 1935 were $12,000 on gross transactions of only $69,000. That bowling alley in Cicero should give some other organizations an idea.

ſ   ſ   ſ

The National Broadcasting Company apparently has a rather low idea of the cultural interests of the members of the Department of Superintendence, judging by its part in the Sunday evening program.

ſ   ſ   ſ

Superintendent Glenn of Birmingham handled with commendable skill the panel discussion of the Yearbook on the Social Studies. Finally, hats off to President Stoddard for his originality and skill in building the convention program, especially for his three-cornered political demonstration.

It developed that the weeklies would not be as fat with advertising as the monthlies had been, but they carried enough to justify their existence for four years. By school year 1959 the weekly issues were down to eight pages, with most advertisers directed to the swollen monthly issues. The eight-page weekly issue was necessary to carry certain advertisers, however, including those buying "teleguide" pages. In addition each weekly issue carried two teaching guide pages — "Education News of the Week" on page one, and a page for a "transparency master." The teleguide pages, purchased by TV producers, promoted forthcoming programs having curriculum application, such as *Jane Eyre, Saint Joan, Hamlet, Victoria Regina,* and several hundred others, including original TV dramas of merit, such as the Hallmark series.

A transparency master consisted of a one-page, heavily lined, black-and-white drawing, chart, graph, or map that teachers could use with overhead projectors for a greatly enlarged image on the classroom wall. Teachers used these as springboards for class discussion of topics featured in the related student edition. Both transparency masters and teleguides proved very popular, and the teleguides continue to this day, providing income to reduce the annual cost of supplying the teacher editions. Transparency masters, now usually called "skills masters" or "activity masters," appear infrequently, as space is at a premium in these days of high production costs.

Upon the departure of Gallant for freelance work in 1957, the editorship of *Scholastic Teacher* was turned over to his assistant, Howard Langer, with Boutwell ever in the wings as consultant.

After eight years Langer left for a job with Civic

Education Service in Washington, and Boutwell again found himself in the saddle — this time on a shared-time basis with the title "acting editor." Soon, "acting" was dropped, and a few issues later "editor" became "publisher." Despite the shifting titles, the work got done. As mentioned elsewhere in this account, Boutwell's imagination and drive made him a valuable member of any unit — if his title were waterboy, it wouldn't have stopped him from pouring out a stream of ideas for new products.

Despite the advertising gains made by Advertising Director Jack Coyle and his successor, Richard Copeland, the deficit on *Scholastic Teacher* persisted. Income from circulation was negligible, as only about 31,000 of the 400,000 press run were "paid singles" (single subscriptions for the Scholastic teacher edition of a given magazine — mainly *Senior Scholastic*, from libraries). All the rest were sent to teachers having bulk subscriptions (10 or more) to a Scholastic student magazine under the time-honored policy of supplying bulk subscribers with the teacher edition at no extra cost.

Obviously, it wasn't free. The Audit Bureau of Circulations considered it paid. For example, if the teacher ordered 20 subscriptions to *Junior Scholastic* at $1.50 each, he or she received the 20 student editions and one teacher edition with the student edition bound in, and was billed $30. The Audit Bureau of Circulations considered the payment to be for 21 subscriptions; thus the Bureau's reports included all 21 as paid subscriptions. The total sum came within its rule of recognizing a subscription as paid if the publisher collected at least 50 percent of the single-subscription price of all copies ordered: *Scholastic Teacher* income was credited with the income from the paid single subscriptions.

Upon the departure of Boutwell from *Scholastic Teacher* a second time, a new editorial lineup was announced. Loretta Hunt Marion, who had been associate editor and later editor of the elementary school edition, was named editor. Derek Burleson, who had been working with John Studebaker in the Professional Relations Division, served as editorial director; and Melvin Barnes, who succeeded Studebaker as vice president in charge of Professional Relations, presided over the whole thing. Marion and her staff produced a succession of smartly written and edited monthly issues with four-color covers and an array of advertising that rivaled the flush issues of the Boutwell-Kerkmann days.

All this augured well for a rejuvenated *Scholastic Teacher*, with the prospect that the annual deficit would be cut to the point where it could be justified as a reasonable "service expense."

That day would not come. In 1973 the problem was intensified by a decision of the U.S. Postal Service (replacement for the U.S. Post Office Department) that *Scholastic Teacher* would no longer be eligible for second-class postal rates, which had always applied to the company's magazines except the "controlled circulation" *Scholastic Coach*.

In making its new ruling, the Postal Service declared that the contents of a supplement had to be germane to the contents of its parent periodical and that *Scholastic Teacher*'s content was not germane. Would it be eligible for second-class entry if it were to become an independent magazine not called a supplement? No, said the Postal Service, which did not consider the circulation of

Scholastic Teacher "paid." Now it would cost an additional $15,000 per issue to mail *Scholastic Teacher*. Even so, the company decided to continue the magazine in the hope that increased advertising revenue would reduce losses to a "manageable level." That level was unattainable during school year 1973–74, so it was decided that the January 1975 issue would be the last. Excerpts from the announcement to the staff follow:

> For more than a year, we have been studying ways to reduce the losses on the monthly *Scholastic Teacher*. We made surveys to determine whether we could charge extra for the monthly *ST*, or whether we could turn it into a paid circulation magazine and still continue to furnish the circulation base that was deemed essential by the advertising sales department.
>
> We made these studies because one year ago we were ordered by the U.S. Postal Service to begin payment of controlled circulation rates on the monthly *ST* which had previously been accepted at second-class rates along with the student magazines. This added a cost of $15,000 per issue above the second-class rates and proved to be the final unendurable burden.
>
> Reluctantly we have concluded that we cannot reduce the losses to a manageable level with our present publishing formula. We have therefore decided to discontinue the monthly *Scholastic Teacher* as a separate publication after the January 1975 issue is published. In its place we plan to expand our weekly service to teacher-subscribers by adding pages to the teacher editions of each magazine. . . .
>
> We shall do all we can to make our expanded weekly teacher editions a more valuable professional service to our readers. We shall continue to carry advertising in the weekly teacher editions to

cover some of the cost of the expanded editorial content that will be helpful to teachers of social studies, language arts, science, and others in their respective subject matter areas and at their grade levels.

The demise of *Scholastic Teacher* under the weight of increased costs largely brought about by its loss of second-class mailing status did not end the company's interest in getting the Postal Service to approve one of the other Scholastic magazines for second-class rates. There remained the problem of mailing costs for the magazine *Forecast for Home Economics*, which in 1973 had been deprived of second-class status as the teacher edition of *Co-ed*. Like *Scholastic Teacher, Forecast* had been included at no extra charge with orders from teachers subscribing to 10 or more copies of the related student edition — in this instance, *Co-ed*. A teacher ordering copies of *Co-ed* for 10 students at $1.95 each received in the one package the 10 copies, a desk copy for herself, and a copy of that month's issue of *Forecast*—and was billed $19.50 for the lot. This amply met the qualifications for paid subscriptions set by the Postal Service and by the Audit Bureau of Circulations that no less than 50 percent of the total subscription price of magazines in the offer be paid by the subscriber. Even so, *Forecast* lost its second-class status as an edition of *Co-ed*. That was the rub—the "edition" label. The Postal Service saw *Forecast* as an independent periodical, not sufficiently germane to the content of *Co-ed* to be called an "edition" of it.

Conferences and correspondence between Darwin Sharp, director of Mail Classification of the U.S. Postal

***Forecast* Spared the Same Fate**

321

Service and Nicholas Kochansky, periodical manufacturing director of Scholastic's School Division, paved the way for a resolution of the problem in Scholastic's favor. It was agreed that *Forecast* would not be designated an edition of *Co-ed*,* that the word *free* would not be used in any reference to the combined subscriptions (*Forecast* and *Co-ed*), and that the terms of the subscription offer would be fully explained in the official postal notice published in every issue of the magazines. As required by postal regulations the combination price worked both ways; that is, a single subscription to *Forecast* at $8 included a subscription to *Co-ed* at no extra cost.

With these conditions understood, the Postal Service in December 1976 approved *Forecast*'s application for second-class entry and refunded Scholastic $60,180.66 of the fees paid during the period in which it was paying the higher "controlled circulation" rates for mailing *Forecast*.

Two years had passed since the folding of *Scholastic Teacher*, which probably would have survived its cost distress had the remedy that brought such relief to *Forecast* been applied in time.

*It became "The Teacher's Aid for *Co-ed* Classrooms."

CHAPTER XX

Here Come
the Divisions

THE company was well along in years — in its early
forties — before organization structure reared its
many heads. During the 1920's, 1930's, and 1940's
Scholastic followed the pattern of organization found in
most newspaper and magazine publishing houses: an
editorial department, a circulation department (sales and
order processing), an advertising department, and a business department — each with an editor or manager who
reported to the president/publisher. In the case of
Scholastic, the publisher knew everybody by name down
the line, and no one could be hired or fired without his
consent. He was his own manufacturing manager, dealing with paper supply houses, haggling with printers,
and cultivating the goodwill of the Postmaster General's
office in Washington. This simple organization prevailed
even for a few years after the company got into the book
business in a significant way with the Teen Age Book
Club in 1948 (Chapter XV). The then-director/editor of
the club — Martha Huddleston — reported directly to
M. R. Robinson, along with a few other department
chiefs of the magazines and Agnes Laurino of accounting
and order processing.

It was the booming book club business that began

rearranging this fireside setup. In 1962 what had been the magazine and book editorial departments were reorganized into curriculum departments at the junior/senior high school level (social studies, science, language arts, home economics and guidance, sports and physical education) and, at the K–6 level, an elementary department without curriculum sections. William Boutwell and Jack Lippert shared the supervision of this setup, with Boutwell overseeing mainly the book side of the business and *Scholastic Teacher* (Chapter XV, "The Book Business"). They and M. R. Robinson as chairman comprised the Editorial Committee. Departments for noneditorial functions continued pretty much as they were: general administration, including personnel; advertising; circulation promotion; accounting; field operations; book operations; order processing; and manufacturing.

When the curriculum organization for junior/senior high school editorial was set up, Robinson said that it was for a trial run, to be revised as needed. The need soon developed, and by 1965 a reorganization drawn up by President Don Layman and Executive Vice President John Spaulding was approved by the Management Operations Committee (MOC). This too, said MOC Chairman Robinson, would be experimental. It was the first big step toward what would 12 years later become a full divisionalization of the company. The 1965 plan called for six publishing divisions, each with a publisher or director at its head. In five of the six, the head was not responsible for the editorial function. The exception was Division III (*Scholastic Teacher,* Folkways Records, Professional Books), where Boutwell presided over editorial and everything else up to the point of order processing and accounting. The five book club editors reported to their two appropriate editorial directors (Hauser of Language Arts and Cary of the Elementary Department). Book club editors were in fact as closely involved with Goldberger of Division V as with their editorial directors. There was an editorial director for each of the curriculum departments at the high school level, with one director, Margaret Hauser, heading two departments. Dick Robinson was associate director of the Language Arts Department, and would succeed Hauser as director so that she could concentrate on the Home Economics and Guidance Department with its two magazines and supplementary materials.

On December 12, 1966, after a year and three months of this first divisional setup, M. R. Robinson sent this urgent request to the management members of the board of directors:*

> We have now been operating under the divisional set-up for a full fiscal year, plus the past three-and-a-half months. In my remarks to the shareholders, I mentioned that we all recognized that numerous flaws in operations had become apparent under the divisional structure and that these were being reviewed.
>
> I believe we all agree that the divisional set-up has succeeded well in at least one of its stated objectives, namely to give younger members of the staff greater responsibility and the opportunity to display initiative and gain executive or administrative experience.
>
> Reducing the size of certain areas of responsibility into divisions that could be delegated

*Donald Layman, Herb McCracken, John Spaulding, John Studebaker, William Boutwell, Agnes Laurino, and Jack Lippert.

made it possible for less-experienced administrators to encompass fully the responsibilities of a division. Having each division head responsible to an experienced executive and member of the Board of Directors was planned so that each of the division heads could be directed by and could lean upon, as needed, someone who had handled the job himself.

In meetings of the Management Directors we have discussed some of the operating flaws that developed. Examples of cross-over problems between divisions, frictions that have developed, communication failures, etc., have been reviewed and efforts have been made to seek better co-ordination — and cooperation — between division heads and staff without stifling their initiative . . .

This memo is not merely an invitation, but is an urgent request directed to the management members of the Board. I would like each of you to prepare a memorandum outlining — in as complete form as you wish to make it — your suggestions for revising the organizational structure, with particular reference to the divisional set-up under which we have been operating. Your memo may be limited to suggestions for bettering the operations of the present system, or it may reflect a new approach to the organizational structure. . . .

"Suggestions for bettering the operation of the present system" were forthcoming from all management members of the board of directors. All agreed "on the need for the organization to be restructured," but were in "serious disagreement about the way we should restructure [it]," as Robinson stated in a memo of April 7, 1967, to the management directors. "Thus it has become apparent," he wrote, "that the Chief Executive Officer will have to make decisions on which there is not likely to be full agreement." He then went on to explain the organization structure of several publishing houses with strong education divisions, whose chief executive officers he had interviewed in order to get a perspective on some of the features of his proposed structure.

The upshot of this was authorization by the management directors for a new organization structure, basically the work of M. R. Robinson, which called for further consolidation of editorial and operational functions by putting them in two divisions—the Elementary Division and the Junior/Senior High School Division—instead of having them scattered in five divisions. Instead of numbers, the company's several divisions were given titles, as follows:

Elementary Division: Sturges Cary, publisher; Richard Spaulding, manager.

Junior/Senior High School Division: Jack Lippert, publisher; Nicholas Kochansky, manager.

General Business Division (cashier's office, order processing, data processing, Circular Mail, warehousing/shipping of nonperiodicals, management of buildings/real estate): Top responsibilities divided among Donald Layman, John Spaulding, and Agnes Laurino.

Library and Trade Division: Morris Goldberger, publisher.

Professional and Public Relations Division: Within a year to be assigned to Melvin Barnes, successor to John Studebaker.

International Division: Ernest Schwehr, director.

Field Operations Division: Kent Allison, director.

M. R. Robinson had given considerable study to the structure existing in some houses that organized the editorial/operations functions by curriculum groupings in a vertical structure from kindergarten through grade 12. That is, instead of having two divisions, one for elementary school and one for high school, there would be one "el-hi" division, within which would be the social studies department, language arts department, science department, etc. The editorial director of each would head the team to produce materials that ran the whole gamut, kindergarten through high school. Robinson decided against this because "presently we have no social studies program for the elementary schools except as the periodicals touch that curriculum area. Our only math item is the Studebaker arithmetic, and our elementary science program is limited to science inserts in the periodicals plus some popular science books for the book clubs.... Eventually I have no doubt that. . .we might move in the K–12 direction." Elsewhere in the same memo he said: "We are quite likely to move in the K–12 direction."

The organization of editorial/operations into Elementary and Junior/Senior High School Divisions split the book club lineup: See-Saw, Lucky, and Arrow book clubs were assigned to the Elementary Division; the Teen Age and Campus Book Clubs to the Junior/Senior High School Division.

The Junior/Senior High School Division was organized in curriculum departments—language arts, social studies, science, foreign languages, home economics and guidance, sports and physical education—each with an editorial director. Thus the editorial director would be responsible for magazines, books, and any other related products. For example, Dick Robinson, as editorial director of the Language Arts Department, had responsibility for all products classified as "language arts" at the junior/senior high school level: Teen Age Book Club, Campus Book Club, the magazines *Practical English* (later *Voice*), *Literary Cavalcade, Scope,* the Literature Units, and other text products.

The next organizational overhaul (1971) took the company close to the structure M. R. Robinson foresaw in 1967 when he wrote, "We are quite likely to move in the K–12 direction."

The 1971 reorganization replaced the Elementary Division and the Junior/Senior High School Division with the umbrella School Division, counterpart of what other educational publishing houses had been calling the el-hi division. Richard Robinson was named publisher and Richard Spaulding, manager, with Steven Swett as promotion director. Their domain included all the magazines, book clubs, and text materials. Kochansky was named manufacturing manager for the magazines; Holahan, for books. Field Operations, under Kent Allison and later Jefferson Watkins, became part of the new School Division.

Responsibility for advertising-space sales, which had been split between Clayton Westland (for the student weeklies and *Scholastic Teacher*) and Arthur Neiman (for *Co-ed, Forecast for Home Economics,* and *Scholastic Coach*) was consolidated under Neiman, and Westland was assigned to a new post: vice president, Corporate Development. Within a year he would take charge of Scholastic International (foreign study and travel).

In the summer of 1974 when John Spaulding could

M. Arthur Neiman, vice-president, Educational Periodicals Division, has headed numerous departments and divisions of the company since joining it in 1945.

no longer continue his work (he died on September 4), the divisions he formerly managed (International, Scholastic International, and Library and Trade) were transferred, respectively, to his brother Richard, to George Milne, and to Richard Robinson, newly elected president. In this emergency situation it was decided that the most effective organization would be one in which the company's major operating activities would be divided into five top-level areas, three of which would be called *groups* and two would be called *divisions*. However, within two of the three groups would be units called *divisions*, one of which incorporated the book clubs with Michael Hobson as publisher. The five in the hierarchy were:

Education Group (including magazines and texts), under Richard Robinson.

Book Club, Trade, and International Group, under Richard Spaulding.

Finance, Operations, and Manufacturing Group, under George Milne.

Field Operations Division, under Richard Spaulding.

Professional Relations and Administrative Division, under Melvin Barnes.

Because the responsibility for managing the company had been thrust so quickly on Richard Robinson, Richard Spaulding, and George Milne, it was necessary to involve others in top-management functions. Andrew W. Bingham, who had been vice president and editorial director of Encyclopaedia Britannica Education Corporation, was appointed to the position of editorial administrator of the School Division (effective February 1, 1975).

An Educational Periodicals Division was formed to include advertising, marketing, and manufacturing—but not editorial—with Steven Swett as publisher. Home economics was again given division status, and Carolyn Bishop was recruited to serve as publisher (Chapter XIV, "The March of Magazines").

As the retirement of Thora Larsen approached, her work as corporate secretary would be taken over by Charles Brock (who was employed as corporate counsel, elected vice president, and later put in charge of the International Division).

Upon the resignation of George Milne, executive vice president for Operations and Finance, in October 1975, Richard Robinson announced that the New Jersey staff would report to him on a temporary basis; Bob Cloutier, head of Book Manufacturing, would report to Richard Spaulding; and Kochansky, head of Magazine Manufacturing, would report to Steven Swett. In the Englewood Cliffs office at the time was Ernest T. Pelikan of the Arthur Young & Company auditing house, who was working as a consultant to Scholastic on the problem of inventory control. He would soon join the staff as head of Operations and be elected vice president. Within a year the post of chief financial officer would be filled by Martin Tell, who had been vice president of Finance and Administration for the Starline Optical Company, and who earlier had worked for Cellu-Craft and Coopers & Lybrand.

In September 1977 a significant change was made in the organization structure to achieve fully integrated and separate divisions for periodical publishing and text publishing. The announcement by Richard Robinson appears on the next page.

A new Text Division will be formed incorporating the editorial, marketing, and business sides of text publishing, including our more than one hundred Scholastic representatives in Field Operations. Vice President Andrew Bingham, formerly Editorial Administrator of the School Division, is named Publisher of the new Text Division. Reporting to him will be Jeff Watkins, Vice President and Director of Field Operations, and Ron Stenlake, who is named Manager of the Text Division with responsibility for business, promotion, product management, and market research. Text editorial directors and text art and production will also report to Bingham.

The Educational Periodicals Division, formed a year and a half ago to include advertising, marketing, and manufacturing, will now assume editorial responsibility for the twenty-seven magazines* published by the division. Vice President Steven Swett is Publisher of the Educational Periodicals Division. Reporting to him for editorial will be Sturges Cary, Vice President and Editor-in-Chief, and Claudia Cohl, who is named Editorial Administrator of the Division.

Russ D'Anna, Vice President and Director of the Audiovisual and New Media Department, will assume new responsibilities focusing in part on TV and film development and on the role of new media in education. This new assignment will be the subject of a separate memorandum. In addition to these new responsibilities, Russ will continue to direct the Audiovisual Department, which becomes a separate department of the company. The Audiovisual Department will produce audiovisual programs for marketing by the Text Division.

*Not all the Scholastic magazines were included in the dominion of the new Educational Periodicals Division. The exceptions: *Co-ed, Forecast for Home Economics*, and the nonclassroom magazines *Wow, Bananas*, and *Dynamite*.

Field Operations was assigned to the Text Division, as that comparatively new branch of Scholastic's business was deemed to require the greater part of the time of the field salespeople — although they were advised to continue to find opportunities for the sale of magazine subscriptions, book club memberships, and Readers' Choice programs.

Four other publishing divisions remained as before: the Book Club Division, Michael Hobson, publisher; the General Book Publishing Division, Morris Goldberger, publisher; the International Division, Charles Brock, acting publisher; and the Home Economics Division, Carolyn Bishop, publisher.

In concluding his announcement, Richard Robinson said:

> Scholastic's publishing objectives become in large part the responsibility of each of these divisions. Yet there is and must also be a common bond among them—a sense of a larger Scholastic that touches all our programs. Primarily, this common bond consists in understanding that our business relies on the support of teachers and parents, and on the care we take in communicating with each individual young person who reads or sees what we create.

Within a year of the establishment of the Text Division and the Educational Periodicals Division, with Field Operations assigned to the former, a major shift in the assignment of Field Operations was announced by Richard Robinson. Excerpted from his announcement of July 6, 1978:

> Field Operations, which formerly represented all of Scholastic's school programs, now will concentrate solely on representation of Text,

Audiovisual, and Readers' Choice programs. A plan is being formed to analyze how Scholastic's magazine and club business may best be represented by field selling.

This decision was reached after a long analysis of the changing role of Field Operations. Last summer, in announcing the decision to incorporate Field Operations in the Text Division, we traced the development of Scholastic's resident representative system from its inception in the late 1940's. At that time, John W. Studebaker, Scholastic vice president for Professional Relations, organized a group of part-time resident representatives who called on schools on behalf of Scholastic's magazines and later its book club programs. By 1960, the Scholastic representative program was organized into six regions with regional directors including Jefferson Watkins (Northeast), Kent Allison (North Central), Charlie Schmalbach (Midwest), Dan Thompson, later succeeded by Mac Buhler (Southwest), Ben Olliff (Southeast), and Gordon Studebaker, later succeeded by Ken Allard (Far West).

During the 1950's and 1960's, Scholastic magazine and book club programs grew rapidly, aided by the efforts of the Scholastic representatives calling on schools and teachers throughout the United States. In the 1960's and early 1970's, Scholastic developed its supplementary text business and Readers' Choice paperback sales to the point where these programs became a significant part of the company. The back-to-basics movement and Scholastic's decision to move more fully into the basic text area led to the organization in the summer of 1977 of a Text Division which included Field Operations. During the 1977–78 year, it has become increasingly clear that we must focus the mission of Field Opera-

tions even more completely on Text and Readers'
Choice programs. This need for concentration
stems from several different factors.

1. As we move more and more into basic publishing, we must be assured that there is a group of
   people dedicated to marketing our new text
   programs, which can be sold only through
   personal representation. The responsibility for
   the development and marketing of texts has
   been placed on Andy Bingham and the Text
   Division.

2. Scholastic's growing product line, including
   magazines, book clubs, supplementary text
   and audiovisual programs, paperback programs, and basic texts, has become too complex for a single Scholastic representative to
   handle. . . .

3. The publishers of the Educational Periodicals
   Division, the Book Club Division, and the
   Home Economics Division have become increasingly concerned about the diminished
   priority and attention of Scholastic representatives to magazines and book clubs. Accordingly, these publishers have expressed a wish
   either to have more time of the existing field
   organization or to have the opportunity to organize a different approach to field selling of
   their programs. The decision to have Scholastic representatives concentrate on texts and
   Readers' Choice makes it possible for Scholastic to study the proper way to organize a field
   representation program for magazines and
   book clubs.

To formulate a plan for magazine and book
club selling which would be separate from the

Text Field Operations Division, Scholastic is fortunate to have the help of James B. Carsky, who will be consulting with Scholastic for the period July to December, 1978, on this project. . . . He will be working closely with Steve Swett, publisher of the Educational Periodicals Division, Mike Hobson, publisher of the Book Club Division, and Carolyn Bishop, publisher of the Home Economics Division. He also will be interviewing regional directors and other members of Scholastic Text Field Operations to determine their views on how magazines and book clubs may best be sold at the building level through personal representation.

In 1978 Mac Buhler was appointed national sales manager of Field Operations, Text Division, and in 1979 Karen Lautenschlaeger, formerly with American Book, was appointed director of national sales planning.

CHAPTER XXI

Attacks!

FEW were the years during Scholastic's first half-century when the company was not under attack by some individual or organization objecting to the choice of topics (usually social and political issues over which the American people were aroused and divided in their opinions) or to the manner in which a topic was presented (allegation of bias).

The word "attack" is used here to mean action much more concerted and threatening than the occasional letter of protest over an article or book. An attack usually called for banning the offending magazine or other Scholastic product from further use in the school or in the entire school district. District-wide and city-wide bans did occur. During the 15 years prior to 1946 — when Scholastic took over operation of the Teen Age Book Club and launched *Practical English, Prep,* and *Scholastic Teacher* — there were just four possible targets for attack: *Senior Scholastic, Junior Scholastic, World Week,* and *Scholastic Coach.* The first three, concerned mainly with the social studies, were much more vulnerable to attack than the sporting *Scholastic Coach,* yet even that unlikely dispenser of burning issues was accused by a competing publication of spreading Communist propaganda (Chapter V, "*Scholastic Coach*").

Most of the attacks came from the extreme right of the socio-political spectrum, whose activists—especially during the New Deal (1932–40), the Cold War period from 1946, and the McCarthy eruption of the early 1950's —were wont to label "Communist," "Communist sympathizer," or "fellow traveler" anyone who didn't see eye-to-eye with them on such issues as peaceful coexistence with the Soviet Union, support of the United Nations, and attainment of civil rights for all Americans. Publishers of textbooks and school periodicals were especially suspect if their material raised questions over the status quo of social and economic conditions. Activists of the extreme right believed strongly — and no doubt sincerely — that topics related to the Soviet Union should not be discussed in the public schools, even at the high school level, for fear students might be converted to the Communist ideology.

Fear of communism was epidemic and perhaps reached its peak during the early 1950's, when Senator Joseph R. McCarthy of Wisconsin made headlines with charges of Communist influence in places high and low. Lesser demagogues at local levels heeded the McCarthy alarm by arousing suspicion against known liberals including ministers, teachers, writers, school administrators, librarians, and politicians. To some swept up by the McCarthy hysteria, the display of a classroom map showing the Soviet Union marked the teacher suspect of being a Communist. Or, if this seemed farfetched in view of the teacher's unblemished record of loyalty to flag and country, the accusation would be something less severe, such as "soft on communism," "unwitting dupe of Com-

338

munists," "leftist-" or "Communist-leaning."*

Perhaps these wild-swinging accusations against liberals can be explained by the difficulty of identifying the genuine Communists, most of whom did not wear membership cards on their chests. At its peak there were said to be 55,000 Communist party members of the total U.S. population of 150,697,361 in 1950. As far as the Scholastic management knew, there was only one member of the staff ever to be a member of the Communist party, and this was not known until he had left the company less than a year after being hired in 1938. Nothing he wrote that appeared in *Scholastic* or *Junior Scholastic* could possibly have been construed as "Communist propaganda."

Generally, if the decision to use or not to use *Scholastic* was left to the teachers in face of an attack by some civic or patriotic organization, the teachers would continue its use and be backed by their principals. But they could not do so if a ban had been officially ordered by the school board. In every instance, bans affecting Scholastic were lifted in time—most within a semester—but for some it took a year or more. In the meantime Scholastic's officers and its representatives in the field continued their efforts to have them lifted.

Let it not be assumed that Scholastic was always blameless in these situations, for there were instances— as the following summary will show—where the editor

*Some teachers in the Washington, DC, high schools, when *Scholastic* was banned by the board of education in 1936, showed their disgust over the action by turning the faces of their Euro-Asia maps against the wall so that the U.S.S.R. would be invisible.

made a "palpable error" of judgment over what was appropriate for school use or over the fairness of a presentation of a controversial subject.

The handling of and response to attacks required the utmost in courtesy and careful letter preparation, and often involved travel to meet with boards of education, school administrators, teachers, and, occasionally, students. This called for vast amounts of time on the part of editors, field staff, and company officers, especially the vice presidents in charge of professional relations—John W. Studebaker when he came on the scene in 1948 and Melvin W. Barnes in February 1969. They were quick to go into action, first on the telephone, then with telegrams, letters, and usually with an offer to put in a personal appearance. These prompt responses were invariably appreciated by school superintendents and their staffs, who were frank to say they needed help. And almost to the man or woman, they wanted to help Scholastic.

Outrage Over a Prizewinner
The first attack of major proportions bore no relationship to the political or economic situation of the time— the Depression—but it did impinge on the religious beliefs and sensitivity of many people.

The flareup came with the publication of the May 2, 1931, student-written issue of *The Scholastic*, announcing the results of that year's Scholastic Writing Awards and publishing the winning entries. First prize in the familiar essay category was awarded to a 17-year-old junior at West Seattle High School, Seattle, WA, by the name of Frances Farmer. You need read no further than the title of her essay to get an idea of the extent of the resulting outcry on the part of teachers. Her essay, "God

Dies," was voted the first prize of $100 by the four outside judges: a Penn State English professor, the editor of *Life* (a humor magazine), the director of the Holliday School of Writing, and a poet.

Robinson had discussed with Managing Editor Kenneth M. Gould the risk involved in publishing the essay and advised, but did not order, him not to publish it. In her autobiography *Will There Really Be a Morning?* Frances Farmer* gave four pages to the episode, stating "When the essay was published . . . all hell broke loose. The national press picked up the story, and within a week I began to receive letters from all over the country." So did Scholastic.

The essay appeared in the third from the last issue of the school year, and its publication at that time probably had a less-damaging effect on subscriptions than would have resulted had it been published early in the school year—when cancellation for that year's subscription undoubtedly would have come from many schools. The circulation of 85,132 at the time represented a gain of 17,890 over the year before. "God Dies" no doubt had a considerable braking effect on the rate of circulation growth for

---

*Frances Farmer went on to fame and misfortune in the 1930's and 1940's, starring in 19 movies and three Broadway plays, then through overindulgence in alcohol, family antagonisms, and disillusionment with Hollywood to imprisonment and physical collapse. She appeared to be on the road to rehabilitation when she developed cancer of the throat and died in 1970. Her frank and frightening autobiography, *Will There Really Be a Morning?* was published posthumously by Putnam's. She wrote, apropos "God Dies": "I had unwittingly released a monster. . . . A prominent minister announced that he was going to destroy the creeping atheist among our nation's youth. . . . He pictured me as a tool of Satan . . . and said 'If the youth of Seattle are going to hell, Frances Farmer is leading them there.' "

the following year, when the gain was only 1,653, for a total of 86,785. A year hence—school year 1932–33—would find the circulation almost doubled to 151,240, much of which could be attributed to the merging of the former American Education Press publications *Current Literature, World News, Current Topics,* and *Magazine World* into *Scholastic.* Of course, there were many new teacher-subscribers who either had not heard of the "God Dies" brouhaha or were indifferent to it, plus others who had been subscribers and who, after a year's absence, decided that the value of using *Scholastic* outweighed any feelings of outrage they had over the essay.

The uproar over "God Dies" failed to elicit a district-wide ban on *Scholastic* in Seattle or anywhere else, although there were subscription cancellations from some schools, mainly parochial. Scholastic had applied for and was granted a display booth at the annual meeting of the National Catholic Educational Association to be held in Philadelphia, but because of the "God Dies" essay the association cancelled the arrangements. Nevertheless, Robinson went to the convention—boothless—to see leaders of the association about the problem. He came away satisfied that they would not carry the censure any further. There soon developed a beneficial relationship between Scholastic and the association, a result of which was the inclusion of a representative of the association on Scholastic's National Advisory Council.

Thirty years later, *Senior Scholastic* would present a major article entitled "Is God Dead?" without one protest. A balanced, factual article on the "God Is Dead" movement of the time, it dealt with the same concept as Frances Farmer's prizewinning essay.

God Dies

By Frances Farmer, West Seattle High School, Seattle, Washington

First Prize, Familiar Essay Division, Scholastic Awards :: Teacher, Miss Belle McKenzie

NO one ever came to me and said, "You're a fool. There isn't such a thing as God. Somebody's been stuffing you." It wasn't a murder. I think God just died of old age. And when I realized that he wasn't any more, it didn't shock me. It seemed natural and right.

Maybe it was because I was never properly impressed with a religion. I went to Sunday school and liked the stories about Christ and the Christmas star. They were beautiful. They made you warm and happy to think about. But I didn't believe them. The Sunday School teacher talked too much in the way our grade school teacher used to when she told us about George Washington. Pleasant, pretty stories, but not true.

Religion was too vague. God was different. He was something real, something I could feel. But there were only certain times when I could feel it. I used to lie between cool, clean sheets at night after I'd had a bath, after I had washed my hair and scrubbed my knuckles and finger nails and teeth. Then I could lie quite still in the dark with my face to the window with the trees in it, and talk to God. "I am clean, now. I've never been as clean. I'll never be cleaner." And somehow, it was God. I wasn't sure that it was . . . just something cool and dark and clean.

That wasn't religion, though. There was too much of the physical about it. I couldn't get that same feeling during the day, with my hands in dirty dish water and the hard sun showing up the dirtiness on the roof-tops. And after a time, even at night, the feeling of God didn't last. I began to wonder what the minister meant when he said, "God, the father, sees even the smallest sparrow fall. He watches over all his children." That jumbled it all up for me. But I was sure of one thing. If God were a father, with children, that cleanness I had been feeling wasn't God. So at night, when I went to bed, I would think, "I am clean. I am sleepy." And then I went to sleep. It didn't keep me from enjoying the cleanness any less. I just knew that God wasn't there. He was a man on a throne in heaven, so he was easy to forget.

Sometimes I found he was useful to remember; especially when I lost things that were important. After slamming through the house, panicky and breathless from searching, I could stop in the middle of a room and shut my eyes. "Please God, let me find my red hat with the blue trimmings." It usually worked. God became a super-father that couldn't spank me. But if I wanted a thing badly enough, he arranged it.

That satisfied me until I began to figure that if God loved all his children equally, why did he bother about my red hat and let other people lose their fathers and mothers for always? I began to see that he didn't have much to do about hats or people dying or anything. They happened whether he wanted them to or not, and he stayed in heaven and pretended not to notice. I wondered a little why God was such a useless thing. It seemed a waste of time to have him. After that he became less and less, until he was . . . . nothingness.

I felt rather proud to think that I had found the truth myself, without help from any one. It puzzled me that other people hadn't found out, too. God was gone. We were younger. We had reached past him. Why couldn't they see it? It still puzzles me.

A year before the publication of "God Dies," *The Scholastic* published four short poems by Thomas Hardy in its April 13, 1929, issue, including one that had brouhaha potential. But as far as the record shows and memory recalls, it passed unprotested. It appeared in the feature, "The Poetry Corner," edited by Orton Lowe.*

Christmas 1924
by Thomas Hardy

"Peace upon earth!" was said. We sing it,
And pay a million priests to bring it.
After two thousand years of mass
    We've got as far as poison-gas.

*Orton Lowe had been M. R. Robinson's English teacher at Wilkinsburg High School and later became supervisor of English for the Commonwealth of Pennsylvania.

Ban Over Langston Hughes

The first city ever to put an official board of education ban on *Scholastic* was Long Beach, CA, an action taken early in 1932 on a charge by the Long Beach Ku Klux Klan that *Scholastic* was a vehicle for promoting communism through the publication of poetry written by Negroes including James Weldon Johnson, Countee Cullen, Gwendolyn Bennett, and Langston Hughes. The Klan's objection was not to the poems *Scholastic* published, but to those it didn't. Hughes, who wrote passionately about Negro life and interracial relations in America, was the principal target: He was accused of being a Communist—if not an actual party member, a purveyor of Communist ideology through his vigorous verse and stories. Moreover, he had recently been welcomed in the Soviet Union. Any such visit by an American liberal at that time was considered by the radical right as *prima facie* evidence of one's affinity for the teachings of Marx and Lenin.

Because of serious company problems at home (Chapter III), Robinson was delayed several months in going to Long Beach to try to have the ban rescinded. Armed with copies of *Scholastic*, including those in which Orton Lowe and Dorothy Emerson (successive editors of the *Scholastic* feature, "The Poetry Corner") had written about Hughes, Robinson called on the superintendent in Long Beach. He explained *Scholastic*'s background, ownership, etc., and its purpose in presenting to high school English classes material about distinguished contemporary American writers — regardless of color, sex, religion, or ethnic origin. Whereupon, the superintendent said he would recommend lifting the ban at the next meeting of the board of education. This was done in time to attract advance subscriptions for school year 1932–33.

The second ban of *Scholastic* was in that noblest of American cities, our nation's capital. On December 2, 1936, the school board of Washington, DC, forbade the use of *Scholastic* in District schools on the allegation that it "advocated communism" and "spread pacifist propaganda." The latter indictment was based on an editorial published three years earlier in *Scholastic*'s Armistice Week issue of November 11, 1933. The editorial, "This Business of War," is reproduced on p. 352.

From the Nation's Capital

The District of Columbia school board took this action despite the recommendations of a special Scholastic Magazine Committee of administrators and teachers set up by Superintendent of Schools Frank W. Ballou, to continue *Scholastic* on the approved list of publications.

A tangle of events—involving a citizens' committee "to expose communism in the schools," two Congressional committees investigating instructional materials used in the District schools, and the appearance of Robinson before these committees—preceded the action of the District's board of education and are pertinent to an understanding of why the board voted to ban *Scholastic*. A summary of these events follows.

In December 1935 Attorney George Sullivan of Washington, DC, representing the Committee on Communism of the Federation of Citizens' Association of the District of Columbia, submitted a report to the Board of

M. R. Robinson presenting his reply to charges of "subversive tendencies" to the Washington, DC, Board of Education: Frank Ballou, superintendent of the District schools (left); and Mrs. Henry Grattan Doyle, president of the Board (December 16, 1936).

Education accusing *Scholastic* of being "Communistic" and demanded that the board of education bar the magazine from the schools because the use of *Scholastic* conflicted with what was familiarly known as the "Red Rider" (a rider to the District appropriation bill forbidding the payment of money to a teacher who teaches or advocates communism).

Sullivan also pointed to the presence of Harold Rugg of Teachers College, Columbia University, as *Scholastic*'s social studies editor as evidence of Communist influence. The objection was not to the articles Rugg wrote for *Scholastic*, but to his social studies textbooks, which were widely used in the high schools.

The board of education referred the charges to Superintendent Ballou, who appointed a committee of teachers and supervisors of the Washington high schools to make an investigation of *Scholastic* and its editorial policies.

In February 1936 this committee of teachers and

supervisors gave Robinson an opportunity to answer the charges, which he did in depth. The following week Robinson appeared before the Subcommittee on District of Columbia Appropriations, Thomas Blanton, chairman, and was accused by the members of fostering communism. A complete report of this hearing was published in *Hearings Before the Subcommittee of House Committee on Appropriations* (74th Congress, second session).

Later the District of Columbia Subcommittee on Education of the House of Representatives held hearings on the Sisson bill, which was designed to repeal the "Red Rider." During these hearings Sullivan again charged *Scholastic*, together with other magazines and books, with fostering communism in the schools and being in conflict with the "Red Rider." This committee gave Robinson an opportunity to file a reply to the charges. His reply was published in the *Hearings on the Sisson Bill Before the Subcommittee on Education.*

The committee of teachers and supervisors appointed by Superintendent Ballou submitted its report on June 10, 1936. It was returned to the committee so that they might examine copies of *Scholastic* issued during the fall of 1936.

On November 17, H. A. Smith, assistant superintendent of schools and chairman of the committee, submitted to the superintendent its final report. It concluded: "The committee recommends that *Scholastic* be retained on the list of magazines approved for classroom use." The committee dismissed entirely any charges of communism or subversive or un-American editorial attitudes. The committee also reported to the board of

WORTHY PROTEST

MAURICE R. ROBINSON of Pittsburgh, editor of the "Scholastic" magazine, has secured permission to carry before the District of Columbia board of education his protest against the banning of that publica- from Washington schools.

We doubt that a public body which was foolish enough to make such an order in the first place will be wise enough to rescind it. However, we admire Mr. Robinson for having the courage of his convictions and also for taking steps to reveal the existence within portions of our educational system of the sort of intolerance which prompted the order.

"Scholastic," a Pittsburgh institution, has been widely recognized as a useful adjunct of the schools. It has been intelligently edited, with a broad respect for freedom of speech and of teaching and a commendable tolerance of the opinions of all. It has sponsored many commendable educational activities.

The District of Columbia school board has cleared the publication of charges of "subversive tendencies" and has held that the banning was caused by "too definite an editorial policy." In short, it expressed views. It had ideas. And the D. C. school board would protect pupils from ideas. (Which, incidentally, would bar from the educational system the works of most leading authors and a large part of the classics.)

About the most serious thing "Scholastic" has ever done is to exemplify the teachings and obligations of the Bill of Rights and to support the principles of academic freedom. The ban against it is a startling demonstration of the Fascist threat which hangs like a pall over America's educational institutions. Freedom of thought and of education are the first objects of Fascist attacks.

From *The Pittsburgh Press*, April 25, 1936.

education that "on one point, however, *Scholastic* does avowedly advocate only one side of the question: that is, 'encouragement of a national popular will against war.' "

The report went on to say, "Although this avowed policy of the editors to use the magazine as a medium through which to develop peace-mindedness among high school students by showing the horror, waste, and futility of war might be called 'indoctrination,' yet it is based on what is, in fact, a fundamental American ideal; and, hence, the committee cannot condemn *Scholastic* for the stand which it takes on this particular question."

On November 18, 1936, the superintendent of schools submitted the teacher-committee report on *Scholastic* to the board of education in these words: "the Superintendent recommends that the Board of Education accept the report of the Committee on *Scholastic*."

At its meeting on December 2 the board of education, by a vote of seven to one, refused to adopt the committee's report, citing the editorial from the November 11, 1933, issue entitled "This Business of War" as their main reason for doing so.

As soon as Robinson heard of the board's decision, he telephoned its president, Mrs. Henry Grattan Doyle, to request a hearing. It was granted and scheduled for the afternoon of December 16. No barrister appearing before the Supreme Court could have been better prepared than Robinson was for that hearing. His "brief" was a 4,000-word document (plus appendices) explaining his purpose in publishing a magazine for high school students, his bewilderment over the board's concern about something that had been published three years before and over the board's rejection of the report of the special committee of administrators and teachers exonerating *Scholastic* of communism. Robinson's three paragraphs on this point are worthy of note:

> Most pertinent of all to this discussion, it seems to me, is the fact that almost a year ago, at the suggestion of the Board of Education, the Superintendent appointed a large and doubtless capable committee of teachers and supervisors to study the charges brought against *Scholastic*; and also to make a thorough investigation of the magazine to determine whether or not it should be retained on the list of magazines approved for classroom use in the District high schools. That committee worked over a period of several months studying a period of six years, for some of their references go back to 1930.

The committee presented to its chairman and through the chairman to the Superintendent, a scholarly and documented report. The care with which they must have studied the magazine is apparent throughout the 10 pages of the report. Innumerable references and quotations show that the committee tackled the subject without prejudice and without fear. They sought to make a thorough and accurate appraisal of the magazine and its editorial attitudes. The committee based its study on instructions and standards issued to them by the Superintendent of Schools. This committee was not concerned with paragraphs and sentences lifted from their context but with the spirit of the magazine. The report that they made to the Superintendent completely dismissed the charges of communism brought against *Scholastic* and although they pointed out the desire of the editors "to develop peace-mindedness among high school students," they added that "this attitude is based on what is in fact a fundamental American ideal; and hence the committee cannot condemn *Scholastic* for the stand which it takes on this particular question."

Surely the members of this committee cannot be condemned as pacifists wishing to poison the minds of Washington high school students; nor can the Superintendent of Schools—with a full knowledge of the anti-war references—be similarly condemned for recommending on November 18 that the Board of Education adopt the report of the teachers' committee.

Robinson also expressed bewilderment over being charged with being both Communist and pacifist. "They are entirely exclusive terms," he said. "We cannot possibly be both. If hatred of war, opposition to war, and the things that make for war are defined as pacifism, then I doubt if there are more than a handful of Americans who would not be classified as pacifists."

He told the board members, "If you are to be fair in analyzing the editorial balance of *Scholastic,* you should study all of its editorials, and if you did so, you would realize the injustice of the accusation that 'the sole and exclusive purpose of *Scholastic* is to wage a campaign against war.' " He added:

> During the four-and-one-half years prior to the summer of 1936, we published 93 editorials—three of them were devoted to the general subject of war and peace. Each of the three appeared during the week celebrating the Armistice of 1918. I do not apologize for those three editorials. In fact, considering the importance of the subject of war, perhaps I should apologize for having so few editorials on that subject in four-and-a-half years. But the point I wish to make is that if you are to analyze accurately and justly the editorial balance of *Scholastic*, then you should study all of its editorials. Last spring, with an editorial assistant and a stenographer, I spent five full days making a survey of the editorial content of *Scholastic* covering a period of four-and-one-half years.

Robinson then proceeded to classify the 93 editorials, and because this classification is an indicator of the range of topics considered important by Editor Robinson and Managing Editor Gould, it is offered here. Another reason for including this list is its significance in understanding a major change in *Scholastic* policy that was to follow early in the 1940's, when editorials were discontinued. This was done in order to avoid the possibility of prejudicing students in support of the *Scholastic* position on critical

SCHOLASTIC

VOLUME 23, NUMBER 7   The National High School Weekly   NOVEMBER 11, 1933

This Business of War

An Editorial

YES, this is Armistice Day. Fifteen years ago Saturday the big guns ceased booming on the Western front. It is time to take stock. Just where do we—the high school generation of America—stand on this war business, anyhow? This issue is devoted to an effort to answer that question.

It does not need a fortune-teller to perceive that the world is nearer today to another war of ghastly proportions than at any time since 1918. We had better begin by admitting what any military advocate will immediately point out: (1) Japan has made an all but fatal breach in the peace machinery laboriously built up through the League of Nations, the World Court, the Kellogg Pact, and innumerable conferences. She has overrun a third of China, and is steadily strengthening her grip on the Asiatic mainland. (2) Republican Germany, harassed by the harsh provisions of the Treaty of Versailles, by reparations, economic collapse, and loss of border states, has installed a Fascist government whose avowed aim is to restore her old militarist power and spirit, has broken with the League, and has begun rearming to challenge her former enemies whose failure to live up to their treaty obligations gave her this excuse. (3) The long-drawn-out efforts to bring a genuine measure of disarmament out of the conferences

$1,300 for One Bomb

at Geneva have met with almost total failure through the rivalries of imperialistic powers. (4) More men today are under arms throughout the world, and greater budgets, totalling 5 billion dollars a year, are being spent for war preparations, than in June, 1914. (5) Under the stress of four years of worldwide depression, the nations, including America, have withdrawn within themselves, raised tariff barriers, and fostered a policy of economic nationalism which has in the past inevitably led to war.

These things cannot be successfully denied. From them, many sober people are being gradually driven to a belief that all peace efforts are useless, that war is imminent, and that the only safe course for the United States is isolation and large-scale preparedness. It is not easy to preach disarmament in a world of unmuzzled mad dogs.

To all these there is but one answer: Another major war will so decimate everything we know as civilization that life will survive, if at all, only on the lowest animal level. The presses of the world are thundering with proof of it. A reading of two books described in this issue—*Cry Havoc!* and *What Would Be the Character of a New War?*—should convince any half-way intelligent person that a second world war will blot out the planet. In 1914 fighting was essentially the same as it was in Napoleon's time—or Genghis Khan's, or Cæsar's. In 1918 it had escaped into the air, the laboratory, and the zones behind the lines. In 1950 these "blessings" of modern science, if uncontrolled, will have destroyed the human race.

What is the answer for a conscientious citizen of a democratic republic? Extremists are never popular. But the passion and logic of Beverley Nichols' great book force us to the inescapable conclusion that war will never be ended except by a mood of fanaticism. There is only one time to stop a war, and that is before the war fever gets us. Two groups could end war if they would—the women of the world, and its young men. There are some signs that a ferment is working in these groups. Votes taken recently in numerous English and American colleges show that nearly fifty per cent of some student bodies would refuse to go to war under any circumstances.

We are not asking high school students to adopt last-ditch pacifism. But we think they should know enough about war to respect sincerity wherever they find it. And we believe the time has come for the youth of America to adopt a program on which students of good will can unite. Here are four possible planks:

1. We will not fight in any war unless the mainland of the United States is invaded by a foreign foe, or unless by international agreement against an aggressor state.

2. We will not fight in any war which has not been declared by majority vote in a nation-wide referendum.

3. We will not accept conscription of our bodies for the army or navy without an equally complete conscription of the capital and profits of industry.

4. We will maintain to the end our right to determine our own conduct by independent thinking.

What do you think?

issues of the day. Since "all positions" (all sides of a controversy) would be represented in the magazine's basic content, the position of the *Scholastic* editors would *ipso facto* be there, although not labeled as such. Thus *Scholastic*—a teaching instrument—would represent the "model" teacher who taught all viewpoints of a serious controversy, but advocated none. To most leaders in social studies education, this was considered the posture a teacher should take.

Analysis of 93 Editorials in Scholastic Between January 1932 and May 1936

Personal enrichment. These include editorials devoted to moral standards; the wise use of leisure; application to studies; the appreciation of and the taking advantage of cultural opportunities; health and the importance of care of the body. (Under this heading *Scholastic* published 43 editorials.)

School life. These editorials concern problems of behavior within the school; relationship to fellow students, to the teachers, and to the administrators; and the problems relating to extracurricular activities of all sorts, including creative work. (10 editorials)

Vocational opportunities for youth. (Three editorials)

Free public education. Its opportunities; its place in a democracy. (Five editorials)

The necessity for a scholarly approach to the study of national and international problems and the necessity for young people to study these problems in order to become intelligent citizens. (11 editorials)

Invitations and pleas to participate as citizens in the life of the community and the nation as a patriotic American. (Eight editorials)

War and peace. (Three editorials)

Economic or political subjects. (Under this heading — although the four-and-a half years covered included a period of stress and depression when these problems were foremost in the minds of each American — we published seven editorials.)

Statement on the editors' attitudes toward national and international problems. (Three editorials)

Good news! It took four months to get it, but Robinson's reasoning was persuasive. On April 7, 1937, the Washington, DC, board of education rescinded the ban on *Scholastic* with the following resolution:

That the Board of Education rescind the action it took against the magazine, *Scholastic,* at the Board meeting held December 2, 1936.

A second motion was then put and passed, "approving the use of the magazine, *Scholastic,*" in the English classes of the District of Columbia public schools.

Perhaps the letters from Robinson, McCracken, Gould, and other members of the staff to members of Congress had some influence on the board, which after all got its money to operate the schools from Congress. Eleanor Roosevelt was also helpful. Robinson went to see her in the White House, and she said she would see what she could do about getting the ban lifted.

A year or so later, in quite another connection, she did something else for Scholastic without any formalities, after reading the first issue of *Junior Scholastic* in September 1937. She gave it a favorable notice in her syndicated newspaper column, "My Day."

The third city to have the honor of banning *Scholastic* was Topeka, KS, and again Robinson would appear before a board of education.* The Topeka board's action got its impetus from a pamphlet widely distributed to boards of education by an organization called the Public School Association, headed by Dr. Amos A. Fries. It was an organization well-known for its sniping at public school systems, especially for what it considered their wasteful use of the taxpayers' money. This circular contained accusations that material published in *Scholastic* was Communist-inspired and espoused the Communist way of life.

As soon as he heard of the Topeka ban, Robinson telephoned the high school principal, Willard H. Van Slyck—a director and later president of the Department of Secondary School Principals, National Education Association—to ask for an opportunity to discuss these charges with him and any others he wished to include. Van Slyck invited Robinson to attend the next meeting of the board of education—Thursday of that same week in November 1938—and to stay at his home in Topeka. It was to be a night meeting, and Robinson arrived in Topeka in plenty of time to visit each member of the board in his or her (there was one woman member) office or

A Retired Army Colonel to the Rescue

* *Nostalgic Coincidence Dept.:* Pittsburgh Superintendent of Schools William M. Davidson—in whose office in the summer of 1920 Robinson got the idea for a high school paper and who helped him get it started—had been superintendent of Topeka schools in 1892.

home and give each a bound volume of a year's issues of *Scholastic*. "I asked only one favor of each member of the board," he wrote in a report soon afterward, "that he read as many of the editorials and articles as he possibly could before the board meeting that night at eight o'clock." Here again, the charge was that *Scholastic* was espousing the Communist way of life.

After passing out the bound volumes Robinson returned to his hotel and spent the afternoon writing the statement he planned to read to the board that night. He never got to read it. Two members of the board were retired Army colonels. When the meeting was called to order, one of the colonels asked for the floor and said:

> Since I made the motion on the evidence presented at our previous meeting to ban *Scholastic* from our high school, I wish to tell you that this afternoon and early this evening I have read not isolated words and phrases, or even scattered paragraphs from *Scholastic,* but I have read page after page, editorial after editorial, and article after article—certainly the equivalent of 10 or 15 complete issues of the magazine, including the issue containing the disputed passages which Mr. Robinson did not hesitate to give me. I wish to make two motions: First, that our action of last week be reconsidered and second, that we reinstate *Scholastic* magazine with our approval and that we order copies of it for the board room. I wish to give three reasons for making these motions: (1) That I consider our judgment of last week hasty, ill-advised, and based on insufficient data, for I find a balanced ration in this magazine which I highly recommend. (2) We have a highly competent superintendent of schools, high school principal, and staff of teachers who have

356

chosen this magazine and recommend its use. If we have no confidence in their judgment— whose business it is to study and know the best materials available for use in our schools—then rather than instruct our teachers and our administrators, we should choose new ones. (3) Most important of all, it occurred to me today that the gods of fate must be laughing at us; for it is indeed a comic situation for us to presume that something the editor of *Scholastic* writes, or something that we forbid our children to read, can possibly alter the course of human affairs.

Shortly afterward, Robinson wrote: "It took high and genuine courage to say what that colonel said to his fellow board members in the presence of the press."

The colonel's motions were passed unanimously. The Topeka ban had lasted one week.

Attack and Retreat

A second instance of an attack followed by a retraction* occurred in 1940 when the September issue of *The American Legion Magazine* came out with an article headlined "Treason in the Textbooks," listing *Scholastic*

*In 1937 Major John L. Griffith, commissioner of athletics of the "Big Ten" Intercollegiate Conference and publisher of *The Athletic Journal*, a competitor of *Scholastic Coach*, sent a letter to the heads of sporting goods companies that advertised in *Scholastic Coach*, calling their attention to a report prepared by the Civil Council of Defense of California that identified Scholastic with the "many forces of communism at work in the schools of America today." On threat of legal action by Scholastic, Major Griffith wrote a letter of apology for "acting rather hastily in sending out a copy of that report without having made inquiry to ascertain whether those charges were true or untrue. Upon investigation I find those charges to be untrue." This was sent to all who received his first letter (Chapter V, "*Scholastic Coach*").

among some 20 books and magazines considered "objectionable for school use" by the Legion's Americanism Commission. Vigorous protests from Robinson and many friends of *Scholastic*—including Legionnaires—were registered with the Legion's editorial office in New York and national headquarters in Indianapolis, resulting in an apology from the Legion's managing editor in a letter to Robinson. Robinson distributed this along with his own statement to all schools subscribing to *Scholastic* and *Junior Scholastic*, then published it in the September 30, 1940, issue of *Scholastic* "Teachers' Section" and *Junior Scholastic* "Teachers' Companion." For years Scholastic representatives would be questioned about the listing by administrators and teachers who had heard of it from local Legion posts, but did not know of the retraction.

It would be debated from time to time in the Scholastic office whether attacks from the extreme right or left wings of political activism didn't do as much good as harm for circulation growth. But those who thought that growth came out of it were outnumbered and outranked by those who preferred to achieve growth by less arduous processes. It would also be pointed out that school administrators (as distinguished from boards of education), although almost always on Scholastic's side, would be ever so grateful not to have these disputes on top of so many others they must deal with.

For several years after the end of World War I Robinson had been a member of the Legion—the Downtown Businessmen's Post in Pittsburgh—but had resigned years before the article "Treason in the Textbooks" appeared in the Legion magazine. He did so because he objected to the Legion's growing involvement in politics.

358

Legion Magazine Retracts

Withdraws Scholastic From List of "Objectionable" School Texts

IN the September issue of *The American Legion Magazine,* an article entitled "Treason in the Textbooks" by O. K. Armstrong, was accompanied by a "partial list of the textbooks which your *(The Legion's)* Americanism Commission finds objectionable." *Scholastic* was included in the list, as were Carl Becker's *Modern History,* Beard and Beard's *U. S. History,* several textbooks by Harold Rugg, and a number of other textbooks, pamphlets and magazines, in cluding the *American Observer* and the other periodicals of our esteemed com petitor, Civic Education Service.

We immediately protested against this aspersion on the Americanism and patriotism of the editors and publishers whose contributions to education were thus attacked under a headline containing the word "treason." And specifically, we demanded that *The American Legion Magazine* publicly withdraw the name of *Scholastic* from the published list of "objectionable" ,school texts. There is reproduced here a copy of the Legion editor's retraction.

Photolithic copies of this letter have previously been mailed to schools using *Scholastic,* but *The American Legion Magazine* has a circulation of a million copies reaching every hamlet of Amer ica, and we urgently request the help of all our readers in calling this retrac tion to the attention of fellow-teachers. administrators, and pupils (asking them to tell their parents) so that this unjust publicity may be at least partially corrected. We urge you, too, to note and announce that the periodicals of the Civic Education Service have been given a similar letter of retraction. No announcement, at this time, has been made about other texts which may be withdrawn from the list.

Space does not permit a full discussion of the article and the list. We commend the editor of the *Legion Magazine* for his sincere desire to correct the errors called to his attention. Consequently, we shall attribute the published findings either to careless reporting, or the failure of the author to make a thorough investigation of the texts included in the list, or to his placing blind and unjustified faith in the person or persons who compiled the list.

Determined as we are, and as we shall be always, to uphold the principle that education and the choice of educational materials shall be entrusted only to the hands of trained and competent educators, we do not oppose the right of the *Legion Magazine,* or individual Legionnaires to investigate the subject matter taught in public schools and the materials used by educators to attain their educational objectives. This is a democracy. All citizens have the right to speak and be heard on how public moneys are expended. Our dearly held tenet of freedom of expression must be upheld no matter at what cost.

But thoughtful educators will be deeply concerned about "blacklists" published with the implied backing of organizations as powerful as the Legion. The implications are frightening. A kind of unofficial censorship of all a school may teach or students may read could result. And it will happen here, unless educators refuse to be influenced by such "blacklists" until after they themselves have arranged for an independent, impartial, intelligent investigation of the charges. In directing such investigations, require the charges to be specific. Despise innuendo, demand scholarly documentation of every charge, and insist that the accused is innocent until proven guilty.

Because of the experience *Scholastic* has had with this and similar incidents, we plan further discussion of the subject in future issues. Meanwhile, since by implication, although without foundation, our Americanism has been questioned, we shall repeat here again something we have said in these columns many times, both in actual words and by exemplification through the entire contents of our magazines:

We sincerely affirm that if anyone associated with *Scholastic* attacks the American way of life and government as described in the Constitution of the United States, or expresses disbelief in the rights of individuals to their freedom as described therein, or if such an associate ever advocates the overthrow of our government, he will be refused any opportunity to express himself through our columns, and we shall oppose him with every ounce of energy and influence we can command.

Maurice R. Robinson
Editor-Publisher
Scholastic Magazines

From the September 30, 1940, Teacher Edition, *Scholastic.*

The American
LEGION
MAGAZINE

Editorial Offices—9 Rockefeller Plaza, New York

September 20, 1940

M. R. Robinson, Editor-Publisher
Scholastic
220 East 42nd Street
New York, N. Y.

Dear Mr. Robinson:

The American Legion Magazine expresses its regret that Scholastic was inadvertently included in the list of publications said to be objectionable for school use, which appeared in connection with the article entitled "Treason in the Textbooks," by Orland K. Armstrong, in the September number, 1940, of this magazine.

Upon investigation and review of several numbers of Scholastic the editors are of the opinion that this publication should not have been included on such a list.

The editors of The American Legion Magazine find nothing in the publication which is un-American or otherwise objectionable for school use, although in all fairness to The American Legion Magazine we must say that the writings elsewhere of an occasional contributor to Scholastic do not always meet our approval.

Very truly yours,

BOYD B. STUTLER
Managing Editor

Later he would question whether he did the right thing: "Perhaps I should have stayed to fight from within."

In recalling *The American Legion Magazine* episode 35 years later, Robinson said: "I believe this one caused the largest percentage of cancellations of any attack we have had before or since."

The available circulation records do not reveal the extent of the cancellations, but they do show the circulation year by year without reference to the cause of ups and downs. The Legion attack came at the worst possible time for *Scholastic*—at the beginning of the school year when many teachers were placing orders and when all teachers who had ordered earlier had the right of cancellation. That year (1940–41) the circulation of *Scholastic* fell by nearly 3,000—from 198,752 in 1939–40 to 195,951 in 1940–41. *Junior Scholastic*, which was not included on the Legion list, had a gain of 5,675 to 107,584. For school year 1941–42, *Scholastic* recaptured the lost circulation of the year before, bettering it by 1,000.

Enemy of Satan and Scholastic

An editorial in the *St. Louis Post-Dispatch* of August 5, 1939, hailed the departure from that city of the Reverend Mary H. Ellis, who had included *Scholastic* in her campaign to rid St. Louis of influences she considered damaging the morals of its citizens. From pulpits in various churches she aroused her audiences to sign a petition to the superintendent of schools demanding the removal of *Scholastic* from the list of approved material. It had the desired effect—for about a year. After the Reverend Ellis left St. Louis, the *St. Louis Post-Dispatch* proposed that the ban on *Scholastic* be lifted:

DEPARTURE OF A GREAT CRUSADER.

The Rev. Mary H. Ellis, the 4-foot 10-inch crusader equipped with a 10,000-volt larynx, has departed for parts unknown. Barging down from Philadelphia last fall, she found St. Louis to be a most sinful city and direly in need of her methods of reform. Grimly she took the gauge of battle.

Raids right and left on book stores and magazine stands failed to make a case. Efforts to "reform" burlesque and the theater merely increased box office receipts. Exhortations for women to stay off bathing beaches, abandon cigarettes and "do all their dancing at one end of town while the men do theirs in the other," fell on deaf ears. Advice that pajamas be discarded for the purer old-fashioned nightgown had no effect on department store sales. But a complaint to Superintendent of Instruction Henry J. Gerling that the words "hell" and "damn" sometimes appeared in Scholastic, a high school weekly with a big national circulation and an advisory board including such men as Eduard C. Lindeman and Frederick L. Allen, bore fruit. Mr. Gerling promptly banned it.

Now that this energetic but rather ineffective enemy of Satan has gone to greener fields, perhaps Mr. Gerling will venture to lift the ban on Scholastic and thus remove the last ludicrous trace of the great reform movement that failed.

Within a few days after the appearance of the editorial, Robinson went to St. Louis to see Superintendent Gerling about lifting the ban. He did lift it on September 6, 1939, and notified Robinson in the following letter:

Sept. 6, 1939

My dear Mr. Robinson:

Last year a very large number of petitioners presented to me a protest against the use in our high schools of the magazine, *Scholastic*. The petitioners were concerned over specific statements that they considered objectionable from the standpoint of the language used or the

362

thought expressed. A protest made by hundreds of persons placed upon me, I thought I had the obligation temporarily, at least, to restrict the offering of the magazine by the schools to their pupils. The schools were not requested to cancel their subscriptions. In fact no general restraining order was issued. Suspension of use was all that was intended.

Since early last spring the magazine has been studied by high school supervisors. A group of intelligent citizens not members of our staff also gave us the benefit of their advice. Neither they nor I approached the problem in a spirit of censoriousness.

As a result of the studies that have been made and from my own conclusions I am writing to say that the magazine *Scholastic* will be restored fully to the position it occupied prior to the action which I took last year.

I cannot conclude this statement without expressing to you any appreciation of the objectivity with which you discussed with me an action of major import to you. Your attitude was not a minor factor in bringing to me the conviction that *Scholastic* is intended as a magazine that invites the interest and stimulates the intellectual activities of high school pupils.

Very truly yours,

Henry J. Gerling,
Superintendent of Instruction

Birmingham

The longest ban of a Scholastic magazine, as far as company records show, came out of the Deep South — Birmingham, AL. The cause of it was *Senior Scholastic*'s issue of February 23, 1948, bearing the subtitle: *Special Issue on Inter-Group Relations . . . Brotherhood Week,*

Feb. 22–29. The photograph on the front cover (shown on p. 366) set the tone of the issue — a plea for the end of segregation of blacks and whites and for the extension of civil rights to all Americans regardless of race. A majority of the Birmingham school board voted to ban the magazine, citing a number of articles and illustrations as being objectionable, among them: "How to Stop Hate Mongers in Your Home Town" by Hodding Carter; "High Hurdles for Minorities," staff-written; a cartoon feature, "Henry's Back Yard," based on the pamphlet *Races of Mankind* by Ruth Benedict and Gene Weltfish and on the animated film *Brotherhood of Man*; "How Crackpots Spread Hatred," by Ross Eichelberger with illustrations by staff artist Charles Beck; and "Boy Dates Girl," a popular feature of *Senior Scholastic* for many years, by Margaret Hauser, writing under the *nom de plume* Gay Head, and illustrated by Katherine Tracy.

The Birmingham ban was reported by the local press, carried on the wire services, and elicited editorial comment favorable to Scholastic. This editorial from the March 10, 1948, issue of the *Birmingham News*, shown opposite, stated the case to the apparent satisfaction of most Birmingham teachers and students, and certainly to the Scholastic staff.

One Birmingham teacher, when asked what she was using in place of *Senior Scholastic*, answered: "This editorial in the *Birmingham News*."

A few days after word of the Birmingham ban reached Scholastic, Robinson called a meeting of the staff to express his views on the situation. He felt that the special issue violated Scholastic's editorial credo in that it was heavily propagandistic, it made no mention of the

364

The Banning Of Scholastic

Senior Scholastic is a magazine especially edited for use as discussion material in the nation's high schools. It is edited and published in New York. Its editor-in-chief is Kenneth M. Gould. He visited Birmingham last year at the invitation of a group of Birmingham's teachers and addressed them at one of their professional meetings. *Scholastic's* national advisory council includes Dr. L. Frazer Banks, Superintendent of Birmingham's schools. The magazine has been used as a basis of discussion in the classrooms of city and county schools for more than a decade.

Last week a citizen, Frank Bainbridge, who has a child enrolled in one of Birmingham's high schools, took exception to some of the material in the issue of the magazine for Feb. 23, 1948. The general subject was Brotherhood Week. Mr. Bainbridge wrote a letter of protest to the Birmingham School Board. He asked the board to examine the "cheap political yellow sheet," declared that in his opinion it was devoid of any literary value, and that it advocates "the repeal of our segregation laws and endorses the president's so-called civil rights program." He asked the board if it approved the spreading of such ideas among the school children of the city. Mr. Bainbridge also pointed out that one section of the magazine featured questions and answers on problems of conduct of boys and girls together. He objected to the periodical's handling of questions about whether or not a high school student should kiss a girl after a date. His protest against the magazine is on the basis of morals and race presentation.

* * *

Last Friday the School Board took up the matter of Mr. Bainbridge's letter. President F. D. McArthur, after examination of the offending issue, agreed with Mr. Bainbridge's position. So did William J. Christian and Lawrence Stevens, members of the board. Mrs. J. A. Dupuy, another member, said that she did not agree with certain matters in the one issue, but stated that she did not approve condemning the magazine wholly on the basis of one issue. Dr. Banks agreed with Mrs. Dupuy and said that he did not recollect that such material as was objected to had appeared before. He urged that the board not condemn the magazine for use in the schools at this time. The board then voted on a motion objecting to further "circulation of the magazine in the public schools of the city." Messrs. McArthur, Stevens and Christian voted in favor of the motion. Mrs. Dupuy did not vote. Dr. Banks is presently formulating a letter to all high school principals banning the official use of the magazine hereafter in their schools.

A number of the school system's patrons have expressed regret at the action of the board in banning the official use of the magazine. At least a dozen high school teachers have indicated that they believe the magazine has considerable value. They object to the banning of it, believing that its presentation of any controversial material is always dispassionate. One teacher said that largely because of the magazine and other materials used, there had been every evidence in the schools that issues can now be discussed without hysteria. The feeling expressed by several others is that if the School Board does not feel that teachers can handle delicate matters satisfactorily in the classroom and in outside discussion groups, then the board is showing very little confidence in the teachers' abilities.

* * *

The News believes that the board acted hastily in banning the magazine without wider discussion and greater knowledge of its editorial policy over the years. Dr. Banks does not know of any other protest than that made by Mr. Bainbridge. Mr. Bainbridge's specific objection has to do with only one issue; he has not observed the magazine for a length of time.

The board did not ask for competent outside opinion on the matter. It listened to what Dr. Banks had to say, but it did not call in any teacher who had used the magazine in the classroom and it did not ask the opinion of any students who had read it and discussed it.

The News believes that the action of the board was summary. It believes it should have withheld judgment till other opinion could have been consulted. It regrets the action of the board. It believes such action is not in accord with the American tradition of free expression. It believes that the action will be widely resented in the city by many of the schools' patrons, by many of the teachers in the system, and by many of the students thus deprived arbitrarily of discussion material which has been found useful and stimulating for many years.

From the March 10, 1948, *Birmingham News*.

COMBINATION EDITION

Senior Scholastic

FEBRUARY 23, 1948 • VOLUME 52 • NUMBER 4

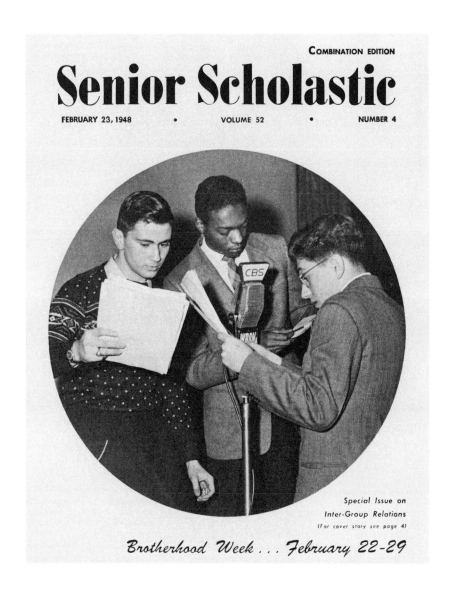

Special Issue on
Inter-Group Relations
(For cover story see page 4)

Brotherhood Week . . . February 22-29

South's point of view, and — especially in one feature, "How Crackpots Spread Hatred" — gave readers in southern states the feeling that they were being called fascists. He said that the topic of brotherhood could have and should have been handled in a spirit more in keeping with its name, avoiding the accusatory approach.

To the staff Robinson said that he would soon go to Birmingham to meet with Superintendent Banks, the school board, teachers, and students. He told of the telephone talk he had just had with Dr. Banks:

> It lasted more than a half hour, and I shall not attempt to give you a "total recall" of that conversation. But I would like to tell you of some of the points that were made by Dr. Banks, a well-informed, intelligent, soft-spoken educator. He has been and is a friend of Scholastic. I asked for his frank reaction and got it. Without attempting to quote him exactly, I shall tell you what he said:
>
> The schools belong to the public. They must be operated primarily to the satisfaction of the parents whose children are sent to them and who are compelled to attend. When the parents find cause to criticize the way the children are being educated and resent the instructional materials placed in those children's hands, the faculties and administrative officers of the schools are put under fire. They must either defend the content of the materials placed in the hands of the children or change the materials. Usually they automatically defend anything they have done. After all, they chose the materials and do not wish to admit they have been careless in making their choices. But when the uproar is too great or when they find it difficult to defend, in their entirety, the materials they have chosen, they have nothing else to do but withdraw them. Since in most cities all one has to do is to convince the majority of a small school board that the materials were unwisely chosen, school officials are almost always in a vulnerable spot.
>
> Having said this, Dr. Banks went on to point out that he opposed the action of the board as being too hasty and urged delay for further study. But he knew it was hopeless to try to defend some

of the material in the magazine that had been criticized. He could defend Scholastic chiefly on the grounds of our long record of excellence. He himself regretted to say that he felt we had failed in this instance because we were insensitive to the problems of a southern educator who must deal with the parents of his community.

Notwithstanding the editorial and articles in the Birmingham papers and the support of school principals, teachers, and students with whom Robinson met in Birmingham, the board of education did not lift the ban on *Senior Scholastic* until 1951. While in Birmingham, Robinson met with Superintendent Banks and members of the school board, and later wrote to the board chairman to thank the members "for the fine spirit they showed in granting me the privilege of a conference." To Banks he wrote: "I thoroughly enjoyed my time with you. It seemed almost worth having the Birmingham 'problem' because it gave me the opportunity to get to know you and other fine Birmingham people."

The attitude of many students toward the ban was well-stated by Dorothy Powell, a senior at Phillips High School, in this letter published in the *Birmingham News*:

March 19, 1948
To the Editor of the *News*:

When I read that *Scholastic* magazine had been barred from use in the Birmingham schools, I was stunned, and when I read the reason, I was completely confused. All of my life — all through school — I have been taught that education is the basis of tolerance. Step by step, it has been shown to me that a person should be judged by his ability and not his race or religion. Now, just as I am about to graduate, the very people who supervised these teachings defeat what I am sure was one of their main purposes. I am completely at a loss to understand their action.

In the first place, *Scholastic* is a literary magazine — and is considered as such by the teacher and pupils. There is no controversial article presented that is not seen from all sides. That is one of the aims of education.

As far as the value of the magazine is concerned, the students realize they will miss a lot of good reading and there is a deep feeling of resentment among most of them.

In the second place, Birmingham is a cosmopolitan town. There are people living here from all parts of the nation, and I see no logical reason for a very few short-sighted people to set us back to the grudges of the Civil War.

Dorothy Powell
Phillips High School

A week after Robinson returned from Birmingham, Scholastic librarian Lavinia Dobler, who had experience as a Scholastic subscription representative in Brooklyn and had taught English in Puerto Rico, paid courtesy calls on many of the administators and teachers Robinson had seen. She talked with them about *World Week* and *Practical English,* which, along with *Junior Scholastic,* had uneasy status in the Birmingham schools — suffering from guilt by association. Many in the Birmingham school community had the impression that all Scholastic magazines might be banned for the 1948–49 school year, as Labor Day had come and gone and the board of education had "not yet taken official action on approval of publications for the coming school year," as Banks wrote to Robinson on August 30, 1948. He added, "The list was presented to them, but we were not able to get enough copies of *World Week* for them to examine it. We have written for some sample copies which should reach us almost any day now. Thank you for telling me about your new publication *Literary Cavalcade.* . . . Send me about eight copies in order that we can consider it also." The board approved *World Week, Literary Cavalcade,* and *Junior Scholastic;* but three years passed before the ban on *Senior Scholastic* was lifted.

Dobler spent three days in Birmingham, then went to Atlanta, GA, and Charlotte, NC, to visit administrators and teachers to see if the Birmingham ban was having any influence on their attitudes toward Scholastic. They knew about the matter, as their local newspapers had carried the story. But no one in those cities or elsewhere seemed excited about it. Atlanta Superintendent Ira Jarrell, when asked by the *Atlanta Journal* what she thought of the ban in Birmingham, said: "If anybody wants to use *Scholastic* here, they can do so. The Birmingham action sounds silly to me."

When the Birmingham case erupted, Superintendent Banks was a member of Scholastic's National Advisory Council. Although Banks made no move to resign, Robinson—in deference to him—removed his name from the mastheads in the magazines.

Word from the Committee on Un-American Activities

The appearance in 1936 of a magazine called *Champion of Youth* (soon to be changed to *The Champion*), carrying the name of Kenneth M. Gould, Scholastic's managing editor, as a member of its advisory board, brought allegations years later that Scholastic was under control of an editor who was either a Communist or a Communist sympathizer. *The Champion* was published by the Young Communist League, but when Gould agreed to serve on the advisory board, he did not know that. Upon learning that it was a Communist publication, he resigned as an advisor, but by that time (1937) *The Champion* was on its last legs. A brouhaha over his indiscretion took 15 years in coming. When it did, the occasion had a somewhat unsettling effect on the Scholastic staff, as it sprang from the feared Committee on Un-American Activities of the U.S. House of Representatives. Word had reached the Committee in 1952 that the name of Kenneth M. Gould appeared on the advisory board of the long-defunct Communist youth magazine, and Congressman Harold H. Velde, Committee chairman, asked Gould for an explanation. He responded with the following:

Affidavit

I was born in Cleveland, Ohio, in 1895, and have been an editor, writer, and lecturer in the fields of secondary, higher, and adult education for more than 36 years. My father, the late Rev. Frederic A. Gould, was a Methodist Episcopal minister. I am a graduate of the University of Pittsburgh and hold an M.A. degree from Columbia University. I have been on the staff of Scholastic Magazines for 27 years, and was formerly associated with the Missionary Education Movement of the United States and Canada, the American Public Health Association, the Rockefeller Foundation, and Time, Inc.

I understand that my name has been cited in a report of the House of Representatives Committee on Un-American Activities as having been "an advisory editor of a Communist front youth publication." The facts in the matter are as follows:

In 1936 I was invited to become a member of

the advisory board of a new monthly magazine to be entitled *Champion of Youth* (the name was later changed to *The Champion*). It was published in New York City for two years only—1936 to 1938. I accepted because the magazine was represented to me as being devoted "to the aspirations and interests of the young people of the United States." It was not indicated at any time, either in its masthead or otherwise, that the magazine was sponsored by the Young Communist League or any other subversive organization. If it had been, I would have refused.

The advisory board, which contained a number of prominent figures (none of whom I recognized as being supporters or sympathizers of communism), was never called together. It was not consulted on editorial policy and had no control of the content of the magazine. It gradually became apparent to me from the contents of the issues that some, at least, of its active editors and contributors were either Communists or Communist-inspired. My suspicions were aroused by these facts, and I asked that my name be dropped from the board. About this time, however, the magazine was completely discontinued.

In the light of the revelations and events of the past fifteen years, it is clear that my acceptance of membership in this board was a mistake in judgment, although I was motivated at the time by purely humanitarian considerations.

I have never been a member of the Communist Party nor of any Communist front organization, and have never had the slightest sympathy with Communist principles or methods. I hate communism for what it has done to human beings, to truth, to freedom, and to the chances of peace in our time.

I am a homeowner and taxpayer in Scarsdale, New York, where I have lived for 21 years; a veteran of World War I; and am listed in *Leaders of American Education, Who's Who in Education,* and *Who's Who in America.*

I should be glad to testify to the truth of any of the above statements under oath, or before a legislative committee.

(Signed) Kenneth M. Gould
Editor-in-Chief
SCHOLASTIC MAGAZINES

The affidavit appeared to satisfy the Committee that Gould was not fair quarry in its search for subversives, and he and his Scholastic colleagues were relieved to read Congressman Velde's prompt acknowledgment of it, quoted in part as follows:

The Committee acknowledges with thanks your affidavit in which you state the facts relating to this matter. . . . The Committee is glad to have your explanation . . . and to learn from it that you have never been a member of the Communist Party, nor of any Communist front organization, as well as your assurance that you have never had the slightest sympathy with Communist Party principles or methods.

Though this ended the matter as far as the House of Representatives Committee on Un-American Activities was concerned, repercussions came from others who presumably had not heard of the Gould affidavit and Congressman Velde's reply — or if they had, considered the matter still open. California too had its Un-American Activities Committee (of the California state legislature) and in 1941 issued a report on the Gould listing on the masthead of *The Champion.* For years Scholastic continued to receive inquiries from California school systems, such as this one from Newport Beach District Superintendent Roy O. Anderson to Robinson (January 7, 1955), stating in part:

> It has been brought to my attention that the Eighth Report of the Senate Investigating Committee on Education of the California State Legislature, 1941, reports on page 55 that "Kenneth M. Gould is listed as Advisory Editor of the *Champion of Youth,* a Communistic party periodical for Youth." This refers to page 196 of the 1948 report by the California Committee on Un-American Activities. Mr. Gould is also referred to as the author of *Windows on the World.*
>
> Will you please advise me if this is the same Kenneth M. Gould who is listed as Editor-in-Chief of *Junior Scholastic* magazine?
>
> Pending receipt of your reply, we are withholding copies of *Junior Scholastic* from the classroom, in the event that this is the same Kenneth M. Gould, and, unless the California Committee on Un-American Activities has been officially established as having been in error in its reference to Mr. Gould, we wish to cancel our subscription to the *Junior Scholastic* magazine immediately and request the refund of the unused portion of the subscription price. If the California Committee on Un-American Activities has been established as having been in error in regards to Mr. Gould, please supply me with factual data concerning this.

The data were supplied, and the superintendent wrote back saying: "Your letter of January 15, 1955, regarding Mr. Gould has been received. I appreciate your prompt reply and am very happy to receive the reassuring information which you sent. I presented this material to the school board and they feel satisfied that we should continue the use of Scholastic publications in our classes."

A headline and article on page one of the January 21, 1955, edition of *The Fresno* (CA) *Bee* was clipped by the Scholastic representative there and sent to Studebaker at Scholastic. It read:

> ### *Pastor Brands Magazine Red; Schools Deny It*
>
> Rev. August Brustat, a Lutheran minister, has charged the *Scholastic* magazine, which is used in some Fresno schools, is carrying the Communist line to students. But a librarian in the Fresno County Free Library and a school official said they can find no evidence the magazine is subversive.

The Reverend Brustat had been critical of Scholastic for some time directly from his home pulpit, Trinity Lutheran Church in Scarsdale, NY, the hometown of Scholastic Editor-in-Chief Kenneth Gould and Vice Chairman and Senior Vice President Herb McCracken. According to the item in *The Fresno Bee*, Brustat charged Gould with "carrying the Communist line to students," and that "Scholastic was organized by Communists." Brustat was active in the Scarsdale Citizens Committee, whose purpose was to expose Communists or their "sympathizers" allegedly at work in the community.

After reading the item in *The Bee*, Robinson wrote to Pastor Brustat at his home in Scarsdale, asking for an opportunity to discuss with him the newspaper report

375

"indicating that you have disseminated some inaccurate statements about Scholastic magazines." Brustat promptly replied, "I shall be happy to comply with your request and invite you to my home. . . . Should you desire a companion to accompany you, that would be entirely satisfactory to me."

Robinson wanted McCracken to accompany him, and they met with Pastor Brustat, who had a Scarsdale friend with him. Brustat told Robinson and McCracken that he had been misquoted by *The Fresno Bee,* and in a letter to Robinson confirming this wrote: "The news item reports that I called *Scholastic* 'red.' This is not so. Nor did I say that *Scholastic* was organized by the Communists. I stated that *Champion of Youth* was organized by the Communist conspiracy. The confusion may have arisen because I correctly pointed out that Kenneth M. Gould was on the Advisory Board of this *Champion of Youth* during the entire period of its publication and was so listed on its masthead, while at the same time he continued his association with Scholastic Magazines."

When Robinson returned to the office, he asked Studebaker to telegraph *The Bee* to ask if they could verify the statements attributed to Brustat. Studebaker received the following telegram from W. E. Lockwood, managing editor:

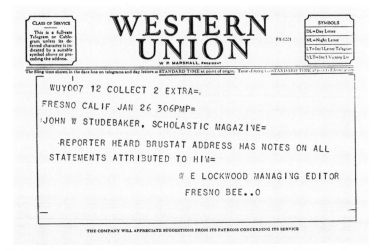

Scholastic's representative in Fresno, Harold Hughes, stayed close to his telephone in the days following the item in *The Bee,* talking to administrators, teachers, and Robert Rees and Arthur Corey of the California Teachers Association. "None of my phone callers seemed to take the attack seriously," Hughes reported to Robinson in New York.

An organization called the Citizens Council tried to get *Junior Scholastic* banned by the Fort Worth, TX, school board because, as claimed, "it teaches one world citizenship and not nationalism." On November 14, 1956, Joe L. Munn, secretary of the group, appeared before the board to renew his protest against the use of *Junior Scholastic*:

"Leftist-Leaning"
Junior Scholastic

> I want to repeat my objections because of leftist leanings in this magazine. I have checked further and have found that Kenneth Gould, Editor-in-Chief of the magazine, has one citation by the Un-American Activities Committee in California and that he is on the editorial board of the *Champion of Youth,* a communist front magazine. The *Junior Scholastic* is leftist because it teaches one world citizenship and not nationalism, which is the thing that has built this nation.

Some seven months earlier Munn appeared before the board to object to the March 15, 1956, *Junior Scholastic,* with its article on segregation and its reference to Ralph Bunche. Munn charged that Bunche had been "cited for un-American connections." The 1,800-word *Junior Scholastic* article, "America Faces a Problem: The

377

Supreme Court Decision — Historical Background and Summary of Recent Developments," referred to Bunche in one sentence as follows:

> Many Negroes have risen to important positions in education, science, literature, music, sports, and other fields. One example is Dr. Ralph Bunche, who is Under-Secretary General of the United Nations.

Neither Superintendent of Fort Worth Schools J. P. Moore nor the board of education could see *Junior Scholastic* the way the Citizens Council saw it, and they declined to take the action demanded.

A *Junior* Victory in Omaha

In the spring of 1963 Dan J. Whiteside, an attorney from Omaha, NB, launched an attack on *Junior Scholastic* for its presentation of controversial issues and petitioned the school superintendent and board of education of School District 66 in Omaha to discontinue its use. Whiteside examined *Junior Scholastic* issue by issue for the school year 1962–63 and prepared an extensive critique of many of the articles during that period, among them articles on the United Nations, the Hungarian freedom fighters, China, Cuba, the test-ban treaty and others. He viewed these articles as "biased and deceptive" in what he considered an attempt to subvert readers to a favorable opinion of the Communist nations. His objection was solely to *Junior Scholastic*'s "political content," and he said, "I find nothing else objectionable. I cannot concede that the disadvantages of this publication are outweighed by its advantages. . . . *Junior Scholastic* does have a theme. I find that theme to be: communism is not without some merit. The best I can say for *Junior Scholastic* is that it is presenting a sort of incompetent brand of 'instant history.' "

In the same report to the board of education Whiteside said: "I believe that politics has no place in the public schools and therefore would not suggest replacing *Junior Scholastic* with another of its kind. However, if the elimination of *Junior Scholastic* is contingent upon a replacement, I will be happy to undertake the effort."

Several weeks after Whiteside presented his case to the District 66 board of education, he received this letter dated June 18, 1963, from the board:

Dear Mr. Whiteside:

Each member of the school board of District 66 has reviewed most of the copies of the *Junior Scholastic* magazine that have been published during 1963. Some of us reviewed copies that were published in prior years.

It is our judgment that the contents are objectively presented. We do not find the deliberate attempt to indoctrinate that you called to the school board's attention on May 6, 1963.

There are undoubtedly isolated statements published in the *Junior Scholastic* from time to time with which some school board member would not agree. This would be true with any publication.

We appreciate your interest in the content of books and publications used in our schools, although we do not agree with your conclusion concerning the *Junior Scholastic*.

Very truly yours,

Jackson M. Barton
President, Board of Education

Not only did the Whiteside action fail in getting the Omaha School District 66 to cancel its subscriptions to *Junior Scholastic*, but it succeeded in increasing circulation by at least one subscription, as revealed in a letter from Superintendent H. Vaughn Phelps to Studebaker: "I do want to thank you for myself and the Board for your cooperation and help. . . . The President of our Board, Mr. Jackson M. Barton, 2506 South 95th Street, Omaha, indicated to me that he would like very much to subscribe to the *Junior Scholastic* for next year. Would you mind arranging with your distribution department for him to do so?"

Book OK, Banned Nevertheless

The public hears much more about book banning than it does about magazine banning. Obviously there is more of the former to hear about. The book, viewed as more enduring and influential than the magazine, is considered by self-appointed censors to be more dangerous to have around if it is one whose message arouses their ire.

As mentioned further on in this chapter, with five Scholastic book clubs and other branches of the company distributing more than 100 million books every year, few weeks pass (unless it be in the summer) without some teacher or parent objecting to a book. Usually the "objectionable" books will be returned for a refund, and no further action taken by the complainant.

Scholastic has not been entirely free of the problem that arises when a local school board decides to remove a book that had been appraised and approved for instructional use by the school faculty. The Levittown (Long Island, NY) case is worthy of note, not because the school board considered the book unfit for use, but because a majority of its members considered the author unfit to be reaping royalties which they thought he might use to promote Communist activities. The book was *The Sub-Continent of India*, one of 13 in the Scholastic Multi-Text series—paperbacks that pioneered the movement toward school use of paperback books for instructional purposes. Its author was Emil Lengyel: Hungarian-born (1895), naturalized U.S. citizen (1927), author of more than 25 works in history and biography, New York University and Fairleigh Dickinson professor. He had served in the Hungarian army in World War I and had been imprisoned in Siberia for 20 months.

A member of the Levittown school board, a former Navy officer, recalled having seen Lengyel's name on letterheads of several organizations accused of Communist affiliation and on the guest list at a dinner sponsored by another organization so accused. At that dinner Helen Keller sat beside him on the dais.

Upon hearing of the Levittown school board's decision to put the question on the agenda of its next meeting, John Studebaker, on April 19, 1963, sent the following telegram to the board chairman, Robert S. Hoshino:

> IT IS OUR UNDERSTANDING THAT THE QUESTION OF THE USE OF ONE OF OUR BOOKS IN THE LEVITTOWN SCHOOLS WILL BE ON THE AGENDA FOR THE MEETING OF THE LEVITTOWN SCHOOL BOARD NEXT MONDAY NIGHT. THE QUESTION ALSO INVOLVES DR. EMIL LENGYEL, AUTHOR OF THE BOOK ENTITLED THE SUB-CONTINENT OF INDIA. UNLESS THE MATTER CAN BE SETTLED WITH MUTUAL FAIRNESS AND SATISFACTION TO YOUR

BOARD, TO DR. LENGYEL, AND TO OUR
COMPANY IN THE RELATIVELY BRIEF
TIME THAT CAN BE MADE AVAILABLE AT
NEXT MONDAY'S MEETING, WE PROPOSE
THAT YOUR BOARD SELECT A SPECIAL
COMMITTEE OF THREE PERSONS CON-
SISTING OF A CATHOLIC PRIEST, A JEWISH
RABBI AND A PROTESTANT MINISTER TO
STUDY THE PROBLEM AND MAKE A RE-
PORT TO THE BOARD AT A LATER DATE.

> JOHN W. STUDEBAKER,
> VICE PRESIDENT AND
> CHAIRMAN OF THE
> EDITORIAL BOARDS
> SCHOLASTIC MAGAZINES, INC.

The school board declined this suggestion, but invited Studebaker to attend the board meeting. Along with
him went Lengyel (for moral support); Lengyel's son, a
Dartmouth student; and Jack Lippert, then executive
editor. The meeting started at 8 p.m. and ended four
hours later. Both Studebaker and Lengyel addressed the
board, the latter reading from a 1,500-word statement,
some of it recounting his teaching and lecturing for the
War Department during World War II, his anti-
Communist writings, and the banning of his book *1,000
Years of Hungary* by the Soviet Union. Referring to the
charge that he had Communist affiliations, he said:

> When the fascist and Nazi powers seemed to
> be sweeping across much of the free world, I did
> what I could do to alert Americans to the danger.
> Then the Second World War broke out. We
> strained every muscle to win that war. Sometimes

382

I was asked by anti-fascists and pro-Ally organizations to act as their sponsors. Of course, I refused to do so when they appeared to be in any degree Communist-inspired. But I had no means of investigating all of them. Thus, when their purposes seemed to be worthy, aimed at promoting the Allied cause, and when they had other sponsors of established prominence, I let my name be used. I may have been naive in assuming that what counted in such matters was not one's activities and real purpose but one's name as a sponsor on a letterhead. Some time after the war, some of these organizations were placed on the subversive list. Most of them are no longer in existence. I resigned sponsorship of the two that continued to function. I never paid dues to any of them.

I have learned a good deal about the tactics of those who were skilled operators of the subtle processes of subterfuge and infiltration. But *never* would I knowingly have permitted my name to be connected *in any way* with any organization whose purpose was to subvert our American way of life. I just couldn't have been a party to any such traitorous intrigue. My love of freedom, my unwavering devotion to my country, and my natural hatred of the deceitfulness, godlessness, and merciless character of the tyranny of communism and other forms of totalitarianism which have always been abhorrent to me, were ever present in my mind.

Lengyel got a rousing applause from most of the 300 spectators in the school auditorium, but this didn't deter the board from continuing the ban on the book by the margin of one vote.

The ban lasted about nine months, or until a new board was elected by an indignant majority of the voters.

Focus on Scholastic's Purpose

A shot from the "left," or anti-business side of the socio-political front, struck Scholastic in the spring of 1966, fired from an article in a magazine published in St. Louis called *Focus/Midwest*. The article, carrying the headline "The Dirty Business of School Magazines," was by Herbert I. Schiller, research associate professor, Bureau of Economic and Business Research, University of Illinois. In it he asserted that Scholastic was more a business- or profit-oriented enterprise than one devoted to education. "Making money has been the first objective of the company," wrote Schiller, and in straining to support this he pointed to the advertising in Scholastic by "corporations in the billionaire asset club — General Motors, A.T.&T., General Electric, Ford, Chrysler, New York Life Insurance, and the American Oil Company." Ads he also considered inappropriate were "the run-of-the-mill inducements to quaff Pepsi, 7-Up, Coke, or what have you; wear sneakers, eat cornflakes, and consider diamond engagement rings." He also looked upon the Scholastic Awards Program as "the promotion of culture on a percentage basis," objecting to the co-sponsorship of the program by a number of Scholastic advertisers, and naming Eastman Kodak and Sheaffer Pen — the latter, at the time, being co-sponsor of Scholastic Writing Awards.

In his attempt to identify Scholastic as an arm of big business, Schiller looked into the origin and early struggles of Scholastic and observed: "The company kept alive in the lean years of the 1920's and 1930's with capital infusions from a few individuals who were important directors of some of the nation's biggest businesses. Leading stockholder and present chairman of the board of directors of Scholastic Company is Joseph Wood Oliver, eldest son of one of the early financial supporters. Mr. Oliver is also vice president in charge of public relations and personnel of the Pittsburgh Consolidation Coal Company. The publisher, Mr. Maurice Robinson, began his working life as a full-time publicity writer in 1920 for the Pittsburgh Chamber of Commerce."

Schiller's diatribe ran some 3,500 words but had no apparent effect on subscriptions — even in the St. Louis area, *Focus/Midwest*'s publishing base.

Schiller aimed some of his fire at a series of full-page ads Scholastic inserted in *The New York Times, Los Angeles Times*, and *Chicago Tribune* addressed to marketing and advertising executives. In these ads Scholastic — via its Advertising Department — made some statements that were sure to trigger the antibusiness views of a Schiller. In his article he referred to these ads and asked: "Does Scholastic lead a double life? For parents and teachers it stresses educational values. At the same time it offers itself as a medium to commerce for winning the allegiance of young people in an atmosphere that is supposed to be directed toward other ends."

To illustrate, he quoted a few passages from the ads, such as: "New consumers develop product preferences in foods, toiletries, cosmetics, drugs, apparel, automobiles, durables, home furnishings — in a universe apart from adults, centered in school-oriented activities";[*] and: "Today advertisers must convey product information to consumers when the learning process is most acute in order to create brand preferences prior to and simultaneous with adolescence and early marriage."[†]

[*]*The New York Times*, December 1, 1964.
[†]*Ibid.*, April 9, 1965.

Schiller also cited another statement, which he prefaced by this remark: "A curious view of what education is all about was indicated in this promise to the business community (quoting from the ad): 'For brand manufacturers wishing to utilize the learning process to create brand loyalties among the NEW CONSUMERS, no medium is comparable to SCHOLASTIC MAGAZINES.'"

A reply to Schiller's allegations and insinuations was prepared by Scholastic executives to use in answering letters the company might receive as a result of the Schiller article. There were only four. To Schiller's charge that "education has always been second to commerce in Scholastic's priorities," the company replied:

> Service to education has always been and remains Scholastic's number-one priority. Scholastic made no money during its first 31 years, and its present profit on the magazines is 2.15% before taxes. We are not necessarily proud of this, but are merely presenting a fact to discredit Mr. Schiller's wholly false statement. Were we to put profit or "commerce" first, our profit record would have been much better than this. Our board of directors, our officers, our staff, put first and foremost service to the schools. Profit there must be to provide this service on a continuing basis, but it is not the first consideration.

The company decided to prepare a reply for publication in an early issue of *Focus/Midwest* if the publisher, Charles L. Klotzer, would agree to print it. He did. Written by Studebaker, it was published in the September/October issue, 1966. His second paragraph set the stage for his point-by-point response to Schiller's article:

The inaccuracies, distortions, and innuendos in this article leave anyone knowledgeable of Scholastic's contribution to education aghast that such an outburst could come from one identified as "research associate professor in the Bureau of Economic and Business Research at the University of Illinois." Mr. Schiller's research for this article did not even extend to one word of inquiry with an officer of our company, or with any member of our National Advisory Council — educators of recognized standing, some of whom Mr. Schiller names in his article and identifies as "prestigious individuals" and "illustrious educators." That they are. As they are also men of high integrity, one might well ask why Mr. Schiller's research did not extend to them if his interest was in accuracy, scholarship, and fairness.

As far as could be determined, Scholastic had no cancellations as the result of the Schiller article. The four teachers who wrote asking for the company's reaction to the article were answered along the lines indicated above, and they took no further action.

Out of Focus on Student Rights

One might say that some of the attacks were self-inflicted — brought on by the poor judgment or carelessness of editors and a lapse in supervision by the editor's superior. That might be said of one of the earliest examples of poor judgment — the publication of Frances Farmer's prize-winning essay, "God Dies," in 1931 — and one of the most recent, the students' rights issue of *News Citizen*, March 19,1973.

Hundreds of letters, telephone calls, and alarms from Scholastic representatives in the field overwhelmed the executive, editorial, and promotion staffs. Melvin W.

Barnes, vice president, Professional and Public Relations, took charge of the extraordinary measures required to handle the emergency.

About 300 schools and school systems canceled subscriptions or stated that they would not renew their subscriptions for the following year, and many of the schools canceled the entire elementary line — from the kindergarten program *Let's Find Out* on through to *Newstime* and *Junior Scholastic*. Even the book clubs and some of the high school periodicals were caught up in the wave of protests.

An English department head telephoned a cry for help into the New York office: "Can you talk to our superindendent? He's ordered us to return all copies of *Literary Cavalcade* and *Art & Man* and is cancelling all our subscriptions. Don't tell him I called you, but can you explain what happened?" When the situation was explained, the caller said, "I don't see what that has to do with our high school English work." Melvin Barnes made a discretionary call to the superintendent, who welcomed it and, a few days later, called back to say "I think this will blow over."

In addition to handling the telephone calls with apologies and explanations, the company dispatched a letter of apology to the 25,000 subscribing teachers and a statement written and signed by Richard Robinson, which just about covers the situation for this record:

Publisher's Statement

The March 19, 1973, issue of Scholastic *News Citizen*, entitled "Have You Got Rights?" was a special issue devoted solely to the subject of students' rights.

As you know, teachers, administrators, and parents are expressing great concern today that the young people of this country should know more about the subject of human rights — and the accompanying movement toward greater attention to the rights of the individual — but in the United States special attention has been focused on the rights of young people to vote in elections, to participate in government, to express themselves freely on public issues, and make basic decisions about their personal destinies.

Scholastic's Credo and Editorial Platform has for many years stated that "we believe in a democratic way of life with basic liberties and responsibilities for all."

It was in this spirit that the editors of *News Citizen* attempted to tackle this difficult subject. The editors wished to accomplish the following:

. . . to prepare students for the important tasks and responsibilities of citizenship in the years ahead.

. . . to help students understand people's rights to free expression, privacy, and fairness of treatment.

. . . to involve students through a discussion of the student's rights in the concept of rights and responsibilities for everyone.

. . . to make students aware that they had certain rights which would become more important to them as they grew older.

After reconsideration of the article, Scholastic editors now agree that we have substantially erred in the following ways:

. . . The article was presented in a way that could create conflict between the student and his school.

. . . The article was presented in a manner not suitable for fifth-grade students.

. . . At the fifth-grade level, students would understand the concept of rights better if presented by describing a situation or by relating an incident, with emphasis on open-ended discussion.

. . . The article was presented too much in terms of the student's rights and too little in terms of the student's responsibilities.

. . . The article gave too little attention to the habits and beliefs of the majority of people in communities in the United States.

. . . The article did not adequately explain why certain rules or standards may exist in the school setting, nor did it present the view of the administrator or teacher.

Despite our failing in the March 19 issue of *News Citizen*, we believe it is possible to present the idea of students' and individual rights in our periodicals. In fact, we believe we have the responsibility to address important topics. However, Scholastic believes we erred in the way we presented the subject of students' rights in *News Citizen*. We hope that teachers, administrators, and parents who have rightly been offended by this error will understand that we are trying to do a fair, balanced job in an important area of social understanding, and that we will occasionally make a mistake. When we do so, we admit our failing. And we hope our subscribers will not be influenced by one error in judgment from a basic commitment to Scholastic and to the important subjects our periodicals present.

In an effort to counterbalance some of the problems noted above, we will run in a May issue of *News Citizen* an article about the *responsibilities* of young people.

Please write or call one of the following individuals if you wish to discuss this statement or need additional information. [Here were listed the names, addresses, and telephone numbers of three fellow officers.]

We are truly sorry for this mistake. Thank you for your understanding. Attached is a copy of Scholastic's Credo and Editorial Platform, which we try our best to live by.

Richard Robinson
Vice President and Publisher
School Division

This statement, along with the telephone calls put through by Barnes' team and the work of regional directors and representatives in the field, had the desired effect on many of the schools that had canceled subscriptions. It was estimated that about 80 percent of them reinstated their subscriptions.

One cannot measure the loss of prestige to Scholastic, but the circulation loss following the ill-fated issue was appreciable. The drop-off in *News Citizen* subscriptions for the next two years was plain to see: They dropped from 831,000 at the time of the trouble to 813,228 the next year, and to 757,334 in school year 1974–75. *Newstime* and *Junior Scholastic* also had substantial losses for the next two years, but the lower-elementary-grade periodicals held their own or had gains.

Out of the hundreds of protest letters, one has been pulled for its amusement value, and only the opening sentences are needed to convey it. It was addressed to Archie R. McCardell, president, Xerox Corporation:

Dear Mr. McCardell:

As a stockholder of Xerox, I should like to call your attention to something which involves the company and is of some concern to me. I understand that Xerox owns Scholastic Magazines, Inc., and I should like to call your attention to their publication entitled *Scholastic Young Citizen*, which carried a major article entitled "Have You Got Rights?" This is a piece of revolutionary propaganda . . . [etc.]

McCardell sent it along to Robinson with a note: "Although this is not the type of mail we like to receive, I thought you should see it since it should have been directed to you originally."

Among the letters received in response to the letters of apology sent to subscribing teachers were 22 from teachers who said they found the issue timely and useful. One expressed the essential message of all 22: "While it may be controversial, I feel the content is such that our students should have the opportunity to know of these rights. . . . I would urge you to continue publication of information that will stimulate discussion of the rights of citizens."

On the book side, perhaps the most serious lapse in judgment occurred in listing a reprint of the book *Trout Fishing in America* by Richard Brautigan on a 1972 Campus Book Club offer. The title was completely misleading, the content having nothing whatever to do with fishing, but, jocularly offered, had a lot to do with lustful living. Following the barrage of teacher and parent protests, all discreetly answered by Editor Mary MacEwen, the hubbub subsided. The degree to which it affected club business was not documented, but it was known that Campus and TAB clubs (although the latter did not offer the book) were banned in some schools because of the listing.

Despite the failure of attempts over a period of 40 **Pete Seeger**
years to pin the Communist label on Scholastic for its **Overcomes**
output in print, was there anything else in the Scholastic
catalog to try it on? There was—in sound—in the
recordings of the noted folksinger Pete ("Where Have All
the Flowers Gone?") Seeger, which were part of the
Scholastic/Folkways collection of 1,400 albums distributed by the company under a lease arrangement with
Folkways founder Moses Asch.

The complaints to Scholastic concerned Seeger's alleged membership in the Communist party. He had been
cited by the U.S. House of Representatives Committee on
Un-American Activities and had refused to answer the
Committee's questions concerning this. Consequently he
was declared in contempt of Congress and went on trial
(March 1961) in the U.S. District Court in New York. He
was found guilty and sentenced to one year in prison by
Judge Thomas F. Murphy. Upon being sentenced,
Seeger declared: "I have never in my life supported or
done anything subversive to my country. I am proud that I
have never refused to sing for any organization because I
disagreed with its beliefs." Seeger went free on bail while
the verdict was appealed. One year later it was reversed by
the U.S. Court of Appeals on the ground that the indictment was faulty.

Most of those who attacked Scholastic for distributing Seeger's recordings did not know the whole story;
they knew only of the contempt sentence, not of the Court
of Appeals' reversal. When it was explained to them,
school authorities were usually satisfied, but some of the
original protestors were not. After about six months, the

complaints became a whimper, then disappeared.

Seeger, who made 40 albums for Folkways, was popular with millions of young Americans. At the time Scholastic received the protests, he was riding a high wave of favorable publicity over his leadership role in the conservation movement, especially for his sponsorship of the good ship *Clearwater*. This was the Hudson River sloop that he sailed into East Coast ports, dramatizing the need for action to restore the viability of public waters.

A Complaint Is Not Necessarily an Attack

Anyone in the business of dealing with the public will get complaints, and if you are in publishing, you probably get more per capita than if you are in the butter-and-egg business. And if you are in publishing for schools, you probably get more than if you are in publishing for the general public.

In the magazine field a complaint that results in a cancellation or an outright ban on future subscriptions can be much more costly to Scholastic than to the magazine publisher whose basic circulation consists of single subscriptions. A typical Scholastic subscriber is a teacher who, on his or her own initiative, subscribes to a classroom set of 20, 30, or 100 copies or an entire school or school system that subscribes to 1,000 or more copies. (Thus, when Scholastic loses a subscriber, it loses "a bundle" in terms of income.) Whatever the quantity involved, the complainant—whether a school administrator, teacher, student, or parent—receives an acknowledgment by telephone, letter, or both, with an explanation of the company's position and an apology where called for.

394

Complaints fall into three main categories: (1) complaints about service—errors in filling orders, late or nondeliveries; (2) complaints about the product, including content of magazines, books, films, etc; and (3) complaints about advertising carried in the magazines.

The company has a carefully worked out set of procedures for handling and responding to complaints. Service complaints are handled by the branch office from which the product was sent, except in the case of magazines. Complaints concerning the magazines (to whatever office addressed) are forwarded to the Englewood Cliffs, NJ, office, where checkers and correspondents process them. Some complainants get a prompt telephone call from that office.

Replies to editorial complaints are the responsibility of the editor in charge of the magazine, book club, or other product. Here too a telephone call followed by a letter can take the heat off before the complainant is moved to refer the matter to the superintendent of schools.

Nearly all complaints about advertising in the magazines are concerned with a certain category of advertising or a specific ad. A few complaints each year object to the inclusion of any advertising at all. (Besides the obvious reason for advertising—revenue—there is the "maturity value" it brings to the magazine, giving it some of the appearance of the magazines young people see at home or in the library.)

From the very first issue of *The Western Pennsylvania Scholastic* in 1920, Scholastic has carried advertising and has never seriously considered not doing so—although none or little is carried by the primary- and middle-grade elementary magazines or by *Art & Man,*

Literary Cavalcade, Sprint, Action, Dynamite, Bananas, and the nine foreign-language magazines.

During the latter years of the Vietnam War, most complaints about advertising focused on that of the armed forces* and of the advertising of diamond rings and feminine hygiene products.

Prior to 1975 the feminine hygiene ads were not accepted in Scholastic magazines other than *Co-ed*, and when they did appear on a trial basis, complaints ran between 15 and 20 a month. Early in 1979 it was decided not to accept these ads in magazines other than *Co-ed*.

The acceptability of a given ad or category of advertising is the province of the Advertising Acceptability Committee. This committee consists of editorial directors, editors, and a representative of the Circulation Promotion Department. They meet as often as the occasion requires, usually when an ad is questioned by the member assigned to screen all incoming ads in proof form or when a complaint is received from sources outside. Certain categories of products are on the *verboten* list, such as tobacco, liquor, and over-the-counter drug advertising.†

The Perils of Publishing   Can a generalization reasonably be made as to the difference between the banning of a magazine and the banning of a book in their effects on Scholastic? When a book is banned by a given school or classroom, it does not usually close the door to the purchase of other Scholastic

---

* These complaints were much less numerous after the discontinuance of the draft in 1974.

†At one time years ago, chewing gum was on the list of products *verboten*.

products by that school or even to other books offered by the company. There are variations on this generalization, and it has happened that the listing of a certain title has caused teachers (perhaps under pressure from parents) to discontinue their book club membership.* In most instances of dissatisfaction—or outrage—over a book, teachers have been content to express it in a letter to the editor and perhaps return the books for a refund, but take no further action.

With 650 titles being offered every year by the five clubs, attracting orders from some 700,000 classroom clubs for 56 million books plus 11 million book dividends, it would be a miracle if a month passed without some teacher or parent objecting to a title, or perhaps a word or two in one of them. ("Out damned spot.") If a character in an Arrow book says "damn" instead of "darn," it is good for a half-dozen letters. "Hell" would bring an avalanche. Heck hath no fury.

The magazines, not the books, have brought about most of the organized attacks. This is understandable because the magazines, being topical, publish material on social issues and national and world problems about

*Among book club titles that have brought a barrage of complaints and cancellations are: *Mary Jane* by Dorothy Sterling, *Trout Fishing in America* by Richard Brautigan, *Slaughterhouse Five* by Kurt Vonnegut, *A Member of the Gang* by Barbara Rinkoff, *And Then What Happened, Paul Revere?* by Jean Fritz, *Ragtime* by E. L. Doctorow, *The Yellow Submarine* (adapted from the movie), and the issue of *Dynamite* featuring the TV celebrity Cher on the front cover (diaphanous gown and all that). *Ragtime* was not offered on the students' list, but was included in the shipping boxes as a teacher's dividend and thus discovered by many of the students, as it is customary in some classrooms to have students open the book cartons.

which there are strong opposing opinions held by the American public. This is not to imply that major book publishers do not have their problems with censorship. Recently Townsend Hoopes, chairman of the American Association of Publishers, expressed deep concern over the high incidence of schools banning all books of a given publishing house because one had been disapproved.

In Scholastic's experience most bans have been of short duration (less than a year). However, an individual teacher may ban a given magazine or book club for the duration of his or her teaching career without this having any effect on the preferences of other teachers in the same school.

Groups of parents have been known to organize protests, and on one occasion several mothers picketed (signs and all) a school to get it to stop using the Scholastic magazine *Scope*. This happened in 1969 at Hare Intermediate School of the Garden Grove Unified School District, Garden Grove, CA. The two signs carried by the mothers said: "GGUSD ENCOURAGES VIOLENCE WITH *SCHOLASTIC SCOPE*" and "*SCHOLASTIC SCOPE* PRAISES KNOWN COMMUNISTS. THIS SCHOOL USES IT." This made news and a photo for the local newspaper, but didn't persuade the school authorities to cancel *Scope*. On the contrary, they voted to retain *Scope* in 10 junior and senior high schools, following the recommendation of a review committee composed of parents, PTA members, and teachers chosen at random.

Around the time (late 1968 and early 1969) of the picketing at Garden Grove, CA, and several other protests over *Scope* by parent groups in California, a group in

Florida calling itself Citizens for Moral Education in Central Florida (Brevard, Seminole, and Orange Counties) registered similar protests with their school boards. The charges were that *Scope* "dwelled on death, atheism, and un-Americanism," and was accused of being "Communistic" and "promoting violence." A printed bulletin in the hands of the leaders of several protesting groups led to the suspicion that their action was getting impetus from some central headquarters. Scholastic regional directors and local representatives pitched in to respond to these charges by appearing before school boards and faculty committees with strong support in letters and telephone calls from the home office. At the time Richard Robinson was editorial director of the Language Arts Department. He prepared detailed responses to the allegations in letters to school officials and statements for use by Scholastic representatives. Typical of these was his paper "Does *Scope* Encourage Violence?"—

Does Scope *Encourage Violence?*

It is often contended that reading about violence causes people to become violent. There is no conclusive evidence that this is true. In fact, it may have the opposite effect on most people. The Kerner Commission, which made a comprehensive study of the effect of news media on the riots in our cities, said: "We believe it would be imprudent and even dangerous to downplay [newspaper and TV] coverage in the hope that reporting of inflammatory incidents will somehow diminish violence." And, after criticizing some media for a lack of balance in reporting the riots, the Commission added: "Our criticisms . . . do not lead us to conclude that the media are a cause of riots, any more than they are the cause of other phenomena which they report."

The question which troubles government leaders, educators, and many others—as well as *Scope*'s staff—is: What should be done to curb violence? It is obvious that there are, as yet, no conclusive answers. In the absence of such answers, *Scope* (November 8, 1968) published an eight-page article called "Violence in America: What Can Be Done About It?" This article reflected our view that the most helpful way of dealing with the topic for our readers is to study the facts, explore the possible causes of violence, and discuss the pros and cons of possible solutions. And we hoped that by presenting the subject straightforwardly and objectively—instead of alienating our readers by moral preachments — we might give them a better understanding of the seriousness of the problem and stimulate a desire to do something about it.

Those who contend that *Scope* by printing stories and plays—as well as articles—about violence is encouraging violence should be aware of the full implications of their position. If they succeed in eliminating *Scope* from English curricula because it deals with violence, then—to be consistent—they must proceed to eliminate other classroom reading that deals with violence at least as much as *Scope*. The victims of such a campaign would surely include some of the greatest treasures of our literature, including much of Twain and of Dickens, most of Poe, much of 20th-century fiction and drama, and all of Shakespeare's tragedies.

It appears, in this latter half of the 1970's, that self-appointed committees of "concerned parents" or "citizens to save our schools" are fewer in number than they were in the 1960's. This may be attributed to the carefully spelled-out procedure most school systems have set up for receiving and passing judgment on complaints by individual citizens' organizations. Usually the school system or individual school has a review committee consisting of lay members as well as the professional staff to recommend to the principal or superintendent what action, if any, should be taken on a complaint.

As we have seen, many of the attacks on Scholastic were allegations that the magazines (mainly *Senior Scholastic* and *Junior Scholastic*) purveyed the Communist ideology. The Cold War of the late 1940's and 1950's put the U.S.A. and U.S.S.R. into a panic of suspicions over each other's motives, the latter to turn the world into a Communist monolith, the former to make it safe for democracy. As mentioned earlier, Senator Joseph McCarthy in the early 1950's fanned the flames of fear and suspicion by charging that Communists lurked in places high and low—including the State Department and the Army. Fear was so rampant that even some palpably innocent of such charges found it discreet to demonstrate that they were not purveyors of communism and stood four-square for the democratic way of life. Scholastic pointed to its record of articles and books explaining the theories and practices of governments under total dictatorships and those functioning under democratic systems. These included: from *Senior Scholastic*, "All Out for Democracy" (1947–48), "Freedom Answers Communism" (1953–54); from *Junior Scholastic*, "What You Should Know About Communism—and Why" (1962–63); and the Multi-Texts, *The Soviet Union and Eastern*

Europe: The Soviet Satellites and Other European Communist Nations (1961). For the magazine articles Scholastic received the Freedom Foundation's distinguished service awards in 1949, 1954, and 1962—"For Outstanding Achievement in Bringing About a Better Understanding of the American Way of Life."

This account of attacks and complaints is not complete, but it is representative of "the troubles we've seen." Certainly some mistakes were made by editors and writers in letting their own viewpoints on highly sensitive, controversial matters influence the printed product—to cause, in some instances, serious difficulties for school authorities with their constituents in the community.

CHAPTER XXII

A Precious Asset

The Scholastic Awards

A program as old as the company itself and one that has contributed vastly to its prestige in American education is the Scholastic Awards. Since the early 1920's these annual competitions in art and writing — and later in photography — have encouraged, recognized, and rewarded students for their work in creative expression.

This early, undated statement of the purpose of the Scholastic Awards serves as the guiding principle for all concerned with the conduct of these programs:

 I. To give those high school students who demonstrate superior talent and achievement in things of the spirit and of the mind at least a fraction of the honors and rewards accorded to their athletic classmates for demonstrating their bodily skills.

 II. To stimulate teachers to give greater attention to the arts of communication and to encourage the creative spirit in young writers and visual artists.

 III. To help develop a genuine appreciation of great literature and fine writing — which appreciation, as all writers know, can best be acquired by one's own self, slaving away at the task of striving to be a writer.

403

The beginnings of the awards can be traced to *The Western Pennsylvania Scholastic*'s second issue (October 29, 1920) with the announcement of a "prize story contest." The word *story* in this instance did not mean fiction but a news feature in the journalistic sense. The announcement read: "The actual cash prizes are three in number: three dollars for each of the three best stories." Robinson recalls that not one entry was worthy of a prize, so none was given.

Two years later during *The Scholastic*'s first year as a national magazine, there was a similar outcome: the short-story contest (this time for fiction) failed to attract entries of a quality to justify publishing any of them. Horace Liveright, the eminent publisher who had been friendly and generous to Robinson when the latter called on him in New York, had agreed to be one of the judges. There were about 300 entries, and Robinson was so disturbed by the low quality that, in choosing seven to send to Liveright, he was impelled to express his feelings in a covering letter, saying in part:

April 24, 1923

I certainly appreciate your kindness in agreeing to serve in the capacity of a judge in our short story contest. Seven stories are being forwarded to you under separate cover. I was quite disappointed in the stories we received for the contest this year. Although there are a large number of them, we could not find five or ten which were really exceptional. The students seem careless in their work and I hope you will not feel that it is too great a waste of time for you to read the calibre of material which we are forwarding to you. I wish you would select the three best stories, sending us your first, second and third choice by letter and indicating the numbers of the stories.

A week later back came the manuscripts from Liveright with this letter:

April 30, 1923

I am sending you by first class mail to-day the seven stories which you sent me to read as a judge.

I can only say that I have never in my life read such a collection of inexcusably poor stuff. I can't with any conscience vote for any of these stories as being worthy of publication even in a magazine edited by 5-year-old girls and boys and subscribed to by morons. Not one of the stories has anything to recommend it. So I refuse to use my vote for the purposes of giving any one of these stories preference over the other or over any others that were submitted for the contest.

Can't you lend dignity to your magazine by fearlessly announcing that the judges felt all of the stories were so bad that no rewards could be made?

Robinson replied, thanking him "for reading the trashy short stories" and saying, "I am going to follow your advice, with the exception that because we advertised the giving of prize money I shall live up to our end of the agreement and send a small check to each of the six that were selected out of the large number of perfectly ridiculous stories."

The final issue of the school year (May 23, 1923) carried the following report:

The Results
of the Short Story Contest

After several readings and re-readings the decision of the judges for the Short Story Contest conducted by *The Scholastic* has been reached. It is with deep regret we make the announcement that the majority opinion of the judges — in which opinion the Editor concurs — is that not one of the stories received is sufficiently superior to any of the others to receive the first prize, and furthermore that not one of the stories is worthy of publication in *The Scholastic* — a magazine that expects superior work from the high school students of America.

Accordingly, in order that *The Scholastic* might live up to its side of the agreement, six stories have been selected from among the hundreds received and the entire amount of the prize money is to be divided among the authors of these six stories. Four of the authors will receive five dollars each and the other two will receive two and one-half dollars each. The winners of the two and one-half dollar prizes are both students in Porto Rican* high schools and their manuscripts showed especial ability.

The judges of the contest were all advisory editors of *The Scholastic:* Horace B. Liveright, President of Boni and Liveright, publishers; Dr. J. W. Searson, Professor of English at Nebraska University; Orton Lowe, Director of English Instruction in the Pennsylvania schools. They decided that although some of the stories showed considerable ability on the part of the authors, yet

*Puerto Rico was spelled *Porto Rico* by most stateside periodicals of the time.

406

none of them gave evidence of a sufficient amount of thorough work, and that it would not be in keeping with the policy and standards of *The Scholastic* to place the stories before its readers as prize-winning examples of short story writing among the high school students of the United States.

Setbacks did not exactly roll off Robinson's back. They shook him, but he had tremendous recuperative powers and, as happened from time to time during the next 50 years, he would absorb the shock and try again on a course improved by experience.

As *The Scholastic* gained in circulation and influence among teachers of English, the number of entries increased, bringing quality along with quantity. Never again would a judge be moved to write, as Liveright did in 1923, that none of the entries was worthy of publication.

After casting his choices for the 1927 prizewinners, one of the judges — Charles Swain Thomas of Harvard — wrote Robinson: "Had I foreseen the difficulties of this task, I should have been reluctant to accept. It is easy enough to judge mediocrity, but it is difficult to decide from the excellent."

Before the terms "Literary Awards" or "Writing Awards" were used for these competitions, the program was announced as competitions for the "student-written number" of *The Scholastic*. The full-page announcement in the February 21, 1925, issue proclaimed:

Another Prize Offer

The Scholastic's first issue in May will be almost entirely student-written. Its contents, from cover to cover, will be selected by the editors from manuscripts submitted in competition by its student readers. . . . Five dollars will be paid to the winner in each competition. . . . Aside from the prizes to be given, this special student-written number will afford teachers an opportunity to prove the prowess of their students. It may be that some one school — whether in the West or the East — will carry off most of the honors. The principal winner may come from one of the country's smallest towns.

Winners came from places large and small, and a considerable number from Kentucky, Alabama, South Carolina, Georgia, and Puerto Rico. The 1925 winning entry in the article classification carried the title "Porto Rico's Independence,"* by Luis Anglade, Guavana High School, Puerto Rico, and was published in the student-written number. An excerpt:

One of our demands is to have as governor a Porto Rican, but our greatest desire is that Porto Rico may be independent. . . . Lately we have taken steps to obtain this recognition from Congress. Now our hopes are that 1926 will be the 1776 of Porto Rican history. Let us wait for what Congress will decide.

Anyone having used the mails in the 1970's will see some irony in an award-winning article by Adrian Huggins of Follansbee (WV) High School, entitled: "The Future of the Airmail" (published in the May 2, 1925, issue of *The Scholastic*). Adrian was gung-ho in his predictions of what air mail would do, but hedged in his concluding paragraph: "This is only fiction — nothing else but

*Luis probably would have spelled it *Puerto*. His original manuscript is not available.

408

fiction — but doesn't it give you an idea of what the air-mail of the future can do?"

For several years in the late 1920's and early 1930's the awards budget was tilted toward a balance by grants of $4,000 from the Carnegie Corporation of New York and $1,000 from *Collier's* magazine. These helped pay administration costs. Numerous firms put up prize money, and some also placed advertising in the magazine. Robinson was reminded of an early angel when he ran into the poet Ben Belitt at a National Book Awards party several years ago in New York. Robinson asked Belitt if he recalled winning a prize for his short story in the 1928 Literary Division of the awards when he was a student at Lynchburg (VA) High School. "Indeed I do," he beamed. "I also remember that the $10 prize came from the Pittsburgh Plate Glass Company."*

Around the time Ben Belitt was in high school and for five years thereafter, prize money for the poetry classification was put up by one of the leading poets of the time (a rich poet!) — Witter Bynner. He paid $100 for first prize, $25 for second prize, and $15 for third prize. He didn't seek the publicity, but Scholastic named the award the Witter Bynner Scholastic Poetry Prize and continued it for nine years while Bynner served as a judge of the poetry classification and chairman of the literary committee of the Scholastic Awards.

There were still other variations in the prizes. For the first five classifications under "The Scholastic Awards" first prize was $100; second prize, $25; and third prize, $15. For the sixth classification — "Community Ser-

*Since 1975, the Writing Awards have been sponsored by Smith-Corona.

vice" — first prize was a bang-up $200; second prize, $50; and third prize, $25. This was a competition for class participation and was explained as follows:

> 6. *Community Service.* For the most constructive project for the improvement of their town or neighborhood, actually carried out or in progress by a school, class, club, or other student group. The project must be described in a report of not over 1500 words, accompanied by photographs, maps, charts, or other documentary proof.

The announcement concluded, in extra-bold type:

Remember the Dead Line—March 20.

Address all manuscripts to

CONTEST EDITOR

The Scholastic

Wabash Building   Pittsburgh, Pennsylvania

(Since the word *baseball* was usually spelled *base ball* back in those days, it is understandable that the closing date for entries in this project was a *dead line*.)

The Writing Awards didn't set out deliberately to make future novelists, journalists, or poets. That it has encouraged a few of them is a happy dividend. The November 1970 *Literary Cavalcade,* an alumni-written issue, contains work of some former Writing Awards winners who became professional writers. Among famous alumni are Joyce Carol Oates, winner of the 1969 National Book Award for her novel *Them*; Pulitzer Prize winner Jean Stafford (1970); Merle Miller; Ben Belitt;

410

Peter Beagle; Joyce Maynard; Bernard Malamud; and the late Gladys Schmitt and Winfield Townley Scott.

The Writing Awards, only one of whose purposes—and an incidental purpose at that—is to uncover potential writers, has given to legions of young people a stimulus for learning to organize their thinking and to express their thoughts competently and creatively in writing. Approved by the National Association of Secondary School Principals, the Writing Awards have become a welcome adjunct to the curriculum and a stimulant to the year's work in thousands of English classes in the United States and Canada.

Scholastic started publishing anthologies of award-winning writings in 1926 with *Saplings,* a collection of the best student writing submitted that year for the Literary (later called "Writing") Awards. It was published annually for 15 years thereafter. For the collection from the 1940–41 Awards, the title was changed to *Best High School Writing: 1941.* This was followed in 1945 by *Young Voices: A Quarter Century of High School Student Writing Selected from the Scholastic Awards*, edited by Kenneth M. Gould and Joan Coyne (who succeeded Ernestine Taggard as literary editor of *Senior Scholastic*). This was not published by Scholastic; Harper & Brothers did it. The Writing Awards anthologies were resumed in 1962 under the Scholastic imprint with *Bittersweet: Stories and Poems from Scholastic Writing Awards*, edited by Jerome Brondfield; *Peppermint: The Best of the Scholastic Writing Awards, Junior Division*, edited by David A. Sohn (1966); *Discovery: The Best from Recent Scholastic Magazines' Writing and Art Awards*, edited by Whit Burnett (1967); *Mad, Sad & Glad: Poems from*

Scholastic Creative Awards, edited by Stephen Dunning (1970); *Teenspell: Stories, Articles, and Poems from Scholastic Writing Awards*, edited by Betty Owen (1973); and *Grab Me a Bus: Award-Winning Poems from the Scholastic Writing Awards*, edited by M. Joe Eaton and Malcolm Glass (1974).

Art as a classification sort of tiptoed into the competition for Scholastic's 1925 student-written number as a single entry for "cover design" among the various classifications in writing: "Submit Your Own Cover Design, Either for One or Two Colors." In 1926 the term "Scholastic Awards" began to be used: "$1,500 in Cash Prizes: Announcing the Scholastic Awards" (Sept. 18, 1926 issue). The classifications included poetry, essay, short story, drama, art, and community service. The art classification offered the George Bellows Memorial Prize "for the best piece of creative art—first prize $100; second and third prizes, $25 and $15.

The Bellows award stimulated a flood of entries in the incipient art category which would soon become a hardy companion to the writing branch of the Scholastic Awards. The magazine had paid tribute to Bellows, who died in 1925 at the age of 42, and reproduced several of his paintings as black-and-white cover illustrations. The widow of the artist, invited to select the jury, chose three of Bellows' artist friends: Eugene Speicher, Robert Henri, and John Sloan.

"I remember how the entries flooded our office in Pittsburgh," recalls Robinson. "We had no room to sort the art entries, so we asked Carnegie Institute to let us have some gallery space for this purpose. After the sort-

412

Art it is! Entries for the 1931 Scholastic Art Awards blocking entrance and hallway to Scholastic office, Wabash Building, Pittsburgh.

ing, we packed up the superior entries and sent them to New York, where Eugene Speicher's gallery unpacked and arranged them for the jurors to see."

The jurors were so impressed with the quality of the work that they urged Robinson to extend the scope of the awards in the visual arts. Wrote Speicher, the jury chairman: "The work had such variety that every encouragement should be given to the project that this competition may be continued. The jury considered it a great pleasure to act for this undertaking and desires to express the best of wishes for the furtherance of the idea."

There could have been no furtherance of the idea without the generosity of Carnegie Institute. With the encouragement of Homer Saint Gaudens, director of the Fine Arts Galleries of Carnegie Institute, and school art leaders, Scholastic launched plans for a big event in the spring of 1928: the first National High School Art Exhibition. Four of Carnegie Institute's Fine Arts Galleries (where hung the famous International Exhibition) would now display the Scholastic exhibition.

They would do so for the next 30 years. During 20 of those years Paul Sarkoff, of Scholastic's Pittsburgh staff, supervised the uncrating, recording, and eventual returning of the thousands of entries. One member of the small Scholastic staff, Abe Savage, simultaneously held three titles during the late 1920's and into 1931: circulation manager, assistant editor, and secretary of the Art Awards. The first to hold the title of director of the Art Awards was Ernest Watson, who was also the first art editor of *Scholastic* magazine (1928–36). He was one of the founders of the art publishing house of Watson-Guptill.

Robinson, aglow over the success of the Scholastic show in the Carnegie Galleries, pondered the prospect of making the Scholastic show international. He broached this brainstorm to Saint Gaudens and Andrey Avinoff, director of Carnegie Institute, and they agreed to take it on. Robinson got off letters to the ministers of education of all the European nations and received acceptances from Germany, Denmark, and Austria for the 1933 show. The European entries were judged separately from the others, and a 14-year-old from Weiner Neustadt, Austria, won first prize in oils. During the second year twice as many countries sent entries, including the Soviet Union.

The Foreign Division was discontinued after two years (except for Canada) because:

1. The company could ill-afford in the mid-1930's adding to the annual deficit of its awards program by continuing a foreign branch which produced no income whatsoever. The main Scholastic Awards attracted some income from advertising in

Sketches by Reginald
Marsh at 1945 Scholastic
Art Awards dinner,
Schenley Hotel,
Pittsburgh. Left to right:
M. R. Robinson; William Frew,
Carnegie Institute; Royal
Farnum, Rhode Island
School of Design; James
Chapin, artist.

Scholastic by art and writing supply houses and from grants of prize money from sponsors of certain categories.

2. There were the added difficulties of clearing entries through customs (they came in duty-free but had to be bonded) and of safely returning them to the ministers of education abroad.

In reminiscence, Robinson said of this episode: "It was foolish and inconsiderate of me to have added another money-losing activity at a time of serious depression and just after Messrs. Oliver and Clapp had salvaged Scholastic for me I suspect it was my press-agent impulse at work" (Chapter III, "Stockholders Ahoy!").

In the early years of the Art Awards the entries could be counted. Then they rose from hundreds to thousands to tens of thousands. The number of pieces pouring out of the schools into Carnegie Institute presented a problem in logistics, as the work had to be returned unless the student-artist indicated that it was for sale. Also, the wide geographical distribution of participants made it impractical for many to see their own works on display in Pittsburgh. Therefore, for the 1940–41 season, it was decided to invite department stores to sponsor preliminary regional exhibitions, and Karl S. Bolander, director of the Columbus (OH) Gallery of Fine Arts, accepted Robinson's offer to join Scholastic in conducting the Art Awards. For a starter, Bolander signed up 11 regional sponsors, and he doubled the number the following year. On this momentum his successors expanded the network until there were 50 or more department stores, newspapers, museums, shopping centers, and TV stations sponsoring regional programs. Their sponsorship fees have helped to pay for the printing, production, and mailing of the rulebooks and other material supplied by Scholastic to the regions. Each region is served by an advisory committee consisting of art educators from its school districts.

In his travels to line up department stores to conduct the regional programs, Bolander dealt with promotion and merchandising managers of the stores. He chose one — Frieda Curtis, who was with the William H. Block store in Indianapolis — to fill the newly created post of national secretary of Scholastic Awards. Since Bolander was on the road most of the time, it was necessary to have someone in New York handling the details of the expanding program. That "someone" became two with the addition of Jennie Copeland to the New York office in 1945. She had taught English and journalism at Robert E. Fitch High School, Groton, CT, and she had the background necessary to coordinate the work on the Writing Awards and to supervise the art scholarship program. In 1958 she was put in full charge of the Art Awards, and three years later was named executive director of the entire awards program. She retired in 1973 and was succeeded as director of the Art Awards by her assistant, Frank Cass, who had joined Scholastic in 1958 as a correspondent in the

Subscription Department. Bolander retired in 1958, the first Scholastic employee to do so under the company's retirement plan, organized in 1954 (Chapter XXIX, "To Talk of Many Things").

From its start as a competition among high school art students for designing covers for the magazine, the Art Awards long ago outgrew the category of a contest. It has become a vast cooperative program for the encouragement and recognition of student achievement in the fine and applied arts as well as a force for the advancement of art education. As Robinson told an interviewer several years ago, "The discovery and encouragement of thousands of talented young people through scholarships and other awards is just a *by-product* of Scholastic Art Awards. Our prime purpose is to promote appreciation of the arts, since we learn to appreciate best by actual participation."

Since 1957 the national exhibition has been held at various locations in New York, including Riverside

Augustus K. Oliver and M. R. Robinson at Scholastic Art Awards dinner, Hotel Schenley, Pittsburgh, 1948.

417

Museum and once at the New York Coliseum as the youth section of "ART USA: 1959." In recent years it has been held annually, except in 1976, at the Union Carbide Exhibition Hall on Park Avenue, New York City. The 1976 show was held in the Chicago Public Library cultural center. For the occasion Mayor Daley issued a proclamation, closing with:

> WHEREAS, the National High School Art Exhibition climaxes the Scholastic Art Awards program of Scholastic Magazines, Inc., an educational publishing house which encourages the arts through its service to American schools....
>
> NOW, THEREFORE, I, Richard J. Daley, Mayor of the City of Chicago, do hereby proclaim the period from Tuesday, May 11 through Saturday, May 29, 1976, as NATIONAL HIGH SCHOOL ART EXHIBITION DAYS IN CHICAGO and urge all citizens to visit the Chicago Public Library Cultural Center to enjoy the creative work of American youth.
>
> Dated this 5th day of April, 1976.
>
> Richard J. Daley

Former Art Awards winners who have achieved professional success are too numerous to be counted. But there are some who are now in the front ranks of the contemporary art world. The 1970 national exhibition included an Alumni Hall of Fame — a graphic listing of 18 outstanding painters, sculptors, and print-makers, including the following artists listed in *Who's Who in America* or *Who's Who in American Art*: Lennart Anderson, Richard Anuszkiewicz, Harry Bertoia, Virgil Cantini, John Clague, James Ernst, Robert Indiana, Jacob Landau, Robert McCloskey, Joseph McCullough, Philip Pearlstein, Sidney Simon, William A. Smith, Elbert

M. R. Robinson and Frank Stanton, president of Columbia Broadcasting System, examining prize-winning jewelry, National High School Art Exhibition, Scholastic Awards, at Union Carbide Gallery, New York (1967).

Weinberg, and Charles White. Others who have received national and international recognition include Peter Lupori, Ruth Adler Schnee, and Clarence Van Duzer.

Eight of them — Anuszkiewicz, Bertoia, Ernst, Indiana, Landau, McCullough, Pearlstein, and Smith — attended the 50th anniversary party of the Scholastic Art Awards in the Union Carbide Exhibition Hall, New York, on June 9, 1977, and paid tribute to Scholastic and Robinson there and at the luncheon in the Waldorf Astoria Hotel. To conclude the tributes, the following letter from Carter Brown, director of the National Gallery of Art, was read by his associate Howard J. Adams:

Dear Robbie:

I would like to join with the many students and friends who gather today at the 50th National High School Exhibition to offer congratulations for your enviable record of supporting young artists in America. Over the past 50 years — almost twice as long as the National Gallery — the Scholastic Awards have provided the encouragement and recognition young men and women need to develop their talents to the full, and you have been the leader, inspiration, and force not only for the award, but also for *Art & Man*, yet another innovation in art education in which the National Gallery has been a very proud partner.

Please accept my best wishes and congratulations on behalf of the trustees and staff of the National Gallery of Art.

Sincerely,

J. Carter Brown

Carter Brown's reference to the partnership of the National Gallery of Art and Scholastic in publishing *Art & Man* prompts mention of the occasion in 1936 when the National High School Art Exhibition was held in the National Gallery of Art (then housed in the Smithsonian Institution). The 1936 exhibition had been moved there after its closing in the Carnegie Galleries in Pittsburgh.

It took a lot of money to pay for the Art Awards, too much for Scholastic to undertake without the financial help that came from so many sources throughout the years. Some of the country's leading art schools provided scholarships; manufacturers of art supplies and other companies interested in art education donated cash awards, and some bought advertising in the magazines.

The Photography Division of the Art Awards, sponsored by Eastman Kodak, has been separated for national

Maurice and Florence Robinson with daughter Barbara at opening of National High School Art Exhibition, Scholastic Awards, Union Carbide Gallery, New York (1967).

Judges of graphic design, Scholastic Art Awards, 1976. Scholastic art directors William Radio, Mary Jane Dunton, Richard Leach.

judging and has its own exhibition. In recent years this has been held at the Eastman Kodak Exhibit Hall in New York on the Avenue of the Americas at 43rd Street, directly facing Scholastic's headquarters at 50 West 44th Street. Eastman Kodak's staging of this show achieves the utmost in dramatic effect from the several hundred winning photographs. Visitors, among them professional photographers and representatives of the press, have expressed amazement at the quality of the work being done by high school students. Traveling exhibits prepared by Eastman Kodak show the prizewinning photographs to school and community groups throughout the country.

For 10 years until 1949 music was included in the awards program, and in its later years the music competition was conducted with the cooperation of the Music Educators National Conference and Columbia Records, under the direction of William D. Boutwell. It was discontinued because of the difficulty in judging the mounting volume of entries, all submitted in musical notation. Today the question of the practicability of reviving the Music Awards is being considered. As a feeler, a category in music — lyrics and music for an original song — was added to the 1975 Writing Awards with gratifying results. Entries were submitted on musical staff paper with the lyrics typed in.

Back in the hardship years of "slow flow" cash, the question would be raised as to the value of the Scholastic Awards in terms of that most persistent of lines — the one at the bottom. The value of the awards could never be measured in terms of dollar "net income." Some say the newspaper publicity alone, in every town and hamlet boasting a winner, is worth the investment in time and talent, even though an occasional newspaper may omit the name "Scholastic" or spell it with a lowercase *s*. A value more basic is its appeal to the school administrations, the English and art departments, parents, and students. To the extent that the awards fulfill Robinson's purpose in starting and continuing them despite their drain on the exchequer, these programs have become one of Scholastic's precious assets.

Robie, the man who is responsible for the whole mess

Gropper

Sketch of M. R. Robinson by William Gropper made during Scholastic Art Awards dinner, Hotel Schenley, Pittsburgh, 1945. Gropper was one of the judges.

CHAPTER XXIII

The Winning Pages

JUST as the company had survived its first 15 years without a formal editorial credo or platform, it reached the threshold of its 50th anniversary before adopting a corporate emblem — a colophon. It was no doubt the approaching celebration that stirred the Management Operations Committee (MOC) in 1969 to move apace toward a decision on an emblem to represent Scholastic's spirit as well as its achievement. Not that the company hadn't given some thought to a colophon during its first half-century; in the 1950's and early 1960's there were several campaigns conducted among art directors and others on the staff to enlist ideas and sketches for a corporate colophon. Many were submitted, none chosen. In the meantime several departments of the company printed their own characteristic letterheads (*Scholastic Coach*, *Co-ed*, *Scholastic Teacher*, Teen Age Book Club, Four Winds Press, Scholastic Book Services, and others).

An illustrated letterhead first appeared in 1931 soon after American Education Press became half-owner of Scholastic. The illustration (right) showed students at their desks. This appeared in the upper left-hand corner, flanked by "The SCHOLASTIC: A National Magazine for the High School Classroom" and three addresses: "155 E.

44th St. New York City/40 So. Third St. Columbus, O./ Wabash Bldg. Pittsburgh, Pa." After the divorce (Chapter VI, "From Cash Slow to Cash Flow"), Scholastic returned to letterheads without illustration until 1940 when the letterhead shown above appeared. Although never adopted as the official colophon or trademark, this design was widely used on business forms, and the treasurer, Agnes Laurino, put it on company checks. It would be many years before a colophon would officially be adopted. The "flying pages," now the registered company mark, was at first tentatively adopted—tentative in that, at the time of adoption (1969), it was approved only for use during the 50th anniversary celebration year 1970–71.

The flying pages design was the work of Morton Goldsholl, a well-known graphic designer who had been commissioned by the company to submit designs. He came up with about 30, varying widely in motif and structure. As the MOC got down to the serious business of making a selection, it invited all staff members to contribute designs, and many did. Two artists were in the running right up to the final decision. In fact, each artist was actually MOC's first choice at different times during July and August 1969, as the members swerved from one to the other of the three designs: (1) the curved, wide band of color in the shape of an S designed by Robert Schaefer, then art director of the elementary magazines and submitted by him in the name of the art service he had organized, RS Associates; (2) the squarish, bold S

424

figure incorporating the shape of two books by Arthur Beckenstein, an artist in Scholastic Book Services; and (3) Goldsholl's flying pages. One, then another, was the first choice of MOC, until, at a meeting on August 20, 1969, the committee voted by a narrow margin to choose *two*! The flying pages design was chosen for use during the 50th anniversary year (1970–71); thereafter, Schaefer's broad, flowing S was to be the official emblem. All three are included in the group shown on the right.

Designed by Robert Schaefer, then art director of the elementary magazines.

As submitted, the left-hand page of Goldsholl's flying pages was solid black, and the right-hand page consisted of curved lines of random, so-called "idiot" type. These were replaced by the titles of Scholastic's (then) 31 magazines, five book clubs, and other products and programs including American Adventures, Reluctant Reader Library, Folkways/Scholastic Records, Individualized Reading Program, Curriculum Units, Filmstrips, Let's Start, Four Winds Press, Citation Press, Contact, Literature Units, Multi-Texts, Self-Teaching Arithmetic, Scope Skills, Sports Books, Action, Great Issues, and *Toute la bande*. As you can see, this filled the page and proved impractical as new product lines proliferated. Within two years after its first use (it had even been painted on the transparent glass entrance doors on each floor at 50 West 44th Street), the right-hand page was converted into solid color, as Russell D'Anna took over responsibility for applying the design to all possible surfaces. Under his direction new letterheads and envelopes were designed and a color was recommended for the right-hand page. He called the color "greige" — something in the twilight between gray and beige. By this time (1972) MOC had voted to adopt the flying pages for continuous use. The divisiveness that had existed among MOC members over the final choice

Designed by Arthur Beckenstein, an artist in Scholastic Book Services.

Goldsholl's flying pages.

was overcome by their favorable response to Dick Robinson's reasoning in support of the flying pages, which he put down in a memo to the ad hoc colophon committee. He wrote:

1. *The flying pages as a shield.* The flying pages could be considered a symbol rather than a denotative description of our business — a shield rather than a page. It could be said that the "page" recognizes our origin in print, but the flying pages can stand for the shield of the company, its way of doing things.

2. *The flying pages as superior design.* The feeling of flight plus the gravity of print — this seems to me an ideal feeling for our logotype, which I also believe to be the best-designed of the three in question. I believe it is the best design when enlarged, showing up well on magazines, books, records, signs, letterheads, book boxes, envelopes, visiting cards, magazine wrappers, SR kits, checks.

3. *A symbol, not a letter.* All S's, in my eyes, have an industrial look. Many don't look well enlarged. With thousands of other companies using letters as symbols, a mark like the flying pages is more distinctive than a letter.

4. *The concept of multiplicity.* I believe what characterizes Scholastic the most is the variety, the multiplicity of things we do. The pages convey this better than an S.

5. *Flight — but with the feeling of scholarship, authority, experience.* We have always been an innovative company editorially, coming up with the breakthrough, the new idea — from the periodical to the paperback. Yet we also are experienced, knowledgeable, reliable. The flying pages carry both the feeling of going somewhere, moving, flying — and the stability and solidity of experience.

CHAPTER XXIV

Never Home
for Thanksgiving

THE chapter title speaks not the whole truth. "Mose" Robinson had been home on Wallace Avenue, Wilkinsburg, for Thanksgiving dinner for the first 17 years of his life. Then came Dartmouth, interrupted by war service, then back to Dartmouth, then back to Wilkinsburg in the spring of 1920 to the job with the Pittsburgh Chamber of Commerce and, with a suddenness for which he was not quite ready, to Vol. 1, No. 1 of *The Western Pennsylvania Scholastic*. By November 1922 Scholastic had gone national to become *The Scholastic*, a curriculum-oriented magazine. That year Robinson started attending national conventions of educators, the first being the National Education Association meeting in Boston. The following year he attended the convention of the National Council of Teachers of English in Detroit. He has attended every one since and has hosted a Thanksgiving dinner at nearly all of them.

From the 15 or 16 guests at the first dinner this affair has grown to a multitude that can only be accommodated in the largest hotel ballrooms. There were 1,600 guests at the 1977 dinner in New York's Americana Hotel. After dessert and coffee the guests heard the only speech on the program — Robinson's greeting and his description of how it all started:

Good evening. As those of you who have previously attended this annual affair know, this is the only "speech" here this evening . . . my annual speech, unchanged, gray-bearded and hoary with age — the same one I gave last year in Chicago, the year before in San Diego, the year before that in New Orleans — and back over the years in every major city.

When I first began to attend NCTE conventions in the flapping twenties, I became more and more distressed to see NCTE members eating Thanksgiving dinner alone or in groups of three and four in the public dining rooms of the hotel. Thanksgiving had always been a very special day in my home, a joyful day climaxed by a bounteous family feast. So, another book salesman and I — of course we called ourselves publishers — decided to do something about the doleful Thanksgiving days at NCTE. This college friend, Dick Pearson, then of Harper's, and I began to gather other friends together in a private dining room for a sort of family feast. The next year, more lonesome away-from-homers joined us. The news spread. More friends said, can't we come to the party? After that, the numbers grew and grew and grew . . . and . . . where it all will end, I know not — but I hope it will not stop.

The first time that this affair was organized in advance of the convention was when NCTE met in Memphis in 1932. Stella Center was then the president. We arranged ahead of time for a private dining room in the old Peabody Hotel. We had one big, beautifully cooked turkey with all the trimmings on the table. There were 15 or 16 persons present. In the group — in addition to my friend Orton Lowe — were two who later became

presents of NCTE: Walter Barnes of NYU and
Mark Shattuck of Detroit. Then and there we all
agreed that it was a delightful idea, and we made
plans to repeat the affair in Detroit the following
year. But none of us even dreamed it would ever
look like this.

The popularity of the Scholastic parties at the NCTE
conventions and goodwill they created encouraged Kenneth M. Gould, at the time managing editor, to gather "a
few teachers and friends" around him for breakfast during the 1939 meeting in Kansas City of the National
Council for the Social Studies (NCSS), which hitherto
had survived without sustenance from Scholastic. NCSS
also held its meeting over the Thanksgiving holiday, and
on this occasion Gould had about 30 for a Saturday breakfast (among them Harold Rugg of Teachers College, Columbia University, a Scholastic contributing editor whose
textbooks had stirred up considerable protest from con-
servatives during the Depression of the 1930's). For the
1940 convention at Syracuse, Gould held the breakfast on
Thanksgiving Day for some 40 guests, including Henry
Steele Commager of Columbia University, frequent contributor to *Scholastic*. The first Thanksgiving dinner at
NCSS was a buffet affair in Indianapolis in 1941, just two
weeks before Pearl Harbor. Despite wartime travel restrictions the 1942 meeting was held, and Gould presided
over "tea and a buffet supper" at the Pennsylvania Hotel
in New York City.

If it is true that tea was the strongest beverage served,
it was the last time on record that the NCSS and NCTE
Scholastic dinners were not preceded by a cocktail hour.
Of course, during the Prohibition decade of the 1920's,

Robinson would spirit into the hotel a few bottles he had obtained at his favorite New York speakeasy, Manny's Restaurant, on the Lower East Side.* The 1932 party in Memphis would be the last during Prohibition, and for that party Pearson of Harper's carried the bottles by train from New York to Pittsburgh, where Robinson awaited him. The bottles were transferred to Robinson's REO† and the two men drove off to Memphis, where the 15 or so Scholastic/Harper guests were gently stimulated before sitting down to dinner (the expense of which was shared by Scholastic and Harper). However, the next year for the 1933 convention in Detroit, they had a much larger group (at least 50), and when Pearson submitted his expense account showing half the cost of that party, the Harper treasurer raised hell about it. That ended the sharing, and the parties thereafter became all-Scholastic. Pearson was always welcome at the Scholastic parties and usually attended them, sometimes bringing several of his Harper authors.

A characteristic of the dinners is their freedom from commercials. Some of the staff have seen this as a missed opportunity for at least a little plug for the company's products. They won a point when they got an okay to place

* The restaurant on Forsyth Street was named after co-owner Manny Wolfe who concocted a rum-based cocktail that became so popular with Robinson and his coterie of friends that they introduced it to their favorite barkeeper in Pittsburgh. There Frederick Bigger, a Pittsburgh city planner, dubbed it the Robinson Special: Combine juice of one fresh lime, one jigger of white or light rum, and one jigger of apricot brandy; shake well and serve with crushed ice in a wide-mouthed 10-ounce glass.

† The REO was one of 68 different makes of automobiles in its heyday — 1908–1938. "REO" is an acronym for the pioneer auto builder R. E. Olds.

on each of the 125 tables at a recent social studies convention a cardboard centerpiece listing the titles (but not the prices) of Scholastic social studies products. None of the guests or NCSS officers commented on this, so it was assumed they had considered it unostentatious.

In his speeches at the end of NCTE dinners, Robinson would refrain from any reference to Scholastic, even to the point of not identifying himself as its head. He would give his name, as there was no master of cere-

An Invitation to Our
Annual Thanksgiving Parties

at the Conventions of

The National Council of Teachers of English November 27-30, 1968	or	The National Council for the Social Studies November 27-30, 1968

Teachers who are subscribers in classroom quantities to any of the Scholastic family of magazines, chairmen of English or Social Studies departments in those high schools using classroom quantities, or Teen Age Book Club, Campus Book Club, Arrow Book Club, Lucky Book Club or See-Saw Book Program sponsors are cordially invited to these annual social events.

ENGLISH COUNCIL (Reception and Dinner) Sheraton-Schroeder Hotel Milwaukee, Wisconsin November 28 (Thursday) 5:15-7:30 P.M.	SOCIAL STUDIES COUNCIL (Reception and Dinner) Sheraton-Park Hotel Washington, D.C. November 28 (Thursday) 5:15-7:45 P.M.

R.S.V.P. (Please send acceptance form as soon as possible. Your guest card for one admission will be mailed to you before the conventions. Acceptances must be received by November 15.)

- -

SCHOLASTIC MAGAZINES, 50 West 44th St., N.Y., N.Y. 10036

Gentlemen:

I accept with pleasure Scholastic's invitation to the annual Thanksgiving party. I plan to attend the

☐ **National Council for the Social Studies convention, Washington, D.C.**
☐ **National Council of Teachers of English convention, Milwaukee, Wisc.**

Name_____

School_____City_____State_____Zip_____

Home Address_____

City_____State_____Zip_____

I use: ☐ Sr. Scholastic ☐ World Week ☐ Jr. Scholastic ☐ Practical English ☐ Scope ☐ Science World ☐ Literary Cavalcade ☐ Young Citizen ☐ NewsTime ☐ News Explorer ☐ News Trails ☐ News Ranger ☐ News Pilot ☐ Let's Find Out ☐ other_____

I sponsor: ☐ Teen Age Book Club ☐ Arrow Book Club ☐ Campus Book Club ☐ Lucky Book Club ☐ See-Saw Book Program

monies except him. His speech at the 1968 party in Milwaukee was the first at which he presented himself as Robinson the Elder, because by that time his son Dick had become known to the guests. On that occasion M. R. stepped up to the microphone and said:

> Good evening:
> May we pause for a few moments for a brief message from our sponsor who, as in the past, shall be nameless.
>
> My name is Robinson. I now must always add: Robinson, the Elder; in fact, I should say the Elder, Elder. I am here as spokesman for your host of the evening. I bid you a hearty and cordial welcome.
>
> As I turned to typing my notes for this occasion, I found it almost impossible to believe that it was five years ago this Thanksgiving that we dined in San Francisco. On that occasion I said it was somewhat of a special anniversary for me, because it had then been 40 years since I attended my first NCTE convention; and I added that it had been my good fortune to be able to attend every year since then when and where the convention was held. Now it is 45 years since I attended my first NCTE convention in 1923. . . .

Direct (and discreet) "sell" takes place in the exhibit area, where publishers and other school suppliers display their products, greet visitors, and stir up business. The staff working the Scholastic booth must be prepared to handle requests for dinner tickets from delegates who did not obtain them through regular channels — by mailing in the coupon published in the magazines' teacher editions and book clubs' teacher memos. The coupon asks the respondent to state what Scholastic product he or she subscribes to. Many of the delegates who ask for tickets at the booth subscribe to none. They are likely to be university professors or instructors in schools of education, in a position to influence their students in their choice of instructional materials when they become teachers.

Company budget balancers annually ponder the mounting expense of these NCTE and NCSS parties. How much are we talking about? At 1977 costs, just multiply 1,500 by about $15 for dinner and drinks (give or take a couple of dollars, depending on the hotel). Add to this round figure 17 percent gratuities, sales tax, and the cost of getting a staff of 20 or so there and keeping them for three to six days. Add 75 percent of that total (for the NCSS party), and you have the rough grand-total cost of the two parties. Is it worth it? Reading the bundles of thank-you letters that follow the parties and reflecting on the goodwill generated inclines one to feel that the "professional relations" value alone justifies the expense.

There is an anecdote worth recording in connection with the expense of holding these parties. Robinson was asked whether he had tried to get other publishers to share in hosting and paying for the NCTE party. "I certainly did," he said, "and it was in 1950 in Milwaukee. By that time the whole affair was getting bigger and bigger, so I went to some of my friends in the publishing business to suggest that all the publishers get together and next year invite everybody who registered at the convention for a big Thanksgiving buffet — entertain the entire convention. I suggested this mainly for a reason other than shared expenses: There was a feeling on the part of some of the publishers that Scholastic had what you might call a monopoly, with our name attached to what many considered the highlight of the convention. Several felt that Scholastic had an unfair advantage, and told me so. Three or four of the publishers I spoke to showed extreme interest in the idea of joint sponsorship, so — along with 10 or 12 other publishers — I met with them in the Hotel Schroeder the day after our Milwaukee party, and we talked it over. As we neared the end of the discussion, one publisher seemed to answer for everybody by saying: 'Well, you can count us out because even if we all pitched in to finance this affair, everybody would still call it the Scholastic Party.' " That broke up the meeting.

On the occasion of the Scholastic dinner during the 1970 meeting of the National Council of Teachers of English in Atlanta, 31 past presidents and the incumbent marked Scholastic's 50th anniversary by presenting a scroll to Robinson inscribed:

To our honored friend
and genial host
M. R. ROBINSON
affectionately known to thousands
as Robbie
in grateful appreciation of his generosity,
modesty, and unselfish concern for his friends,
among whom we have the privilege
to subscribe ourselves
*on behalf of all the others**

* Robert C. Pooley, NCTE president in 1941, made the presentation speech. Six years later in Washington, DC, the year of America's bicentennial celebration, past and present leaders of the National Council for the Social Studies also paid tribute to Robinson in a speech delivered by James P. Shaver, president, at the Scholastic dinner in the Sheraton Park Hotel, November 5, 1976.

CHAPTER XXV

Getting Students' Opinions

SCHOLASTIC has been conducting opinion polls among junior and senior high school students for more than 35 years and continues to do so, presently under an arrangement with The New York Times Special Features Syndicate for distribution of a weekly column based on poll results. About 70 newspapers and the American Broadcasting Company have subscribed to this service.

Forerunner of the Scholastic poll was the National Youth Poll conducted in October 1940 in cooperation with the Civics Research Institute of Washington, DC. Five questions were presented, including one on Presidential preference: Roosevelt or Willkie. These questions were published in the October 21, 1940, *Scholastic* (which marked the 20th anniversary of its founding). Students were asked to write their answers on separate pieces of paper and deposit them in a box on the teacher's desk. They were also asked to take the questions home and have their parents write answers and return those ballots to the teacher. The teacher filled out a report form and sent it to the Civics Research Institute for national tabulation, to be published in *Scholastic*. The five questions from Poll No. 1 for school year 1940–41 and the responses, as published in the December 16, 1940 issue, were:

■ QUESTION 1: Do you think that the United States will be drawn into the war in Europe?

Total number voting: Students, 9,618; Parents, 2,304.

	Number	Yes	No	Undecided
Boys	4,006	55.8%	31.9%	12.3%
Girls	4,554	52.2	28.4	19.4
Unclassified*	1,058	50.1	25.2	24.7
Fathers	1,114	56.6	30.0	13.4
Mothers	1,190	49.2	29.7	21.1
All voters	11,922	53.3	29.6	17.1

■ QUESTION 2: Do you think that all high schools should give students instruction in the mechanics of automobile driving?

Total number voting: Students, 9,649; Parents, 2,284.

	Number	Yes	No	Undecided
Boys	3,965	81.2%	16.1%	2.7%
Girls	4,593	82.9	13.5	3.6
Unclassified*	1,091	83.1	13.0	3.9
Fathers	1,094	75.2	21.3	3.5
Mothers	1,190	77.1	18.1	4.8
All voters	11,933	81.1	15.5	3.4

*This group includes the votes of students that were reported but not divided to indicate how many were boys and how many girls.

■ QUESTION 3: Do you think that there should be a law requiring all cars and trucks on the open highway to go at least 25 miles an hour?

Total number voting: Students, 9,500; Parents, 2,273.

	Number	Yes	No	Undecided
Boys	3,931	68.5%	29.2%	2.3%
Girls	4,502	61.4	34.1	4.5
Unclassified*	1,067	58.4	35.9	5.7
Fathers	1,095	67.6	29.8	2.6
Mothers	1,178	64.5	29.3	6.2
All Voters	11,173	64.4	31.8	3.8

■ QUESTION 4: Who is your choice for President, Roosevelt or Willkie?

Total number voting: Students, 9,978; Parents, 2,499.

	Number	Roosevelt	Willkie	Undecided
Boys	3,934	57.4%	41.4%	1.2%
Girls	4,520	59.3	39.0	1.7
Unclassified*	1,524	61.5	36.5	2.0
Fathers	1,254	66.7	32.1	1.2
Mothers	1,245	66.1	32.1	1.8
All voters	12,477	60.4	38.1	1.5

■ QUESTION 5: Who do you think will win the Presidential election, Roosevelt or Willkie?

Total number voting: Students, 9,423; Parents, 2,315.

	Number	Roosevelt	Willkie	Undecided
Boys	3,934	69.0%	29.5%	1.5%
Girls	4,415	71.3	26.4	2.3
Unclassified*	1,074	69.9	26.7	3.4
Fathers	1,131	75.3	23.5	1.2
Mothers	1,184	76.4	22.6	1.0
All voters	11,738	71.3	26.8	1.9

★ ★ ★ ★ ★ TEACHERS EDITION

Senior Scholastic

SENIOR

VOL. 42 NO. 13   MAY 3-8, 1943

Institute of Student Opinion
Organized by *Scholastic*

WILL *this* war finally be the war to end all wars?
You can make it happen. Your convictions, as well as your actions, will help to shape the world's destiny.

Is Congress efficient? Does it obey the will of the American people? Should 18-year-olds vote? Do high school students know enough about American history to be good citizens?

Scholastic believes that your opinion on these and other timely questions is important to the future of the United States and the whole world of nations. What you think and do will help determine whether we shall live in peace and security or die in war and chaos in the world of tomorrow.

Scholastic believes that the opinions of youth should be accurately determined and widely publicized. And now they will be! We have organized the Scholastic Institute of Student Opinion through which high school students of America can register their opinions.

Already 728 schools representing more than a half million students have joined the Institute. No dues or fees are attached to membership. Every student may vote. Ballots are kept strictly anonymous.

In each school, the school paper will conduct the poll. All school papers, whose names *Scholastic* has on file, received membership invitations. All schools are welcome, and if the faculty advisor of your paper did not receive an application form, we shall be glad to send one. Application should be made before May 12th in order to be in time for the first poll, which must be completed during that month.

Send for application form to
Scholastic Institute of Student Opinion,
220 East 42nd Street,
New York, N. Y.

By the time the 1944 election came around, Scholastic had organized its own Institute of Student Opinion (ISO) with Margaret Hauser, then an associate editor, as director. In every Presidential election since 1940 except one,* the students participating in the Scholastic poll have picked the candidate who won the election, usually by a percentage very close to that of the country at large.

The system of registering students' opinions through ISO has varied over the years. During the early years the poll in each participating school was conducted by the faculty advisor and student staff of the school newspaper. The ballots were supplied by Scholastic, and each school got as many as it requested. Boys and girls were polled in equal numbers, and the results for each school were tabulated at the school and reported to Scholastic on a master form.

With from 800 to 1,500 schools polling between 75,000 and 200,000 students, this caused a great deal of clerical work at Scholastic, straining the exchequer to the point where a decision was made to change the procedure to one more selective, or "scientific." Under the guidance of a professional statistician, Scholastic chose a sample of junior and senior high schools by geographic, socioeconomic, urban, and rural demographics so that each area and group would be fairly represented in the national poll. For about seven years the ISO was conducted according to this solidly based system. But after Scholastic had put a

*The election outcome that the ISO students failed to predict was that of 1948 — Truman vs. Dewey. Of the 80,000 students voting, 46.29 percent picked Dewey, 38.76 percent, Truman. This corresponded to the outcome of the Gallup and Roper polls, both of which predicted Dewey the winner. ISO students gave Henry Wallace 4.90 percent, Strom Thurmond, 1.42 percent, and Norman Thomas, 0.78 percent.

highly qualified statistical expert on its full-time staff to conduct ISO (which by 1964 had become a part of the newly formed Scholastic Research Center), operating costs continued to mount and the poll was changed back to the voluntary system: Any school desiring to participate could do so by conducting the poll from ballots printed in the magazine.

Beginning in 1976 Scholastic has conducted polls four or five times during the school year, with an average of 25,000 students participating in from 400 to 600 junior and senior high schools coast to coast. The title was changed to the National Institute of Student Opinion (NISO), and the company employed a full-time coordinator — Arnold Rubin — who prepares the questions with the assistance of a committee of Scholastic executives and editors and a representative of The New York Times Syndicate. Poll results are distributed to about 70 newspapers subscribing to the service, and Scholastic is compensated on the basis of each newspaper's circulation. Under this system Scholastic, as conductor and copyright-owner of each poll, reaps thousands of columns of publicity in newspapers with a total circulation of about 12 million coast to coast. Each of the polls consists of approximately 12 questions and provides a sufficient amount of material for newspaper syndication on a weekly basis, using the responses to one question for each weekly release. Scholastic also obtains comments on the questions from individual students and persons of renown, and these are used in the weekly releases. Betty Ford, James Schlesinger, Donald Rumsfeld, Joyce Brothers, George Meany, Ernest Noble, and Kenneth E. Clark have been among those quoted.

CHAPTER XXVI

From Hot to Cold

A Successful Transition

E ARLY in the 1960's the publishing industry began departing from using the system of typesetting that had stood for hundreds of years — the arrangement of letters, figures, or other characters on wood or metal blocks to form words and sentences. The new system eliminates the metal blocks* and in their place uses film to which images of the letters of the alphabet, etc., are transferred photographically. This is photocomposition, called "cold type" to distinguish it from the hot type that came into common use during the late 19th century with the invention of the linotype machine by Mergenthaler. It was called "hot" because the metal used for the slug on which a line of words was formed was very hot when it emerged from the pot of molten metal, the lifeblood of the linotype machine. Photocomposition eliminated the need for the molten-metal/hot-type stage, substituting the much faster camera and achieving considerable economy in time and money, unless the system created its own problems, as new systems are wont to do.

Always interested in cost reduction in order to keep prices at a level that encouraged quantity purchases by

* Wood was commonly used before metal.

at our corner

IT IS 6:20, Tuesday evening, October 4, '49. The three pages of "Understanding the News" for the October 12th issues of *Senior Scholastic* and *World Week* are being teletyped from "our corner" to a big, modern printing plant in Dayton, Ohio—the McCall press.

Yesterday afternoon at 4 o'clock, printing plates, or "shells" or "mats" of all pages except the late news for *Senior Scholastic, World Week* and *Junior Scholastic,* were sent to Dayton by overnight express in a special box rushed to Grand Central Terminal, New York, from the composing room of the Western Newspaper Union plant, three blocks away.

The "mats" from which printing plates were made for this week's issue of *Practical English* (in which we publish no late news) were shipped to Dayton late last week.

Tonight, or rather about two o'clock tomorrow morning, the last copies of the October 10th issue of *Newsweek,* our distinguished contemporary, will roll from the battery of high-speed two-color presses at McCall's. As rapidly as the *Newsweek* printing plates can be snatched from the presses, a double set of *Junior Scholastic* plates will be fastened to one press and a single set of *Practical English* plates to another.

Pressmen will thread newsprint from huge rolls through the maze of inked rollers, dryers, and folders. Soon the presses will roar into high speed. Behind the press, additional rolls of paper will be lined up ready to be spliced to the emptying rolls ahead—without a stop—as each hungry press eats up more than a mile of paper every six minutes.

Junior Scholastic will run "two-up." Duplicate sets of plates have been made so that two complete magazines may be printed simultaneously on a large press. Copies of *Junior* will rush from the presses at the rate of 26,000 complete magazines an hour.

Meanwhile, *Practical English* will be running on another press—and copies will be delivered at the rate of 16,000 each hour until the run is completed. While *Practical English* is being printed, the last-minute news for *Senior Scholastic* and *World Week* will be set in type and printing plates made. The moment *P. E.* is completed tomorrow (Wednesday) afternoon, October 5th, *Senior Scholastic,* then *World Week,* will take over the press. The speed of 16,000 complete magazines an hour will be maintained.

Then, the bindery and mailing room staff will move in. Magazines will be stapled, trimmed, and wrapped.

Within 72 hours from the time this copy is teletyped, 700,000 copies of our weekly classroom magazines will be in mail cars moving to all sections of the U. S. Some packages will have already been delivered to the schools. An airplane will be carrying copies to Hawaii.

But here I am writing of what is going to happen. It is now 7:28 p.m., Tuesday, October 4th. The girl at the teletype has finished typing the news. Her sharp call reminds me the deadline is here. "Where's that copy, Mr. R?" she calls. "Hurry, we must send it now. The subscription department wants to use the teletype to wire today's late orders!"

M. R. Robinson

PRESIDENT AND PUBLISHER

the schools, the company had changed typesetting houses and printers a number of times over the years in order to reduce costs-per-page without losing good service. Don Layman and Dick Holahan, "true believers" in the future of cold type, led the company to shift two of its magazines from the hot-type shop of Sterling Graphic Arts, formerly the Western Newspaper Union, to a newly organized photocomposition outfit: Foto-Comp, Inc., which took basement space in one of the skyscrapers that began transforming Sixth Avenue (Avenue of the Americas) from a street of saloons and pawnshops into a canyon of metal and glass superstructures. Foto-Comp was started by the two Dunn brothers, who had set up such a system for Time-Life Books.

Photocomposition had proved its value for setting long columns of routine copy such as for catalogs, telephone directories, and straight bookwork in which lines were of even length and in the same typeface. Note that the images of letters on film were still to be called type, although it was not what the dictionary called type — "a rectangular block, usually of metal or wood, having its face so shaped as to produce, in printing, a letter, figure, or other character." In the photocomposition sense, type could be defined as "the image of a letter, figure, or other character photographed on film from which could be produced the sensitized plate for printing."

Although it was an efficient process for setting galleys of straight or routine copy, efficiency was slow in coming in the composition of type for magazine pages

"At Our Corner" column, which appeared in *Scholastic Teacher* after William Boutwell took over the editorship in 1947, commented on company procedures and programs of interest to teachers. Most were written by Boutwell and M. R. Robinson. This one, from the October 12, 1949, issue, appeared during the years in which *Senior Scholastic, World Week,* and *Junior Scholastic* gave high priority to expeditious coverage of late news by teletyping it to the printing plant in Dayton, OH.

443

with as many as 10 different typefaces per page, uneven lines, heads and subheads, halftone and line illustrations. Scholastic's production staff—Jane Fliegel, Barbara Kellogg, Eve Sennett, and others—assigned to Foto-Comp's workshop to read proof and give the final OK on pages, were at their wits' end trying to get the work out on time to meet the printing deadline at the McCall plant in Dayton, OH. In this situation it was understandable that the photocomposition system was not getting a very warm reception by Fliegel, Kellogg, Sennett, and company. They were ready to go back to hot type, from which the other Scholastic magazines had not departed.

Nicholas Kochansky, as manufacturing manager for the magazines, was eager to relieve the production staff of its tribulations without necessarily giving up on the photocomposition experiment. Perhaps one of the other houses that had recently started up in photocomposition could do an efficient job. One, whose president, Harold Altmayer, had been doing business with Scholastic as head of Tonemakers, Inc. (a photocopying, not a photocomposition, house), had recently launched a second company to do it named Compu-Graphic Corporation. In order to take over some of the Scholastic work, he needed capital for new equipment and proposed that for $150,000 Scholastic could have 33⅓ percent of Compu-Graphic's voting stock.

M. R. Robinson set up a special committee consisting of George Milne, Holahan, Kochansky, and Richard Spaulding "to investigate investment in Compu-Graphic." Within three months, on December 5, 1969, the committee recommended "that the Executive Committee of the Board of Directors authorize the investment of $150,000, terms to be negotiated." In photocomposition the committee saw "a process which, if effectively developed, could save substantial amounts in typesetting and improve flexibility and quality," and in the link with Compu-Graphic an opportunity "to develop people, expertise, and management abilities, part of which will become available for acquisition by Scholastic should this become desirable."

The Executive Committee endorsed the recommendation, and all that was needed to complete the transaction was to negotiate the terms. For this a negotiating committee was set up consisting of Milne as chairman, Holahan, and Kochansky. They wrote to Altmayer, saying: "If your prices are indeed competitive, Scholastic would be awarding you not only *Senior Scholastic* but one or two other weekly magazines, depending on your capacity to handle them."

Altmayer came back with prices at least 30 percent higher than Scholastic was paying Foto-Comp, Inc., for its film setting and Sterling Graphic Arts for its hot-type setting. Kochansky expressed his disappointment over this in a telephone call to Altmayer, followed by innumerable conferences with Holahan and sometimes Milne attending. Still Altmayer could not produce prices close enough to competitors' to satisfy Holahan and Kochansky. In a memo dated February 13, 1970, they reported to Milne (and thus to the Management Operations Committee, M. R. Robinson, chairman) that it was "in the best interest of Scholastic to break off the negotiations with Compu-Graphic Corporation. We do not believe it would be prudent business judgment to invest any capital in Compu-Graphic. We have arrived at this position reluctantly and after more than seven weeks of painstaking

445

negotiations. What began with such promise of success has turned into a real disappointment. . . ."

Milne, unwilling to accept this as a terminal case and sensing an opportunity in the one-third ownership to put Compu-Graphic on a businesslike basis, prevailed upon Kochansky and Holahan to return to the bargaining table with Altmayer. This they did, and a prolonged task it was. But with each successive meeting, Altmayer — desperately in need of the immediate financing — came down in his prices stage by stage until by June 25, 1970, Kochansky would report: "Agreement reached with Compu-Graphic today to reduce prices by adopting a billing method satisfactory to Holahan and me, putting their service in line with competition, at least theoretically. The agreement calls for setting *Scope* and *Junior* at Compu-Graphic for 70–71." Indeed that happened, but it was a slow operation, resulting in many missed deadlines. Altmayer was short on work-force, as he was keeping the payroll low in order to meet the competitive page-rate and still make a profit. Now any profit (or loss) would be one-third Scholastic's. Milne, Holahan, and Kochansky went on the Compu-Graphic board of directors. Holahan would keep in close touch with the work that took place in a building just a five-minute walk from Scholastic headquarters at 50 West 44th Street.

In March 1972 Compu-Graphic had to change its name on demand from a manufacturing firm in the same business that proved prior use of the unregistered title. Under its new name, Advanced Typographic Systems, Inc. (ATS), Harold Altmayer continued as president, continued doing quality work, and continued running a deficit operation. As Milne wrote to the Management Opera-

446

tions Committee early in 1973: "ATS has bumped along all winter with a small gain or a small loss. . . . The major problem is its inability to get additional outside business."

Conditioned to profits on his successful operation of Tonemakers, Altmayer began wearying of the struggle for ATS to make money. He let Milne know that he would consider yielding to Scholastic — his job and his shares of ATS stock. With most, if not all, of Scholastic's production personnel high on prospects for the future of photocomposition, the board of directors approved the proposal to acquire Altmayer's ATS stock, to accept his resignation, and to reorganize the company.

Scholastic acquired 210,000 shares, with two of Altmayer's working associates — Werner Barusek and Rodney Kohn — retaining a piece of the ownership (20,000 shares each).

In April 1974 Holahan, who was nearing retirement from Scholastic, was elected president and chief executive officer and a member of the ATS board along with Barusek and Kohn. The board was well-stocked with Scholastic staffers — Dick Robinson, chairman, Charles Hurley, Jane Fliegel, Barbara Kellogg, Paul King, Nick Kochansky, and Ray Naimoli.

Under the reorganization ATS acquired new equipment including a new Mergenthaler VIP (Variable Input Phototypesetter) and developed the technical skills and efficiency needed to take over the typesetting of all of Scholastic's junior and senior high school English-language student magazines, plus *Scholastic Coach* and *Forecast for Home Economics*. ATS also took on an increasing amount of Scholastic book and brochure composition in addition to book and catalog work for other publishers. What Layman, Holahan, and Kochansky envisioned in 1965 as the type "wave of the future" had finally come to pass for Scholastic, now in possession of its own photocomposition house. For the first time, ATS broke even on its operations for the fiscal year ended August 31, 1976.

As press runs of the magazines moved into the millions, the idea of Scholastic owning its own printing facility occurred to company officials. Once the seed germinated, it began to sprout — not the whole plant but a couple of shoots, each costing $1,500,000. These presses were direly needed, but the company had hoped to persuade McCall to buy and install them. McCall would do this only if Scholastic would sign a long-term noncancellable printing contract. Scholastic elected to buy the presses: two Goss four-color offset presses, installed in 1965 in the McCall plant and operated under contract by McCall personnel.

McCall leased time on the Scholastic presses to print some of its other work when the weekly runs of several of Scholastic's magazines had been finished. Five years later the presses were sold to McCall, as considerable investment was needed to rebuild them for improved color work and it was impractical for Scholastic to undertake the expense. McCall had plenty of other equipment to handle the Scholastic work.

Scholastic does own a piece of a printing plant — 25 percent of the voting stock of a Dayton company called United Color Press, formerly Otterbein Press. As Otterbein, it was owned by the Methodist Church Publishing House, which printed church periodicals and took in out-

448

side commercial work, including Scholastic's book club promotion kits. Otterbein, finding itself in that no man's land between tax-haven and commercial profits, decided to get out of the printing business, and it was offered for sale to its employees and customers. Scholastic jumped in along with *Billboard*, the entertainment industry periodical, and Don Layman went on the board of directors to represent Scholastic. When Layman retired, George Milne took his place, and now Richard Spaulding represents the company. Scholastic's interest now exceeds its stock investment, as United Color prints all nine of its foreign-language magazines, several of its other magazines, and millions of copies of promotion materials for the five book clubs.

Hobart M. Corning, superintendent, Washington, DC, schools, and the Reverend Monsignor Frederick G. Hochwalt, director, Department of Education, National Catholic Welfare Conference, at the 1957 meeting, National Advisory Council.

Richard M. Clowes, superintendent, Los Angeles County Public Schools, speaking at 1978 meeting, National Advisory Council. Next to him, Brother John D. Olsen, executive director, Secondary School Department, National Catholic Educational Association; and Charlotte Ryan, president, Massachusetts Parent-Teacher-Student Association.

1968 National Advisory Council. Left to right, sitting: John W. Letson, superintendent, Atlanta Public Schools; William H. Curtis, superintendent, Manchester, CT, Public Schools; James A. Hazlett, superintendent, Kansas City, MO, Public Schools; Sidney P. Marland, president, Institute for Educational Development. Standing: John W. Studebaker, chairman; Melvin W. Barnes, superintendent of schools, Portland, OR; Ellsworth Tompkins, executive secretary, National Association of Secondary School Principals; Paul F. Lawrence, chief, Division of Higher Education, State Department of Education, CA; C. Albert Koob, executive secretary, National Catholic Educational Association; M. R. Robinson.

CHAPTER XXVII

Advice and Consent

M. R. Robinson has always held the notion that advisory boards are meant to advise, not just to lend prestige to the masthead. His first encounter of this kind was with the western Pennsylvania high school principals, from whom in 1920 he sought and received consent for Scholastic to be the official publication of the Western Pennsylvania Interscholastic Athletic League (Chapter I). By 1923 he had set up the first body of "advisory and contributing editors" for *The Scholastic*. Among the 11 members were high school principals, college professors, the president of the National Council of Teachers of English, two Pennsylvania State Education Department officials, the publisher Horace Liveright, and Donald F. Stewart, a Liveright editor who took on a freelance assignment to edit the "Scholastic News Caldron," a regular feature of the magazine.

By early spring of 1928 the Scholastic directors, acting on a suggestion by Robinson, authorized him to invite a group of distinguished educators to attend a meeting in Pittsburgh to discuss the prospect of organizing "an editorial council for the Scholastic Publishing Company."

Robinson already had in mind the identity of the

Scholastic's English Advisory Board with editors, 1940. Left to right: Jack Lippert, associate editor; Carol Hovious, San Benito County H.S., Hollister, CA; Ernestine Taggard, associate editor; Kenneth Gould, editor; Charles Swain Thomas, Harvard; M. R. Robinson; Marquis Shattuck, director of Language Education, Detroit; Mabel Goddard, Arsenal Technical Schools, Indianapolis; Max J. Herzberg, principal, Weequahic H.S., Newark, NJ. Robert Frost, the poet, and Dorothy Canfield Fisher, author, were absent. At the time, Scholastic was published in three editions: advanced English, social studies, and combined.

distinguished educators he would invite to this meeting, as he had had lunch with them in Boston a few weeks earlier at the annual meeting of the American Association of School Administrators. The Boston luncheon had been set up by Robinson's friend and counselor, Pittsburgh Superintendent of Schools William Davidson, and it had included Superintendent Weet of Rochester, NY, Superintendent Cody of Detroit, Dean Judd of the University of Chicago School of Education, and Dean Withers of New York University School of Education. It was this group (including Superintendent Condon of Cincinnati who was unable to attend the luncheon) that would meet with Oliver, Clapp, Robinson, and McCracken at the University Club in Pittsburgh on May 12, 1928, to discuss the prospects for Scholastic's growth. Oliver had the group for dinner that night at the Pittsburgh Golf Club. Soon after this meeting, on May 21, the Scholastic directors invited Superintendent Davidson to summarize the outcome of the May 12 meeting: Dr. Davidson declared that "the

Left to right: James E. Allen, commissioner of education, New York State; George B. Brain, dean of education, Washington State University; M. R. Robinson; during luncheon, 1967 meeting, National Advisory Council.

unanimous opinion of the educators was that there is an almost unlimited opportunity for the development of the periodical idea for the public schools."

The educators named above, with the exception of Judd, became the Board of Supervising Editors, to be announced in *The Scholastic* as follows:

> The Scholastic Publishing Company has the honor to announce the appointment of the following Special Editorial Board of distinguished educators who will actively supervise the educational policies of all the Scholastic publications beginning with the school year 1929–1930:
>
> Randall J. Condon, former Superintendent of Schools, Cincinnati.
> William M. Davidson, Superintendent of Schools, Pittsburgh.
> Frank Cody, Superintendent of Schools, Detroit.
> Herbert S. Weet, Superintendent of Schools, Rochester.
> John W. Withers, Dean, School of Education, New York University.

In September 1940 a reorganization of the advisors was announced: What had been the Board of Supervising

Editors became the National Advisory Council, which would continue to consist of top-level school administrators. At the same time, two other boards were formed, each consisting of teachers, department heads, and curriculum specialists — the Advisory Board for Social Studies and the Advisory Board for English. Soon *Junior Scholastic* would have its own advisory board, and as Scholastic launched new magazines or purchased others, each would have its own advisory board. These boards met in New York annually until 1964, when the meetings were changed to a biannual schedule. The National Advisory Council, however, continues to meet annually.

Each of Scholastic's five book clubs has an editorial board of teachers, librarians, and other professionals in education qualified to advise the editors on book selections, reading trends, and students' interests.

National Advisory Council, 1957 meeting. Left to right, standing: Jay Davis Conner, associate superintendent of public instruction, California; Eric N. Dennard, superintendent of schools, Waco, TX; Monsignor William McManus, the National Catholic Conference; Henry H. Hill, president, George Peabody College for Teachers, Nashville, TN; Lloyd S. Michael, superintendent, Evanston Township H.S., Evanston, IL; E. B. Norton, president, State Teachers College, Florence, AL; Benjamin C. Willis, general superintendent of schools, Chicago, IL; John H. Fischer, superintendent of public schools, Baltimore, MD. Sitting: Herold C. Hunt, Harvard; Galen Jones, director, Council for Advancement of Secondary Education; John W. Studebaker, vice president/chairman of editorial boards; M. R. Robinson.

CHAPTER XXVIII

Scholastic Unit
Newspaper Guild
of New York

SINCE its earliest days the Newspaper Guild of New York has had a unit at Scholastic representing magazine editorial employees. The unit was formed in 1937 within a year of the formation of the American Newspaper Guild under the noted journalist Heywood Broun. The first president of the Scholastic unit was Marcus Rosenblum, a member of the editorial staff and editor of Scholastic's short-lived *Highschool* (Chapter XIX, "Lesson Plans, Teacher Editions").

The Scholastic unit functioned as best it could for the first two years without a contract or agreement of any kind except management recognition. One evening in 1938 Robinson invited all 17 members to his narrow apartment on East 89th Street for an evening of informal talk and refreshments, constituting further recognition by the management of the unit's presence and purpose. There followed an exchange of memoranda between the unit and Robinson on points to be considered in framing a "running agreement," as it was called in Robinson's memorandum of February 8, 1940. It became, in effect, the first contract between Scholastic and the Guild, and is remarkable in several ways, not the least of which is the absence of a salary scale. The Guild had submitted a

455

salary scale, listing minimums for each of the editorial categories, but Robinson responded that there was "no prospect during the present school year [1939–40] of Scholastic Corporation's being able to meet those minima, much as the management and the owners would like to do so." Robinson was willing to include in the contract the current salaries being paid the editorial staff, but the Guild did not wish to have what it considered a low scale (compared to the scales in contracts it had with New York newspapers and other magazines) exposed in a written document.

Another noteworthy feature of the first contract was management's acceptance of the principle of the "Guild shop," according to which a Guild member in good standing was bound to remain a member, having no opportunity to resign. Six years later management held out for and won a revision of this so that a Guild member could resign during a specified two-week period without prejudice to his standing as a Scholastic employee. This, at the time and for years after, was referred to as the "escape period," but later was called the "resignation period." Management won the provision for escape/resignation following a controversy with the Guild over its demand that Owen Reed, then editor of *Scholastic Coach,* be dismissed for not paying his Guild dues. (At the time dues were not deducted from payroll checks.) Reed was not dismissed, and the 1946 contract and all since have included a resignation clause.

The first Scholastic–Guild contract to provide for pay increases — without mention of a salary scale of minimums — was signed May 21, 1942, and stated "The

Publisher agrees to grant salary raises of 15 percent above the salary that each employee received in May, 1941. These raises shall be effected as follows: 7½ percent as of February 1, 1942; 7½ percent as of October 1, 1942. No such raise to be less than $5."

The first specific salary scale appeared in the contract for school year 1943–44, and it evolved out of recommendations by the National War Labor Board to which Scholastic and the Guild had appealed to settle their dispute over job classifications and minimum salaries. The Board was empowered by law to determine whether salary increases would be permitted and, if so, how much. The hearings were held before Hearing Officer Jules J. Justin, appointed by the National War Labor Board. Scholastic Corporation was represented by M. R. Robinson and Jack Lippert; the Guild's New York office by attorney Sol D. Kapelsohm and Guild organizer Thomas J. Murphy; and the Scholastic Guild Unit by its chairman, Julian Whitener. The Board's recommendations for salary minimums by job classification were accepted by Scholastic and the Guild, and appear on the next page.

In 1950 the Guild conducted a vigorous campaign among certain noneditorial employees in an attempt to expand the membership of the Scholastic Unit and put it in a position to represent all departments of the company. The Guild distributed cards to noneditorial employees to obtain their opinions as to whether they would join the Guild. The outcome of this balloting prompted the Guild to send a letter to the company on August 19, 1950, stating that "a majority of your employees in the noneditorial departments, other than Subscription Service

SALARY RECOMMENDATIONS OF THE NATIONAL WAR LABOR BOARD FOR SCHOLASTIC EDITORIAL DEPARTMENT EMPLOYEES, SEPTEMBER 9, 1943*

Classification	*Weekly Mimimum Rates and Wage Brackets*
1. Stenographers	Start: $23; after 1 year: $26
2. Researcher-Writer	Start: $30; after 1 year: $35
3. Librarian	Start: $35; after 1 year: $40; after 2 years: $45
4. Library Clerk	Start: $25; after 1 year: $27.50; after 2 years: $30; after 3 years: $35
5. Production Men†	Start: $40; after 1 year: $43; after 2 years: $48; after 3 years: $53
6. Production Assistant	Start: $25; after 1 year: $28; after 2 years: $30; after 3 years: $35
7. Artist	Start: $40; after 1 year: $43; after 2 years: $48
8. Assistant Artist	Start: $30; after 1 year: $35; after 2 years: $40
9. Writers, copy-readers, and editorial staff	Start: $50; after 1 year: $53; after 2 years: $58
10. Editors	The minimum wage of editors shall be not less than the highest minimum wage established for any other classification herein.

*The amounts recommended were, in the main, a compromise between what the Guild requested and what Scholastic offered.

†This is verbatim phrasing from the hearing officer's report, and not the phrasing of this writer, the Guild, or Scholastic. At the time, Scholastic's production department was headed by Sarah Gorman, and included Jane Russell (Fliegel) and Julian Whitener. Sarah Gorman had succeeded Eric Berger as production chief when he became editor of *World Week* in 1942.

and Fulfillment, has selected the Newspaper Guild of New York as its collective bargaining agent." The letter also stated that the Guild desired to enter into "negotiations with you as soon as possible for the purpose of modifying the present editorial contract to cover these noneditorial departments." Management replied on August 30, 1950, saying: "Since we have no way ourselves to verify your claim to represent certain Scholastic employees, we suggest that arrangements be made for an election by secret ballot as provided by the laws of the United States government." The Guild did not reply to this letter but applied directly to the New York regional office of the National Labor Relations Board for an election. NLRB officials arranged a meeting, to be attended by both Guild and Scholastic representatives, to discuss the petition. The Guild asked that employees of the Subscription Service Department be excluded from the voting. Scholastic raised no objection to this, but the NLRB did: It would not certify an election that excluded a department of the company. Soon thereafter the Guild notified NLRB that it was withdrawing its request for an election.

Several days later the Guild announced to Scholastic employees that "in a short time, an election will be held at Scholastic under the direction of the National Labor Relations Board. . . . All Scholastic employees will vote whether or not they want to have the Guild cover all departments of Scholastic, instead of just the Editorial Department as at present." This caught management by surprise, since it had received no word from the Guild about reapplying for an election. Robinson immediately sent a message to the Unit Officers.

To the Scholastic Unit of the Newspaper Guild:

We have been informed that you have advised the employees of Scholastic that there is soon to be an election here at which all employees will vote whether or not they want to have the Guild cover all departments of Scholastic, instead of just the editorial department.

In view of the long and unusually pleasant relationship between the Guild and Scholastic, we were disappointed in the fact that we had to discover this information from a source other than the Guild. We learned of the proposed election when we were asked by certain employees about the Guild's request that they sign a card applying for Guild membership.

If we *are* going to have a secret election, we see no reason — prior to the election — why anyone should be asked to sign a card which may imply a promise or obligation to vote a certain way. We do not deny the Guild's right to seek memberships in advance of an election. But we believe that such a procedure destroys the fundamental reason for a secret election.

We would like to make a proposal to you and the Guild. If the members of the Scholastic organization are going to discuss the subject of whether they wish to be represented by the Guild, let's make an honest effort to do a straightforward educational job of it. Let's conduct the discussion out in the open in a true democratic spirit.

There are many good arguments in favor of unions. There are likewise many good arguments against them, and this is especially true in a small organization like Scholastic.

Accordingly, let's discuss the "pros" and "cons" of this subject in a spirit of good comradeship. Please read Management's statement on Union Membership on page 19 of Scholastic's

460

office policies [a copy of which is given to each employee]. We say in that bulletin: "You need have no fear from Management if you join any union. Nor need you have any fear from Management if you do not join any union." We mean that and we mean it BOTH ways.

We propose, therefore, that the Guild and Scholastic Management agree promptly on an approximate date for the NLRB election. We propose that a meeting be held to be attended by all members of our organization. The meeting would be held on company time in a mutually acceptable place. We propose that the Guild and Scholastic Management divide the time at the meeting exactly in half, perhaps 30 or 40 minutes for the Guild and the same number of minutes for Management. We propose that we agree that neither the Guild nor Management will conduct any other meetings except the open "town meeting" which we jointly organize and conduct.

There is no reason — in an organization like Scholastic — for the question of "union membership" to be discussed in corridors, stairways, rest rooms, etc. Why not display some of the spirit on which our own business is based? That is: open and frank and honest discussion of divergent points of view. Then a secret vote. Why should we not respect an honest difference of opinion about the desirability of joining an organization?

We propose this sane and straightforward and adult method of carrying on an educational program concerning union membership at Scholastic in a spirit of goodwill and in a desire to advance the best interests of Scholastic Magazines and all its employees. Our energies, our time, our skills should be directed toward improving our products, our service, our sales techniques. The best interests of the entire staff and of the business itself are most effectively served when we devote ourselves to advancing the growth and financial strength of Scholastic.

After all, the stockholders and officers of Scholastic are not getting rich. Our stockholders —for most of our 30 years—have been putting up money to pay decent salaries to all of us. Let's not act as if Management and employees of Scholastic are "enemies." All of us who wish to build a satisfying career at Scholastic know that our personal advancement will come only with the progress of Scholastic itself. That's been true for 30 years and will continue to be true.

We hope you will accept the proposal contained in this letter — or some modification of it which you might like to suggest.

There was a prompt and positive response from the Guild to Robinson's proposal, and the parties met to discuss it. They agreed to do it without the NLRB. It would be a gentlemen's and ladies' agreement: (1) to hold a meeting in a neutral place (Adelphi Hall, 74 Fifth Avenue, on December 13, 1950, 3 p.m.); (2) to have a neutral chairman — Howard L. Hurwitz;* (3) to include the

---

*Howard Hurwitz, then a teacher in the Social Studies Department of Seward Park High School, was well known to Scholastic executives and editorial staff, as he worked in the Scholastic office several hours every Thursday after school, preparing the teaching guide for the social studies content of *Senior Scholastic*. Later he became principal of Long Island City High School, where he established a reputation as a disciplinarian. He had wide community and parental support for his policies and means of maintaining a well-behaved, productive student body. In 1976 he attracted national attention when he refused to readmit to his school a disruptive student and was suspended by the chancellor. Students and parents boycotted the school for three days until Dr. Hurwitz was restored to his position.

462

Subscription Service and Fulfillment Department employees, but not the Editorial Department employees; (4) to identify each person eligible to vote (a total of 72); (5) to vote by a secret ballot; (6) that a majority would determine the outcome; and (7) that each side would have 45 minutes to present its case.

Seventy of the eligible 72 employees voted, and the count was 45 to 25 against the proposition that the Guild represent all noneditorial employees as well as those in the Editorial Department. It had been stipulated in the "Attestation of Good Faith," which both parties signed prior to the meeting, that the Guild would engage in no further activity to enlist the support of noneditorial employees "for a period of at least 12 months from the date of the election [December 13, 1950]." Contracts have been signed by the Guild and Scholastic ever since covering only magazine editorial employees of the company.

The Guild has never struck Scholastic, although negotiations for contract renewal have often been protracted and dangling long after the date of expiration. As of May 1977, 82 of the 111 eligible employees on the magazines' editorial staffs are Guild members. The editorial administrator, editor-in-chief, and editorial directors are exempt, under the terms of the contract.

Chief negotiator for Scholastic until 1944 was M. R. Robinson, who gave up this role after some particularly frustrating bargaining sessions. He was succeeded by Kenneth M. Gould and Donald E. Layman. Upon Layman's retirement in 1971, John P. Spaulding headed the Scholastic team, which usually consisted of two others: the editor-in-chief or executive editor and the personnel director. Paul A. King, director of Administrative Services, succeeded Spaulding in 1973 during the illness that led to Spaulding's death on September 4, 1974. Upon King's retirement in 1978, Richard Spaulding, executive vice president, and Carol Rafferty, vice president and corporate director of personnel, conducted negotiations for management.

Chairpersons of the Scholastic Unit, Newspaper Guild, in the order of their appearance, are listed below. The first date is the year during which the chairperson took office. A term usually overlapped into part of the succeeding year.

Marcus Rosenblum, 1936–38
Arthur Gorman, 1939–40
Ernestine Taggard, 1941–42
Julian Whitener, 1943
Herman Masin, 1944
Frank Latham, 1945
Eric Berger, 1946
Irving Talmadge, 1947
Herbert Marx, 1947–50
Sturges Cary, 1951
Patricia Lauber, 1952
Robert Stearns, 1953
Mary Dirlam, 1954

Sarel Eimerl, 1955–56
Lucy Evankow, 1957–58
Carol Drisko, 1959–60
William Lineberry, 1961–62
Patricia Stoddard, 1963
Gene Berg, 1964
Carl Proujan, 1965–67
Jim Barsky, 1968
Anita Soucie, 1969
Dona Kaminsky, 1970–74
Carole Thielman, 1974–78
Bryan Dunlap, 1978—

CHAPTER XXIX

To Talk
of Many Things

TO promote observance of the 300th anniversary of high school education in America in 1935, the Department of Secondary School Principals of the National Education Association set up a Celebration Committee with Calvin O. Davis, professor of Education at the University of Michigan, as chairman. Maurice R. Robinson of Scholastic was named chairman of the Publicity Committee and William D. Boutwell, chief of the Editorial Division of the U.S. Office of Education, assistant chairman. Others on the committee of 15 included leading school administrators at state and city levels, professors of education at Columbia Teachers College and the University of Michigan, and the headmasters of Boston Latin School and Boston English High School.

A Tricentennial Special

Besides contributing its president to the work of this celebration, Scholastic produced a 128-page, cardboard-covered, special Celebration issue printed on coated stock. *Scholastic* had become a weekly magazine in September 1933 (circulation, 132,000). This February 23, 1935, issue appeared in the regular weekly sequence and was sent to every subscriber. Ten thousand additional copies were sold at 50 cents each — a good sale in that Depression year.

Robinson's acceptance of the chairmanship of the

Publicity Committee and his intuitive decision to publish a Celebration issue were characteristic responses to opportunities to associate with educators — "to win them to our side," as he put it. It has been a way of life with the Scholastic leadership since that meeting in the summer of 1920 with the principals of the western Pennsylvania high schools.

Robinson opened his 1,500-word foreword to the Celebration issue with these two paragraphs:

> With this Celebration Book, *Scholastic* pays tribute to a three-century-long struggle which began formally in 1635, when Boston Latin School, forerunner of the present American high school, established free, public education for the first time in the modern world. Efforts of public high schools to teach youth how to work, to think, and to play have not always availed against civic apathy, but universal, democratic education has endured in principle for three hundred years as a major factor of the American dream. The creation of an enlightened citizenry, capable of providing a life of peace and abundance for all, is still the hope of those who have not altogether succumbed to selfish interest or hopeless cynicism.
>
> The plan of this book is to show how secondary education has expanded its historic role in society and how it now performs that role. It is hoped that this work may open a few windows on the problems of the high school and its heroic possibilities as the moulder of America's destinies.

Vocational Sideline In 1944 the company signed a contract with the American Vocational Association (AVA) to furnish publishing services for its official publication, *American Vo-*

cational Journal (*AVJ*), issued monthly starting with the January 1945 issue. "Publishing services" included all phases of the operation — editorial, advertising, printing, and subscription fulfillment — with the reservation that the Association had the right to final approval of editorial content through its executive secretary, L. H. Dennis. He also held the title of editor-in-chief of the editorial board of the Association, which consisted of AVA regional representatives from its eight curriculum departments. Each editorial-board member was responsible for preparing articles and news items relating to his or her field of specialization.

As has happened to other houses in which the publisher did not have final responsibility for a periodical's content, this structural weakness strained the working relationship between AVA and Scholastic to the point where continued affiliation seemed useless. Scholastic exercised its option to cancel the contract in the spring of 1948 upon payment of a $1,000 penalty to AVA. Scholastic lost $64,000 in the four-year operation (the loss of $24,441 in 1945–46 was the peak and $8,700 in the last year, the low) including the $1,000 penalty for cancellation.

Scholastic benefited from this experience, for two of the men who had recently joined the company had held key roles in the operation of *AV Journal* — Donald E. Layman as publisher and William D. Boutwell as managing editor. After one year on *American Vocational Journal* in its Washington office, Boutwell was transferred to the Scholastic office in New York — then in the Daily News Building on East 42nd Street — to develop the teacher editions of the weekly magazines. He would soon convert these once-a-month teacher editions into *Scholastic Teacher*, "Monthly Magazine for the Teaching Profession" (Chapter XIX, "Lesson Plans, Teacher Editions").

With *AV Journal* returned to its owners, Layman was free to give his full attention to main activities of the company as it headed into a 25-year period of expansion. He was with it all the way, building the advertising linage in the weeklies and demonstrating executive and leadership qualities that led to his election to the board of directors, to executive vice president, and to president.

Now Playing in the Little League

In another instance Scholastic entered into an agreement with a nonprofit organization — The Little League Baseball, Inc.—to provide publishing services for its periodical, *The Little Leaguer*. The difficulties encountered in the arrangement with the American Vocational Association were avoided in this later collaboration (1953–55): The Little League provided the editor — Robert H. Stirrat — whose office was at Little League headquarters in Williamsport, PA, but who worked in the Scholastic office for five or six days prior to lockup of each of the six issues per year. Scholastic provided art, production, and advertising-sales services, and it billed the Little League on a cost-plus basis. After two years the Little League decided it could do the whole thing in Williamsport at a figure less than that paid to Scholastic. It had been a friendly, workable arrangement, which had been expected from the start — for both organizations shared Herb McCracken as a director.

From 1956 and for a period of seven years thereafter **Collaboration** Scholastic published the proceedings of the annual meet- **with IRA** ings of the International Reading Association (IRA). The organization, a merger of the International Council for the Improvement of Reading Instruction and the National Association for Remedial Teaching, held its first meeting in Chicago in May 1956 with a registration of 2,300 teachers, supervisors, and others involved in the growing problem of reading disability. Toward the end of the two-day meeting Jack Lippert approached William S. Gray, IRA's first president, and Nancy Larrick, who would succeed him, to express the hope that the proceedings would be published. He offered Scholastic's services to this end, and they were accepted. The 176-page Volume I, under the title *Better Readers for Our Times*, was edited by Gray and Larrick, with Sarah Gorman handling the production in the Scholastic office. Scholastic assumed responsibility for publishing and promotion costs, put a price of $2 on the book ($1.50 for additional copies to the same address), and came out with a profit of around a thousand dollars, which it turned over to IRA. Scholastic published the next six annual volumes with the same understanding and better profits, and then yielded the role to IRA, which by that time had established a prolific publishing unit in its Newark, DE, office.

The headquarters house organ, *Scholastic Ink*, made **On the House** its appearance in 1959 as the successor to *Hi There, Scholastic,* which was launched in 1947 under the joint editorship of William Favel of the editorial staff and Hil-

Scholastic Ink
A NEWSLETTER FOR SCHOLASTIC STAFF MEMBERS
DECEMBER 1964

New Books will Feature Initial Teaching Alphabet

Early in February Scholastic will have available the first ten books being published by the company in the new Initial Teaching Alphabet (i/t/a). Developed in England by Sir James Pitman, this alphabet has just recently been introduced into American schools.

Spectacular results are claimed for the new system in teaching children to read much earlier than has been possible with the conventional alphabet. One of the confusing factors at present is that letters have different sounds in different words. This difficulty is overcome in i/t/a by adding symbols -- "letters" -- to the regular alphabet which stand for individual sounds. There is no difficulty in children making the transition from i/t/a to the regular alphabet once they have learned to read, the developers of the new system find.

The first ten titles Scholastic is issuing in i/t/a all appear on the company's regular list. They are: ZANY ZOO, by Norman Bridwell; THE BIGGEST BEAR, by Lynd Ward; LUCKY AND THE GIANT, by Benjamin Elkin; OLAF READS, by Joan Lexau; CLIFFORD, THE BIG RED DOG, by Norman Bridwell; BIRD IN THE HAT, by Norman Bridwell; THE LITTLE FISH THAT GOT AWAY, by Bernadine Cook; INDIAN TWO FEET AND HIS HORSE, by Margaret Friskey; TONY'S TREASURE HUNT, by Holly and John Peterson; THE ADVENTURES OF THE THREE BLIND MICE, by John W. Ivimey.

> **merry cristmas and a happy nue yeer**
>
> in i/t/a

SPAULDING VISITS IRAN

Bouncing around in a British Land Rover through "some of the most desolate" territory imaginable, spending nights in crude accommodations in little Iranian villages, eating goat cheese, chelow kebab, and other dishes not included in the average American diet, all may seem completely unrelated to publishing and editing, and to the problems of book and periodical houses. But to John P. Spaulding, vice-president of Scholastic, Product Sales, they were very much related recently.

Iranian village elders, children proudly surround local Literacy Corpsman (in uniform, center) on school steps in Amirabad, outside Isfahan, Iran. Village head man is seen at right, rear. Photo by John Spaulding.

For three weeks, ending November 12, John was in Iran "on loan" from Scholastic to Franklin Book Programs, Inc., a nonprofit organization for book-publishing development, serving as a consultant to help in planning for the publication of periodicals and books for use in the government of Iran's ambitious literacy program in rural areas.

With the help of the Franklin staff and outside advisers such as John Spaulding, Iran is endeavoring to teach more children and adults to read, and then to furnish them with magazines and books so they will have a chance to use and improve their new-found knowledge. At present, reports John, there is little or no printed material of any kind to be found outside Iran's cities.

(Continued on page 7)

House organ, December 1964. Wesley Callender, editor.

degarde Hunter, personnel director. In 1950 Thora Larsen, secretary to M. R. Robinson, accepted the editorship of *Hi There, Scholastic* on Robinson's promise that he would leave the city fairly often so that she could have time to bring it out on a regular frequency. He did, and she did — for most of that decade. A new personnel director in 1959, Alex McWilliam, relieved Larsen of the editing

470

responsibility, although she continued as associate editor into the early years of the successor, *Scholastic Ink*.

The title change to *Scholastic Ink* in 1959 was the result of a contest among employees. Out of hundreds suggested, the one submitted by Herman Masin, editor of *Scholastic Coach*, won the $25 first prize, which he turned over to the Damon Runyon Cancer Fund. Masin had more than a prizewinner's interest in the house organ. For about a year around 1949–50, while Scholastic's offices were at 7 East 12th Street, Masin, with the art assistance of Charles Beck, produced an unofficial house organ. Its title was as sassy as its content: *The 12th Street Rag*, after the Dixieland classic by a composer named Bowman. Only one of the Scholastic survivors from those days recalls the circumstances that brought about a second house organ to compete, so to speak, with *Hi There, Scholastic*. Masin's recollection is that he and Beck considered *Hi There* too pedestrian for the youthful Scholastic staff and decided to show what could be done with a livelier production. It is regrettable that copies of *The 12th Street Rag* cannot be found.

Upon the resignation of McWilliam in 1960, Paul King became personnel director and assumed responsibility for *Scholastic Ink*. At various times he had members of his staff serving as editor, among them Barbara Cooley, Carol Rafferty, and Pat Coleman. Then editorial-staff members Wesley Callender and Julia Piggin took over, followed by Seaver Buck of the office administration staff, and then by Dick Pawelek, who held the post along with his other responsibilities until relieved in 1976 by Pat Estess, a freelance writer/editor. The back issues of *Hi There, Scholastic*, and *Scholastic Ink*, and the house organs of Scholastic's branch offices and foreign subsidiaries* provide a rich source of company history, especially in the reports of work that was done and biographical sketches of the employees who did it.

Education Update

Early in 1978 the company published the first issue of a periodical called *Education Update,* edited by Sonia Levinthal, director of Public Relations. Three issues were published during the year. The eight-page, controlled-circulation newsletter — sent to school administrators, curriculum specialists, and others in education leadership — provided professional comment on, and analyses of, developments in curriculum and methodology along with information about Scholastic's programs.

Articles and interviews appearing in the first three issues included: "The SAT Score Decline: What Can Be Done About It," "RIF Spurs Reading and Community Involvement," "Living the Law," "Basic Competency Standards — Their Effect on School Curricula," "Reaching the Reluctant Reader Through the Media," "Mainstreaming," and "Classroom Guidelines from an Experienced Teacher."

Book of 20 Best Stories (1941)

Ernestine Taggard, Scholastic's literary editor, selected 20 of what she considered the best stories that had been reprinted in *Scholastic* since it became a national magazine. Under the title *Here We Are,* with a foreword by Dorothy Canfield Fisher, Robert M. McBride & Company published them in 1941. The stories were by

* *Cliffdwellers* in Englewood Cliffs, NJ; *Mo-Link* in Jefferson City, MO; *SCHOL* in Pleasanton, CA; *Ashton's Circus* in Australia; *Ashco Roundup* in New Zealand.

472

outstanding writers of the era, among them: Sinclair Lewis, Dorothy Parker, John Steinbeck, Ring Lardner, William Saroyan, Katherine Brush, Jesse Stuart, Irwin Shaw, Ruth Suckow, Katherine Anne Porter, Marjorie Kinnan Rawlings, Stephen Vincent Benet, and Sally Benson.

A paperback edition of *Here We Are* was issued under a new title—*Twenty Grand*—by Bantam in 1947, and put on the Teen Age Book Club list. Twenty years later, a revised edition edited by Mary MacEwen was published by Scholastic Book Services, and offered by the Teen Age and Campus book clubs. The title was changed slightly, from *Twenty Grand* to *20 Grand*.

The Advertising Factor

Advertising has been very important to the company's economy on the magazine side of Scholastic's business — which until 1948* was virtually the only income-producing side. *The Western Pennsylvania Scholastic* in its two years carried as much advertising as its entrepreneurs could sell. Its successor, *The Scholastic*, depended considerably on ad income to keep it afloat and to give its high-school-age readers a magazine with a major characteristic of those their parents subscribed to. Scholastic's magazines, by their editorial quality and relevance to the aims of the schools, provided a very special environment for advertising, which schools would accept

---

*1948 was the year Scholastic took over operation of the Teen Age Book Club from Pocket Books, Inc., a landmark in the product diversification that would lead to five book clubs, the Four Winds Press, *Readers' Choice Catalog* sales, text and audiovisual products, and more than 25 additional periodicals (see pp. 513–17).

Edward Chenetz, associate publisher and advertising director, Educational Periodicals Division.

under such auspices.* Here Scholastic had an obligation and responsibility that it dutifully met by its Advertising Acceptability Committee's surveillance of ads scheduled for publication.

The extent to which paid advertising contributes to the revenues of the magazines carrying it is shown below for a given year.

SUBSCRIPTION AND ADVERTISING INCOME
FOR FISCAL YEAR ENDING AUGUST 31, 1977
(school year 1976–77)

Magazines	Subscription Income and % of Total		Advertising Income Net and % of Total	
Senior Scholastic, Search, Scope, Voice, Science World, Literary Cavalcade, Junior Scholastic, Newstime	$17,249,000	82.6%	$3,641,000	17.4%
Scholastic Coach	197,000	28.1%	505,000	71.9%
Co-ed and Forecast for Home Economics	1,746,000	37.1%	2,964,000	62.9%

Publishers of the Land, Unite!

Long before Scholastic published anything that could qualify as a textbook, it became a member of the young American Textbook Publishers Institute (ATPI). This organization consisted of 28 textbook publishing

---

* It should be noted that not all Scholastic magazines carry paid advertising — as distinguished from house advertising of the company's own products and services, which all the magazines carry from time to time.

A laughfest of past presidents of the American Textbook Publishers Institute during annual meeting, Seaview Country Club, Absecon, NJ, 1965. Left to right, front: M. R. Robinson; W. Bradford Wiley, John Wiley and Sons. Second row: Alden Clark, Franklin Book Programs; R. W. Hill, South-Western Publishing; Emerson L. Brown, McGraw-Hill; Parke H. Lutz, Holt, Rinehart & Winston; William E. Spaulding, Houghton Mifflin; Burr L. Chase, Silver Burdett. Standing: Andrew McNally III, Rand McNally; Craig T. Senft, Silver Burdett; Austin McCaffrey, executive director, ATPI.

houses when it was organized in 1942, among them Macmillan, American Book, Houghton Mifflin, Ginn, Webster, Winston, Silver Burdett, D.C. Heath, and Scott, Foresman. Scholastic became a member in 1946, and it was no doubt Robinson's long friendship with Richard Pearson* of Macmillan and William Spaulding of Houghton Mifflin that paved the way for Scholastic's admission to this textbook group. Within a few years it would include every major textbook and reference-book house in the United States (and a great many minor

---

* Pearson was one of the three Dartmouth seniors who in 1920 worked up a dummy for a national college magazine which got no further than that (Chapter I, "Origins of Scholastic").

475

ones). It would change its name to American Educational Publishers Institute (AEPI) in 1968 and two years later merge with the American Book Publishers Council to form the Association of American Publishers (AAP).

M. R. Robinson had served on the board of directors of ATPI, was elected president for the 1962–63 term, and represented the Institute on a visit to publishing facilities in the Soviet Union in August/September 1962. John Spaulding, Scholastic president from 1971 until his death on September 4, 1974, was elected AAP chairman in April 1974.

Scholastic has been a member of two other publishers' organizations since the early days of their formation: the Magazine Publishers Association* and the Classroom Periodical Publishers Association (CPPA). At the peak of its membership CPPA included the following publishers of school or Sunday School periodicals: Amer-

---

*On September 15, 1970, at a luncheon at the Plaza Hotel in New York, the Magazine Publishers Association presented its Henry Johnson Fisher Award for distinguished magazine publishing to Maurice R. Robinson and to Roy E. Larsen, vice chairman of Time Inc. The citation for Robinson stated: "Maurice R. Robinson has earned a secure place in that select group of Americans who are distinguished as founders of magazines which in their own lifetimes achieved the pinnacle of prestige and influence — an accomplishment made possible by their talents to weld editorial, circulation, advertising, and business aspects of publishing into a successful enterprise. For 50 years, Maurice R. Robinson has profoundly influenced the education of America's youth, and the company he founded now publishes 35 different magazines with a combined circulation of over 12 million copies per issue. For his notable contributions to the magazine industry and his dedication to the highest standards of journalism, Mr. Robinson is nominated by his fellow editors and publishers to receive the Henry Johnson Fisher Award during the Fall Conference of the Magazine Publishers Association."

ican Education Press, Columbus, OH; Civic Education Service, Washington, DC; David C. Cook Publishing Company, Elgin, IL; George A. Pflaum, Dayton, OH; Scholastic Magazines, Inc., New York, NY; Standard Publishing Company, Cincinnati, OH; Young America Magazines, Silver Spring, MD. Until his retirement in 1971 Donald Layman was the principal Scholastic representative in both of these organizations and served as a director and secretary of MPA for two years. He was influential in having the Scholastic Research Center conduct a survey for MPA on the use of all media, especially magazines, as teaching resources in secondary schools (1970). Upon Layman's retirement, Arthur Neiman became the Scholastic representative in MPA and Clinton Smith in CPPA.

Through its counsel, Counihan, Casey & Loomis in Washington, DC, the work of CPPA was directed toward preserving preferential second-class postal rates for educational and religious school periodicals. Actually, the United States Post Office Department, at the behest of Congress, had provided preferential rates for these publishers before they formed an association. However, continued united action was needed to defend and uphold the rationale for those preferential rates against any and all efforts that might arise to eliminate them. CPPA continues to function with a membership of five publishers: American Education Publications (Xerox), Columbus, OH; David C. Cook Publishing Company, Elgin, IL; Standard Publishing Company, Cincinnati, OH; Scripture Press Publications, Inc., Wheaton, IL; and Scholastic Magazines, Inc. In 1977 this organization changed its name to Classroom Publishers Association.

Scholastic has for many years been a member of the 87-year-old Education Press Association of America (ED-PRESS). Former Scholastic editors William D. Boutwell and Loretta Hunt Marion have served as officers of this organization. The membership of about 500 includes general publications covering broad topics in education; publications for young people; journals of educational associations, professional societies, and colleges; and special-subject publications for classroom use. ED-PRESS makes annual awards to member organizations for "excellence in educational journalism"; Scholastic and its editors have been the recipients of many.

Pension Plan   In 1950, prompted perhaps by the 30th anniversary of Scholastic, the officers of the company felt a growing personal concern about the age of some of their loyal and dedicated associates who had been with Scholastic for 15 years or more and would reach retirement age within another 10 to 20 years. All members of the staff were covered by Social Security from its inception in the thirties, but the officers and directors were fully aware of the inadequacy for decent retirement of the *then-projected* Social Security payments that members would get at age 65. A retirement plan to supplement Social Security was developed, approved by the board of directors, submitted to the Internal Revenue Service for approval, and finally put into effect on June 30, 1954.

When the plan was adopted, the resources of the company were modest indeed. However, the plan was made retroactive to the date of initial employment of each member of the staff, except for those few who had been employed prior to 1931. The company thus incurred at that point what is known as a "past-service liability" of $208,312, which would be "funded" with interest over a 10-year period.

As the company grew and its financial structure strengthened, the benefits for both past and future service to members of the retirement plan have been substantially improved. On June 30, 1962, the plan was revised at additional cost, and the "past-service liability" increased to over $500,000 to be funded with interest over a 10-year period. On June 30, 1970, the company once more improved the plan with a revision which again added substantially to current expense and also sent the "past-service liability" soaring over $800,000.

Membership in the plan is voluntary, and all employees are eligible after one year of service. Although the company pays most of the cost, members also contribute to the plan. If any member leaves the company prior to being "vested" under the Employee Retirement Income Security Act, all his or her own payments into the plan are returned with interest. In 1954–55 the company paid $37,706 into the plan; employees paid $3,462. In 1975–76 the company contributed $492,439 to the plan while employees paid $80,493.

It is impossible to generalize about the annual payments an employee will receive upon retirement under the present (1977) Scholastic pension plan. Many factors are involved, such as age at time of employment, salary changes during employment years, and the retirement option selected. But here are two examples:

1. A person who is employed at age 30, retires at age 65, and whose average annual salary for those years is

approximately $10,000 would receive annual retirement income for life of approximately $5,250.*

2. A person who is employed at age 30, retires at age 65, and whose average salary for all those years is approximately $15,000 would receive annual retirement income for life of approximately $8,110.*

These payments would be in addition to Social Security payments from the U.S. government, to which both the company and the employee contribute and to which the employee is entitled upon retirement.

Scholastic retirement payments and Social Security payments could be supplemented by additional payments upon retirement for all Scholastic employees who were members of the profit-sharing plan (described below) and who had elected to leave their profit-sharing funds invested until retirement.

Profit-Sharing Plan   Three years after the initial pension plan became effective, the board of directors said, in effect, that if the company could increase profits, they would also approve a profit-sharing plan to sweeten the retirement payments above those provided in the pension plan. A profit-sharing plan was approved in principle by the board in 1957, and it became effective September 1, 1959.

The details of the profit-sharing plan were worked out after months of study and a review of then-existing plans approved by Internal Revenue Service. Employees

*As an indication of how the present plan has been improved over the original plan adopted in 1954: the employee in example 1 would have received $2,870 annually instead of $5,250; the employee in example 2 would have received $4,620 annually instead of $8,110.

were then given the opportunity to express their preferences concerning certain aspects of the projected plan. It
had to be flexible so that it would adapt as the company
grew; thus the basic plan now is almost the same as the
plan as it was originally designed. It is directly related to
the total *revenues* of the company. The plan said, in effect,
that seven percent of the gross revenues should first be
set aside and called "profit reserve before federal income
taxes." This profit reserve was needed first to pay corporate income taxes, which usually required about 50 percent of it. The balance was reserved for additional working capital, half to be plowed back into the business (perhaps to buy land, construct a building, develop new products, etc.) *and* half to pay dividends to stockholders.

Whatever profits were left *above* seven percent were
also to be shared by the corporation and the members of
the profit-sharing plan. For example, here are figures for
the first year the plan was in operation (fiscal 1959–60):

Total revenues (sales) 1959–60		$10,821,741
Profit reserve (before income tax) of 7%		757,522
Pretax profit in 1959–60	865,940	
Minus profit reserve	757,522	
Profits shared by corporation and members of profit-sharing plan	$108,418	
50% of this amount, paid to the members of the plan: $18,070 in cash (⅓); $36,139 deferred (⅔)	54,209	

That year there were 80 members of the profit-
sharing plan. They each received a total of four-and-one-

third weeks' pay: 1.44 weeks in cash and 2.89 weeks in deferred credits.

At that time only full-time employees who had worked at Scholastic for five years or more were eligible for membership in the profit-sharing plan. Eligibility was reduced from five years to three in 1962–63, to two years in 1963–64, and to one year in 1976–77. Eligibility for the *cash* portion of the profit-sharing is limited to those with five years or more of service.

The figure of seven percent of total revenues as a before-income-tax reserve for the corporation prior to any profit-sharing is not sacrosanct. The board of directors, *at its discretion*, may authorize profit-sharing when pretax profit is *less* than seven percent, but it may *not* authorize it if pretax profits do not exceed five percent of total revenues.

All employees in the United States regardless of their positions become members of the plan when they meet the eligibility service requirements. In fiscal year 1975–76 there were 778 members of the plan, among whom $579,000 was distributed.

In fiscal year 1976–77 employees who were paid by the hour were added to the profit-sharing plan if they had been employed for a year or more and worked a minimum of 1,000 hours during the year. (The plan formerly had been limited to salaried employees.) This change again increased the number of participants in the plan, and for the fiscal year ending August 31, 1977, there were 1,073 members of the plan who shared $615,000.

During the 18 years the plan has been in effect — from 1959–60 through 1976–77 — there were three years in which there was no profit-sharing. The total paid to members of the plan in the 15 payment years was more than $3,800,000.

The basic distribution is not in cash, but in deferred credit, allocated to each member of the plan — based upon salary — and deposited with a trustee (presently the Bank of New York) to the individual member's credit. The member does not pay income tax on these funds until such time as they are withdrawn or paid to the member after he or she retires or leaves the company. Except upon retirement, a member of the plan may not withdraw the funds credited to his or her account until fully "vested," which requires a minimum of 10 years' membership. Payments in cash are made at the discretion of the board of directors and are granted only to those who have been employed for a minimum of five years. These payments are related to the profit-sharing plan but, unlike the deferred payments, are taxable to the recipient in the year in which they are paid — and thus are similar to a cash bonus. Until 1977 the funds deposited with the trustee for each member were managed and invested by the trustee in various stocks and bonds. A revision of the plan in 1977 gave members options under which they could designate certain types of securities in which they wished their portions of the funds to be invested, including the right to invest up to 50 percent of each member's portion in the common stock of Scholastic Magazines, Inc.

Five-Year Dinner

Ever since 1955, with the exception of one year (1974), the company's New York office has held a dinner for employees of five or more years' continuous service. After the Englewood Cliffs warehouse and office build-

483

Steve Swett, publisher, Educational Periodicals Division, at five-year dinner, 1978.

ings were opened (1959 and 1963), New Jersey and New York employees joined in the same dinner, usually held at a New York hotel but on several occasions at a country club in New Jersey. The program has consisted of (1) a cocktail hour; (2) a dinner supreme; (3) awards to employees who have reached their 20, 25, 30, 35, 40 years of service;* (4) a brief report by the president on the company's condition and usually an announcement concerning profit-sharing; (5) dancing to a five-piece band.

From about 60 employees attending the first dinner in 1955, the attendance reached 320 at the Pierre Hotel, New York, in 1976. As of August 31, 1976, there were 601 employees in the United States and Canada with five or more years' service. Branch offices west of New Jersey and the Canadian company hold similar annual dinners, luncheons, or barbecues. Retirees are invited, and many attend. There were 111 living retirees at the time of the 1976 dinners.

Happy Birthday, Everybody

All Scholastic employees get a birthday greeting and box of candy from the company with the greeting card signed by the chief executive officer, a custom that goes back more than 35 years. M. R. Robinson explained how this came about:

> The suggestion was made by Miss Norma Carman who was my secretary — following Miss Thora Larsen's temporary departure due to ill-

*In earlier years the awards were sterling-silver plates, later they were items of the employees' own choice within a price limit, and more recently, cash.

484

ness in 1941. Miss Carman also served as personnel officer — as had Thora. I had been wishing "happy birthday" to Herb McCracken and a few other members of the staff whose birthdays I knew — like Ken Gould and Jack Lippert (to both of whom I gave cigars), to Margaret Hauser whose birthday was the same day as Ken Gould's, and to a few others.

Miss Carman asked me why I didn't wish all members of the staff a happy birthday. I quickly agreed. So she set up a procedure. At first there was only a birthday card. Later on, after Thora returned, a single rose in a holder was placed on the desk of a "birthday girl." The men got a 1½-ounce bottle of liquor or cigarettes. I signed each birthday card by hand for many, many years. Getting a rose on a desk for women, or knowing who smoked or liked liquor and who didn't, became too, too much! (One of the women objected to having the "announcement" of her birthday in the form of a rose on her desk, but everyone else seemed delighted with the idea.) As the company grew, the signature had to be printed and we finally standardized on the small box of candy.

The A.K. Oliver-Scholastic Charitable Trust

In 1962, on a proposal by M. R. Robinson, Scholastic's directors authorized the establishment of the A. K. Oliver-Scholastic Charitable Trust in memory of the Pittsburgh publisher and civic leader who for many years was a principal financial backer of Scholastic and chairman of its board of directors (Chapters II and III). The Mellon Bank was named trustee, and an initial contribution of $20,000 was made by Scholastic to the Trust. Thereafter, from time to time, the Scholastic directors authorized a percentage of the company's profits be allotted to the Trust so that it could continue to aid "such

485

charitable, religious, scientific, literary, or educational purposes as in the judgment of the Committee shall be in furtherance of the public welfare," as stated in the agreement with the trustee bank. The committee referred to, known as the Trust Committee, has from the beginning consisted of three top officers of the company. The major function of the Trust Committee is to review and act upon the recommendations of the Advisory Committee as to the grants to be made by the Trust. The Advisory Committee receives requests for grants from many sources and involves Scholastic's branch offices in assuring a nationwide distribution of the available funds. The Advisory Committee membership represents different branches of the company's operations.

The Trust Committee almost always approves the recommendations of the Advisory Committee and authorizes the bank trustee to issue checks in the amounts stated. It is the policy of the Advisory Committee in recommending contributions to give special consideration to educational programs, particularly in the field of elementary and secondary education.

The Maurice R.
Robinson Fund   The Maurice R. Robinson Fund was set up in 1960 on the initiative of its namesake, who contributed over the first nine years a little more than 25,000 shares of his Scholastic stock to the Fund. In 1969 the Fund sold 25,000 of these shares and purchased other securities in order to diversify its holdings and improve the amount available for its annual grants. In accordance with regulations of the Internal Revenue Service, a tax-free charitable fund or foundation must pay out annually an amount

486

at least equal to its income. Since 1970 and up to 1978 Robinson has given additional shares of his Scholastic stock to the Fund to bring its present holding of Scholastic stock to 23,300 shares.

The purpose of the Fund, as stated in the certificate of incorporation, is "to employ the funds and assets . . . not for profit but exclusively for educational, scientific, and charitable purposes." The emphasis has been on grants to educational institutions. The Fund's trustees are empowered to select the grantees and determine the amount given to each. The trustees in 1978 were Melvin W. Barnes, Sturges F. Cary, Jack K. Lippert, Sidney P. Marland, Jr., and Florence L. Robinson. The Bank of New York is the Fund's custodian/investment counsel.

Unlike the A. K. Oliver-Scholastic Charitable Trust, the Maurice R. Robinson Fund is financially independent of Scholastic Magazines, Inc. It is mentioned in this history because of the use of Scholastic stock in setting it up and because that stock was donated by Scholastic's founder and chairman.

In deciding on a subject for his Ph.D. dissertation at Stanford University in 1973, Richard C. McCormac chose Scholastic for reasons that emerge in the introduction and final chapter of his dissertation.* Excerpts from both follow.

"Unique Among Publishers"

* The dissertation carried the title "Influences on the Publication of Current Events Materials." It was submitted to the School of Education and the Committee on Graduate Studies of Stanford University, and was published in May 1974.

487

From the Introduction:

The subject of this study is Scholastic Magazines, Inc., a company which deservedly can be described as unique among publishers of educational materials. Corporate amalgamations, changes in ownership, changes in management have not yet affected this company. It is still controlled and operated by the man who started the organization in 1920, Mr. Maurice R. Robinson. Furthermore, it has remained steadfastly dedicated to educational enterprise throughout its entire existence. . . .

A major emphasis of this study will be to determine the amount of input received by Scholastic from professional educators. Not only will the quantity of information be ascertained but also its relevance to the final decisions as made by Scholastic. Scholastic Magazines has been, and continues to be, a highly successful educational publisher. The relationship between information obtained from educators and the company's success will be an important aspect of this study.

From Chapter VII (Concluding Chapter), "The Style of Achievement"

The purpose of this study has been to examine the major decisions which Scholastic has made over the years with regard to their secondary-level social studies periodicals. Although interesting and historically valid, that as the sole basis for this thesis would be inadequate. Thus an additional objective was to determine whether logical generalities could be extracted concerning those factors which influenced Scholastic in making the decisions analyzed.

A major factor — and this is patently reasonable — is the influence which financial considerations have on publishing decisions. Obviously, finances are one of the more crucial (if not the uppermost) considerations affecting Scholastic's decisions. Businesses (and not just publishing businesses) simply don't operate very long if income fails to exceed expenses. Certainly financial considerations carried substantial weight in each of the decisions analyzed in this study.

The initial determination to form *Scholastic* was based on the availability of a market, with the expectation of a commensurate financial reward. *Junior Scholastic* and *World Week* both came into being for a similar reason. Even the acquisition of the periodicals of Civic Education Service was motivated partially by the necessity to improve Scholastic's financial position in relation to competition.

The financial drain represented by serious circulation declines was largely responsible for the amalgamation of *American Observer, World Week,* and *Senior Scholastic.*

Finally, the previous financial success of *Scope* was an instrumental factor in the decision to start the new magazine *Search.*

It is understandable and logical that finances play the type of role which they do. Idealistically, this may be unacceptable, but reality dictates otherwise. This is not necessarily a negative factor. If one accepts that private enterprise has a legitimate position in society, and the publishing business is a proper representative of private enterprise, then the desire to obtain a financial gain should be expected and accepted.

The fault lies in placing total reliance on the financial ledgers to arrive at decisions. Happily, this was not true at Scholastic; two other major bases were instrumental in the decision-making process.

First, the opinions of the professional community were a powerful influence at Scholastic.

The strong thread of educators' opinions runs through every major Scholastic decision, and the effect was of sufficient import to suggest that this influence would be one reliable measure of any comparable publishing enterprise.

This influence, of course, can be positive or negative; preferred and accepted, preferred and ignored, or simply never solicited. Scholastic chose the first course, and has profited by accepting the advice of the professional educator. As has been shown throughout this dissertation, Scholastic repeatedly has gone to the professional educator through its advisory boards and National Advisory Council to ascertain information pertaining to their publications. In addition to being reactors or sounding boards for Scholastic ideas, these groups as well as others have initiated input into Scholastic. Some of this input has been very formalized, such as the curriculum conference held in the spring of 1971, which was open-ended in terms of what Scholastic was asking. Other input comes more indirectly to the company through field representatives, school visitations by company officials, national conferences, and communication from the practicing teacher. Ideas which came from the field and later resulted in action by Scholastic included the suggestions for creation of *Junior Scholastic,* of *World Week,* and of *Scope.* . . .

Secondly, the "personality of management" has been a significant influence in the overall decision-making process.

The emphasis throughout this analysis on M.R. Robinson's influence may have led to the conclusion that he alone was the "personality" who dominated management decisions. This would be incorrect. Rather, it has been the Scholastic management team which sets the tone. Certainly, in the early days this was primarily Robinson's bailiwick and his personal influence was clear in the *American Observer* decisions, but with the expansion of Scholastic and the resulting growth of management-level positions, the operational climate has sprung from a conglomerate of ideas, opinions, and suggestions.

Robinson is still very much on the scene, and this undoubtedly has been a strong (though lessening) influence. The key will be when he is no longer actively involved. Appearances suggest that management will remain essentially the same — searching, innovative, creative, in close touch with the educational community.

Whatever its future outlook, the management philosophy evidenced throughout those years scrutinized by this study reveals a strong and positive influence on company decisions — and certainly how management perceives its task and its responsibilities should be a valid measure of any firm in a similar enterprise.

Scholastic's management, if not unique, certainly can be defined as bold, often experimental, expansionist. Risk has been a constant companion. Creating the business involved considerable risk; expanding to the national level was equally tenuous. Creating new publications at precarious times was no less risky. Perhaps the decision involving *American Observer* is the best example of Scholastic's management tone — the willingness to maintain the publication against the pragmatic logic of immediately merging it with *Senior Scholastic;* the long, introspective examination of 1970–72, involving inquiry, declining circulation, continuation versus amalgamation — all suggest basic independence and the desire to experiment; these are the real indicators of management's philosophical position.

At the Top   Upon the election of Richard Robinson as president
and Richard Spaulding as executive vice president of the
company in 1974, Jack Lippert wrote the following biographical sketches for that year's *Annual Report to the
Stockholders*. (In 1975 Richard Robinson was elected
chief executive officer to succeed his father, M. R. Robinson, who continued as chairman of the board.)

Richard Robinson

As Dick Robinson wrote in an autobiographical sketch prepared for our sales representatives,
he "unofficially joined Scholastic" the day he was
born, May 15, 1937. But the first regular
paycheck came 25 years later when he became
assistant editor of *Literary Cavalcade*. One of his
earliest recollections from childhood is of his
father, M. R. Robinson, at home evenings reading
proofs of pages that were to go to the foundry the
next day. In the years between that "early recol-
lection" and his joining the staff in 1962, Dick fell
or jumped into a variety of experiences in and out
of school: elementary school in his home town,
Pelham, NY; then to Phillips Exeter Academy;
Harvard College, A.B. 1959, Phi Beta Kappa (English major); followed by a graduate year at St.
Catherine's College, Cambridge University. During vacations and a "sabbatical" from Harvard he
broadened his American experience by working
in printing plants, mailing rooms, on construction
jobs as bricklayer's helper and cement inspector,
and out West to work in a lumbermill and as
switchman on the Rock Island Railroad.

From Cambridge, Dick went to Evanston
Township High School in Illinois to teach 11th
and 12th grade English, and that's where he was
when the assistant editor of *Literary Cavalcade*
resigned. Editor Jerry Brondfield, after a futile
search for a qualified candidate for the job, asked

what I thought of notifying Dick Robinson of the job. Did I think he would be interested? I said it only costs four cents to find out. Jerry, who had been impressed by Dick's contribution to an advisory board meeting (a group of high school English teachers), wrote to Dick. He responded from Evanston to say that he was very much interested, and would like to talk with Jerry when he came to New York during the Easter school recess. I decided to inform M. R. Robinson of these developments, and his response was terse and firm: "Leave me out of it." So we did.

It didn't take long for Dick Robinson to demonstrate the leadership and publishing acumen which led to ever greater responsibility. Within six months he was named editor of Scholastic Literature Units. Eighteen months later he was involved in the pilot studies that led to the launching of *Scholastic Scope*, which turned out to be an instant success under his editorship. Soon, Editorial Director Margaret Hauser who had charge of two major departments — Language Arts and Home Economics/Guidance — called on management for relief, and asked that Dick be named associate director with a view to becoming director if he turned out to be as good at program development as he was at editing. He was. He moved from editorial director to publisher of the School Division and vice president in 1971; was elected to the board of directors in 1972; publisher of the Education Group in 1974; and was elected president by the board of directors at its meeting October 15, 1974. Outstanding among his qualifications to lead the company are his grasp of the educational process and the initiative that takes him into the schools to confer with teachers and administrators, seeking guidance in directions the company should go in developing new materials of instruction and incentives to reading.

Dick lives with his wife, Katherine, editor of *Scholastic Scope*, in a brownstone house they restored on West 88th Street in New York City. He plays tennis, squash, jogs in Riverside Park, and swims in the Atlantic.

Richard Spaulding

A look at Dick Spaulding's years of experience with the company reveals a range of assignments in nearly all phases of the business. His first job in 1960, fresh from active duty with the U.S. Air Force Reserve, was as a Scholastic representative in northern Virginia, calling on teachers and school administrators to sell our products. He was soon moved to the New York office to start on a succession of jobs that gave him a breadth of experience invaluable to one who would within a few years head up major departments of the company. These include office manager; administrative assistant to the executive editor; manager of book clubs; manager of the School Division with responsibility for manufacturing, marketing, and related operations—at which time (July 1971) he was elected a vice president.

A performance report on Dick Spaulding made by his supervisor six months after starting on the job in New York listed his "strongest points" as "great initiative; is systematic, persevering, intelligent; careful approach to problem solving." The report form asked for a listing of "employee's weakest points," and was filled in as follows: "Tends to run with the whole ball without ducking as much as an individual in a new spot should." Another boss of his, five years later, when asked if he would agree to the transfer of Dick wrote: "I would hate to lose him out of my division (where he makes me look good), but I

Left to right: Richard Robinson, president and chief executive officer; M. R. Robinson, chairman of the board; Richard Spaulding, executive vice president.

have to say that I think he could handle most any job in this company with credit."

Now advanced to executive vice president at age 37, Dick is the administrator to whom report five vice presidents in charge of the following operations: Library and Trade; Book Clubs; International Subsidiaries; Field Operations; and Study-Travel Programs.

Dick Spaulding attended elementary and high school in Winchester, MA, and was graduated from Amherst College in 1959. He lives with his wife, Emilie, and three daughters (aged 4, 7, and 8) in the village of North Tarrytown, NY. They escape as circumstances permit to Lake Winnipesaukee, NH, to lay another wall to the house they are finishing, to play tennis, and to sail their 14-foot Hobiecat.

Note: The above biographical sketches were written in 1974, the year before Richard Robinson, then president, became president and chief executive officer.

Reflections and Addendum
by M. R. Robinson

I asked for the privilege of adding to Jack Lippert's story of Scholastic some of my personal reflections as I reviewed the page proofs of the final version, after having read drafts of each of the chapters. I also wished to include an addendum to this chronicle because of omissions that were evident to me as I finished reading the completed book.

Jack was the right choice to write the Scholastic story. With the exception of myself and Herb McCracken, Jack devoted more years to Scholastic than anyone else. He was a part-time staff member from 1923 to 1926 and full-time from 1931 until his "official" but only partial retirement three years ago when he began to write this history.

I say "began," for his presence in the office resulted in frequent interruptions of his writing and research by his being asked to handle miscellaneous tasks in every emergency that arose and to assist the new young editors and managers who frequently sought his help and advice. The long delay in the publication of this chronicle is no reflection on the productive capacity of Jack Lippert.

In his Preface Jack refers to my urging him to be critical of my shortcomings "even more than you may like," for in my 55 years' association with him I knew him to be divinely kind to his fellows. Now as I read the entire document I realize that his response, "There was no reason . . . to censure" me, contains truths he had not intended.

I'm sure that Jack did not wish to picture me as a bungling, amateur publisher, but the reprinting, in heavy, unedited doses, of documents and other source material of the first 20 years of Scholastic is itself ample testimony to the naiveté (to put it kindly) of the central figure in this history. My ignorance of the hard economic facts of the magazine publishing business, of the large amounts of capital needed to establish a viable publishing enterprise was, in retrospect, appalling. So at my present age, as I read I can reflect upon this book as a tale of the survival of an often-near-death magazine business. It could well be described as "the trials and tribulations of a young innocent who desperately wanted to be an editor and publisher and was fortunate enough to keep the enterprise afloat with the help of devoted friends, talented and loyal associates, and unbelievably patient financial backers."

Thanks to and appreciation of those who financed Scholastic come first in my reflections, for no matter how dedicated and talented a staff may be, only money can supply paper, printing, postage, and salaries. The willingness of Gus Oliver and George Clapp to forgive my errors in judgment and suffer through my unrealistic economics made me eternally grateful to them. Had they been investing in Scholastic for the purpose of making a profit, it is likely that their patience would have been exhausted shortly after the stock-market crash of 1929, but to suffer losses through the Depression of the thirties was a severe test of their dedication to education, for it was on that ground that their support had been sought and given. That there are financial rewards for the descendants who inherited what once seemed worthless pieces of paper is a source of personal gratification, as has also been the continuing support of Joe Oliver who, as a member of the board, has represented the six children of Augustus K. and Margaretta W. Oliver. They are, besides Joe, Margaretta (Schroeder), Janet (DeCamp), George, William, and Jack. I am deeply grateful for their solid backing of the company and their loyalty to me.

Before I leave Jack's Preface, I must correct a decidedly inaccurate statement. He wrote, "In a history written by an insider, the writer will err on the side of omission when it comes to his or her own role in it. The present writer applied very little of this kind of restraint in the pages that follow." Although Jack is one of the most honest persons I know, it would be impossible to convince him that he wasn't being honest when he wrote that. As every colleague who reads this book and with whom Jack worked in his near 50 years at Scholastic will know, Jack's contribution to Scholastic's growth, achievements, and prestige is greatly understated in this chronicle. He dutifully records his first freelance relationship with Scholastic beginning in 1923, his full-time employment in 1931 as the first editor of *Scholastic Coach,* and (in 1937) of *Junior Scholastic,* but he neglects his role as the publishing director and editorial sparkplug of every new Scholastic periodical from the *Coach* in 1931 to *Scope* in 1964, especially the six elementary school periodicals and our entries into home economics. He pays tribute to those named editor, but he was the leader, in effect the publisher, and became a superb spokesman in communicating Scholastic's editorial philosophy to teachers and school administrators. As his colleagues will also testify, members of the staff of whatever rank did not hesitate to go to him with their problems, whether personal or work-related, knowing that Jack's unfailing patience, his instinctive warmth, and his sense of fairness assured them a sympathetic hearing. It is little wonder that every member of the staff admired and respected him as their leader, teacher, and friend. It was characteristic of Jack in quoting widely from Thora Larsen's earlier document to omit the tribute to him. A wish to supply at least a part of that omission prompted this "reflection."

Also, as is apparent to the reader of this book, Herb McCracken, Ken Gould, and Jack Lippert formed with me the quartet that was really "Scholastic" for its first 20 years. So, in my reflections there are some personal words I wish also to add about Herb and Ken.

I got to know Herb through Norman MacLeod, who from my early childhood was an intimate and lifelong friend. Norm entered the University of Pittsburgh two years before I finished high school and when he failed to persuade me to join him there, he cheered my choice of Dartmouth and made sure that I joined the Dartmouth chapter of his college fraternity, Delta Tau Delta. Norm and I volunteered for the Army together in 1917 but were separated at the end of basic training. After the war he got a job at his university (Pittsburgh). About the time I was finishing college in June 1920, Norm heard of a job opening at the Pittsburgh Chamber of Commerce and suggested I apply. I got the job. Later, when I was seeking an associate on Scholastic, it was Norm who suggested that Herb would be a good partner. How right he was! Herb and I were indeed a complementary pair. Herb was a superb athlete, acclaimed in basketball and track, and most of all as a nationally known football star. (I had tried hard but failed to make even the freshman tennis team at Dartmouth.) Herb was a gregarious extrovert, an active participant in numerous clubs, organizations, and institutions. Although I was not exactly a recluse, I had few of the essential attributes needed to be a successful salesman or outgoing public figure. For that role Herb had all the estimable and none of the disagreeably aggressive characteristics apparent in some salesmen.

As Jack points out, Herb's fame as an athlete helped open the doors of prominent Pittsburgh business leaders and University of Pittsburgh alumni, but opening the door is useless if the intruder's character — especially his integrity, his resolute belief in his mission — is not as evident as an acknowledged athletic prowess. Herb did with consummate skill what I would have been unable then to do in approaching and winning the initial support of men like Messrs. Clapp, Oliver, and Snyder, and later in establishing Scholastic's image in the world of sports and in the New York advertising fraternity. In short, I could not have made it without Herb. He probably would have needed me in much the same way in winning the support of the academic world. We were both naive. Only a year or two ago, Herb confessed to me that in the early days he thought I really knew much more about the publishing business than I did. Having spent a lot of time in the composing and press rooms of printing plants — and knowing the "vocabulary" — I probably acted as if I knew a lot more than I did, perhaps even believed it myself. Our mutual loyalty and respect along with a willingness to sacrifice through difficult years certainly helped. Anyhow, together we accomplished, with the unfailing help of our associates, much more than either of us dared hope. Despite our differences and, at times, severely strained relations through more than 55 years, we also remain the best of personal friends.

Even as Herb and I had complementary skills, Ken Gould as the fourth member of the early quartet supplied the qualities of a genuine scholar which none of the other three of us sufficiently possessed. To Herb's extroversion and Jack's journalistic flair, Ken added for me a publisher's essential ingredient of sound scholarship and academic distinction. After a fashion, I was a scholar, a history major, a rather wide but not intense reader with special interest in literature and art, but Ken was a dedicated scholar, a worthy member of the highest intellectual fraternity. I met him in 1923 when he was the first university editor at the University of Pittsburgh. He was a mere seven months older than I. We became personal friends. My admiration for him led to my enlisting him as a contributor to the fledgling *Scholastic* and later to my convincing him to leave the academic world and become managing editor — on January 1, 1926. For 35 years Ken led the writing staff of an expanding organization in a steady and determined pursuit of editorial excellence. His job description in the forties and fifties, even after he became editor-in-chief, is but a clue to the prodigious worker he was. His assignment from September through May included: "take full responsibility for planning, assigning, and editing four or five special theme issues of *Senior Scholastic;* write every week a major article for the history behind the headline series; read carefully for accuracy and editorial policy the drafts of every news and special article prepared for the three social studies magazines; closely supervise two of the three social studies editors; serve on a two-man team to handle negotiations with the Newspaper Guild." To that schedule were added the miscellaneous duties of the editor-in-chief such as planning meetings with consultants and advisory boards and attending several educational conventions every year, often as a speaker. My personal feelings about Ken's matchless contribution to Scholastic were well expressed by Jack Lippert when, in a talk to the editorial staff a few years before Ken's full retirement and Jack's succeeding Ken as editor-in-chief, Jack said: "Having had a happy and harmonious relationship with Kenneth Gould — on and off the job — for 30 years, I consider myself especially privileged to have had more than my share of a rare experience; and I wish that somehow the 30 years could now be apportioned among the younger members of our editorial staff, so that each could have the advantage and pleasure of working with and getting to know, in one man, a fine person, a scholarly teacher, and an editor of rare talent."

In my first decade as editor-publisher there were others I wish to mention in these reflections who briefly but importantly participated in the molding of the early *Scholastic* and to whom I owe a debt of gratitude.

One was Anya Freedel (later Mrs. Anthony W. Smith III), my first full-time employee, an exceptionally bright, highly competent, intelligent young woman who suffered with me during the trying years from 1921 to 1927 as secretary, bookkeeper, office manager, and the first corporate secretary and treasurer.

Another was Penelope Redd, highly respected art critic of two Pittsburgh newspapers (*The Post* and *The Sun*) who, beginning in 1923, was for four years a part-time associate editor and a regular contributor to the magazine. Her enthusiasm for emphasizing the arts in the magazine heightened my personal interest in art. Her reputation as an art historian and critic helped to win the consent of artists like John Sloan, Eugene Speicher, Robert Henri, and others to serve on our selection juries when we organized the first National High School Art Exhibition.

Other associates from the earliest days of Scholastic, including Ruth Fuller Sergel, Abe Savage, and Ida and Jay Schein, are also mentioned in Jack's text. Memories of them and many others who worked with me in the twenties and early thirties are still fresh in my reflections. But if I were to continue to describe the special contributions of the scores of other associates who strongly supported my career as a publisher, I would be writing another book. So I shall not pursue that course beyond the very beginnings of Scholastic. However, I cannot end this personal comment on the book without naming two other associates who worked closely and directly with me during their entire careers at Scholastic.

As Jack's chronicle sharply reveals in the chapter, entitled "Incompetence Alleged," there was an essential ingredient missing for 20 years in the "quartet" I referred to earlier. That ingredient was superbly supplied by Mrs. Agnes McEvoy Laurino, a skilled accountant, a prodigious worker whose zeal for productivity coupled with accuracy was more than equalled by her warm personality, her thoughtfulness, and her kindness. It is rare indeed to find in any executive a strict disciplinarian who is also beloved, as Agnes Laurino was by her entire staff. From 1941 until her death in 1967 Mrs. Laurino dedicated most of her life — especially after the early death of her husband — to Scholastic. Jack's history portrays some of her activities, but there is no way to describe the contribution she made to the economic health of Scholastic. I personally owe her double appreciation because she also took charge of my personal finances. She said she was doing it to relieve me from such minor details and to free me for the pressure of my executive responsibilities. But I suspect it was her measurement of my accounting skills. So as I reflect on my life, I again gratefully pay tribute to my friend and co-worker, Agnes McEvoy Laurino.

My other close associate during her entire Scholastic career, and indeed for almost her entire working life, was Thora Larsen. From 1938 — except for a long illness partially caused by overwork — until her retirement in 1976, Thora was my personal assistant and secretary. When she wrote our brief history in 1960, *The First Forty Years of Scholastic*, she characteristically omitted her identity as the author, an omission I revealed in a footnote to that pamphlet. I also vouched for the accuracy of its content, for I knew Thora would verify every statement by carefully searching files, bound volumes, and other records in the Scholastic archives. I then added some words I wish to have republished in this history: "I wish to say *thanks* to my good and loyal secretary who has been my strong right arm for 20 years. She sheltered me from unnecessary controversy when she knew other problems were engaging my every waking moment; she tempered in transcription my dictated memos and letters when they were done in moments of annoyance or anger; she answered difficult letters when I hadn't the time to prepare carefully worded replies; and best of all she was unmoved by attractive offers to leave me and loyally stayed on to become our corporate secretary too."

For 16 more years after I wrote that tribute, until she asked for early retirement in 1976, Thora Larsen continued with constantly improving administrative and writing skills to do all she had been doing for the many previous years. She also handled the demanding responsibilities of corporate secretary through those years when the company threaded its way through the unfamiliar, intricate maze of registering in 1969 as a publicly held corporation and later functioned under the regulations of the Securities and Exchange Commission. Occasionally a lawyer or corporate executive with whom Thora's work brought her in contact would ask about her college and were amazed to learn that her formal education ended with high school. The need to conserve her physical energies for her job because of a collapsed lung was a rather happy excuse for indulging in unlimited reading and study in leisure hours and gave her the equivalent of a post-graduate education and further qualified her for her expanded role in the company. I am deeply indebted to many co-workers but to none more than to Thora Larsen.

It is probably apparent to anyone who has thus far read these "reflections" that I privately feel that the book gives me more personal credit than I really deserve and is inadequate in portraying the supporting roles of my associates. While the book does expose my naiveté as a neophyte publisher and does record 35 years of the company's getting into difficult straits (chiefly financial) and yet extricating itself, the book includes no criticism of the quality of my performance as a publisher. Because I was aware of these omissions as I read the draft chapters of this book, I suggested to Jack that he recognize in his Preface that this is a chronicle rather than the work of a historian whose responsibility requires the inclusion of at least some degree of critical appraisal of the subject. Fortunately the book contains no comparison with or reference to the achievements of my contemporaries like Henry Luce and Roy Larsen of *Time* or Dewitt Wallace of *Reader's Digest*, who founded their magazines a few years after Scholastic.

Raw resource material — documents, financial records, old correspondence — on which to base a different sort of Scholastic history is in our files, though it would have few readers and would serve no purpose. I would not be the unbiased person to write such a treatise, but I know all too well the mistakes, the errors in judgment, that I (and my associates) made in our trial and error experiments, many of which brought bitter disappointments, shook our faith in ourselves and our products, and severely tested our resilience. With the aid of some of my long-time associates I have tried to pass along to our successors a full confession of our publishing sins. Perhaps they will benefit from an awareness of the many errors we have made.

An associate who read the first draft of these reflections chided me for what he termed a "recital of my shortcomings," brought me the Bible, pointed to a verse in Ecclesiastes and read, "There is nothing better than that a man should rejoice in his own works; for that is his portion." So, lest I appear to lack any pride in my accomplishments, I shall add some other observations.

After the first 15 years or so of publishing *Scholastic* I got to know many other publishers, some of whom became good friends. Frequently some of the knowledgeable ones questioned me about my having chosen to enter the hazardous field of publishing a magazine for youth. Why I happened to enter the juvenile field is correctly told in the first chapter of this book. Why I adhered to it may cast doubts on my perspicacity or convict me of bullheaded stubbornness. In my very first decade as publisher I saw around me dramatic examples of the hazards of publishing a magazine for the young. I saw the final days of the *Youth's Companion* after 109 years of considerable success. I witnessed the last days of *The American Boy*, of *John Martin's Book*, and of the *Open Road for Boys*; the struggles of *Child Life*, and the gasping breath of the revered *St. Nicholas* which I vainly tried to keep alive long enough to seek its use in elementary schools. I saw *Boy's Life* and *American Girl* kept alive by the subsidy of tax-free organizations. I certainly was not blind to the problems of the field. The reduction in the number of children in the average family was a known statistic, and I remembered in contrast, as the fifth of six children in our family, how many years the *Youth's Companion* and *St. Nicholas* continued to be renewed for our home.

I was not blind, but I was convinced I knew the reasons for the demise of the privately published juvenile magazines. I firmly believed they failed because, with the exception of library subscriptions, the selling and renewing of single subscriptions in smaller families and thus for only a couple of years, was economically unsound. I saw the solution in the school buildings of the country, which year after year furnished a new mass enrollment freshly renewing the market. The solution: Win the support of teachers and school administrators by demonstrating that a carefully edited magazine can be an effective teaching tool and can update and supplement textbooks, especially in the curriculum areas where the rush of human events and new inventions and discoveries invalidated many texts. One teacher meeting four or five classes a day was a prospect for 100 or more subscriptions — one bill, one renewal, a shipment in bulk to the school instead of 100 invoices and 100 individual wrappers.

This was not an idea I originated. *Current Events*, founded by C. P. Davis, had been published for public elementary schools since 1902, and it had been preceded by others, including the *Young Catholic Messenger* for parochial schools. *Literary Digest* had been sold in bulk to high schools beginning in World War I. But there had been no nationwide organized plan to win the nation's top responsible educators personally to endorse and support the classroom use of magazines. That, as I saw it, was the challenging task publishers of children's magazines had to tackle if they wished to build an economically sound enterprise. That's why I early sought — and later won — the support of hundreds of the nation's influential educators and the direct participation of many of them in Scholastic's programs. I just wasn't wise enough to realize how difficult a task that would be nor how long it would take.

I would not wish to imply that I was alone in seeking school acceptance of periodicals for the classroom in the twenties and thirties. The son of the founder of *Current Events* continued and expanded his father's program

(Chapters VI and VIII), and Walter Myer published his first eight-page paper in 1925. Some adult magazines also began to promote bulk subscriptions to high schools as a secondary market.

Perhaps Scholastic's unique contribution is best described by Jack in Chapter XXVII, "Advice and Consent." Our involvement of the upper echelon of curriculum specialists in improving the teaching effectiveness of our products led to our creation of magazines for specific disciplines such as world history, U.S. history and government, business English, literature, home economics, science. We were then able to win the support of more and more school administrators, culminating with the full-time participation of John W. Studebaker, U.S. Commissioner of Education; Pearl Wanamaker, past president of the National Education Association and Washington State superintendent of Public Instruction; and later Melvin W. Barnes, superintendent of schools of Portland, OR. This support and that of teacher subscribers to the magazines also helped win the acceptance of our pioneer programs of classroom book clubs as an effective technique for encouraging children to read.

In addition to the problem of school acceptance, I was not sufficiently aware of the editorial limitations imposed on a magazine that must meet the restrictions of the classroom and that a school's confidence in the magazine's integrity and freedom from bias was a prerequisite to entering its doors without prior review. I was slow also in learning that the taboos concerning many types of advertising in classroom periodicals would limit revenues from this essential source, as would the negative attitude of many major advertisers toward young people as an attractive consumer market. This list of a few of the hazards facing a publisher of children's magazines may partially answer the question of why it took so many years to erase the red ink from Scholastic's ledgers.

I dare no longer "reflect" lest I'm prompted to wish to share many more memories of my life with Scholastic. Jack properly omitted from this chronicle any biographies of the participants except when related to the business or its products. But before I stop, I do wish to include a few more personal words. I am thankful for having had strict parents who taught me the self-discipline I needed and whose own good health and concern for mine endowed me with a working life span that has permitted me to see the slow-growing vineyard of Scholastic begin to bear fruit far beyond the level it had attained by the time I reached the normal age for retirement. I am grateful to a loyal staff of associates named and unnamed in this book. My early associates willingly shared what they termed my "pie-in-the-sky" optimism and patiently made personal sacrifices to keep Scholastic alive through many difficult years.

My life in gradual retirement has been enriched as my son Dick became an active participant in the company's management. Dick was 37 when, upon the untimely death of John Spaulding, the board of directors elected him president and later elected him chief executive to succeed me. Any misgivings I may have had over whether he had yet acquired sufficient publishing experience to fill the post have been replaced by an utmost confidence in him, an esteem I believe is shared by our management colleagues and the staff.

Above all I wish to express my deep, heartfelt thanks to my wife Florence for her devoted understanding and support and for patiently putting up with my frequent neglect of her and of my responsibilities to the home and family as I gave almost all my waking hours to bring to maturity my adolescent dream of wanting to be an editor and publisher.

Appendices

1920	*The Western Pennsylvania Scholastic* (became *The Scholastic*, Sept. 16, 1922; *Scholastic*, Sept. 19, 1931; *Senior Scholastic*, Mar. 8, 1943)
1924	*Better Busses*[2,3]
1925	First student-written number
1926	Scholastic Awards
1929	*The World Review*
1930	*St. Nicholas*[2,3]
1931	*Scholastic Coach*
1932	*Camp Director*[2]
1935	*Highschool*[2,3]
1937	*Junior Scholastic*
1942	*World Week*[2]
1944	*Scholastic Debater*[2]
1946	*Practical English* (became *Scholastic Voice*, 1969)
	Scholastic Teacher[2]
	Prep[2]
1947	Scholastic Bookshop[2]
1948	*Literary Cavalcade*
	Scholastic Radio Guild (became National Scholastic Radio-Television Guild in 1952)[2]
	Teen Age Book Club (operated by Scholastic under contract with Pocket Books, Inc., until acquired in 1951)
1952	*JAC/Junior American Citizen* (became *Newstime*, Dec. 1952)

[1]A magazine or other property acquired and immediately discontinued is not listed here. See pp. 518–19, "Scholastic Acquisitions."
[2]No longer published or offered.
[3]First issue after acquisition by Scholastic.

513

1952	*Practical Home Economics*[3] (became *Practical*
(cont'd)	*Forecast for Home Economics,* Sept. 1963; *Fore-*
	cast for Home Economics, Sept. 1966)
1954	*Summertime*[2]
	Listenables and Lookables[2,3]
	The Globe-Trotter[2] (Scholastic published *The*
	Globe-Trotter: Official Bulletin of the United Na-
	tions Stamp Clubs in collaboration with the UN.)
1956	*Co-ed*
1957	*Explorer* (became *News Explorer,* Sept. 21, 1960)
	Arrow Book Club
1958	Campus Book Club
1959	*Science World*[3]
1960	*Science World, Jr. Edition*[2]
	News Pilot
	News Ranger
	News Trails
	Science World Book Club[2]
	Scholastic Literature Units
1961	Lucky Book Club
	Vacation Fun[3]
1962	Self-Teaching Arithmetic Books
	World Affairs Multi-Texts[2]
1963	*Merry-Go-Round*[2]
	Foreign-language periodicals (U.S. and Canadian
	distribution rights from contract with Mary Glas-
	gow & Baker, Ltd.)
1964	*Scope*
1965	*Young Citizen*[3] (became *News Citizen,* 1972)
	Four Winds Press
	Folkways Records (under licensing agreement with
	Moses Asch)
1966	See-Saw Book Club
	Story[2,3]
	Great Issues Series[2]
	Let's Find Out

[2]No longer published or offered.
[3]First issue after acquisition by Scholastic.

1967	Better Buymanship Books[2]
	Scope Skills Books
	Reluctant Reader Library
1968	Citation Press (became part of the Library and Trade Division in 1970, which is now General Book Publishing Division)
	Contact
	Curriculum Units[2]
1969	Toute la bande[4]
	Junior Review[2]
	American Observer[2,3]
	Civic Leader[2,3]
	Headline Focus Wall Map[3]
	Scholastic Coach Athletic Services
	Scope Visuals
	Self-Teaching Tennis Workbooks
1970	*Art & Man*
	Action Unit
	American Adventures text program
	Art & Man Filmstrips[4]
	Art & Man Units[4]
	Black Literature
	Enrichment Records
1971	Action Libraries
	Bill Russell's Basketball Films[4]
	Creative Expression
	Scope Plays
1972	Clifford Filmstrips[4]
	Search
	Scholastic International (student/teacher travel program)[2]
	Firebird Collection
	Five Children & Five Families[4]
	Individualized Reading from Scholastic
	Margaret Court Instructional Films[4]
	Pleasure Reading Libraries

[2]No longer published or offered.
[3]First issue after acquisition by Scholastic.
[4]Audiovisual program.

1972	World Cultures text program
(cont'd)	World Cultures Filmstrips[4]
1973	American Adventures Filmstrips[4]
	Beginning Concepts/1 & 2[4]
	Black Culture[4]
	Discovery[4]
	Double Action Unit
	Elementary Skills Books
	GO — Reading in the Content Areas
	I Can[4]
	Images of Man[4]
	The Life That Disappeared[4]
1974	*Dynamite*
	Bilingual Early Childhood Filmstrips[4]
	Dimension[4]
	Eye Openers[4]
	Kindle[4]
	Literature of the Screen
	Reading Comprehension
	Science World Visuals
	Search Simulations
	Search Skills Visuals
	Sprint Libraries
1975	*Bananas*
	Sprint
	Beginning Concepts/People Who Work[4]
	The American Experience
	Becoming Yourself[4]
	Family Living[4]
	Human Issues in Science[4]
	Mass Communication Arts
	Reading Diagnosis[4]
	Scholastic Literature Filmstrips[4]
	Scope Activity Kits
	Search American History Plays
1976	*Wow*
	Explore[4]
	Opportunity[4]
	Worldview[4]

[4]Audiovisual program.

1977	*Action*
	Adventures in Science[4]
	American Citizenship text program
	American Literature
	Beginning Concepts/Science[4]
	Double Action Libraries
	Health & Safety Filmstrips[4]
	Listening Skills[4]
	New Action Unit
	Real Life Reading
	Spelling Monsters[4]
	World History text program
	World History Filmstrips[4]
	Teachers' Book Service
1978	*Wheels*
	American Citizenship Filmstrips[4]
	Arithmetic Skills
	Basic Soccer Filmstrips[4]
	Feeling Free[4]
	Living Law
	Practical English (skills handbooks)
	Real Life Math
	Scope English
	Social Studies Skills
	Sprint Reading Skills
	Sprint Starter Libraries

[4]Audiovisual program. (During the period 1973–79 Scholastic's Audiovisual and New Media Department [Russell D'Anna, director] received more than 40 awards from film festivals held in the United States and abroad.)

Scholastic Acquisitions

(Magazines, Teen Age Book Club, Enrichment Records, Headline Focus Wall Maps)*

Year	Title	Acquired From	Notes
1924	*Better Busses*	Brian Boshier	Sold to F. C. Andresen, 1925.
1929	*The World Review*	Kable Bros.	Sold to American Education Press, 1930.
1930	*St. Nicholas*	Century Co.	Sold to Kable Bros., 1932.
1931	*Magazine World*	American Education Press	Acquired as a part of merger agreement between AEP and Scholastic for shared ownership of the Scholastic–St. Nicholas Corp. The four periodicals were discontinued, and *Scholastic*'s masthead carried the line: "*Scholastic:* Combined with *Magazine World, Current Literature, World News, Current Topics.*"
	World News		
	Current Topics	,,	
	Current Literature		
1935	*High School Teacher*	Brown and Reese	Title changed to *Highschool* upon acquisition.
1938	*Our World Today*	National School Publications, Inc.	Discontinued upon acquisition; subscription obligation of 4,300 met by substituting *Scholastic.*
1948	*Teen Age Book Club*	Pocket Books, Inc.	Title changed to TAB Book Club, 1968.
1952	*Practical Home Economics*	Lakeside Publishing Co.	Merged with *Forecast for Home Economics,* 1963, and title changed to *Practical/Forecast for Home Economics,* then to *Forecast for Home Economics.*
1954	*Listenables & Lookables*	Morris Goldberger	Became a department in teacher editions.
1959	*Science World*	Street & Smith	In continuous publication since acquisition.
1961	*Background*	LeRoy and Anita Hayman	Was published fortnightly by the Haymans in Chicago for high school social studies classes, discontinued upon acquisition, and subscriptions filled by either *Senior Scholastic* or *World Week.* Starting with issue of May 13, 1965, *World Week* carried the title "Combined with *Background*" in order to protect rights to title. Upon acquisition of *Background,* Scholastic employed LeRoy Hayman as associate editor of *Junior Scholastic.* He became editor in 1964; later editor of social studies books and *American Observer.*

Year	Title	Company	Notes
1963	Forecast for Home Economics	McCall Corp.	Merged with Practical Home Economics, 1963, and title changed to Practical/Forecast for Home Economics, then to Forecast for Home Economics.
1965	Young Citizen	Civic Education Service	Title changed to News Citizen, 1972.
1966	Story	Whit and Hallie Burnett	Intended as a quarterly, Story was discontinued after one issue, May 1967. A rather intensive promotion campaign yielded few subscriptions. Title was used for an annual book issued 1968–71.
1969	American Observer	Civic Education Service	Merged with Senior Scholastic, 1972.
	Junior Review		Merged with Junior Scholastic, 1969.
	Civic Leader	"	Discontinued, 1972.
	Headline Focus Wall Map		In continuous publication since acquisition.
1970	Artist, Jr.	Artist, Jr., Inc.	Discontinued upon acquisition, and mailing list used in promotion of Art & Man magazine (first issue, Oct. 1970).
	Enrichment Records	Martha Huddleston	In continuous stock since acquisition.

*Pages 234–35 in Chapter XIV, "The March of Magazines," list the Scholastic magazines in current publication (1978).

AGREEMENTS

Under publishing services agreement:

American Vocational Journal (American Vocational Association), 1945–48.
The Little Leaguer (Little League Baseball, Inc.), 1953–55.

Under licensing agreement:

Bonjour, Ça va, Chez nous, ¿Que tal?, El sol, Hoy dia, Das Rad, Schuss, and *Der Roller* (Mary Glasgow Publications, Ltd., London), 1963 —.

I Spy booklets (Charles Warrell, London), 1957–60.

Folkways Records (Moses Asch), 1966–73.

OFFICERS

Scholastic Publishing Company (a Pennsylvania corporation)

A.E. Freedel	Secretary and Treasurer, 1921–29
Paul E. Hutchinson	Secretary, 1930–35; Counsel, 1922–35
G. Herbert McCracken	Vice President, 1922–35
Augustus K. Oliver	Treasurer, 1932–35
M.R. Robinson	President, 1922–35; Treasurer, 1930–31

St. Nicholas Publishing Company (a Pennsylvania corporation)

Paul E. Hutchinson	Secretary and Treasurer, 1930; Secretary, 1931–32
G. Herbert McCracken	Vice President, 1930–32
M.R. Robinson	President, 1930; President and Treasurer, 1931–32
Ida Schein	Assistant Secretary and Assistant Treasurer, 1930–32

Scholastic—St. Nicholas Corporation (a Pennsylvania corporation), became Scholastic Corporation, 1932

Raymond Black	Assistant Treasurer, 1942
William C. Blakey	Secretary, 1931
John T. Broderick	Assistant Treasurer, 1951–55
Norma Carman	Assistant Secretary, 1943–44
Preston Davis	Treasurer, 1931
Hildegarde B. Hunter	Assistant Secretary, 1945–46
Paul E. Hutchinson	Secretary, 1932–55
Marie L. Kerkmann	Assistant Secretary and Assistant Treasurer, 1941–43
John J. Lang	Assistant Treasurer, 1939–41

520

Thora Larsen	Assistant Secretary, 1939–41; 1946–55
Agnes M. Laurino	Assistant Treasurer, 1942–48; Controller and Assistant Treasurer, 1949–53; Controller and Treasurer, 1954–55
Donald E. Layman	Vice President and Director of Sales Promotion, 1948–53; Vice President and Director of Advertising, 1954–55
Jack K. Lippert	Vice President and Director of Circulation, 1949; Vice President and Coordinator of Editorial and Circulation Promotion Departments, 1950–52; Vice President and Executive Editor, 1953–55
Mary E. McAvoy	Assistant Treasurer, 1949–55
G. Herbert McCracken	Vice President, 1932–46; Vice President and Treasurer, 1947–53; Senior Vice President, 1954–55
Dudley Meek	Vice President and Treasurer, 1954
Augustus K. Oliver	Vice President, 1931; Treasurer, 1932; Chairman of the Board and Treasurer, 1933–46; Chairman of the Board, 1947–53
Joseph W. Oliver	Chairman of the Board, 1954–55
Elizabeth M. Retta	Assistant Treasurer, 1947–55
C.E. Richards	Assistant Treasurer, 1931
M.R. Robinson	President, 1931–55
Ida Schein	Assistant Secretary, 1932–33
I. Jay Schein	Assistant Treasurer, 1936–38
Blanche L. Shawcross	Assistant Treasurer, 1941
Clinton R. Smith	Assistant Treasurer, 1954–55
John W. Studebaker	Vice President and Chairman of Editorial Boards, 1948–55

*Scholastic Magazines, Inc. (a New York corporation
into which was merged Scholastic Corporation,
a Pennsylvania corporation, 1956)*

Melvin W. Barnes	Vice President, 1968–76
Andrew W. Bingham	Vice President, 1975—
Carolyn Bishop	Vice President, 1976—
William D. Boutwell	Vice President, 1960–69
Charles Brock	Vice President and General Counsel, 1974–75; Vice President, General Counsel, and Secretary, 1976—
John T. Broderick	Assistant Treasurer, 1955—
Sturges Cary	Vice President, 1968–77
Jack W. Coltrain	Assistant Treasurer, 1969
C. Richard Cryer	Vice President, 1973—
Russell D'Anna	Vice President, 1974—
Morris Goldberger	Vice President, 1968—
Walter J. Heussner	Assistant Treasurer, 1958–62; Controller and Assistant Treasurer, 1963–75; Treasurer, 1976—
Michael Hobson	Vice President, 1974—
Richard V. Holahan	Vice President, 1961–73
Paul E. Hutchinson	General Counsel and Assistant Secretary 1956–69
Paul A. King	Assistant Secretary and Associate General Counsel, 1970–77
Nicholas Kochansky	Vice President, 1974—
Thora Larsen	Secretary, 1955–75
Agnes M. Laurino	Treasurer, 1956–67
Donald E. Layman	Vice President, 1956–60; Executive Vice President, 1961–62; President, 1963–70
Jack K. Lippert	Vice President, 1956–62; Senior Vice President, 1963–69; Vice Chairman of the Board, 1970–72

522

Kathleen H. Lyons	Assistant Secretary, 1976—
Joan Marcelynas	Assistant Treasurer, 1972—
Alan J. Marmorek	Assistant Controller, 1977–78
Mary E. McAvoy	Assistant Treasurer, 1955–56
G. Herbert McCracken	Senior Vice President, 1956–60; Vice Chairman of the Board 1961–69; Chairman of Executive Committee of the Board, 1970—
George H. Milne	Vice President and Treasurer, 1969–74
Raymond Naimoli	Assistant Treasurer and Controller, 1970—
M. Arthur Neiman	Vice President, 1968—
Joseph W. Oliver	Director, 1956—; Chairman of the Board, 1956–62; Chairman of Executive Committee of the Board, 1963–69
Ernest T. Pelikan	Vice President, 1976—
Carol A. Rafferty	Vice President, 1977—
Elizabeth M. Retta	Assistant Treasurer, 1955–71
M.R. Robinson	President, 1955–62; Chairman of the Board and Chief Executive Officer, 1963–74; Chairman of the Board, 1975—
Richard Robinson	Vice President, 1971–73; President, 1974; President and Chief Executive Officer, 1975—
Ernest Schwehr	Vice President, 1973–77
Clinton R. Smith	Assistant Treasurer, 1955; Controller and Assistant Treasurer, 1956–62; Vice President, 1963—
John P. Spaulding	Vice President, 1961–66; Executive Vice President, 1967–70; President, 1971–74

Richard M. Spaulding	Vice President, 1971–73; Executive Vice President, 1974—
John W. Studebaker	Vice President, 1956–67
Steven C. Swett	Vice President, 1974—
Martin Tell	Vice President and Chief Financial Officer, 1976—
Jefferson Watkins	Vice President, 1974—
Clayton C. Westland	Vice President, 1968–76

DIRECTORS[1]

Scholastic Publishing Company

George H. Clapp	1924–31
N.E. Degen	1922–23
A.E. Freedel	1923–24
Paul E. Hutchinson	1922–25
William R. Jarvis	1922–23
Charles McK. Lynch	1931
James T. MacLeod	1923
Roscoe T. McCormick	1924
G. Herbert McCracken	1923–31
Augustus K. Oliver	1925–31
M.R. Robinson	1922–31
William Penn Snyder, Jr.	1925–31

St. Nicholas Publishing Company

F.G. Blackburn	1930–31
George H. Clapp	1930–31
Charles McK. Lynch	1930–31
G.H. McCracken	1930–31
Augustus K. Oliver	1930–31
M.R. Robinson	1930–31
William P. Snyder, Jr.	1930–31

[1]First names or initials appear as listed in corporate records.

524

Scholastic–St. Nicholas Corporation

F.G. Blackburn	1931–32
William C. Blakey	1931–32
George H. Clapp	1932
Preston Davis	1931–32
G. Herbert McCracken	1932
Augustus K. Oliver	1931–32
M.R. Robinson	1931–32

Scholastic Corporation

George H. Clapp	1933–43
John E. Crawford	1943–48
Paul E. Hutchinson	1933–55
Thora Larsen	1954–55
G. Herbert McCracken	1933–55
Augustus K. Oliver	1933–54[2]
Joseph W. Oliver	1948–55[3]
M.R. Robinson	1933–55

Scholastic Magazines, Inc.

Melvin W. Barnes	1968–76
Edward E. Booher	1976—
William D. Boutwell	1961–70
John C. Burton	1968–72[4]
Richard M. Cyert	1972–76
Fred H. Gowen	1965–78
C. Talbott Hiteshew, Jr.	1968—
Paul E. Hutchinson	1955–70
Thora Larsen	1955–56
Henry A. Laughlin	1957–65
Agnes M. Laurino	1963–67
Donald E. Layman	1957–71
Jack K. Lippert	1957–73

[2]Chairman, 1933–53.
[3]Chairman, 1954–55.
[4]Rejoined board, December 1977.

G. Herbert McCracken	1955—
Sidney P. Marland, Jr.	1976—
George H. Milne	1969–74
Joseph W. Oliver	1955—[5]
M. Richard Robinson, Jr.	1971—
M.R. Robinson	1955—[6]
John P. Spaulding	1963–74
Richard M. Spaulding	1974—
John W. Studebaker	1957–67
Barbara D. Sullivan	1974—

[5]Chairman, 1956–62.
[6]Chairman, 1963—.

PEREGRINATIONS OF SCHOLASTIC HEADQUARTERS

Pittsburgh offices

Sept. 1920–Jan. 1921	Sewing room, second floor of parents' home, 715 Wallace Ave., Wilkinsburg, PA
Jan.–Sept. 1921	Keenan Building (Desk space courtesy of Ketchum & MacLeod, later to become Ketchum, MacLeod & Grove, fund-raising and advertising agency)
1921–24	Bessemer Building *
1924–31	Wabash Building
1934–39	Chamber of Commerce Building
In 1931 Administration and Editorial Departments joined the Advertising Department in the company's new quarters in the Commerce Building, 155 East 44th St., New York. That was the time of split own-

*The Advertising Department moved from Pittsburgh to New York in 1928, taking up quarters in the offices of the Educational Advertising Co. (George Bryson, president) at 11 West 42nd St. Herb McCracken was the sum total of the department until its move to New York, when Sol Z. Oppenheim and Marie Kerkmann joined him.

ership between Scholastic–St. Nicholas Corporation and American Education Press (AEP). For that 11-month period, the circulation fulfillment operations were moved to the AEP plant at Columbus, OH, but the promotion/copywriting for circulation development was done at the Scholastic offices in New York under a budget controlled by the company treasurer, AEP's Preston Davis, in Columbus. With the divorce of AEP and Scholastic in June 1932, Circulation Fulfillment returned to Pittsburgh (Wabash Building) and in 1934 moved to the Chamber of Commerce Building, owned by A.K. Oliver. It stayed there until 1939, when it moved to the McCall printing plant in Dayton, OH.

New York offices

1931–35	Commerce Building, 155 East 44th St., corner of Third Ave.
1935–40	Crystal Building, 250 East 43rd St., corner of Second Ave.
1940–48	Daily News Building, 220 East 42nd St.
1948–51	Fairchild Publications Building, 7 East 12th St.
1951–53	351 Fourth Ave.
1953–62	33 West 42nd St., facing Bryant Park. Second floor, formerly Aeolian Hall, occupied by Administration and Editorial. Accounting, advertising, and subscription occupied third and fourth floors.
1962—	50 West 44th St., Hippodrome Building, so called because it was the site of the huge entertainment palace, the Hippodrome, razed in 1943.

ORDER-PROCESSING AND DISTRIBUTION CENTERS
(Years in Which New Buildings Were Occupied)

Englewood Cliffs, NJ	Warehouse, 1959; Office Building, 1962
Pleasanton, CA	1964
Jefferson City, MO	1968
Richmond Hill, Ontario, Canada	Scholastic-TAB Publications, Ltd., 1968
Southam, United Kingdom	Scholastic Publications, Ltd., 1974
Auckland, New Zealand (rented building)	Ashton Scholastic,* 1969
Gosford, New South Wales, Australia	Ashton Scholastic,* 1973

*Ashton Scholastic is the title used publicly. The corporate title is H. J. Ashton (Pty.) Ltd., for Australia; H. J. Ashton Co., Ltd., for New Zealand.

SCHOLASTIC EMPLOYEE POPULATION
AS OF JUNE 1978

Offices	Full-Time Employees	Daily Part-Time Hourlies
New York, NY	539	37
Chicago, IL	10	0
Englewood Cliffs, NJ	404	298
Jefferson City, MO*	79	137
Pleasanton, CA	21	64
Dayton, OH	10	1

*Includes short-year employees in full-time column.

Los Angeles, CA	3	0
Richmond Hill, Ontario Canada[1]	101	31
London and Southam, United Kingdom*	64	11
Auckland, New Zealand	31	20
Gosford, New South Wales, Australia	56	42
Totals	1321	641

*Includes short-year employees in full-time column.

In addition to the above there were, as of March 1, 1979, three field selling groups in the United States; one known as Scholastic Text Representatives, 94 in number, half of whom are independent contractors; one known as Magazine/Book Representatives, 15 in number, with more to be recruited (the book part of their assignment refers to the book clubs); and one known as Trade Representatives.

Under the Text Representative plan, the United States is divided into six regions, each with a full-time director who recruits and trains the representatives within a given region. The regional directors report to Mac Buhler in the New York office.

James Carsky and Carol Haney of the New York office recruit and train the Magazine/Book Representatives, assisted by Charles Schmalbach, director of the Midwest region, wearing two hats in the service of Scholastic. He has been with the company since 1946, and is one of the original regional directors.

The Book Club/Trade Division has six full-time Trade Representatives and six on a contract arrangement, reporting to James Brewington in the New York office, working the retail and wholesale book markets.

50 YEARS OF HEADLINES FROM SCHOLASTIC*
(A Selection)

Date of Issue	Headline
10/22/20	"Girl Cheerleaders New Idea This Season: 'If Our Older Sisters Can Vote, Why Can't We Lead Cheers?' Said Cheerleader Interviewed"
11/5/20	"'Better Speech' Week Is Observed by All Schools"
11/19/20	"Bolshevism Feeds on Publicity Given It" "Washington Girls Now To Have Own Athletics" "Movement Planned To Better Auto Education"
10/6/21	"Latin Cannot Be Listed With Dead Languages"
10/27/21	"League High Schools Will Take Action on Disarmament"
1/19/22	"Interest in Wireless on Increase at Latrobe"
4/27/22	"Why It Pays To Study Music"
11/11/22	"The Big Four — Passing Figures of the Greatest Political Drama in History" (Lloyd George, Clemenceau, Orlando, Wilson)
1/15/23	"President Harding's Last Words"
3/3/23	"The Wonders in a Pharaoh's Tomb" (Tutankhamun tomb discovery).
3/17/23	"The Soviets on Trial Before the World"
11/10/23	"John Barleycorn at Bay"
2/9/24	"Lenin, Red Premier, Dead"
3/8/24	"Oil, Oil, Oil — The Great American Scandal" (Teapot Dome)

*From *The Scholastic, Scholastic,* and *Senior Scholastic.*

10/21/40	"America Accepts Japan Challenge — Strong Steps To Protect U.S. Pacific Interests Give Pause to Japan"
11/4/40	"Schools Make Us Strong: Education for the Common Defense" (editorial)
3/24/41	"Canada at War Is Still the Greatest Playground in the World" (full-page advertisement of Canadian Government Travel Bureau)
4/14/41	"Your Part in Defense" (guest editorial from Laconia [NH] High School) "Yugoslavia Fights for Freedom"
9/15/41	"Nazi–Soviet War Gives Britain Breathing Spell — Hitler and Stalin, Once 'Neighborly Friends,' Are Now Locked in the Greatest Battle in History Affecting the Fate of the World"
12/15/41	"War Is Declared by U.S. and Japan" (Dec. 8, following Japan's attack on Pearl Harbor, Dec. 7)
1/5/42	"United States Enters the Second World War" (U.S. declares war on Germany and Italy a few hours after they declared war on the U.S., Dec. 11)
5/21/45	"World Order Wins 'Beachhead' at San Francisco — 46 Countries Lay Foundation for the United Nations"
10/21/46	"Judgment Day at Nuremberg: 21 Top Nazi Leaders Convicted"
10/28/46	"Is Europe Going Communist?"
3/17/47	"Why Can't They Read and Write?" (Most English teachers in high school stated that their students did not read, write, or speak well.)
9/29/47	"Freedom But Not Peace for India; Two Sovereign States Born: India and Pakistan"
2/16/48	"Will Mohandas K. Gandhi's Murder Unleash New Horrors in Strife-torn India?"

2/28/48	"Shall We Take the Wraps off Margarine? A Factual Discussion of the Butter vs. Margarine Controversy"
9/22/48	"Report from Israel by Irving DeW. Talmadge" (Eyewitness story of the new nation by Scholastic's Foreign Affairs Editor)
10/12/49	"Two Chinas" (Communists proclaim People's Republic of China; Mao Tse-tung, Chairman)
2/8/50	"Must We Build the Hydrogen Bomb?"
3/15/50	"'I Saw This Happen' by Maurice R. Robinson: One Man's Memories of the Last 50 Years" (mid-century comment)
9/20/50	"We Are at War: U.N. Fights To Crush Communist Aggression" (Korea)
4/15/53	"Mr. Universe." (Albert Einstein publishes latest revision of his theory of relativity.)
9/15/54	"School Segregation Ruled Unconstitutional"
12/2/54	"McCarthy 'Condemned': U.S. Senate Votes To 'Condemn' the Wisconsin Senator for 'Tending To Bring the Senate into Dishonor and Disrepute'"
10/18/57	"Earth's New Red 'Moon'" (Sputnik)
5/3/61	"Death on Cuba's Beaches" (Bay of Pigs invasion)
12/6/63	"Johnson Takes Oath as Nation Mourns Kennedy"
2/21/64	"Smoking and Cancer — A Verdict"
1/7/65	"New Panama Canal Treaty Proposed" (by President Johnson)
2/11/65	"With *Senior Scholastic*'s Editor in Vietnam" (Roy Hemming)
4/1/65	"Alabama: The March to Montgomery. Civil Rights Marchers, Led by Martin Luther King, End 54-Mile March From Selma."

4/8/65	"Should the Government Compensate Crime Victims?"
5/6/65	"Paying the School Bill — With Help from Uncle Sam" (Aid to Education bill signed by President Johnson)
9/15/65	"Men on the Moon"
11/4/65	"Storm at Home" (student protests over Vietnam War)
12/9/65	"The World's Refugees — Living With Heartache and Hope"
9/21/67	"Urban Riots: Hottest Summer Yet"
9/21/67	"Israelis Rout Arabs" (Six-Day War)
9/28/67	"The Draft: Who, When, Why?" (Vietnam War)
10/5/67	"Fact Sheet on Newly Independent Africa"
3/28/68	"Vietnam: Why Are We There?"
4/25/68	"From Berkeley to Bangalore — Teens in Dissent" "Martin Luther King, Jr., 1929–68: Assassination Shocks Nation"
10/29/69	"Students' Protests: How Far Is Too Far?"
3/9/70	"Some Straight Talk about Drugs."
10/5/70	"Skirmish over 'Peace' Symbol"
10/19/70	"50 Years . . . Oh, You Kid!" (50th anniversary issue)

Index

535

B

542

House organ, 469–72
Housman, A. E., 164
Houston, TX, 215
Hovious, Carol, 452
Howlett, Margaret, 229, 230
How To Judge Motion Pictures, 238
How To Star in Basketball, 73
How To Use Your Library, 238
Hoy dia, 234, 285, 519
Huddleston, Martha, 241–43, 245, 246, 248, 249, 250, 268, 269, 314, 323, 519
Huggins, Adrian, 408–409
Hughes, Harold, 377
Hughes, Langston, 164, 344
Hughes, Terry, 295, 296, 297, 301, 302
Human Issues in Science, 516
Hungarian freedom fighters, 378
Hunt, Alfred E., 50
Hunt, Herold C., 156, 454
Hunt, Pearson, 184
Hunter, Hildegarde B., 469–70, 520
Hunter-Bone, Maureen, 207
Hurley, Charles, 73, 218, 447
Hurley, Richard J., 245
Hurwitz, Howard L., 462
Hutchins, Robert, 102
Hutchinson, Paul E., 21, 45, 65, 108, 113, 116, 180, 520, 522, 524, 525

I

I Can, 516
Illinois, University of, 384, 387
Images of Man, 516
Incorporation of Scholastic, 19, 44–45, 49
Independent, 37
Indiana, Robert, 418, 419
Indianapolis, IN, 358, 416, 429
Individualized Reading Series (IRS), 269, 271–72, 425, 515
Institute for Educational Development, 450
Institute of Student Opinion (ISO), 439–40
Internal Revenue Service, 191, 192, 478, 480, 486
International, Scholastic goes, 279–302
International Business Machines (IBM), 173, 266

International Council for the Improvement of Reading Instruction, 469
International Reading Association (IRA), 469
International Telephone and Telegraph (IT&T), 173, 175
Investment Observer, The, 115
Ireland, 286
Irwin, John, 279
I Spy booklets, 519
Issues Today, 222, 223
Italy, 305
Izod, Alan, 296, 297, 301, 302
Izod, Olive, 296, 297

J

Jackson, Kathryn, 206, 207
Jamieson, John, 127
Japan, Scholastic products in, 302
Jarrell, Ira, 370
Jarvis, William R., 44, 524
Jefferson City, MO, office, 264, 265, 266, 472, 528
John Martin's Book, 508
John's Island, SC, 132
Johnson, Alba B., 27
Johnson, Eleanor, 187
Johnson, James Weldon, 344
Johnson, Phillip, 233
Johnson, William, 218
Jones, B. F., 52
Jones, Edward W., 30
Jones, Galen, 454
Jones, Guy and Constance, 248
Journal Publishing Company, 18
Judd, Dean, 452, 453
Junior American Citizen (JAC) 124, 205, 513. *See also Newstime.*
Junior Review, 122, 123, 207, 216, 217, 223, 240, 515, 519
Junior Scholastic, 101, 125, 126, 128, 143, 154, 202, 204, 217, 223, 233, 235, 239, 242, 245, 253, 313, 318, 339, 355, 358, 361, 369, 370, 374, 378–80, 388, 391, 401, 443, 446, 454, 474, 513, 519; advertisers in, 121–22, 213; attacks on, 337; attempted ban of, in Ft. Worth, TX, 377–78; circulation of, 99, 100, 115, 121, 122–23, 125, 128, 148, 196, 206, 217; content of, 161, 166;

546

New American Library, 249
Newark, DE, 469
Newark, NJ, 241
New Castle (PA) High School, 37
New Deal, 338
New Guinea, 296
New Haven, CT, 229
New Orleans, LA, 428
Newport Beach, CA, 374
News, book club, 313
News Citizen, 124, 235, 387–91, 514, 519. *See also Young Citizen.*
News Explorer, 235, 514
Newspaper Guild of New York, 96, 100, 455–64, 503
Newspaper Publishers Association, 225
News Pilot, 206, 207, 235, 514
News Ranger, 206, 207, 235, 514
Newstime, 124, 203, 204–205, 206, 207, 235, 253, 281, 388, 391, 474, 513
News Trails, 206, 207, 235, 514
Newsweek, 32, 175
Newton Junior College, 158
New York City, NY, xi, xii, 20, 83, 91, 105, 129, 139, 208, 215, 217, 241, 243, 266, 269, 270, 274, 295, 296, 298, 358, 365, 372, 377, 393, 404, 409, 413, 417, 421, 430, 454, 459, 476, 483, 494, 501; Public Library, 245
New York City, NY, office, 59, 76, 81, 84, 145, 146, 188, 215, 238, 247, 261, 285, 304, 388, 416, 424, 467, 483, 495, 526, 527, 528, 529
New York Coliseum, 418
New York Department of Education, 450
New York Herald-Tribune, 65
New York Post, 68
New York Society of Security Analysts, 117
New York state, 166, 250, 253, 522
New York Times, The, 77, 78, 143, 189, 223, 385
New York Times Special Features Syndicate, The, 435, 440
New York University, 34, 63, 72, 381, 429, 452, 453
New York World, 68
New York Yankees baseball club, 66

New Zealand, 285, 293, 472; sale of Scholastic products in, 295–97, 300
Nickerson, John, 218
Noble, Ernest, 440
North Tarrytown, NY, 496
Norton, E. B., 454
Noyes, E. Louise, 245

O

Oates, Joyce Carol, 410
Oatman, Eric, 229
Officers: of St. Nicholas Publishing Company, 520; of Scholastic Corporation, 520–21; of Scholastic Magazines, Inc., 522–24; of Scholastic Publishing Company, 520; of Scholastic–St. Nicholas Corporation, 520–21
Oh, You Tex, 248
Oldmeadow (marketer), 302
Olds, R. E., 430
Oliver, Augustus K., 58, 64, 65, 85, 97, 99, 182, 188, 254, 417, 452, 498, 499, 501, 520, 521, 524, 525, 527; American Education Press and, 90–94; biography of, 51–52, 56; as financial backer, 60, 75, 78, 107, 121, 415; Forum of American Youth and, 104, 105, 106; management-consultant firms and, ix, 106, 125, 133–50; "Report on *Scholastic* Magazine" and, 71; as Scholastic stockholder, 51, 54, 55, 96, 102, 103, 108, 109, 110, 181
Oliver, A. K.,– Scholastic Charitable Trust, 485–86, 487
Oliver, George, 497
Oliver, Jack, 497
Oliver, Joseph Wood, 56, 113, 114, 116, 119, 177, 182, 183, 184, 384–85, 497, 521, 523, 525, 526
Oliver, Margaretta W., 497
Oliver, Mrs. Augustus K., 185
Oliver, William, 497
Oliver Twist, 247
Olliff, Ben, 334
Olsen, John D., 450
Omaha, NB, 378–80

Robinson, Maurice R. (*cont.*)
Education Press, 194–96; Reflections, Addendum by, 497–512; *St. Nicholas* and, 65; sales letter by, 37–38; Scholastic Bookshop and, 239; Scholastic going national and, 19, 21–42; Scholastic organization and, 323, 324, 325–28, 329; *Science World* and, 211–14; sharing of sales representatives and, 155–57; states purpose of *Scope,* 214–15; study/travel project and, 307; Teen Age Book Club and, 242–43, 246, 249, 250, 252; tricentennial of high school education and, 465, 466; *The Western Pennsylvania Scholastic* founded by, 4–6; *The World Review* and, 61–64; Writing Awards and, 9
Robinson, Maurice R., Fund, 486–87
Robinson, Rachel, 14
Robinson, Ralph, 14
Robinson, R. B., 14
Robinson, Richard, 76, 118, 211, 219, 226, 325, 329, 392, 432, 447, 492, 496, 511, 523, 526; biographical sketch of, 492–94; elected president, chief executive officer, 277; flying pages and, 426; named editor of *Scope,* 216; named publisher of School Division, 329; *News Citizen* protest and, 388–91; *Scope* protest and, 399–400; study/travel program and, 308
Robinson, William, 14
Robinson, William Walker, 76
Rochester, NY, 63, 257, 260, 452, 453
Rockefeller Foundation, 371
Rockford, IL, 257, 259
Rock Island Arsenal, 3
Rock Island Railroad, 492
Roosevelt, Eleanor, 101, 354–55
Roosevelt, Franklin D., 133, 152, 167, 435, 437
Roosevelt High School, Des Moines, IA, 158
Roper poll, 439
Rosenbloom, Jonathan, 207
Rosenblum, Marcus, 312, 455, 464
Rosten, Stanley, 294
Roxbury, MA, 27
RS Associates, 424
Rubin, Arnold, 440

Rugg, Harold, 312, 346, 429
Rumsfeld, Donald, 440
Runyon, Damon, Cancer Fund, 471
Ruppert, Jacob, 65–66
Rushen, Bryan, 290
Russell, Bill, Basketball Films, 515
Russell, Jane, 126
Russell, Ruthanna, 208, 210
Russia, 305
Ryan, Betsy, 254
Ryan, Charlotte, 450
Ryan, Linda, 300
Rynearson, Edward, 5, 27, 34

S

Sacramento, CA, 275
St. Catherine's College, 492
St. John's University, 73
St. Louis, MO, 215, 315, 361, 362, 384, 385
St. Louis Post-Dispatch, 361, 362
St. Nicholas, 60, 65–66, 75, 79, 80, 84, 85, 87, 89, 93, 95, 181, 508, 513, 518
St. Nicholas Publishing Company, 65–66, 75, 80
Salary scale, 456, 457, 458
Sales districts, 155, 158
Sales representatives, 155, 158, 243, 334, 515; sharing of, 156–57
Salt Lake City, UT, 303
Salvation Army, 17
San Benito County High School, Hollister, CA, 452
Sandburg, Carl, 164
San Diego, CA, 428
Sandoe, Nichol M., 20
San Francisco, CA, 215, 242, 263, 269, 432
Santa Barbara (CA) High School, 245
Saplings, 237, 273, 411
Sarkoff, Paul, 129, 414
Saroyan, William, 473
Satire, 274
Savage, Abe, 504
Sayre, Harrison M., 81, 89, 190
Scarlet Letter, The, 247
Scarsdale, NY, 60, 372, 375, 376; Citizens Committee, 375

X

Y

Z

Text photoset in Primer and Century by
Advanced Typographic Systems, Inc.
Printed on Mohawk Superfine Text, soft white,
and bound by Halliday Lithograph
of the Arcata Group. Cover and jacket
printed by Duenewald Lithograph Company.